Story Summary

Sarah Hammond is the overprotected daughter of passionate Massachusetts abolitionists. Matt Slade is the orphaned son of hardscrabble Texas settlers. Sarah knows about every Civil War battle from studying newspaper accounts. Matt fought in the bloodiest of them under Generals Longstreet and Lee. If Matt and Sarah ever crossed paths, it should have been for an unremarkable moment. He would tip his hat. She would nod and pass on by.

Except that as survivors of a Comanche attack, Matt and Sarah spend far more than a moment together. They come to know each other, depend on each other and love each other. Humiliated by Sarah's love for "Rebel trash," her jilted fiancé extracts a revenge so vicious, he boasts that he destroyed the young lovers. Did he? Or when Matt and Sarah meet again years later, can they put their lives and their love back together?

Sing My Name

Ellen O'Connell

This book is a work of fiction. Names, characters and incidents are the product of the author's imagination. Any resemblance to actual events or persons is strictly coincidental. Some of the places mentioned do exist; however, descriptions may have been altered to better suit the story.

ISBN-13: 978-1456450915
ISBN-10: 1456450913

Sing My Name

Rebel and Yankee

1867

1

AN EXPLOSION OF PAIN woke Matt.

"I got him, Barney! I got him!"

The stranger who had kicked Matt in the ribs shoved a gun in his face, and the man's triumphant shout reverberated in Matt's throbbing head. Behind the lethal menace of the gun barrel, black eyes set too close in a pockmarked face glittered with malice.

Matt spoke softly, hoping to defuse whatever was happening. "You've got me, sure enough, but why on earth do you want me? Nobody else does."

"Hah!" With the sound, his captor spewed spit and foul breath, exposing a mouth full of tobacco-stained teeth. Matt fought a wave of nausea.

A heavier, swarthier man approached, iron handcuffs swinging from one hand. Matt tried again. Maybe this one had some sense.

"If you fellows think I'm worth getting, you must have me mixed up with somebody else. If it's thieving you're up to, the horse is all I've got. Take him."

"You should have got rid of that horse yourself, you damn fool. He'll help hang you—if you live that long. Poster says dead or alive, so you make trouble, and we'll collect on your carcass."

Now the sinking feeling in Matt's stomach had nothing to do with his hangover. This was trouble, far worse trouble than losing a good horse.

"I never did anything that would get my name on a poster," he said flatly. "You need to read it again more careful."

"Hah! Show him, Barney. Show him how he's gonna make us rich."

Barney grinned, showing his own set of stained teeth, and pulled a folded piece of paper from a shirt pocket, unfolding it with great care.

As Barney waved the paper at him, Matt had time to read only the largest words: "$1000 REWARD" and "DEAD OR ALIVE."

Snatching the paper back, Barney refolded it, returned it to his pocket and tucked it in with the same great care. "Maybe you could kill a whole family and do as bad to them as Comanches and get away with it, except you didn't kill them all. Some old man made it, even scalped like you did him, and he saw you and he saw that horse. And the Yankee paymaster you robbed saw the horse. Did you think the Yankees wouldn't put out a reward for you after that?"

"I didn't kill anybody, and I didn't rob anybody," Matt said. "When did all this killing and robbing happen?"

"As if you didn't know. Couple of months ago, near Fort Grissom. You going to claim you've never been there?"

"I haven't. I've been working at the freight company only a couple miles from here since late winter. If you ask there, they'll tell you I've been there six days out of every week. No way I was anywheres near Fort Grissom two months ago."

"We're not asking anywhere. That poster describes you, and it describes your horse. Line-back red dun with a star and two hind stockings. How many like that are there? Man about thirty, brown hair, blue eyes, couple inches over six-foot, two hundred twenty pounds. You're not fast-talking your way out of this. That's you."

"No, it's not me. Let me stand up and take a good look. There's lots of men in Texas with brown hair and blue eyes, but the army measured me an inch shy of six-foot."

Matt saw no reason to mention that he'd been seventeen when the army did the measuring.

Standing up slowly, he held his arms out to the sides to give them a good look. "Look at me. I turned twenty-two this past winter. Soaking wet and with a full belly I'd still never get near two hundred pounds. Put me on the scale at the feed store in town, and I bet you that horse the needle doesn't get to one seventy."

Uncertainty flickered momentarily in Barney's black eyes, but it passed, and something ugly and calculating spread across his face.

"So you looked older and bigger to some farmer laying in the dirt with a bullet in him and his scalp torn off. Now you shut up and come along peaceful or all they'll have to identify is your body and the horse. Right now it's easier to haul you off alive so's you ain't swelling up, stinking and starting the flies, but you fuss and Hank and me will put up with the stink."

Matt did shut up then. If he succeeded in convincing these two they had the wrong man, they'd kill him so he couldn't convince anyone else. The sheriff in town was one of the Yankees running Texas now, but he had a reputation as a fair man. He'd straighten this mess out.

Matt made no protest when Barney locked the cuffs on his wrists, searched his pockets and found the combination of saved wages and poker winnings he carried with him for lack of anywhere else to keep it.

"Got nothing but the horse, you lying son of a bitch! You still got most of what you took off them people."

Hung over or not, Matt saw the blow coming and threw himself back to the ground. He rolled clear of Barney's first kick, but Hank held him for the second and third.

Last night Matt had celebrated a winning streak at poker a little too much. Making a dry camp here instead of riding back to the bunkhouse at the freight company seemed sensible at the time. Hank and Barney hauled him to his feet and prodded him onto one of their own spavined jugheads.

The two men argued briefly over who would ride the red dun gelding. Barney won the argument with a curse and threw his considerable weight into the saddle so hard the horse grunted.

When Barney spurred the horse straight west, Matt's roiling stomach sank even lower. "Town's east of here. Where you going to turn me in?"

"Hell, we ain't going to let no carpetbagger sheriff get that money and keep it. We're going to Fort Grissom, right to the Yankees giving that reward. The easier you make it, the longer you stay alive."

Swallowing hard, Matt said a grim goodbye to the freight company job, the first decent one he'd found since the war, or before it for that matter. Best forget the horse and the money too. The plain truth of it was he'd gotten uppity lately with a good job and a fine horse and since last night even enough money to buy one of those

Spencer repeating rifles he coveted. Now he needed to forget those things and get down to what he was best at.

Surviving.

2

"MISS HAMMOND!"

Sarah jerked her head back around to face the makeshift table of boards set across wood crates. She stared at her plate of unappetizing food, not wanting to see prim disapproval all over her chaperones' faces.

"They're kicking him again," she said.

"Good," Anna Royer said. "Hanging is too quick and easy for one like that."

"But...."

"What must we say to make you understand?" Lydia Lowell whispered. "He killed a whole family. And what he did to the women—it was as bad as the Comanches." Giving emphasis to her words with an exaggerated feminine shudder, the pretty young woman slid her glance to Mrs. Royer for approval.

At first Mrs. Royer's outspoken opinion and Mrs. Lowell's dark hints had silenced Sarah, but after three days of watching Hank and Barney Webb starve, hit and kick their prisoner, distress was beginning to outweigh her timidness. She stabbed a piece of the tough meat on her plate in frustration, then pushed it off the fork, continuing to toy with her food.

"Really, dear, if your appetite were always so dainty, I do believe you might lose that baby fat before we arrive at Fort Grissom."

The remark brought Sarah's head up. Her cheeks burned at mention of the layer of extra flesh that plagued her, yet knowing the other woman intended the deliberate cruelty to reduce her to an obedient jelly added a flush of resentment.

"Good evening, ladies. Once again, I apologize for the rough fare." Lieutenant Dennis Broderick, the officer in charge of their cavalry escort, placed his own plate and cup on the boards and prepared to join them for the meal. Continuing his sociable conversation with the other two women, he nodded stiffly at Sarah then ignored her. She took the opportunity for another peek back over her shoulder.

Soldiers sat in clusters here and there. Every one of them ate the stew made from stringy antelope with more enthusiasm than Sarah could muster. Hank and Barney Webb had joined Alvaro and Jake, the guides, as they usually did for meals.

The bounty hunters stuffed United States Army food into their swarthy faces with great speed and no manners. Exactly how long would a man have to go without washing to become that filthy? Months? Years?

Their prisoner had certainly had no chance to wash since the dirty men wheedled their way into traveling with a cavalry escort. They never let him have enough water to drink. Yet even with the strong lines of his jaw and lower face blurred by more beard growth each day and the coarse, cheap fabric of his clothes stained and dusty, he looked a whole lot cleaner than his captors.

The only one in the camp not eating, he sat where they had pulled him off his horse in a bruising fall, legs bent, elbows on his knees, head in his hands, the ugly handcuffs hanging from his wrists. Sarah had not seen the Webbs offer him water, but she knew if they did, they ripped the canteen back out of his hands before he got more than a swallow.

Upset by the sight, almost overwhelmed by her own sense of helplessness, Sarah turned to find all eyes on her.

"Lieutenant...," she began, only to be immediately interrupted by Mrs. Royer.

"If I had any idea that you so lacked good sense and ordinary manners when your family first asked me to accompany you, I would have made my excuses. No wonder your poor parents worried about scandal if you married quickly in the East. You're going to involve yourself in scandal here in the middle of nowhere."

Finished with her furious criticism, the woman only paused for breath before issuing an ultimatum. "If you persist in your disgraceful interest in that criminal, you will spend every day of the remainder of our journey in splendid isolation, and I shall feel compelled not only to write to your family but to have my husband speak to Major Macauley."

Sarah couldn't believe her ears. The insult was as vile as it was baseless. When Carter Macauley had received orders to Fort Grissom only days after the announcement of their engagement, it was he who opposed a hastily arranged wedding that might cause talk. It was Carter who located wives of officers who would be traveling to Texas to join their husbands to serve as chaperones.

Finally finding her tongue, Sarah said, "You cannot seriously think my interest in that young man is unseemly. He...."

"Young man, is it? How exactly has your close study of him led you to an evaluation of his age?"

"It doesn't take close study," Sarah said indignantly. "I have brothers. He moves the same way they did when...."

"Oh, so it's the way he *moves* you've been studying, is it?"

"Ladies, ladies, please."

Fair complected anyway, Broderick blushed as pink as any school girl right through his short, blond beard. "Mrs. Royer, I'm sure Major Macauley is aware of the emotional vagaries of young girls, but he's right to have complete faith in your steadying influence. And yours, of course, Mrs. Lowell."

Lydia Lowell giggled. Expecting intelligent conversation out of Mrs. Lowell would be as foolish as expecting kindness out of Mrs. Royer. Broderick's voice pulled Sarah away from her uncharitable thoughts.

"And there is no need for further recrimination. I've done everything I can, and they have treated him better today. So let's put this behind us and finish our meal. None of us wants a repeat of last night's unpleasantness, do we?"

He took his seat and picked up his fork as if those words settled the matter. Anna Royer threw Sarah a smug look over the rim of her tin cup, sure of her victory.

Beginning to simmer to a stew finer than the mess on her plate, Sarah decided they were absolutely right about one thing—there was not going to be a repeat of last night. Then she had gone to Broderick, sure his duties had kept him from noticing the cruelty of the Webbs.

"I have no control over civilians, Miss Hammond," he had said, refusing to involve himself.

Reason did not move him, and in the end, Sarah had resorted to childish begging, continuing until Broderick gave in just to silence her. Stiff and angry, he went to the Webbs, but he spoke only a sentence or two, and when he left they were laughing, poking each other with their elbows, and gesturing toward her. Having those men even look at her made Sarah want to hide under a wagon cover and not come out for the rest of the trip.

Without meaning to, Sarah looked back over her shoulder again, this time straight into pale blue eyes so brilliant their color was distinct across the distance and in the fading light. As she stared in surprise, one of those eyes closed, stayed closed long enough to leave no doubt, and opened again. Teeth flashed white against tanned skin and dark beard.

Sarah straightened and pretended interest in her food. No corset had ever made it as difficult to breathe as that smile. And he had winked at her! That starved, beaten *murderer* had winked at her!

They had all seen it, of course. As soon as Mrs. Royer got her mouth out of that tight, grim line, or Mrs. Lowell got hers closed, they'd start with even more insulting criticism. Sarah decided not to wait.

"Lieutenant, are you going to talk to those men again?" she asked politely.

"No, Miss Hammond, I am not, and perhaps Mrs. Royer is right that we need to find a safer place for you for the rest of the trip."

Sarah didn't reply but rose, picked up her plate and cup and started for the cook fire.

Broderick followed, already worried. "What are you doing?"

"I need a second helping."

The cook jumped to his feet. Sarah smiled at him and shook her head. Heaping her plate with as much stew as it would hold, she balanced several biscuits on top, poured coffee almost to the brim of her cup and stirred in two heaping spoonfuls of sugar. Before she turned and started across the campsite, Broderick realized her intention. He kept pace with her, walking sideways to argue, his long legs scissoring.

The Webbs got to their feet, also aware of what she intended. They stood over their prisoner, looking uglier and meaner with every step she took. Twenty feet, ten. Broderick seized her arm, forcing her to stop. Coffee sloshed.

"Let go of me, Lieutenant."

"If you persist, I will physically restrain you."

"In that case, *Lieutenant* Broderick, I hope you have an explanation ready for *Major* Macauley as to why you found such action necessary to stop me from a harmless act of charity when you could easily accomplish the same thing with one order."

"How exactly do you think I can force civilians to behave in a manner that suits *you*, Miss Hammond?"

"You can explain to them that unless they mend their ways, they won't be allowed to accompany us in the morning. There must be enough rope in the wagons to leave them right here, all trussed up for the Comanches to find. Perhaps we could deliver their prisoner to the authorities ourselves and share the reward."

"The hell you say," Barney Webb snarled. "You get that interfering little bitch away from here, soldier boy."

Broderick's aggravation switched from Sarah to Webb in a flash. "Mind your language, Mr. Webb, or I may give serious consideration to Miss Hammond's suggestion." He held out his hands toward Sarah. "Give me those, and go back to the other ladies. I will deliver them. You have my word."

The delivery of a single plate of food no longer seemed a worthy goal. "He's going to have three meals a day and enough water like everyone else."

"I will assign a man to see to it."

"And there will be no more hitting, no more kicking and no more pulling him off that horse head first."

"And you will turn around, return to the other ladies and stop concerning yourself with this matter."

Recognizing a better bargain than she had started out to get, Sarah handed over the plate and cup and turned away, careful never to look at the man on the ground. Shaky from head to toe already, she didn't dare risk the effect of those eyes or that smile again.

MATT WATCHED THE girl approach with increasing delight. The closer she got, the better she looked. Surely if the mass of hair under her bonnet fell free, it would be not a curtain, but a cloud. The dark eyes he'd thought were brown were really blue, the darkest blue of the night sky. Her voice was a light and lovely thing, and her accent intrigued him.

As she turned away, he tore his eyes from her long enough to take the plate and cup. He watched her walk back across the camp and listened to Broderick telling the Webbs that humoring the fiancée of a Yankee major was necessary, no matter how any of them felt about it.

Wolfing down the food, Matt tried not to think about how much he envied some Yankee officer. That girl was sure enough on her way to becoming a special kind of lady.

Later that night Matt shifted his aching body against the wheel of Jake and Alvaro's wagon. Days ago he had given up looking for weakness in the axle Barney fastened the cuffs to at night. He had also stopped avoiding kicks or punches from either Hank or Barney. Avoiding a blow provoked a second, less casual. Better to make sure there was contact the first time. So far he'd succeeded in minimizing his damage. Maybe he hurt all over, but he didn't have broken bones.

Better still, tonight his belly was full and his thirst was slaked, thanks to the girl he thought of as Boston. He knew she was from Boston the way he knew about the other women, by listening to the kind of talk going on right now between the guides and the Webb brothers.

He blocked out most of the foul talk by concentrating on his own thoughts. Like every other man in the camp, Matt spent a good part of every day following the women with his eyes. Unlike most, he didn't favor the full-figured, raven-haired one. Her milky skin was flawless all right, so were marble statues, and the woman he called Sourpuss struck him as every bit as hard.

The fluffy one with light brown hair and wide always-surprised-looking eyes had her admirers too. So ladylike, he'd heard the soldiers say. Well, he hadn't been around women all that much, but Puppydog sure looked useless to him. Maybe if he attended tea parties he'd feel different, but all that giggling and posing must get pretty tiresome, and the way she kept looking to Sourpuss as if for a pat on the head was downright irritating.

Then there was Boston. His own age, maybe a little younger, until tonight she had seemed timid and unsure of herself. A little bit of a thing, she was shorter than the other women, even with the mass of blonde hair piled high on her head. Her hair wasn't gold but the color of oats left standing in a winter field. There was a round softness to her, an indescribable sweetness.

A man who could spend a lifetime wrapping himself around all that sweetness, burying himself in it, might get a long ways toward forgetting what an ugly place the world could be. And, of course, some Yankee major was going to do just that. Those Yankees really did get a hard hold on every fine thing.

He had winked at Boston without thinking. She was so obviously fretting, and getting herself in trouble doing it. He only meant to reassure her and let her know he was all right, that she shouldn't make more trouble for herself.

Even before she forced the green Yankee lieutenant to show some spine against the Webbs, her efforts last night had gotten him a few swallows of water at the stops today. If he got a chance to escape now, he'd have the strength to take it, and if that was jumping from the frying pan to the fire, well, the Webbs were going to kill him for sure. The Comanches had to catch him first.

The coarse laughter of the men on the other side of the wagon pulled Matt away from his own thoughts. Every night the four of them got together, played cards, jawed and drank. Not only did the Webbs shackle him to the guides' wagon, they put their own bedrolls underneath and slept there. The way Jake and Alvaro had taken to Hank and Barney bothered him. Birds of a feather and all that. Other things bothered him more.

Like this wagon. Maybe a guide wasn't exactly the same as a scout, but guides ought to have saddle horses and ought to be taking a look around now and then. Jake and Alvaro rolled along in line with the other wagons like a pair of little old ladies, only they didn't look like little old ladies. Not that you could hold the way they dressed against them. In this part of the country, the motley combination of Mexican, Indian and American they wore was common enough.

Matt didn't like the way Jake and Alvaro always had liquor to offer Hank, Barney and any of the soldiers they could get to take it either. Was the wagon full of the stuff? And why would they be so generous with it?

They'd let Hank and Barney have more to drink than usual tonight and had a few more themselves from the sound of it. Matt had heard a lot of rough talk during the war, but nothing like this. He wasn't sure he was getting the straight of what they wanted to do to Sourpuss. If so, it had to be an unnatural act.

The men finished with Sourpuss, moved on to Puppydog and disposed of her in short order too. Matt pictured the lifeless white forms used and tossed aside. His jaw tightened and eyes narrowed as Hank started on Boston.

"That Yankee ain't getting any virgin. You could tell from the way she wagged her tail at that soldier boy to get her way."

"Now, all women have certain instincts," Alvaro said. "From that background, the little one is undoubtedly untried."

"Well, I'd like to try her. I'd throw her fancy little ass down in the dirt and crack her right open, and the harder she cried and begged, the more I'd like it and the harder I'd give it to her till she couldn't cry no more."

Matt pulled restlessly against the handcuffs, wishing he could wrap the chain around Hank's dirty throat. Alvaro's voice came again, oily and knowing.

"So she got her way tonight. There's no profit in revenge, my friend. If all three women were ours for the taking, we should use the older ones and save the little one. She's worth too much."

There was a harsh hiss. A warning. Jake?

Too drunk to notice anything unusual in the words, Hank just mumbled and went on with his filthy imaginings.

Matt stopped listening. "Worth too much?" What kind of talk was that from half-drunk men in the middle of Texas? Worth too much. He thought of the heavy army wagons lumbering along. Ten to one they carried ammunition and maybe even repeating rifles for the Fort Grissom garrison. Rifles and ammunition with a military escort of green troops, a girl from Boston worth too much, and guides with an endless supply of whiskey. Matt shivered, and the night air had nothing to do with it.

3

SARAH PINNED HER DAMP hair into a loose arrangement on the top of her head and picked up the mirror to see what kind of mess she'd made. Then she sat staring at the reflection of her own troubled face. Bathing had washed away travel dirt, but she had been unable to wash away an uneasy feeling.

Yesterday Lieutenant Broderick's announcement of this stopover had lifted her spirits.

"Alvaro tells me we'll reach a deserted homestead tomorrow afternoon. We'll make an early stop there, and not only will you sleep with a roof over your heads, we should be able to arrange for you ladies to bathe."

Surely the edgy, unhappy feeling gnawing at her had nothing to do with this place. Close to a swift-running stream bordered with trees, the one-room cabin was a fortress of logs. The heavy door and thick shutters could be barred from inside, leaving rifle loopholes as the only openings. Broderick had ordered his men to clean out the place, but there hadn't even been much dust and dirt to sweep off the board floor.

No, the cause of her uneasiness wasn't the place, but people. The absence of the people who had built this homestead bothered Sarah. Why would settlers who traveled so far across this vast, empty land to find a home just pick up and leave? She wished she dared ask Lieutenant Broderick, but except for a frosty yes or no in answer to a direct question, the lieutenant, along with Mrs. Royer and Mrs. Lowell, was shunning her.

The Webbs also counted as worrisome people. Her demand that the Webbs feed their prisoner had resulted in the two ugly men

shunning everyone, even Jake and Alvaro. Day and night, the
bounty hunters kept their distance. Yet the cook assured Sarah they
took plates of food to their prisoner. So what were they up to?

The last rays of the setting sun slanted in through the open
window and struck sparks from her engagement ring. The ring, with
its huge center diamond and two emerald side stones, weighed
heavy on her hand and in her mind. How could Carter think
anything so massive suited her?

Thoughts of Major Carter Macauley deepened her unease. How
was he going to react when Mrs. Royer and Lieutenant Broderick
finished telling him their tales? Carter saw shadows of scandal
everywhere without help from the likes of those two.

Sounds of male laughter and the wail of a harmonica drifted in
through the open window. Evidently the soldiers didn't share her
worries. They would have a roof over their heads tonight too, although only the roof of the barn. If one of the early summer storms
that threatened every afternoon finally brought rain, any shelter
would be welcome.

Sarah put the mirror down and rose to finish dressing. The
soldiers had always been polite to her, but since the scene with
Broderick and the Webbs they had showed her something more—
almost approval? No, that was too fanciful. Still, if the men wanted
to turn the respite from constant travel into a festive occasion, they
could count on her help.

The other women had not waited for her. Sarah walked outside
alone and took a place next to Lydia Lowell on one of the wooden
crates set out for seats. To her surprise the other woman gave her
a small smile. Mrs. Royer showed no sign of softening.

Half a dozen soldiers were dancing to the harmonica music.
Dancing with each other! Sarah laughed out loud. Were enlisted
men forbidden to ask the fiancée of an officer to dance? She hoped
not. She wanted to dance, and she didn't want to dance with
Lieutenant Broderick, not that he would ask her. Sarah tapped her
toe to the music, enjoying herself, until the sound stopped abruptly.

Seconds later Lieutenant Broderick appeared, pushing through
the men with an angry look on his face and a corked jug in each
hand. His sergeant and a corporal followed, throwing a few harsh
words to each side as they came. The soldiers disappeared into the
night one after another.

Broderick stopped in front of Mrs. Royer. "Ladies, I'm sorry but I must ask you to go inside now. A small problem has arisen, and I want to be sure that nothing happens to upset any of you."

"What problem would that be, Lieutenant?" asked Mrs. Royer, as she got to her feet.

Broderick hesitated, then said, "Jake and Alvaro tried to liven the festivities by providing spirits. Fortunately, it was reported to me immediately. The sergeant and I are going to talk to every soldier, and any who gave in to temptation will be disciplined when we reach the fort."

"Your men have been *drinking*?"

"I doubt more than one or two had anything. We've confiscated the whiskey, and the jugs are almost full." He lifted the jugs in his hands slightly.

"Inside, ladies. Please."

Mrs. Royer led the way back into the house, where Broderick thumped the jugs down on the only piece of furniture that had been left there, a rough-hewn table.

"Suppose I make my own bed in here tonight," Broderick suggested. "Since talking to the men will take a while, perhaps you would be so kind as to make arrangements. A curtain? I'll have the sergeant bring blankets."

"Yes, thank you, Lieutenant," Mrs. Royer said coldly. "I think that's a very good idea."

Later that night Sarah lay awake on her narrow cot. She ought to be pleased. Mrs. Royer obviously considered the lieutenant's deficiencies worse than Sarah's own. Perhaps Broderick would be too busy defending himself to even report her bad behavior to Carter.

Somehow none of that mattered much at the moment. All Sarah's vague worries from earlier in the evening had coalesced into fear.

Outside the wind moaned around the house, and horses called back and forth. As the sleepless hours dragged by, she even imagined she heard a wagon leaving, wheels creaking in the night.

Soon she would be a woman, an army officer's wife. Giving way to silly, groundless fears had to stop. This house exemplified safety. The soldiers outside were part of the Grand Army that had defeated the Rebels only two years ago.

Of course the soldiers who cornered Robert E. Lee weren't drunk. *Stop it!* she told herself. *Just stop that.* So a few of the soldiers took a drink, or even two. The rest were sober, alert.

The unshuttered windows let in night air barely cooler than mid-day. So far as Sarah could tell, night never brought much relief from the heat in Texas. If mid-June was this miserable, what would August be like? Thank goodness Carter planned on returning East after his service. Turning restlessly, Sarah plumped her thin pillow again.

"Miss Hammond! If you cannot sleep, the least you can do is be considerate enough to be quiet."

Even pitched low, Anna Royer's voice managed to convey dis-approval, disappointment and superiority.

"Yes, ma'am," Sarah whispered.

She forced herself to lie still then, quietly waiting for the dawn to free her from her uncomfortable bed and her fears.

4

As soon as the black of night lightened ever so slightly, Sarah rose, pulled on her slippers and belted a wrapper over her night dress. Hoping Lieutenant Broderick slept soundly on the other side of the blanket hung to divide the room, she went about her morning routine as quietly as possible, embarrassed to be doing such personal things with a man close enough to hear.

Soon the other women were awake, chatting away as they used the chamberpot, washed and began brushing the night braids out of their hair. Did marriage make everyone less shy about such things?

Reaching for her under garments, Sarah paused mid-motion at the sound of two sharp cracks from the direction of the creek. More of the sounds came, singly and then in series. Anna Royer threw herself at the nearest window.

"Close them. Close them now!" she ordered, panic in her voice. "Lieutenant!"

Even as Sarah moved to close the shutters on the window closest to her, she heard Broderick responding. He didn't sound worried.

"I hear. The men have probably seen coyotes or a wolf. I'll find out immediately."

His reassuring words had no effect on Mrs. Royer. She pulled down the dividing curtain with a single violent motion. Ignoring Broderick, who was still buttoning his trousers, she ran to the window on the other side of the room, Mrs. Lowell right on her heels. Speculating out loud about reasons for the gunfire, Broderick secured the shutters across the last window himself.

His words were given the lie as the door crashed open, and a soldier all but fell through, carrying the limp body of one of his fellows. Another soldier followed right on his heels, then Barney Webb lumbered inside, forcing his prisoner to stay with him by yanking on the handcuffs.

Lydia Lowell, frozen in place across from the open door, made a small sound as of surprise, stiffened and crumpled to the floor. Mesmerized by the sight of blood soaking the thin material of the fallen woman's night clothes, Sarah didn't look up until she heard the door slam.

No one in the room moved except Webbs' prisoner. He lifted the heavy bar into place across the door, ignoring Broderick's order to stop.

"We need to be able to take in the others who will make it here," Broderick said.

"Get your men at the windows. If they see anyone coming, you can open the door for them."

The young killer's deep voice inspired confidence in a way Broderick never had. Sarah found the courage to move.

Kneeling beside Lydia Lowell, taking a cool hand in her own, Sarah smiled down into the pain-filled, frightened face.

"Don't let them get me," Mrs. Lowell begged in a gasping whisper.

"There's nothing to worry about," Sarah lied. "There are soldiers with us now, and we'll be fine. Save your strength."

The wound was terrible, in the center of the chest and spurting bright arterial blood. Without having seen such a thing before, Sarah knew the woman was dying and there was nothing she or anyone else could do. Concentrating on Mrs. Lowell, Sarah ignored the others until raised voices made her look up.

"Give me a gun," the prisoner said. "You need all the help you can get."

"We'll be reinforced by others soon," Broderick said.

"No, you won't. Those are Comanches out there, and half your men were dead before the other half woke up. If anyone's alive, they're holed up in the barn. Give me a rifle."

"You shut up about Comanches, you son of a bitch," yelled Barney Webb. "Shut up, shut up, shut up!"

The prisoner started to turn toward Webb, but the bounty hunter was already swinging his rifle. The wooden stock hit the young man in the side of the head and he fell sideways, slid several feet on the floor, and lay unmoving.

"That was stupid," Broderick said. "We're going to need an extra rifleman before this is over."

Pasty-faced under his filth, Webb blustered. "They killed my brother. They killed Hank, and it should've been him. He talked me into taking him into the bushes just before one of them Injuns came sneaking out and knifed Hank. It was me shooting that murdering redskin that warned everyone. You should be thanking me."

"Thank you, Mr. Webb," Broderick said coldly. "Now I think we need your gun at one of these windows."

Webb walked to the nearest window, but instead of firing through the loophole, tried to look out. "I can't see...." He got no further before his head jerked back, the rest of his body following the arc. He fell silently to the floor, blood and something gray and dreadful spreading from his head.

Bile rose in the back of Sarah's throat. She looked down at Mrs. Lowell, unwilling to take in more of what was happening.

"She's dead, Sarah." Mrs. Royer knelt at the other side of the body and gently pulled the dead woman's hand out of Sarah's.

Sarah met Mrs. Royer's eyes, surprised to see no disapproval or anger.

"Have you ever loaded a gun, or shot one?" Mrs. Royer asked.

Unable to speak, Sarah shook her head.

"Me either. Aren't we a pathetic pair." Reaching out, she touched Sarah's cheek gently. "We must make sure Lydia doesn't prove to be the fortunate one among us."

Gentleness from a woman who had previously subjected her to nothing but criticism and scorn undid Sarah. She huddled on the floor beside the body, her fear turning to terror.

The soldier who had been carried inside never moved from where he was propped against a wall. He was dead or dying. Broderick and the other soldiers moved from window to window. Anna Royer had spoken to Broderick after she left Sarah by the body. Now she crouched near the fireplace.

"The roof, Lieutenant!" a soldier shouted.

All three men turned from the windows and shot into the roof several times. The gunfire was deafening.

In spite of coughing from the gun smoke and gagging from the scents of death, Sarah knew she was whimpering, couldn't hear herself, couldn't stop herself.

She watched one of the soldiers drop his rifle and pick up Barney Webb's. He also pulled Webb's pistol free from its holster.

Seeing this, Sarah glanced toward the body of Webb's prisoner, the murderer who killed like Comanches. He moved! Pushing himself up by his arms slightly, he shook his head, then fell back. *Wake up,* she thought, *wake up and help us.*

One of the soldiers could barely lift his rifle now, his left arm bloody and hanging. He slumped over, and Sarah saw blood spreading across his back as Broderick eased him to the floor.

"Close to the end here, Lieutenant." The remaining soldier said the words matter of factly between shots.

"You take care of yourself. I'll do what else is necessary," Broderick replied in the same tone.

Both men moved from window to window, firing from each in turn. Moments later, the soldier dropped Webb's rifle. He went to the friend he had carried inside, checked for signs of life and returned to a window, sorrow on his face.

After another few shots, he said, "I'm out of ammunition, Lieutenant. You want me to wait?"

Broderick shook his head. "I'm sorry, soldier."

The man said nothing. He pulled Webb's revolver from his waistband, put the barrel in his mouth, and pulled the trigger.

The sudden silence in the house made Sarah more aware of the shrieks outside. Right outside. Close.

Anna Royer walked to Lieutenant Broderick. Neither one said a word. He pressed his pistol to her breast and fired. She smiled as she fell.

Broderick turned to Sarah.

"Miss Hammond."

His cold, formal manner and clear intention panicked Sarah. She threw herself backwards, scrambling into the opening of the stone fireplace, trying to hide. "No!"

Unable to get further away from the man and his gun, Sarah looked up into his contemptuous eyes, ready to argue, beg, but Broderick was the one who spoke.

"You stupid little bitch," he said, then turned the gun on himself.

As his body fell, Sarah tried to push herself even farther back into the fireplace. She was alone, the only sounds those of the Comanches outside, beating on the door and shutters to break through. Except....

Webb's prisoner moved across the floor so quickly Sarah could hardly take it in. He dug in Barney Webb's pocket, pulled out a key and freed one wrist from the handcuffs. Pocketing the key, he left the cuff dangling and turned Webb's body over. A pistol that had been hidden at Webb's back went in his waistband. Crawling from one body to the next, he searched through pockets and cartridge pouches.

He took a rifle from one of the dead soldiers. Sarah watched with disbelief as he pushed bullets into the gun. Where had he found more ammunition?

With a wolfish grin on his face, he poked the rifle through a loophole, took careful aim and fired. After a second shot, the assault on the door stopped, and the sounds outside faded as the Indians moved back. Relief flooded through Sarah, then dissolved as the young killer crawled from one window to the next, staying low, firing a shot without aiming from each one before moving to the next.

Back at Webb's body he took a knife from the scabbard on the man's belt. Then money? Sarah watched in disbelief as he pulled a handful of paper notes and coins from the dead man's pocket and stuffed them in his own.

Between more random shots, he pried at one floor board after another with the knife. Near where Sarah had slept, he stopped, pulled a board out of the floor, then another.

For the first time, he looked at her. "Let's go. Time to move, Boston."

Sarah didn't move. Uncomprehending, she stared at him. He didn't waste more words; he came and got her. As he pulled her out of the fireplace, she yelped. He clamped a dirty hand across her mouth, dragged her to the opening in the floor and pushed her through. Sarah fell into a shallow hole in the dirt underneath the floor. When she rolled over and sat up, cobwebs brushed her face. She whimpered and cowered lower.

The killer stepped down into the hole beside her, fit one of the boards back into place, and dragged something over the floor. Hunching down beside her, he used the knife to fit the second board into position. The darkness was almost total, only faintly lighter along the cracks between the boards. In the small space he bumped into Sarah with every movement.

He kept moving, elbowing her time after time, until a thump sounded from above. As he fitted himself down beside her, still at last, an unmistakable stench filled the air, and liquid dripped down between the boards, dripped onto Sarah's arm and shoulder and on the ground where she sat.

He'd knocked over the chamberpot! Sarah couldn't stop the sound that escaped her as she tried to get away from the filth.

His hand closed over her mouth again. Even pitched low, his voice was harsh. "Not another sound. You understand?"

Sarah managed to move her head enough to nod in spite of his hard hold.

"If they find us, they most likely won't kill you, but they'll hurt you bad. You want to take your chances with them?"

Sarah shook her head violently from side to side. In the dark, the distinctive sounds as he drew back the hammer on the pistol tore across her nerves and left her quivering. The empty iron cuff and chain hanging from his wrist fell across her shoulders, and the barrel of the gun pressed under her chin.

"Me neither," he said. "Now, sssh."

5

SARAH WAS GLAD OF the hand over her mouth. Without it she would never have been able to suppress sounds of distress. How could she have thought he looked even slightly clean only days ago? The stench was overwhelming—of his unwashed body and of the contents of the chamberpot. Behind the pressure of his hand, she sucked the inside of her lower lip between her teeth, bit down and concentrated on not gagging.

Overhead, sounds of the Comanches' success were clear. Wood splintered as the door gave way, triumphant shouts and laughter rang out. The floorboards creaked as the Comanches walked back and forth. Without being able to understand a word, Sarah recognized the gloating and boasting tones. After a while, the voices changed. They became agitated, rose to quarrelsome and finally, angry. The argument continued for what seemed like hours before dying away.

For the first time since early morning, silence descended. Silence except for the sound of her own labored breathing and that of the man holding her. Not only could she hear him, she could feel him. The hole was stifling, the smells unbearable. Just as Sarah lost her struggle not to gag or fight against his hold, he took his hand off her mouth, moved the pistol away, and eased the hammer down.

She leaned forward and cupped her own hand in front of her nose and mouth, breathing deeply. There was no scent on her hand; it didn't help. Gulping air through her mouth, she could *taste* the stink. Even so, she began to feel calmer. Except....

He was moving again. An elbow dug into her once, twice. She jumped at the sound of cloth ripping. The faint light through the cracks no longer looked dark gray but lighter, yellowish. That light disappeared little by little as he stuffed whatever he had ripped up between the boards.

"I need that thing you're wearing," he whispered.

His hands reached for her. Shrugging him off, she managed to squirm out of her wrapper and push it at him.

He gave it back to her almost at once. "I started some cuts with the knife. Rip it into lengths and give them to me."

Unable to understand why he was cutting off the only light, still Sarah obeyed as best she could. The tearing of the cloth played across her nerves like a fingernail across a blackboard. Why didn't the Indians hear it?

"Are they gone?" she whispered.

"They're out of the house. It's on fire."

Fire! Sarah's fear ratcheted right back up. "We're going to burn?"

"Most likely not. The burned out places I've seen, the floor's scorched some but still there. Fire moves up. Smoke's going to be our problem. We need to get these cracks filled."

The burned out places he'd seen?

He filled the cracks, and total darkness made the hole close in even more. As he pushed back down beside her, Sarah cringed against the dirt wall, unable to get away from him, trying to make herself smaller.

A tear ran down her face, and then another. She was going to burn to death in a tiny hole in the ground that a killer had turned into a latrine, a killer who hadn't washed in days and days to start with. Or if she was lucky, she was going to be smothered to death by smoke, or....

"Is there—is there enough air down here?"

"For a while. If I pass out, you push out those boards and pop out of here. If you pass out, I'll do the same. Maybe they'll be gone."

He was joking about it. Joking!

As if he could read her mind, he went on more soberly. "Look, Boston, fretting won't help now. A little while ago we had no chance. Now we've got some chance."

"My name isn't Boston. It's Sarah, Sarah Hammond."

"Pleased to meet you, Miss Hammond. I'm Matt, Matthew Slade."

What he called her didn't matter, and she certainly didn't want to be correcting him and making him angry.

She ventured, "It doesn't matter what you call me. You saved my life. I.... Thank you."

His voice resonated with humor again. "You're looking at it wrong, Miss Hammond. You saved us both when you made old Hank and Barney start feeding me decent. Another couple of days with no food and not much water, and I wouldn't have had the strength to run here from the creek, much less move around once I got here."

Even speaking softly, his heavy drawl was in every word. He dropped the final sound of some words so that what he said sounded like *ole Hank an' Barney start feedin' me decent*. Still, Sarah didn't have the trouble understanding him that she had had with some of the people in Louisiana, even though he called the creek a crick.

"Is that why you saved me?"

"Like I said, you saved yourself. I'm not the one stopped Broderick when he was getting all noble there at the end. I figured you'd want what he was offering."

The memory rose bitter in Sarah's mind, making her feel small, stupid and cowardly again. "I didn't realize.... He didn't explain, even a little bit the way you did. Everything was so awful, and I was so scared. When he pointed the gun at me, I didn't think."

She hesitated a moment, then went on, feeling compelled to tell him, tell someone. "He looked right at me and said, 'You stupid little bitch.'"

"I heard him. Now he's dead and you're alive. Some would say that makes him the stupid one, and you didn't lead a bunch of green Yankees right into a Comanche trap."

Sarah couldn't believe he was casting aspersions on the dead. "They weren't green."

"Greener than spring grass."

"And *you* would know that how?"

"Yankees spent almost four years trying to kill me. At first, we were all green. At the end most of us knew what we were doing. I reckon I can tell the difference."

Two of Sarah's brothers had joined the Union Army after Lincoln issued the Emancipation Proclamation, but even before that, her whole family had searched the papers every day for any scrap of war news. She didn't know as much about what had gone on in the West as the East, but she had a general idea.

"Were you with General Sibley?" she asked.

"Hood."

Sarah sat up straighter, felt the cobwebs and shrank back down. "You were with Hood's Texas Brigade?"

"I was."

Hood's Texas Brigade. General Robert E. Lee's Texans. The very name brought to mind the newspaper accounts of the Cornfield at Antietam, the Devil's Den at Gettysburg. They'd fought for Generals Longstreet and Lee over most of the East, been sent west for Chickamauga and returned to fight through the Wilderness and at Cold Harbor. Had he been there at the end, when the remnants of the Texas Brigade marched at Appomattox? Or had he deserted before then like so many?

The Rebels had fought for an evil cause and were the enemy. Still, it was hard to believe a murderer could have been one of Hood's men. And why should she believe him? He was too young for one thing. The war had been over for two years. Unless....

"Did you enlist the last year or so? Were you there at the end?"

"The end, the middle and the beginning. Eltham's Landing to Appomattox."

She forgot about not antagonizing him. "You're making that up. You're too young!"

"Maybe you Yankees could be fussy about who got a uniform. Down here if a fellow was tall enough to keep a rifle out of the dirt, he was old enough. Then again I sure saw some baby-faced Yankees here and there. Of course, maybe being dead made them look younger."

This—Rebel was making fun of dead Union soldiers. "My brother Will lost an arm at Gettysburg," she said indignantly.

"I'm sorry to hear that, but I reckon somebody else shot him. There were a lot of us there."

Remembering that she didn't want to make him angry, Sarah pressed her lips together. Arguing with a killer so close she could feel him in the darkness had to be even stupider than.... Her mind veered away from those last moments with Broderick, and she changed the subject.

"What did you mean about a trap?"

"Jake and Alvaro weren't guiding Broderick anywhere except where he is right now. They're Comancheros, and they sold the whole bunch of us to the Comanches. I figure we're way off course for getting to Fort Grissom, way too far north and that's because they wanted us here, here where they could get everybody to relax and get some of the soldiers to take their whiskey. Hiring men like that was Broderick's first mistake. He couldn't have asked around about them."

Sarah couldn't argue with him about that. Broderick had never mentioned how he'd come to hire the guides. "What are Comancheros?" she asked.

"Traders. They trade supplies, whiskey and guns for horses, cattle and anything else the Comanches have stolen and want to be rid of. And they trade people. Some of the talk I heard sounded like they planned on selling you down into Mexico."

Daughter of passionate abolitionists, Sarah forgot herself again. "There is no slavery in this country any more. That's why we fought the war. And we won! No one can sell me or anyone else anywhere!"

Her voice had risen.

"Ssh now. Keep it soft."

Chastened, she whispered, "I'm sorry."

His deep voice vibrated out of the darkness again. "A lot of things against the law still happen. Selling whiskey and guns to Indians is against the law. It still happens, and it's going to keep happening, and so will selling people. If they sold you down in Mexico, maybe you'd be lucky and some fellow would take a shine to you, marry you even. Otherwise, maybe you'd wish you'd let Broderick have his way. Life gets ugly sometimes."

"If you knew all that, why didn't you tell someone?"

"I did. Hank and Barney didn't want to hear it. They figured I was just trying to make trouble, escape. And they were right about the escaping part. Jake and Alvaro were their best friends, listening to them brag every night, giving them free liquor. When they couldn't shut me up, that's when they started staying so far away from everybody. Barney was listening a little at the end, though. That's what made him so mad. He knew he got himself and his brother killed because he wouldn't listen and kept anybody else from getting a chance to listen."

Sarah remembered the desperation and fear in Webb's voice as he'd swung the rifle. Shut up, shut up, shut up. "I thought he killed you."

"My head's too hard for that to work as a way to kill me."

There was nothing to say to that, so Sarah asked him one of things she had been wondering about. "How did you know about this hole?"

"Hidey-holes like this are in a lot of these homesteads. The idea is to maybe save some of the young uns if the Comanches come. My folks had one."

"Under the floor?"

"No, we had a space built into a wall, but if there was one here, where else could it be? And not many places like this have board floors. The only other hiding place I could see was the fireplace. Hanging in there like bats until they were gone didn't seem too likely."

He probably wouldn't have had any trouble doing that very thing, but *she* wouldn't be able to even start to climb a chimney.

Another wave of nausea rolled through Sarah, worse than before. "I think I'm going to be sick."

"Breathe through your mouth."

"I am. It's still—dreadful."

"Keep telling yourself that stink is what's between us and a passel of Comanches, and maybe it won't bother you so much."

For the first time it occurred to her that spilling the chamberpot hadn't been some kind of clumsy accident. "You did it on *purpose*?"

"I did. Indians have been finding these hidey-holes and digging Texans out of them for years, but they don't like mucking around in...."

He paused as if searching for an acceptable word, and Sarah couldn't stop herself from saying, "Excrement."

"Ex-cre-ment. There's a ten dollar Yankee word for it. They don't like it any more than anybody else. And after that there was the whiskey."

"What whiskey?"

"Those two jugs on the table there. Once any self-respecting Comanche laid eyes on them, he'd forget all about hunting down stray white folks."

Whiskey. The two jugs that Broderick had confiscated last night had been sitting on the table, Sarah remembered. "Why would whiskey keep them from looking for us?"

"Because they've got a weakness for it. Not one of those Indians would want to take his eyes off those jugs for a second for fear somebody else would get his share. That's most likely what they were arguing about there at the end."

A loud crash above them made Sarah cry out and flinch. "What was that?"

"Roof caved in."

"What if.... What if part of it fell over those boards?"

"Then we're going to die down here."

What was the matter with him? Did he have to be so, so *truthful?*

Sarah didn't want to talk to him any more, didn't want to know the answers to any more questions. He was right that knowing the dreadful smell was part of why she was still alive made it more bearable. So did the fact she couldn't think of anything other than whether there was still a way out of this terrible grave.

She set herself to enduring the heat, her own fear and the fetid air, which no longer seemed to be filling her lungs in spite of her labored breathing. She leaned against the dirt wall, no longer so frightened, no longer even caring much, starting to fall asleep in spite of herself.

His hands on her shoulders, shaking her, brought her awake. "Wake up, Boston. Time to go."

"Go where?" Sarah said muzzily.

He shook her harder. "Are you listening to me?"

"Yes," Sarah said, struggling for air, no longer caring what it smelled or tasted like.

"Good. Those boards are moving up just fine. I'm going to push them all the way up and get out of here as fast as I can. You reach up, and I'll pull you out. Then we're going to run through whatever we find up there straight for the door, you understand?"

"Yes."

"When we get outside, if they're still there, I'm going to use the gun. You still want that?"

"Yes," Sarah whispered.

"If your hair or your dress catches fire, don't run. Get on the ground and roll. Hear me? Don't run."

"Don't run," Sarah managed.

She felt him rising from beside her, the boards flew up, and he was gone. Smoke swirled into the hole, making breathing even more difficult. *He had left her!*

Coughing, struggling to get to her feet, Sarah couldn't make her numb legs work. No matter. Matt reached down, grabbed her flailing arms and pulled. She popped out of the hole like a cork from a bottle.

He never let go. Flames licked the charred walls of the house; the roof was open to the sky. She caught only a glimpse of burned bodies as Matt dragged her through the smoke-filled room, over and around fallen rafters and outside as if she were weightless.

The Indians were gone. Even doubled over coughing, Sarah felt a stab of pure joy. She was alive and breathing clean air! When she straightened, she found herself looking into the same pale blue eyes that had so disconcerted her days before.

Dried blood streaked one side of his face, not quite covering swelling and old bruises. His bare chest sported more bruises, colors from faded yellow to angry red declaring their age. His clothes had gone into the cracks in the floor before her wrapper. The sight of him all but closed her throat with fear.

He looked like a sinister devil—until he smiled, and the sinister devil disappeared, replaced by a charming one whose face reflected the same joy she felt. Sarah looked away, as much afraid of the charm as the menace.

When she looked back he had a key in his hand and was working on the one cuff still on his wrist.

"You not only got the key from Mr. Webb's pocket, you took his money too."

"I did not. The money is mine. They stole it from me the day they stuck a gun in my face, drug me halfway across Texas and all but served me up to the Comanches."

He got the cuff open and dropped the handcuffs where he stood. His wrists were bloody and raw.

"You need to clean those wounds and bandage your wrists," Sarah said.

"They'll get cleaned with the rest of me in a minute. We've got no time for bandages. We've got to round up anything we can use or eat out of what's left here and find a better hiding place before they come back."

"Come back!" Sarah looked around wildly. "Why would they come back?"

"Jake and Alvaro left in the middle of the night, keeping themselves nice and safe, I expect. So right now they're all meeting up again to parcel out the spoils. And sooner or later, somebody's going to say, 'Too bad those two women were dead when we got inside.' And Alvaro's going to say, 'What do you mean two? There were three.' Or maybe Jake's going to say, 'Did you have fun with that one fellow all chained up and waiting for you?' And some Comanche is going to say, 'What are you talking about. Nobody was chained up.' What do you think they're going to do then?"

Sarah didn't want to think about that. She studied the death and destruction around them instead. The grass in the yard had been beaten down by yesterday's activities and did nothing to hide the bodies sprawled by the barn.

The wagon she and the other women had ridden in and that carried all their things lay on its side. Another body slumped over the seat of the half-burned cook wagon, but the rest of the wagons were gone.

"How long do we have?" she asked.

"No way to tell. So we better get a move on. You get down to the creek and scrub up. No use hiding if they can find us with their noses."

Sarah looked down at herself in horror. All she had on was her thin cotton night dress, stained with filth, and one slipper. Here in the bright sunlight she might as well be naked.

"I need clothing," she said.

"I'll get you clothes. You go wash."

"I will get my own clothing," Sarah said with as much dignity as she could manage. "You go start bathing if you want to."

She kicked off the one slipper and headed for the overturned wagon barefoot. The humiliating knowledge of what he must be seeing as she walked away had her legs trembling, until she got close enough to the first body to get a good look.

The body was bloody and mutilated. Spinning in her tracks, she doubled over and retched. Hearing Matt come up behind her, she expected comfort, reassurance.

He took hold of her shoulder and shook. "We've got no time for feeling sorry for them or for us. They're dead, and we're going to be if we waste time. Now, you've got about two minutes to get your own clothes, and then I'm going to pick you up and throw you in that creek and scrub you off myself. And you won't like it."

Sarah tried to glare at him, but her eyes filled with tears and her chin trembled.

Without the slightest sign of sympathy, Matt repeated his warning. "Don't you go puddling up on me now. Get a move on."

He was a killer and a Rebel, and she wasn't about to give him any chance to carry out his threat. After wiping her mouth on a clean place on one sleeve, she marched over to the wagon where her trunks and those of Anna Royer and Lydia Lowell lay open, contents tossed all over the ground.

Wrapping a piece of a torn sheet that had been part of her trousseau around herself with relief, Sarah pawed through the scattered clothing to find her own things. Clothing wasn't hard to find, but her only sturdy walking shoes had burned in the house. She settled for a pair of low-heeled shoes she remembered as being comfortable.

Matt searched one body after another as thoroughly as he had those in the house. Seeing her standing still, he said, "No female frou fraws now. You got clothes. Go wash."

"I need soap."

"Here." A dirty gray lump landed at her feet.

Turning it over in her hand, Sarah protested. "It's lye soap. I want...."

Matt started toward her, nothing charming on his face at all. Sarah clutched her clothes to her chest and fled.

AVOIDING THE SECTION OF the creek where the Webbs had camped, Sarah walked alongside the stream until she found a place where a thick clump of prickly bushes screened her from Matt's view. She expected the small bit of privacy to make her feel better.

Instead her heart started racing and her breathing became ragged. Taking off her filthy night dress and getting into the cold water took more courage than forcing Broderick to confront the Webbs.

She rubbed the harsh soap over herself with frantic speed. The only way to make sure her hair was clean would be to lay right down and submerge herself. Perhaps she could just.... Matt's threat to wash her himself rose in her mind. She lay flat in the water, teeth chattering, rubbed the soap through her hair, and rinsed it out of the thick mass as best she could.

She would use the piece of sheet to dry off, dress as fast as possible and get back to Matt Slade—get back to the wagons. Out of the creek and on the bank by the pile of clothes, Sarah wrapped herself in the sheet and stared in dismay.

Except for drawers, chemise and stockings, her clothes were gone. No corset, no petticoats, no dress. And no shoes. Beside her own under clothing were a soldier's trousers and shirt. She picked up the male clothing and saw several pairs of thick wool stockings, ugly brogans and a woman's sturdy walking shoes, not her shoes, but Lydia Lowell's.

"You get into those things, and I'll cut off the legs and sleeves." Matt came around the bushes without so much as calling out.

She shrank away, gripping the sheet hard. "I can't wear these."

"Sure you can. You try to walk to Fort Grissom in a dress and fancy shoes and you'll be naked and barefoot in a week. Hurry up."

"These shoes aren't mine. They're way too big."

"That's what the stockings are for. You want me to help?"

"No!"

Matt went to the creek and started filling the half dozen canteens he carried. Sarah scurried to the far side of the bushes and dressed as fast as she could in the strange outfit. She barely had the clothes on when he was there with the knife, cutting off more than a foot of trouser leg, uneven and ragged, doing the same with the shirt sleeves. Cutting off the sleeves didn't change the fact the shoulder seams fell halfway to her elbows.

"I can't wear this. The trousers will fall off if I let go of them."

"No, they won't. You need clothes tough enough to stand up to what we're going to have to get through the next weeks. None of your ladies' stuff is going to work, and if the Comanches catch us, what we're wearing won't make much difference."

The soldier's trousers had no belt loops. He fixed that with a few knife cuts into the fabric. Sarah tried unsuccessfully not to stare at the smooth skin of his chest so close to her eyes, the flat brown discs of his nipples so like her own and yet so different.

When he pulled his belt off, her eyes followed the way his trousers slid low on narrow hips. Then he ran his belt around her waist and all thoughts fled except embarrassment. The belt fit, and not in the last hole either.

"There," he said with as much satisfaction as if he'd just finished fine tailoring. "Now you figure out what stockings work best under those brogans or the shoes so you can walk and walk without crippling yourself. And hide that ring. The way it flashes in the sun, the Signal Corps could have used it. If you're done before I am, get back up to the wagons and start looking through them. Everything I found so far that we can use is in a pile on a blanket by the cook wagon. You add in whatever you come up with. Find yourself a hat."

He sat on the creek bank and pulled off his boots. Not wanting to be there when he got to his trousers, Sarah picked up the shoes and stockings and headed back to the wagons. The soldier's clothing felt foreign. The length of her chemise that hung down under petticoats and dress was bunched around her waist and hips.

Nothing she did made Lydia Lowell's shoes fit. The brogans fit, sort of, with two pairs of the heaviest wool stockings pulled over her own cotton stockings.

She was *not* taking a soldier's hat off a dead body. After adding a wide-brimmed straw bonnet of Anna Royer's to the things piled on the blanket, she twisted her engagement ring off, tied it in a handkerchief, and pushed it to the bottom of a pocket.

Some of the things Matt had set aside were a puzzle. She understood the reasons for blankets, knapsacks, rubberized ponchos, matches and spoons, but string, rope, a coil of wire and a tin shaving mug, razor and small mirror? This was the man who had told her she couldn't have female "frou fraws."

And the man who had told her to get busy and look through the wagons. Sarah started sorting through everything still in the tipped wagon and everything that had spilled out or been thrown out.

A small stash of hard candies in with Lydia Lowell's things brought more tears to her eyes, and the tears had her glancing over her shoulder to be sure Matt Slade wasn't around to catch her wasting time on feelings.

She added the small paper packet to the things on the blanket. He would approve of that.

She put a comb, a brush, tooth powder and two bars of glycerine soap on the pile too. If he said anything about those, she'd ask about the razor and shaving mug.

The pile included more of the thick wool stockings, so when she found another pair of her own cotton stockings, she saved those too, and after a moment an extra chemise and pair of drawers.

Having gone through everything in the first wagon, she turned to the second. As she feared, the body in the wagon seat was the cook's. He had always been kind to her. Since the scene with Broderick and the Webbs, he was one of those who had been extra kind. Sarah looked away and walked around to the back of the wagon.

Before she climbed into the wagon, Matt returned. Except for his own boots, not shoes, and a belt with a holster for the pistol and a scabbard for the knife, his outfit matched hers. Of course everything fit the lean, tall length of him and looked—good.

"I would have said even Comanches couldn't get me into one of these blue belly uniforms, but here I am," he said. "I'll go through the wagon. You take anything I hand out and add it to the pile."

Relieved, Sarah carried hardtack, a few dented cans of peaches, a couple of handfuls of dried beans Matt scraped up off the floor, and a few dried apples over to the blanket.

"I was hoping they wouldn't want white man's food, but they must figure they can trade anything a body could eat," he said, jumping down. "I reckon they didn't see how anybody could eat hardtack, because there's enough here to keep us going a while."

Sarah watched him scan the horizon as he'd done before getting into the wagon. "Won't it be too late if you see them?"

"We'll see a dust cloud in the distance first. When we see that, we're out of time and better start running."

He didn't remark on the female things she'd added to the pile, just packed everything into the knapsacks and strapped a blanket and a poncho on the outside of each. Soon Sarah had the lighter knapsack and two canteens around her neck and over her shoulder. Matt carried everything else and started toward the stream.

"What about the bodies?" she asked.

He didn't even stop. "They're in God's hands now. While He's taking care of them, He's going to expect us to be taking care of ourselves, so that's what we're going to do."

Before she could protest, the shoes she'd fussed so much finding a way to fit were around her neck too, the stockings stuffed in the pockets of her trousers, and the trouser legs rolled up to her knees in an absolutely disgraceful fashion.

As she waded into the creek behind Matt, the water swirled cold around her calves. Her feet dug into the sandy bottom with each step, and when he turned upstream, the current pushed against her, adding to the effort it took to go forward.

"Where are we going?" she asked.

"I'm not sure yet, but if we're lucky I'll know it when I see it."

With no idea what he meant, Sarah decided against more questions. Just walking in the water was hard enough.

6

THE CANTEENS AND KNAPSACK grew heavier and heavier. Sarah's lungs and legs burned alike. Soon she would be left behind or have to beg Matt to stop, but she trudged on through the water, putting off the inevitable as long as possible. When he did stop, she almost walked into him, then stood gasping.

"Come on, you sit on the bank a minute. I'll be right back."

She didn't want to stay by herself but was unable to argue or to follow. He left the water, pulled his boots on and walked away. As he grew smaller and smaller with distance, Sarah's fear rose, her mouth went dry. Her breathing, which had slowed, quickened.

What if he left her? She took two steps in his direction, then watched him turn and retrace his steps. By the time he got back, her breathing was almost back to normal.

"Walk around a little," he said. "Over there where the ground is soft."

Sarah followed his directions, leaving several clear prints of her bare feet beside the creek.

"What did you just do? What did I just do?"

"Gave the Comanches something to puzzle over, I hope." He had his boots off and tied around his neck again. "Let's go."

He turned back in the direction they'd come! Was she putting her faith in the survival instincts of a crazy man?

They were almost back to where they'd started, the buildings of the homestead in sight, when he stopped right in the middle of the creek. "Give me those things you're carrying."

More than happy to let him have everything, Sarah handed it all over. He got her knapsack positioned over his shoulders with everything else. Before guilt made her offer to keep carrying the canteens, he said, "Thirsty? We're going to be out of the creek soon. How about a drink?"

Surprised to find how thirsty she was in the midst of all the water, Sarah drank greedily from the canteen he handed her. He drank just as deeply from another, refilled them both and slung them into place around his neck with the others.

"When are we getting out of the water?" Sarah asked.

"Right now." Matt pointed overhead. "See that branch up there? I'm going to boost you up. You grab it and pull yourself into that tree."

Sarah stared up in horror. Yes, a sturdy branch from one of the trees along the creek was hanging right above them. No, she couldn't grab it, or pull herself up, or....

He picked her up with one hand around her ribs just under her right arm, his fingers pressing into the side of her breast, and the other hand between her legs. Holding her like that, he lifted. She shrieked, tried to twist free and ended up grabbing the branch, her scrambling bare feet getting enough purchase on his shoulders to let her pull herself away from his terrible hands and into the tree. He swung up beside her seconds later.

"See that? You can climb a tree just fine." He was laughing at her, laughing. She could see it in those pale blue devil eyes. "Now up there."

Sarah was still shaking her head when she found herself even higher, clinging to the trunk of the tree with all her strength.

He bullied her, he cajoled her, and he manhandled her up that tree and over into one growing close enough to swing to, and then to another and another until they ran out of trees. Sarah clung to the last precarious perch, wishing she had the courage to throw herself down head first and get away from him for good.

Although there were no more trees, a large, dense thicket of bushes grew below them off to one side, the same kind of prickly bushes Sarah had hidden behind when bathing. Matt threw everything he had carried into the middle of the thicket.

"That ought to scare off any snakes."

Snakes!

He looked at her. "You next."

"No."

"Don't be like that. I bet most Yankee soldiers couldn't squirrel up a tree the way you did. This part's easy. If I have to throw you down there, you could get hurt. I'll swing you by the wrists and when I let go, you'll go down feet first and be fine."

"No."

"Yes."

He pried her hands off the tree, grabbed both her wrists in one hand, hung on to the tree with the other and swung her out into nothingness. Too terrified to scream or plead, Sarah watched the ground go by at dizzying speed as he swung her one way, the other, then let go. She fell into the center of the thicket, landing in thorns that tore at her clothes, face and hands. Matt thudded down a few feet away.

"Are you all right?" he asked.

"No!" She was never going to be all right again.

"So what's wrong? Nothing's broken is it?" He pushed through the bushes, started to pull her to her feet.

Sarah hit out at him in a fury. "Don't touch me. Don't you ever touch me again! You pig! You killer! Leave me alone!"

His lips twitched and his eyes gleamed, but he backed away. "If you can fuss like that, you can't be hurt much."

After that, he ignored her and applied himself to arranging the places where they'd broken through the bushes so the gaps didn't show. Sarah watched him pull threads torn from their clothes off the thorns here and there and pocket them.

Finally, down low, he cut away enough branches to make a small, open spot around them. When he was done, he sat down beside her and put his stockings and boots back on.

"Put your shoes back on, just in case, and no more yelling. We won't be able to see them coming from in here, so we have to be quiet and wait."

Sarah said nothing. She was no longer worried about Comanches. In her world, the biggest danger was Matt Slade.

Hours later, Sarah lay on her stomach, face hidden in her arms. At first the only sound had been the occasional buzz of an insect. As time passed, birds began calling back and forth. A cooling breeze rustled through the bushes, and she glanced up to see storm clouds rolling across the sky the way they had every afternoon for more than a week.

She hid her face again. No matter how threatening they looked, the black clouds had never produced more than a few drops of rain. Today the entire sky would probably open and flood the prairie, drowning her like a rat.

Her body was sore and stiffening, her stomach contracting with hunger pangs. The scratches on her face and hands stung. Worst of all, that most private place between her legs that no man but a husband should touch still burned from the feel of Matt Slade's hand.

There had to be some way to erase the memory, to make the swelling and heat between her legs subside. Discomfort and even pain wasn't doing it.

A different sound ended Sarah's self-pitying sulk, one she had heard only inches from her head that morning—the hammer going back on the pistol. She jerked her head up and looked at Matt. Like her, he lay stretched out on his belly. No amusement lit his narrowed eyes. Face set in grim lines, he stared toward the creek as if he could see through the thick bushes.

The birds stopped twittering, but that was just because the storm threatened, wasn't it?

The wind distorted the voices at first, gave the illusion that they were part of the whisper of rustling leaves. As the Comanches grew closer, their voices became more distinct, their words the same incomprehensible cacophony that she had heard overhead that morning.

The voices faded to nothing in the same way they had come, and Sarah collapsed back down in relief until she noticed that Matt had not relaxed. He stayed up on his elbows, listening intently. As day faded into night, Matt kept his intense focus on the bushes between them and the creek.

Long after full dark, Sarah heard the metallic sounds again, knew that he had let the hammer back down on the pistol and that the immediate danger was past. She shivered. Even after the winds of the failed storm, the summer night was warm. Still, Sarah shook.

The memories of Lydia Lowell's face as she lay dying and afraid, of the smile with which Anna Royer greeted death and of the cook's mutilated body rose dark in her mind. She wept, wept silently, with her fist jammed in her mouth to keep grief inside and quiet.

She felt Matt's hands on her and stiffened. He pulled her into the curve of his body, her back to his chest. She waited for his hands to rove, for assault, but he held her without moving. His touch stopped her tears. The quiet, solid warmth of him gradually soothed away her fear and sorrow. Exhausted, she escaped into sleep.

MATT HAD NEVER HELD a woman before. Well, there was this morning, but that didn't count. Sure there had been a few times during the war when he'd danced with a lady or two from nearby towns at some of the parties they held for soldiers, but that little bit of touching wasn't holding. And that visit to the prostitute didn't count at all. That definitely wasn't holding.

Holding Boston—Miss Sarah Hammond—wasn't anything like Matt had imagined. His body had reacted to her so strongly the fire that started in his groin spread until it ran out of places to burn when it got to his scalp, fingertips and toes. He had been careful to position himself so she wouldn't feel his arousal, worked at controlling his breathing so that wouldn't frighten her either, or at least not frighten her more. Strange that something so close to pain could be pleasure.

When she relaxed all the way and her breathing evened out into sleep, his own body calmed, and he spooned her closer. Such a fierce wave of protectiveness swept through him, he almost laughed at himself. Come daylight it might be that the only thing he could do for her would be to take a few extra seconds to kill her before turning the gun on himself. With only five bullets in the gun, he couldn't risk trying to make the first Indian to find them pay for the discovery. Then again, they'd been hard-to-believe lucky so far. Maybe their luck would hold, even though tomorrow the Comanches would have all day to search, not just a couple hours of fading light at day's end.

The odds of getting out of this fix alive were still too small to calculate, but it was hard not to hope. A man who could go through life knowing he had saved a woman like Miss Hammond, knowing she would go on to marry her Yankee, have children, daughters like herself maybe, a man who knew he'd done that could spend the rest of his life knowing he'd done something fine.

Maybe he should have told her about Webbs' mistake, told her he hadn't killed those folks. Telling wouldn't make her believe, though.

Miss Hammond was not fool enough to believe a man who would murder would hesitate to lie. And the plain fact of it was her fear had come in handy today. Without that fear, she never would have made it through the trees, and nothing except the trees gave any hope of escape. They'd made it almost a hundred feet away from the creek and hadn't left a single mark on the ground for Comanche trackers to find.

Maybe his own experience with ladies was limited, but he'd sure heard enough talk about wives, girls at home, sisters and mothers from men during the war. No one ever described such a grand combination of courage and conviction, self-doubt and fears, sweetness and spirit as Miss Sarah Hammond.

One thing about it, staying awake all night making sure she didn't talk or cry out in her sleep was going to be easy. No power on earth could make him sleep through one moment of holding her.

7

SARAH WOKE AT FIRST light. Already awake and moving around in the confines of their thorny, leafy redoubt, Matt had the knife out and was using it to dig a hole. She sat up, realized what he was doing with that hole and spun on her bottom in the other direction. The acrid scent of urine filled the air, and she thought of what he'd said the day before about the Comanches finding them with their noses.

His hand on her shoulder turned her back around. He pointed at her, then at the hole. She shook her head violently. He nodded, then pointed at himself and did a spinning motion with his forefinger.

Not for one moment did she believe he'd really turn his back, but she remembered all too well how he'd ignored her protests and attempts to get away yesterday and bullied her up the trees—and how he'd gotten her down again. She thought about speaking, threatening to make noise if he didn't leave her alone, but the knife in his hand and the look in his eyes chased that idea right out of her head.

Besides, her full bladder ached.

He did keep his back to her as she fumbled with the buttons on the unfamiliar trousers, thankful for the little modesty her chemise provided. As she worked on refastening, the buttons, he turned. She flushed with embarrassment, knowing the sounds had let him track exactly what she did every moment, but she did feel better.

At least he was too busy filling in the hole and scraping more fresh earth over it to enjoy her discomfort. By the time he finished, the scent faded away. The Comanches still weren't going to find them with their noses.

Handing her one of the canteens, Matt opened the sack that contained the few food items they'd found. He gave her a piece of dried apple and one of the hardtack biscuits.

Sarah ate her apple eagerly, but she watched what Matt did with the biscuit before even putting it into her mouth. The thing had the consistency of brick, but if he could eat it, so could she. Chewing on the edges eventually softened it enough she could nibble bits off. To her surprise, when she finished, she felt full.

She settled the whole thing with another drink. As she capped the canteen and put it down, Matt held the packet of Lydia Lowell's candies out to her. His hand was filthy, and she didn't care. Looking into pale blue eyes once again alight with humor, Sarah knew as surely as she knew her own name that he was not a killer, not crazy, and that if there was any chance at all of getting across all the empty miles of Texas to safety, Matt Slade would find a way to do it.

More than that, he'd find a way to make *her* do it. She took one of the candies and smiled at him.

Matt pointed two fingers at her eyes, then circled his hand around, closed his eyes and pointed at himself. A second, slower repetition of the gestures made it clear. He wanted her to watch and listen while he slept! No, she couldn't. She absolutely could not.... She was still shaking her head, still trying to make it clear she couldn't watch on her own when he stretched out on his back and pulled his hat down over his face.

It was like being alone. She scooted a little closer to him. After a while she reached out and touched his sleeve with her fingertips. When he didn't wake, she closed her fingers around the cloth of his sleeve, feeling braver somehow. If he trusted her to watch while he slept, she must really be able to do it.

The sun beat down from straight overhead when they came again. Sarah didn't wait to hear them. As soon as the sounds of the birds stopped, she grabbed at Matt's shoulder. He woke instantly, gun in hand.

No voices came this time, but the quality of the silence crawled up Sarah's spine. She flinched at the muffled sound of a horse snorting.

Glancing at Matt, hoping to see from his attitude that her imagination played her false, Sarah found no comfort in the tense way he watched, turning his head to follow something, someone, moving at the edge of the bushes.

Three times that day the searchers came close. No telltale sound ever gave them away, but the prickling sensation of danger in the air and the way Matt acted were all the evidence Sarah needed. Late that afternoon, storm clouds formed, blacker than ever, and the wind cleared the eerie, crawling feeling out of the air. For the first time, the clouds brought rain.

Mrs. Royer's straw hat dissolved to a sodden, useless mess. Wet through, wiping rivulets of water off her face, Sarah thought wistfully of the ponchos. The rubberized cloth would crackle with every movement, but still.... Long after the rain stopped, Sarah settled down to sleep under the damp blanket Matt gave her, wishing she could trade the clammy wool for the warm, solid feel of him against her back.

In many ways the third day was the worst. The rising heat of the summer day dried out their clothes, but without any sign of the hunters, boredom became the enemy. Sarah feared she would lose control and start babbling—or screaming. In her mind she pushed out through the bushes and danced in circles, shouting at the top of her lungs, or bathed in the creek, splashing without a care.

Matt's restlessness showed in the way he went through the knapsacks, examining one item after another as if he could find something unique in such ordinary things. When he was through, he picked out the brush and comb and gestured at Sarah. If he had expectations of passing the time brushing her hair, he could just give them up!

She took the brush and comb herself and began working at the tangled mass. By the time she had untangled the bottom few inches of her waist-length ropes and snarls, her hands were sore and her arms ached. The maids back home who did this for her made it seem so easy. Sarah sighed and put the comb down. She didn't protest when Matt picked it up and started working where she left off.

His gentleness surprised her. He held each section of hair above where he combed and teased the knots out with patient care. When his hands went still, a peek over her shoulder showed him looking off toward the creek, listening intently. Reassured by his vigilance, Sarah closed her eyes and gave herself over to the sensations, enjoying the occasional touch of one of his hands on her back or shoulder, the feel of the brush running through each untangled section.

MATT HAD NEVER TOUCHED a woman's hair before. He knew folks called the texture of clean hair silky, but Boston's hair wasn't like the silk of a corn tassel or like anything else he could think of either. Back East some of the fancy folk had been dressed in silk, satin and velvet, and he thought he knew which was which but not for sure. Things like that had never mattered much, but now, knowing the right way to describe the blonde cloud in his hands seemed important.

As Matt worked on the tangled mass, he tried to concentrate on the decisions he had to make. If the rain came again today, should they take the chance, give up this hiding place and head out? A storm like yesterday's would let them get away without leaving a trail, but was today too soon? And whether they left today or tomorrow, which way should they go?

If Hank and Barney had gotten the straight of it, Fort Grissom was about as far ahead as the last town was behind, but trying for the fort meant walking deeper into Comanche country, traveling over land he didn't know.

In either direction water would be the problem. The creeks were running full now, but soon most of them would dry up as the rains stopped and full summer heat baked the land. The half dozen undamaged canteens he'd found each held only a couple of cups of water, not enough.

Going back would be easier, and that's where Jake and Alvaro and any Indians helping them would search the hardest. Going forward also meant taking a chance on the Comanches, but maybe only raiding parties with no idea two white folks were on foot out there.

Her hair was almost all untangled now, less of a cloud, smooth and sleek. He stopped worrying about what to do next and gave himself over to the pleasure of feeling it slipping across his hands.

No wonder women kept their hair bound up and hidden. They must do it to protect men from themselves. Getting to do this very often would leave a man so weak kneed he'd never be able to deal with his share of the world's troubles.

SARAH MOUTHED A THANK you at Matt. In spite of several breaks—for a few swallows from the canteens, for one hard candy apiece, for a silent debate waged with sign language about the wisdom of cutting out one particularly dreadful knot with the knife—by early afternoon the brush slid right through her hair from scalp to end.

She expected him to quit then, but he twirled his finger in the turn around sign. She obeyed, no longer afraid of what he might do. What he did was plait the whole length into one thick braid.

She had paid no attention to the darkening sky and rising wind. The afternoon clouds only marked the time of day, and Sarah hoped the clouds wouldn't bring another storm to soak them to the skin.

Her attitude changed abruptly as she watched Matt put the brush and comb back with the other things, fasten the knapsacks and strap the blankets on the outside. All he left out were the ponchos.

The ponchos and a slouch hat! The same kind of soldier's hat she had disdained only days ago. He dropped the hat on her head, grinned as it fell into her eyes, lifted it off, wrapped the braid around her head and tried again.

When the hat fit well enough that way, she half expected him to say, "There," in his fixed-it tone, but he remained silent. Silent, but getting ready to leave this safe place. Her stomach clenched and her heart beat faster.

By the time Matt finished cutting Sarah's poncho short enough so that it didn't drag on the ground, the first fat raindrops spattered across her shoulders.

Thunder crashed and lightning streaked across the sky. Sarah didn't need Matt's signal to stay close behind him. She all but stepped on his heels as he pushed through the bushes. Out in the open, they stood for a moment looking, listening. No one was in sight. There were no sounds except of the storm.

"Let's go."

Even pitched low, his voice made Sarah start. She followed him to the creek, spun in a circle, watching all around nervously as he refilled the canteens.

When Matt headed away from the creek, Sarah started out beside him but couldn't keep up. She fell behind, caught up when he slowed or stopped and waited, then they did the whole thing all over.

Before long, he adjusted his long-legged stride, and they walked side by side at a steady pace. Sarah thanked goodness that she had often walked beside the wagon in days past, but how long could she keep up even this pace?

The rain came down so hard the drops bounced on the ground. The grass underfoot turned slippery. The wide-brimmed hat and poncho kept Sarah's hair and upper body halfway dry, but walking through the tall, wet grass soon had her trousers soaked to the knees.

As the thunder and lightning faded into the distance and the rain slowed, Matt began stopping every so often, studying the landscape.

All Sarah saw was a sea of featureless wet grass. She wanted to ask him what he was looking for, where they were going, a hundred other questions but decided to keep quiet until he talked and use the stops to catch her breath.

The rain dwindled to a drizzle. Matt veered off the straight line of travel he had been setting and led the way to a small clump of bushes. Low and sparse, they didn't begin to provide the kind of hiding place they had been in near the creek.

He dragged one of the canteens through the bushes. Was that to scare off snakes? Did snakes really scare? Sarah didn't know, but when Matt threw their knapsacks down, she relaxed.

"It's not good, but the rain's going to quit any minute. We can't push our luck any further than this."

"They can see us here."

"They'll have to be searching this piece of prairie, and they'll have to get close. Come on. Let's get hunkered down as best we can."

The rain continued for more than a minute but not too much longer. When it ended, the sun chased the storm clouds, and the wet grass glistened. No one could miss the distinct double trail of bent grass leading to this clump of bushes.

"They'll see our tracks," Sarah said.

"Not unless they hurry. That grass will soak up the rain as fast as it can and straighten up overnight, and the ground is washed clean. By morning there won't be any sign left, and I've got a notion most of the Comanches have given up anyway. They'd be happy to catch us and have some fun, but they don't care enough to keep looking for days. It's Jake and Alvaro that aren't going to give up. Maybe they can bribe a couple of the Comanches to help them hunt, but right now every one of those Indians has a big share of the spoils from this raid and wants to get home with it."

"Why won't Jake and Alvaro give up?"

"Because if we make it to Fort Grissom and tell the Yankees who set that trap and helped the Comanches, there'll be no place in the reconstructed United States they can hide. They can maybe run to Mexico, but I'm not sure they'd be safe even there."

"Oh." That made sense, but Sarah didn't want to think about the guides relentlessly searching for them, never giving up.

"I'm sorry I'm slowing you down so much," she whispered, unable to look at Matt as she said the words. "I know you could be two or three times as far away by now without me slowing you down."

He looked up from rummaging through the knapsacks. "You've been listening to too many people like that sourpuss lady. If it weren't for you, those Comanches would be roasting me on a spit right now."

Sourpuss lady? Sarah thought about pretending she didn't know who he meant and decided against it. "Her name was Anna Royer," she said. "She just wanted me to behave the way an officer's wife should, and she was very brave at the end."

"Well, it's a good thing for me she never got you to stick your nose as far up in the air as hers was, and I bet she couldn't climb a tree. I figure the most likely reason they didn't find us is because they knew about you from Jake and Alvaro, and they didn't even think about a lady like you climbing a tree, much less climbing one and swinging over to four more."

"I didn't climb those trees, and you know it," Sarah said. "You pushed me up them, and you took advantage of the fact I was afraid of you."

His teeth flashed white in the dark beard growth then, his eyes full of mischievous recognition of what he'd done. Her stomach did a strange little flipping thing, a thing it had never done before.

"I gave you a little boost to start, but you climbed sure enough. And you're not afraid any more, are you? Why is that?"

Because you held me and didn't take advantage. Because I wouldn't react to a murderer's smile the way I react to yours.

Sarah said, "Because I know you didn't kill those people. Don't ask me how. I just know. Why were Webbs so sure you did?"

"The horse mostly. That red dun Barney rode was mine. The killer had a horse like that, and the poster said brown hair and blue eyes. I'm too young and not big enough in any direction, but they figured if they brought in a body that had been out in the sun a couple of days, nobody'd look too close and they could get their money."

"How could you take the time with the Indians right outside to go through his pockets and get your money back?"

Matt had a can of peaches out, opening it with the knife. "If we get to Fort Grissom, your Yankee will be taking you in, marrying you and taking care of you like a husband should, but for me, maybe some fellows will buy me a drink or two, but that's about all. So there I'd be, hundreds of miles from where I want to be without a nickel to my name for another horse, for food or for anything else."

All the laughter was gone from his face now. "I've been there before, and I'm not going to be there again if I can help it. Besides, I needed to find the key, and he had my gun in the back of his belt."

"What about the bullets you found? They thought they were out of ammunition. That's why they.... I heard them say so."

"Folks always get panicky in a tight spot. I figured they didn't search careful."

They didn't, but you did.

"When you shot the rifle, did you—did you hit one of them?"

"One with each shot. That Yankee rifle was every bit as good as I expected." He gave her a trace of the same fierce grin he'd had on his face as he'd made those shots.

He had two of the awful hardtack biscuits out and handed her one. "Here, soak it in the peach juice for a while. That'll soften it up and make it taste halfway decent too."

It would still taste dreadful, and Sarah knew it, but she smiled as she took the biscuit anyway. "It's good to be able to talk again. I was afraid I'd lose my mind and start screaming."

"You did fine. We'll have to be quiet again as soon as it starts to get dark. Most likely they won't be out looking at night, but there's no use taking any chances."

Sarah nodded and began working on her biscuit. If they could talk until dark, she had a little while to find out some of the things she wanted to know.

They finished the peaches and biscuits, and Sarah watched him rinse the empty can with no more than a spoonful of water and tuck it away carefully. "Why are you saving the can?"

"If we get to where we can have a fire, we can use it to cook the beans."

"Did you learn that in the war?"

He shrugged and shook his head. "Before."

Sarah took a deep breath and asked her most pressing question then. "How could you fight for the Confederacy? How could you fight for slavery?"

He looked away for moment, then met her eyes.

"You make me ashamed to say. The fact is nobody down here talked about fighting for slavery. All I ever heard was how the Yankees were trying to take our rights away and coming down here and telling us what to do. So I figured I'd join the army and I'd get to wear a uniform instead of the raggedy clothes I had, and they'd feed me three decent meals a day, and it would be a fine thing."

He looked off into the distance again. "That was the biggest mistake I ever made. Hunger and I were only passing acquaintances up until then. It was in the army we got to be best friends and bedfellows."

"I'm sorry. I didn't realize settlers here were...." She stopped, unable to think of a polite way to finish the sentence.

"Poor? A lot of them are, but my folks weren't poor; they were dead. They died when I was ten. I was on my own when the war started."

How could she believe something like that? How could anyone? "You were on your own from the time you were ten until you were what, fifteen, sixteen?" The thought appalled her so much her voice rose.

"Sixteen. It was a long time ago, no reason to get all het up about it. No, first I was with these religious folks that took in boys like me. I didn't get away from them for good until I was, oh, fourteen, I guess."

Matt got up on his knees then, as if he needed to do that to see out over the prairie better. Many inches shorter, Sarah could see just fine. He was using the movement as a way to stop her questions. Sitting back down, he changed the subject and confirmed her suspicion.

"Now it's your turn," he said. "Tell me about where you come from. Does it snow every winter in Boston?"

She was going to find out more about the religious folks that he'd gotten away from "for good" and what had happened to his family. Tomorrow. Today she'd already heard enough about a life so far removed from anything familiar.

Until it got dark and they had to be silent again, she told him about her family, about their passion for the abolitionist cause and their sober ways, about the three-story house in Boston that had been home to Hammonds since before the Revolution, and, yes, about the snowstorms that came every winter.

Sarah fell asleep knowing he watched over her and thinking about a boy who had joined the army hoping for decent meals. She thought about what she'd heard about the ragged, starving Confederate Army the last years of the war. If her parents ever saw her anywhere near someone like Matt, they'd each grab an arm and hustle her away as fast as they could. She smiled to herself in the dark. Fortunately, her parents were far away, safe in Massachusetts, because she wanted to know a lot more about Matt Slade.

8

THE NEXT MORNING MATT told Sarah why he'd decided to go on to Fort Grissom instead of back the way they'd come. She wondered if his seeming ignorance of the fact men never explained themselves to women had to do with being orphaned young. Some part of her wanted him to be like her father, brothers and Lieutenant Broderick, to tell her everything would be fine, trust him. Only a small part, though. The rest of her liked this way better.

Still, knowing he planned for the two of them to walk across this empty land that white men didn't travel except in armed groups frightened her even before she understood the problems they would face over food and water.

"How will we find the fort in all this nothingness?" Sarah asked. She had not liked the moist air of Eastern Texas, but the hill country and forests suited her much better than the almost flat grasslands that stretched in every direction now.

"Grissom is one of a line of forts that run north to south. If I'm right and our *guides* led us too far north, and we head southwest we'll hit Grissom, or at least one of the roads or trails near it. If we angle too far south and miss Grissom, we'll still cross some road that will lead to one of the other forts."

"It's hard to believe water is going to be a problem when it rained so hard the last days."

"I know. If we stay lucky the storm season will be a long one, but as soon as the rains stop all but the biggest creeks will dry up, and we can't carry much water with us. Everything I've ever heard is that the country gets drier as you go west. So from here on out, except when we're right at water, we need to be careful with it."

Sarah nodded. "Are we waiting for rain today before we go on?"

"We are. We'll give it at least another day. If we can get a few miles further away without leaving sign, maybe they'll never figure out which way we went."

"What are our chances now?"

"Getting better but still not good," he said soberly. "The land is the biggest enemy now, and Texas is a hard place for folks with no more than we've got."

Since they were talking about hard things.... "Tell me about your family, Matt. You said they had a house with a hiding place in it, so I know they were settlers. Where did they come from? Do you have sisters and brothers?"

Whatever she expected, it wasn't that he would laugh at her. "I think I'm starting to understand why you Yankees won the war. Those poor fellows went home after the first year and said, we've been whipped, and you ladies just threw them right back out and said try again. And then they went home after the second year and said, we've been whipped, and you did the same thing again. And...."

Sarah interrupted him. "And after the third year, they came home, and said, we're winning, and after the fourth year they came home and said, we won."

Matt grinned at her, not at all bothered by what she'd said. "That's the mortal truth, but you had to force them back at it those first years."

"I didn't, but I suppose Mr. Lincoln did," Sarah admitted. "So we're in agreement that I'm not going to give up, and you may as well tell me about your family now and save me asking tomorrow."

"I might as well." He shifted so that they were sitting facing each other instead of side by side. "You watch behind me, and I'll watch behind you."

After a brief hesitation as if to gather his thoughts, he started talking. "My folks came here from Kentucky, started out the day after they married, and they settled a little northwest of San Antonio. Texas was part of Mexico then. My pa was one of those that fought Santa Ana. I had four sisters and two brothers."

He named each one slowly, and Sarah wondered if it was a ritual of remembrance. "What were your parents' names?"

"My father was Thomas, same as my oldest brother, and my mother was Laura."

She bit her tongue, forcing herself to wait for him to go on and not pepper him with questions.

"That whole year was a hard one. The summer before was grasshoppers and drought, and Pa said the winter was the coldest he'd ever seen in Texas. Just when it seemed we'd finally made it through, the sickness came. We all came down with it, one by one. By the time a neighbor stopped by, looking to tell Pa he was giving up and we could have anything he left behind at his place, Betsy and I were the only ones still alive, and just barely at that. So Mr. Greenlow, he threw us in his wagon with what was left of his own family and took us on in to San Antonio. Betsy died the day we got there, and he left me with these religious folks who took in boys like me."

"Orphans."

"Exactly."

"Did he bury your family?" The thought of the bodies they'd left behind in the open still bothered Sarah.

Matt shook his head. "Pa buried Jane, Luke, and Eva. They died before he got too sick to get out of bed. Tom buried Ma, Pa, and Georgia. His body was the only one in the house with me and Betsy when Mr. Greenlow got there. He fired the house and left everything to burn. Don't look like that, Boston. It was the best he could do and pretty decent of him at that."

"If he was so decent, why didn't he take you in, adopt you?"

"He was giving up and going back East where he came from. He'd lost his wife and two youngsters to the sickness himself. He couldn't take on another boy."

"Was it cholera?"

"I don't know what it was. We were sick pretty much every way a body could be sick."

"I'm sorry," Sarah said softly.

"Me too. They were good folks, and my sisters and brothers would have been like them."

"Like you."

"Well, now maybe I'd have been the black sheep. Maybe I am, even if there's only one of me."

He was making fun again, blast him. "How can you do that?" Sarah asked. "How can you treat everything as a joke? Even when we were in that terrible hole, I could hear it in your voice. Don't you take anything seriously?"

He shrugged. "Sure I do, but there's no use fussing over things you can't fix or change, and laughing makes things easier most times. Now it's your turn again. What's this Yankee of yours like? Is he tall and handsome?"

Sarah didn't want to talk about Carter Macauley. She wanted to know about the religious folks he'd gotten away from for good at fourteen. Perhaps prying that information out of him would be easier tomorrow.

"Yes," she said. "He's about your height, and he's very handsome." Studying the lean face looking back at her with interest, she couldn't help adding in her mind, *handsome in a soft, easy-life kind of way.*

"So did he see you at some fancy ball and take one look and know you were the one he wanted for a wife and come courting?"

Incredibly, now he was serious. As if he really thought some man could take one look at her, tight corset not disguising the extra pounds no amount of starving herself had ever melted away, and decide she would be an ideal wife because of the way she looked.

Remembering the way Matt had admitted to shame over the reason why he joined the army, Sarah decided to tell him the truth, the truth she was half-ashamed of herself.

"My family arranged for us to meet because they knew he was looking for a wife, and they knew I met his specifications, and he met theirs."

"Spec-i-fi-ca-tions."

He tipped his head at her as if studying on the word. Sarah recognized the teasing glint and realized he knew perfectly well what it meant. He probably knew every other multi-syllabic word she could come up with too.

"Yes." Unable to look at him as she said the words, she scanned the horizon behind him. "My parents would only let me meet suitable men, and to them suitable means a man with proper political beliefs from a family with the same. And upright, of course. And with means to support a family."

"What are proper political beliefs?"

"They're—we, we're abolitionists."

"Still? Like you said, it's over. You won."

"Reconstruction has to be done properly. Freed slaves need help to build decent lives."

He didn't say anything more, so Sarah went on. "Major Macauley, was never part of the movement, but he was in the war, so that was good enough for my parents, and he was looking for a wife, and he wanted someone of good character from a prolific family."

She gave him a knowing look. "That's pro-lif-ic. I have five brothers and two sisters. My mother is one of ten children, and all but one of her sisters has at least six children."

"So when he met you, he knew he'd never find another girl who fit the bill and was beautiful to boot."

Sarah looked into the light blue eyes, surprised to see he wasn't laughing at her this time. "I'm not beautiful."

"Sure you are. That's probably why Sourpuss and Puppydog gave you such a rough time. They were jealous."

"Jeal...." Sarah stared at him in disbelief. "You haven't been around many women, have you?"

"That depends on how you mean being around. I saw a lot of ladies during the war. There were some that did nursing and some that were just nice ladies that did what they could for us. There weren't any that could hold a candle to you."

Ever since Sarah could remember, her aunts and other family members had always remarked that she had such a pretty face it was a shame she was chubby or plump or some other euphemism for fat. No one ever described her as pretty without the qualifier, much less called her beautiful with a straight face, and she wasn't about to let Matt Slade get away with making fun of her that way.

"I'm not beautiful, and I am fat," she said.

"You're just nice and round. If you think being skinny is good, you're going to find out by the time we get to Fort Grissom."

He actually seemed serious, which made her feel wistful. "Probably not. Not eating has never had much of an effect, and as soon as I start eating again, whatever I manage to lose comes right back." Was she insane? She was discussing her *figure* with a man?

"You'll be surprised. Not getting enough to eat is one thing. Not getting enough to eat and marching across miles of Texas is going to be something else."

"Then you'll waste away to nothing."

"No such thing. I'm used to it. In fact I'm good at it." He grinned at her again, and Sarah couldn't help but grin back.

"So why did you agree to marry him?" he asked. "Did you fall in love with his handsome, pro-lif-ic searching self?"

"Yes," Sarah lied, unable to face telling any more uncomfortable truths.

"Good," Matt said, as if it mattered to him. "Now you need to do the watching all around because I'm going to get some sleep."

Sarah felt more confident of her own ability to watch, but she still held on to a bit of his shirt once she was sure he was asleep.

$$9$$

RAIN DID COME AGAIN the next day. It came early and lasted a long time, enabling them to travel a good many more trackless miles, and after that they kept moving, moving until dark, and moving through the dark. Two nights later, with the canteen water long gone, the gurgle of another creek, swollen from the storms, sounded in the night.

Sarah would have run to the water, but Matt held her back, approached cautiously. After he filled the canteens, and they drank their fill, Sarah expected they would either cross the stream and go on, or settle for the night nearby. Instead he moved back away from the water, choosing another clump of sparse bushes as a resting place rather than any of the thicker growth near the water.

She fell asleep wondering why but too tired to ask, even if she didn't know better than to risk making a sound in the night.

In the morning, he explained. "Water's dangerous this time of year. Sometimes when it rains, the creeks swell up sudden and a wall of water rushes down and takes everything with it. We don't want to be part of that everything." After a pause, he added, "And Indians stop at creeks for water just like us."

Perhaps it was the bright sunlight of the summer morning, but the creek didn't look too fierce when they approached, and it didn't sound dangerous either. In fact it looked inviting.

"Has it gone down overnight?"

"Sure, and it'll go up again later if it rains today."

"Can we wash? I'm so dirty I itch."

"You bet. I'll watch for you, and you watch for me."

He filled the canteens while Sarah made a pile of everything she had carried and dug the extra stockings and clothing out of a knapsack. She didn't care that the water was cold. She barely glanced over her shoulder to make sure Matt's back was turned.

She soaped and scrubbed, dried herself with a blanket and put on the fresh drawers and chemise with pleasure and the dirty trousers and shirt with reluctance. As soon as Matt finished bathing, she'd scrub up the dirty chemise and drawers.

She sat on the bank with her back righteously turned and scanned the horizon ahead of her, to each side, further and further to the left, to the right.

Then she took a guilty peek over her shoulder. Matt was sitting in the water, soaping an arm. He caught her looking and winked at her. Chagrined, she jerked back around as guiltily as she had after that first wink weeks ago.

Not long after that he was beside her, clad only in trousers. "You need to keep watching. I'm not done yet."

Done with what? Shaving. He had the razor and strop out. Sarah forgot her embarrassment and joined him on the stream bank. "Why shave out here? It's going to grow back."

"Why wash out here? You're going to get dirty again."

That silenced her, but after a moment he explained. "The first years of the war it was no problem, I wasn't growing beard yet, but those last years.... It seemed every time things got so busy I couldn't shave that's when bloodsucking critters moved in, and by the time it was all over I had this notion that shaving kept them away. Maybe it's just a foolish notion, but the fact is when my face gets hairy, I start feeling crawly.

"Oh. That makes sense I guess." The muscle and sinew moving in his arm as he stropped the razor mesmerized her. Back and forth, back and forth. When he stopped and started working up the shaving soap, she said, "Don't you need hot water?"

"It would make it easier, but this will get it done."

She held the mirror for him, watching the process with fascination. It wasn't a smooth shave, his skin looked scraped raw where the razor passed, but the dark beard fell steadily away. His jaw was a little long, tapering to a strong chin that seemed quite suitable for a man with such a persistent disposition. His lean cheeks told the same story as the outline of his rib cage and flat, maybe even concave stomach. Sarah forced her gaze up away from that stomach.

His nose was narrow with just a hint of a blade-like convexity along the bridge. It fit perfectly with cheekbones that would be well defined even with more flesh on him.

As his hair dried, she saw reddish glints in the dark brown. The tan of his face and dark lashes emphasized the sapphire of his eyes.

"Are you watching?"

"Yes." She scanned the land behind him to make it true.

"Hold it still. Just a minute more."

The mirror had drooped in her hands as she studied him. Raising it up, she said, "If the Comanches showed up right now we'd feel foolish."

"Not as foolish as if they'd showed up a while back." He finished and wiped the last of the soap from his face with his shirt.

"You looked too," she blurted without thinking.

"Sure I did, and I'm not a bit of sorry. I've never seen anything half so fine." He touched the end of her nose and left a bit of shaving soap there. "Now let's get these clothes washed up, and they can dry while we sleep."

"We're both going to sleep at the same time?"

"We are not. You first, then me. We've got till dark. We'll walk at night and sleep by day. The sun won't get us as bad, and there's less chance of being seen. All we have to do is not stumble over Comanches in the dark."

Of course. That's all we have to do. Sarah tore herself away and began to gathered their dirty clothes.

MATT HAD NEVER SEEN a naked woman before. Well, except for the prostitute, and that didn't count. Come to think of it she never had taken off that gauzy thing she had on, just left the whole front of it open and pushed it out of the way, so that double didn't count.

That tough, bony girl, impatient with the ignorance of a boy who'd never before done what she did a dozen times a day, had aroused his body just fine, but the feelings Boston stirred were something else. Boston made him wonder if his body would ever settle down again, but she aroused other feelings too.

Here he was, combing her hair for a second time. Wet through, it was a few shades darker than when dry. About as dark as the curls of hair he'd glimpsed that covered the secret female part of her. The hair now in his hands had hidden her back as she walked into the water, although her bottom had still been visible. Who would think a glimpse of a backside could turn a man's insides to jelly?

She'd sat down in the water facing his back, and his second cheating look had let him see the front of her, all that smooth white skin curving in all those wonderful ways. Her breasts looked to be a perfect size, just right to fill a man's hand with maybe a little to spare just in case, and her nipples were pinkish, not brown like his own, larger before she got down in the cold water, smaller after.

Cold water made a lot of his parts pucker up too, including his nipples, but it wasn't the same. His hands were shaking, and he laughed to himself. The state he was in right now served him right for looking, looking several times and trying to memorize the sight.

"Matt?"

He started at the sound of her voice. Surely she couldn't read his thoughts, didn't know why he was breathing as if he'd just run a mile.

"Don't you think it's time you tell me about the religious people you were with after your family died? Were they terrible people? Is that why you don't want to talk about them?"

For days now, he'd turned aside her questions on the subject with jokes and questions about her own life. The problem with telling her would be the look of her as she heard it, most likely the same look as when he'd told her his folks died.

Whatever he wanted from Boston, wanted and wasn't ever going to have, pity wasn't it.

Still, right now, with her back to him, he couldn't see her face, and after stealing those glimpses of her bathing, he probably deserved to have to tell it. Thinking about it already had his hands steady, his breathing and the rest of him almost back to regular.

"Sure I'll tell you. It wasn't some orphanage like you've got in your mind. It was just this preacher and his wife, Reverend Joseph Stolfelz and Mrs. Stolfelz." Her hair all combed out, he began braiding. "They took boys like me right into their home, and there were never more than three of us when I was there. Two most of the time. He was a decent preacher so far as I ever saw. I think he believed what he preached."

"So why did you say you were fourteen by the time you got away from him for good then? That sounds like you spent the whole time you were there trying to get away."

"That I did. We all did. We worked at running away the way generals work at winning wars. The trouble was everybody for miles around knew him and knew us, and they'd help round us up before we got anywheres."

"But why were you running away to start with? If he was a good man, and he was taking care of you, why did you want to run away?"

"That was Mrs. Stolfelz. Looking back, I reckon she most likely meant well, but she was one mean lady. She could have had old Sourpuss for breakfast, chewed her up and spit her out. She was sure it was her duty to educate us so that our lot in life would be improved and our souls would be saved. And she was good at it. She got the ain't beat out of me in the first year."

"The ayent?"

"The ain't. You know, your hair ain't dry yet. She wanted us talking fancy. The way you talk would maybe have been good enough for her, but I sure never made her happy, even though she cured me of ain't and some other things. She got me fixed so I can't cuss either."

"She beat you for swearing or for bad grammar? That's, that's...."

"Maybe I shouldn't have said it was beating. She whipped on us with this cane she had. It hurt pretty bad, but it didn't leave us crippled or anything. The cussing was different. She washed our mouths out with soap for that. That was worse."

"I'm surprised you thought so. I wouldn't expect just washing your mouth out with soap to have much effect on you."

He couldn't tell from her voice whether she was teasing or serious. "She didn't just wash our mouths out. First she did that and then she made us eat what was left of the soap. On good days, I could get it to come up again as soon as I got out of her sight. If it got down into your guts, it meant a day or two pretty much living in the outhouse."

Sarah looked back at him over her shoulder, and to his relief all that was on her face was anger. "Doing that to children is a sin itself. Didn't anyone ever stop her?"

"Who?"

"Her husband?"

"I expect he was more afraid of her than we were. We all knew we'd get old enough to get away some day. He's probably still creeping around trying not to make her mad."

"So you were fourteen when you got away for good."

"I was, and you know sometimes I wonder if I really got away or if they let me go. The last time she was whipping on me, all of a sudden I was looking her right in the eye and thinking about did I really have to stand there and take it any more. I wonder if she saw me thinking that, and I wonder if all the boys that got away just got to a size where she figured it was time to let us go."

"Do you think she's still doing that to boys?"

"I expect not. She had gray hair and was pretty stiff in the mornings back then. They talked about moving back to Galveston a lot. They had family there."

"I hope she rots in hell."

"Now, now, that's soap talk."

He tied off the end of her braid, and she turned right around. "You really can't curse?"

"I can do it, but it brings on the taste of soap so strong, I don't."

"I'd think the minute you got away from them, you'd be yelling ain't and cursing at the top of your lungs on every street corner," Sarah said.

"I was young, and I'm a mild mannered fellow, not hard headed like you Yankees."

She laughed then, looking so beautiful something knotted up inside him. If he stayed here, he'd be reaching out, touching. He got to his feet. "You get some sleep. I'm going to see if there's a way to maybe catch a fish in that creek. I'll be right close by."

THE SCENT OF roasting meat woke Sarah in early afternoon, her stomach growling eagerly. Matt had a small fire going and held a branch with pieces of meat skewered on it over the flames. She hurried over and sat beside him. "Is a fire safe?"

"No, but eating raw snake isn't either. As soon as it's cooked, we'll put it out."

Snake!

"You said you were going to catch a fish."

"I said I was going to try to catch a fish. I didn't, but this fellow offered himself up."

"I am *not* eating snake."

"More for me. You can have a biscuit, and I found some wild onions. You can have some of those." He pointed to the empty cans he'd saved. He'd used the wire to make handles for the cans, and they now sat close to the flames, their contents simmering.

"What does it taste like?"

"Like onions, pretty strong."

"I mean the snake meat."

He examined the piece of meat in his hand as if expecting it to give him the answer. "Better than salt pork, not so good as beef. It's meat is all." He looked at her, serious now. "Meat will keep you stronger than hardened up flour and water or vegetables, Boston. Taste doesn't matter much, just getting ourselves out of this fix. I bet you ate clams where you came from, didn't you?"

Well, when he put it that way, yes, she had, and oysters, lobster, and crab, and come right down to it, fish had scales. Sarah ate several bites of onion, then sighed. "All right, give me a piece of that—meat." She gagged at the first bite, thought about how far she'd have to walk that night and how tired it would make her, chewed and swallowed, keeping a sharp eye on Matt the whole time. If he dared to laugh at her....

Laughter wasn't a problem as he handed her the skewer with the rest of the meat and scraped up loose dirt to smother the fire. Satisfied at last, he sat back down, and they shared the last of the meat and onions in silence. Eating snake had to be the worst, Sarah thought. Getting out of this "fix" just couldn't require anything worse.

10

EATING SNAKE WASN'T THE worst. A week later, after they had settled into a routine, walking nights, sleeping days, Sarah woke to find herself facing a problem that had her close to panic. How could she have not expected this to happen, planned for it? Because of Comanches and dead bodies and climbing trees and walking across empty miles of Texas, that's how. And wasn't upset and strain supposed to make it skip a month anyway? There had to be a way to deal with this and keep Matt from finding out, there just had to be.

They'd finished the last of the food from the massacre site days ago. On good days, they ate one meal after she slept and before Matt did. Today was a good day. A rabbit had hopped into one of the snares Matt set early in the morning. That and as much as she could stand of the greens Matt called pigweed would make today's meal a feast.

While he cooked, she should be able to get what she needed out of the knapsack, fold up her spare stockings and stuff them into her trousers. Then while he slept…. Frantically thinking over everything they had with them, Sarah seized on the idea of her chemises. The muslin was soft, and there was a lot of it. That would work. She could bury the used cloth without Matt ever knowing.

At first the plan worked fine. Once Matt was asleep, she got her spare chemise out of the knapsack and took it far enough away he wouldn't hear the cloth tearing.

The hem defied her attempts to rip through it with her hands. Sarah had the cloth in her teeth when a shadow fell across her.

"What are you doing?"

"You're supposed to be asleep!"

"I'm used to you holding on to me while I sleep, so when you snuck off I missed you."

"I don't hold on to you, and I didn't sneak!"

"If you say so. Why are you ripping up your clothes?"

"Because I need.... I need.... It's a female thing, and I need to do it, and you need to go away."

He crouched down beside her, concern on his face. "Are you hurt? What's wrong?"

"I'm fine. I just need to do this."

"Can I help?"

Oh, blast him, yes, he could. Tears welled. That wiped the sympathy right off his face.

"You quit that now. If you're not hurt there's no reason to be puddling up over something we can fix. Whatever it is, if ripping up that thing will fix it, I'll help you rip it up."

He took the chemise out of her hands. "What do you need?"

"I need strips about this wide." She showed him. "I need to make the cloth into, into pads."

He gave her a hard look. "If you've got a sore suppurating some place you're embarrassed to admit, you better get over it and tell me. That kind of thing is dangerous."

"Nothing is sup-pur-at-ing. Is that a ten dollar Rebel word?"

"Boston."

"I *told* you. It's a female thing."

"You've got some kind of female problem that's going to take this much soaking up? Are your kidneys going bad?"

Kidneys. Was he implying.... "No, you nosy parker, it's my monthlies. I'm bleeding!"

That fixed him. The stunned look on his face almost made it worth admitting what the problem was.

"How can you be bleeding and not be hurt?"

"I'm bleeding from inside. I told you."

"It's a female thing." He tipped his head at her, the blank look changing to one of understanding. "Are you telling me human ladies bleed from inside like lady dogs do?"

For long seconds, Sarah stared at him in disbelief. Her fists balled up, and she considered hitting him. "Don't you dare compare me to a dog," she hissed.

"What are you mad at me for? If that's not what you're talking about, tell me what it is."

She started crying then, really crying, and to her surprise, he gathered her into his arms and held her as she howled into his shoulder. "Ah, come on. It can't be that bad. Just tell me, and we'll figure out what to do about it."

By the time she had control of herself again, she'd accepted that she was going to have to educate him on the female cycle. Between subsiding sobs, she did just that.

Matt had trouble with the concept. "How can ladies bleed from inside for a week every month? You'd fall over dead."

"Well, we don't. In all that time you were in the army with men who were married, didn't any of them ever mention anything about their wives being—indisposed—sometimes?"

"They talked about something monthly all right, but it was more like ladies go sort of crazy for a while now and then. Something to do with the moon maybe?"

Sarah closed her eyes. No one could be this obtuse. The last of her tears dried up.

"It has nothing to do with the moon. Different women have different times."

"If you say so." He let go of her, picked up the chemise, and pulled out the knife.

As he cut and she ripped, he said, "You know, I've been thinking. All over Texas, there are lady coyotes and lady wolves, even lady buffaloes, and none of them bother like this, maybe you could just wear one of these things with nothing under. Then you could do what they do and drip across the prairie. It would sure be easier than all this fixing and fussing."

Sarah gasped and looked up. She *was* going to hit him. Except... he was trying without success to keep a straight face. The afternoon sun slanted across him, and his eyes shone bluer than ever, dancing with suppressed laughter. No other man in the world would react this way to such an unmentionable subject, help her without complaining, and tease away her embarrassment.

Sarah started laughing with him. Something slipped and slid inside her, and she fell in love with Matt Slade.

MATT HAD NEVER SPENT a lot of time thinking about ladies before. Well, yes, he had, but not quite the way he was thinking about Miss Sarah Hammond. Not that he wasn't thinking about her the other way too, a lot as a matter of fact. The thing about it was that the more he got to know her, the more he wanted to know.

He lay on his back with his hat over his face, trying to force himself to sleep and not succeeding in large part because the object of his thoughts was sitting with her back turned to him and several feet between them.

Telling her he knew she hung on to him while he slept had been a sorry mistake. Having denied it, she was going to show him how wrong he was, and he missed the slight tightening of the cloth of his sleeve as she took hold, the feel of her fingers against his arm when she relaxed as she always did after a while.

Of course she'd caught him out pretty good too—over the words. She was right that words like prolific and specification weren't unknown to him. At least when it came to seeing them in newspapers or a book or hearing someone else say them. Along with beating the ain't out, Mrs. Stolfelz had beat a lot in.

Using fancy words like that was what he shied away from. For him to talk like that would be uppity somehow. The last time he'd gotten above himself was buying the flashy red dun horse. That had sure ended ugly, although maybe if he could get Boston to the fort in one piece....

The talking they did every morning as they settled into a new place and scouted around for anything that might be edible had already given him a surprising look at her life. Her family was wealthy all right. Just trying to keep track of all the servants she named and what rooms were on what floor of the big house tired him out.

The picture she painted looked dark in his mind, though. That family must care more about faraway causes than about Boston, or why was she traveling across Texas all by herself except for a couple of other ladies she hardly knew? Shouldn't family want to be there when a daughter got married?

Maybe that was why she had been willing to let that Yankee major come courting even after he checked her out like a horseman would check out a broodmare. That would be worrisome except that once he had come courting, the Yankee must have fallen in love with her. Any man who got to know Boston would fall in love....

Her brothers sounded like the same kind of righteous, determined men as her father. The two who had been in the war hadn't come home happy over the victory but bitter over the experience. Maybe her mother was a pretty nice lady, but how much say would she have in a family like that? How had it been in his own family?

He didn't think back on them often. Their faces were no longer clear in his mind most times. Getting past the memory of lying in the filth of his own sickness was a hard thing. He didn't even know how long he and Betsy had lain there, fading in and out of consciousness, waiting to die, knowing Tom was already dead beside them. Then Mr. Greenlow had shown up, cursing and moaning, not wanting to face more death and sickness, but doing what he could.

Some memories were there, and one came to him now, his father running across the yard to his mother as she scattered feed to the chickens. He had been excited about something, excited in a good way, and he took hold of her around the waist, whirled her in a circle and lifted her up. In his mind Matt saw them laughing, laughing the way he and Boston laughed today when he teased her about the coyotes and wolves.

Talk about getting above himself. How exactly had he gone from thinking about Boston to thinking about his mother and father's marriage, any marriage at all?

He felt a slight tightening of his shirt sleeve and smiled to himself under the hat. Minutes later he fell asleep.

11

THE FEEL OF A callused hand across her mouth and another pinning her to the ground brought Sarah awake ready to fight. Only Matt's voice in her ear, so soft it was barely a breath kept her still, "Ssh. Don't move."

His hand moved away from her mouth and very slowly across the inches necessary to pick up the pistol positioned on the ground near her face, and she knew. Moving nothing but her eyes, she saw the line of half-naked brown men approaching, riding by on their spotted horses close enough that she could make out the pattern of the paint on their faces. They rode silently except for the sound of their horses' hooves and an occasional snort. If she could see them so clearly, how could they miss two people hidden among the rocks and bushes to one side of their line of travel? Afraid they would feel the weight of her frightened gaze, she closed her eyes.

The rising sun had already lightened the eastern sky to gray when they'd found this place. By the grace of God, the cover was better than usual, a large patch of bushes on ground scattered with rocks, a few almost the size of her head. Still, the cavalrymen's trousers she and Matt wore had started out bright blue and their shirts white. Yesterday Sarah had hated the ground in dirt that was turning everything grayish brown. Today she prayed they were dirty enough.

The silent parade went on and on. How many of them could there be? Was every Comanche in Texas riding by this very place this very morning? At last they disappeared, or at least they disappeared from the narrow space between two branches that was her window on the prairie.

Matt still didn't move and neither did Sarah. A single straggler on a black and white horse trotted by.

Only the absolute stillness of Matt behind her, his arm heavy across her shoulder and hand holding the pistol so steady enabled Sarah to keep the signs of panic down to the rapid rise and fall of her chest.

Matt's mouth touched against her ear. "Easy now. Just a little longer." He kissed her then, a slight touch of his lips on her neck, and she calmed.

Dear God, don't let that be the only kiss I ever get from him. Just a little longer.

His idea of a little longer didn't match hers. An eternity passed before he moved, sat up and scanned to the horizon in all directions.

"If our luck keeps holding like this, when we get to the fort, I'm going to get in the first poker game I can find."

"Luck? Luck would be if they all stayed wherever they came from."

"Maybe so, but I'll settle for the fact we stopped when we did this morning. If we'd kept going another minute, they'd have cut right across our trail. If they'd come a couple hours later, they might have caught us roasting that fellow over there for dinner."

He nodded toward a thick rattler sunning itself on a flat rock nearby. Not long ago Sarah would have squealed and run. Now she just moved closer to Matt. "Hold me for a minute. Please. I promise I won't cry."

Wordlessly, he pulled her into his arms.

"I'm sorry," she whispered against his neck.

"You've got nothing to be sorry for unless maybe you've been wishing for some more excitement when you're supposed to be watching."

"What I've been doing is thinking you're too cautious, that it's foolish to spend so much time rearranging bushes and rocks and putting out the fire as soon as things are half cooked and walking in the dark when it's so much harder and slower. Luck's got nothing to do with why we're still alive. We're still alive because you're so careful, and I'm slowing you down and making things harder and don't even have the sense to appreciate you."

"You're not starting to puddle up, are you?"

"Of course not," she said, sniffling a little.

He dug a handkerchief out of his pocket and handed it to her. As she blew her nose, he tugged on her braid and grinned at her. "I've got nothing against you appreciating me. Maybe you could do some cooking. Hungry?"

He tipped his head toward the flat rock, and Sarah laughed. "Hungry enough to eat a snake," she said.

THAT AFTERNOON SARAH settled in to watch holding on to Matt's sleeve more firmly than ever before. Pretending she didn't hold on to him while he slept no longer seemed important; holding on did.

The heat of the day pressed down all around. The air shimmered with it. The combination of layered dust and perspiration made her skin gritty, and the way she smelled.... She shuddered thinking about it.

Thank goodness the Comanches hadn't come close enough to find them with their noses, although perhaps they would have except for a slight movement in the air, not enough to call a breeze, just enough to help. Matt might be right about that poker game.

Nothing moved in the hot empty land all around. A few puffy white clouds hung low in the clear blue sky. Even insects hid in dark, cool places.

How did soldiers bear picket duty? Scanning the horizon, Sarah admitted to herself that these last days she had been less than vigilant. Too much of her watch time had been one long daydream about how it would be after they reached the fort.

She could picture it all in her mind—telling Carter she couldn't marry him and giving back the ring, writing to her parents, marrying Matt. There had been that niggling little worry that Matt might not feel about her the way she did about him, but no longer. He had only touched his lips to her neck, such a small, gentle kiss, but enough.

After today, staying alert would be easy. Seeing Comanches up close would scare anyone into staying alert, or perhaps it was knowing what the Comanches would do if they saw her or Matt, or knowing what *Matt* would do if they were discovered and that he could only do it if he had time.

Matt half turned in his sleep, pulling his sleeve out of her grip. Once he settled, she renewed her hold. The hat had fallen off his face, and she studied him. What exactly about him called to her so strongly that she had been unable to stop looking at him, even when she believed he was a killer?

No other man ever had that effect. Certainly not Carter Macauley. Carter had black hair and dark eyes, a high broad forehead and complexion ruddy with health. Her father and brothers had all but adopted him into the family. Her mother and aunts referred to him as a "fine figure of a man." Anything they'd say about Matt would not only be far less complimentary, but would be said with nose in the air and a sniff.

Yet Matt was the one she ached to touch. Watching over him without giving way to the desire to run her fingers over each of the bones so prominent in his lean face, smooth each eyebrow, trace the outline of his lips and kiss him took all her strength.

What would kissing Matt be like? Once she had accepted his proposal, Carter had begun kissing her in a way that frightened her, hard enough to bruise. When he pushed his tongue into her mouth the first time, she tried to pull away. After that she endured. Even knowing how much more intimacy marriage required, she had squelched all doubts. She would come to love him, get used to his ways.

Now she knew. Accepting Carter's proposal had been a terrible mistake. Perhaps she would have gotten used to him, but she could never love him. Love was not something you decided on. Not the part in your mind that made you want to know everything about him, make him forget every bad thing that had ever happened to him, make sure nothing bad ever happened to him again. Not the part in your body that made you ache to touch him, have him touch you.

She traced the lines of Matt's face in the air. Then her air-touch moved down his neck, out across his shoulder, in again along his collarbone, down the breastbone, back and forth across each rib. Air touching only made the ache worse. She wanted to feel the smoothness and warmth of his skin, feel the muscle and tendon and bone under his skin. She wanted to spread her hand out flat over his belly, feel the breathing and life of him. She wanted—oh, she wanted.

As she watched, the clouds to the west darkened to gray and expanded. She urged them on, prayed for rain. The last water they'd come to had been a trickle in the center of the streambed, barely enough to fill the canteens and drink until they were what Matt called "plumped up" again. Plump was one of those words Sarah heartily disliked from hearing it applied to herself too many times. The way Matt used it made her smile.

Perhaps once this ordeal ended, words like that would regain their power to wound. After all, her body had a proven ability to return to plumpness the minute she stopped starving it. Then again, her ideas of how to starve her body to a desirable slimness had been as naive as many of her other ideas. Back home, she considered eating a little less at each meal and going to bed hungry starving herself.

Now she understood about real hunger, not a few gurgles and growls of your stomach in the night, but a dull pain that never went away. Hunger was a force that made you happy to eat those ugly things Matt called crawdads and not sure you wanted to wait for them to cook. Hunger led to the day you lay down to sleep, rested a hand on your middle, and looked down in wonder when you felt your own ribs for the first time.

The clouds spread over more and more of the sky. Perhaps a good storm would mean the next "crick" they came to would be deep enough to bathe. Thinking of the many ways that bathing could lead to touching, Sarah smiled.

12

EXECUTING HER PLAN PROVED much harder than dreaming it up in the first place. Sarah sat and kept watch as Matt bathed in the first water they'd come across in almost two weeks that was more than a sluggish trickle. The situation fit the plan perfectly, but she lost her nerve.

What if he laughed at her? After all she had no more than a vague idea of how to seduce a man. He had called her beautiful weeks ago, but Sarah knew pretty described her better. Her features were regular, but the chin her family called determined on good days and stubborn on bad days kept her face from forming the desired oval shape. Her eyes, large and so dark a blue strangers mistook them for brown or black all the time, were her best feature, but blonde brows and lashes provided no accent.

Then again, Matt did look at the world in a rather unconventional way. Perhaps he did think she was beautiful when he said it. If so, what did that mean now, when he had punched two new holes in her belt in the last weeks so that her trousers didn't slide right off? Feeling her own ribs for the first time had been a pleasure. Seeing them, right there poking up through the skin, didn't seem like such a good thing. In spite of wearing the hat religiously, the last time she'd seen her own face in Matt's shaving mirror it was brown from the sun, anything but ladylike.

When she looked at Matt she wished she could put back the extra flesh that had melted off his body too, but the desire to touch him, have him touch her, never lessened. How did he feel, though? Even if he cared about her, he couldn't love her the way she loved him. No one could love anyone the way she loved Matt Slade.

Her chance passed. She heard him splashing his way out of the water. She kept her back righteously turned to him, but she no longer bothered trying to hide occasional glances in his direction. He didn't pretend much either, and he certainly did get a look on his face as if he liked what he saw.

Sarah sighed. Her plan had been to walk out and join him in the water, to touch his face, kiss him. Surely with both of them there like that, unclothed, he would kiss her back, carry her out of the water and touch her the way she wanted to be touched.

What would happen if she asked him? Nothing. Because she'd never find the courage, or the words, to ask for what she wanted either.

As he pulled the shaving things out of the knapsack, Sarah moved to join him. She enjoyed holding the mirror for him as he shaved, studying him from so close. Today, by the time he took the last swipe with the blade and wiped the soap off his face, her breath came as fast and hard as when she saw the Comanches.

Giving way to these thoughts always brought swelling, heat and wetness to female places. This time was worse than ever before.

Matt tipped his head and studied her. "I thought that rabbit we had yesterday would be enough to make you feel better. There should be some frogs or crawdads here, maybe even wild onion."

"That would be good." The hunger for food was nothing right now compared to the other hunger, the one a braver woman would do something about.

He started combing her hair. Every brush of one of his hands on her back or a shoulder intensified her feelings. Gradually she became aware of the sound of Matt's breathing, as rapid and ragged as her own.

By the time she let herself believe the reason was the same for him as for her, he had finished combing her hair and was braiding the thick, damp mass with practiced speed.

She didn't wait for him to tie the braid but pushed around toward him, cupped one side of his jaw in the palm of her hand and ran her thumb first along his cheekbone, then his lips.

"Matt?"

Maybe the kiss that single word provoked didn't bruise, but it was hard and rough. So were his hands as they explored her breasts and stomach, pulled her down full against him.

At first she tried to touch and explore too, but he overwhelmed her. Sarah had envisioned unclothed bodies gently entwined. The only clothing he removed was hers. Buttons popped as he pulled her shirt over her head. He pushed her trousers and drawers down around her knees and no farther, which offended her so thoroughly she kicked free of them. He showed no answering need to shed his own trousers.

When Matt's full weight pinned her to the ground, Sarah stopped participating in what was happening. The heat of his organ probed between her legs. Her body resisted, didn't seem to be designed to accommodate all that maleness, except that neither Matt nor any part of him cared.

The barrier gave way, and pain overrode every other sensation. Sarah gritted her teeth and dug her fingers into his back, determined not to struggle against him or cry out. By the time the worst of the pain receded, he was finished. He pulled away from her, rolled off, and sat up.

"Sarah?"

She sat up too, tears streaming down her face. If he made a single remark about puddling up, she'd hit him. Better than that, she checked where he'd left the gun and knife when he started to shave.

"Sarah?"

He touched her face, gently now, blast him. And did he have to call her by her name for the first time when she was thinking about shooting him?

"Tell me that's something to do with that monthly thing again and that I didn't make you bleed like that."

There was blood on her thighs, blood and something sticky from Matt on the ground, and she hurt all the way up inside, but the worry on his face dissolved the worst of her anger and indignation. So her daydreams had been just that, foolish, girlish dreams. She still loved him and if he'd touch her face like that afterward....

"Of course you did. That's what happens."

"No, it doesn't. I did it before, and that lady didn't bleed." He hesitated a second and then said, "And she didn't cry. I hurt you, didn't I? That's not what I.... What do we need to do now?"

"We don't need to do anything. It just happens. It happens a woman's first time. The maidenhead tears and there's blood. My Aunt Lucy told me about it."

"I *tore* something?"

"Yes, it's just this little bit of...." Too late Sarah realized she didn't really know what it was. "Skin."

"You're telling me ladies bleed a week every month, and you bleed the first time you.... That can't be right. That's just not right."

"Aunt Lucy said it proves God's a man."

For the first time since their bodies separated, they met each other's eyes. Sarah smiled at him, and to her relief he smiled back and looked more like himself.

"You're sure you're all right?"

"Yes. The bleeding stopped already." Probably it had. It would by the time she stood up.

"Matt, you know that I.... I wouldn't except...."

He stared into the distance, and her heart sank before he said, "I know."

"You don't feel the same?" she whispered.

"I expect I do." He turned back to her, and what she saw on his face made her want to cry again.

"Tell me honest, Sarah. If you were back in Boston, would your folks ever let you meet somebody like me? Not a fellow from Texas who was on the wrong side of the war, but a Yankee who was like me?"

She wanted to lie, wanted to pretend it could have happened some way, but she couldn't look in his eyes and do that. "No. They wouldn't." When he didn't say anything more, she added, "But I did meet you. It's too late for them or anyone else to change that."

"Maybe so, but that doesn't change that all their reasons would be right. Are you really thinking about living someplace like that settlers' cabin, one room, no maids, hauling water, scrubbing and cooking till your hands bleed?"

Sarah didn't answer right away, did really think about it. "If you asked me that when I was still back home, before any of this

happened, I would have said what you think I should. I couldn't
even imagine it, but now, here we are. Here I am. Most of the time
we're hungry and thirsty and filthy. My hands may not be bleeding,
but all the other parts of me seem to be." She grinned at him, and
at least he smiled back.

"Everything that's happened has already changed me so much
there's no way to go back. How could I go back to leading a life like
my mother's after this?"

"Easy. What's happening between us, being out here alone
together, this isn't real, Sarah. If we get to the fort, you marry your
Yankee, and what happened out here will maybe make you happier
with the kind of life he can give you."

"No. Whatever else happens *when* we get to the fort, I'm not going
to marry Carter, so if you don't want me, I'll just be an old maid."

"I didn't say I don't want you. I started wanting you the night you
walked across the camp with fire in your eyes and food in your
hands, and I'm pretty sure I'll feel the same the day I die, but the
world's full of people who never get anything they want. Wanting
makes no never mind. Most of time it just makes the not getting
worse.

"You don't have to worry about not getting. You have me."

He shook his head. "Then maybe it's keeping I don't believe in."

His attitude hurt far more than the rough coupling. None of this
was what she had expected, and it was nobody's fault but her own.
Sarah looked down at herself, naked and smeared with her own
blood, and wondered where her pretty daydreams had all gone.

Matt stood up and pulled her to her feet. "Come on. If we don't
need to do anything else, we need to clean up and get under cover.
If the Comanches catch us like this, maybe they'll die laughing
before they can kill us, but most likely not."

By the time they rinsed off and Matt started a rodent he called a
squirrel cooking over a small fire, Sarah had stopped feeling sorry
for herself. Mostly. So he thought love didn't matter. All she had to
do was prove him wrong. And find out about the other woman he'd
been with who didn't bleed or cry. It must have been after the war.
And hadn't he said something once about being hundreds of miles
from where he wanted to be? Could there be a girl waiting for him
back where he came from?

"Matt." When he looked up, she said, "Tell me about this girl you were with who didn't bleed or cry."

He dropped his gaze back to the fire, and a ruddy flush started across his cheekbones. "That's not something to talk to a lady about."

"I'm not a lady any more. I'm a fallen woman now."

His head jerked up fast at that. "That's not true."

"Of course, it is. What I did today is what makes women fallen."

"You didn't do anything. I did."

"I started it, and you know it. And it doesn't matter what you did. Men don't ever fall anywhere, do they?"

"No, we need hard-headed Yankees to push us where we don't want to go."

She said nothing, just waited.

"It wasn't like you're thinking. It was during the war. You know."

"No. I don't. How could you get to know some girl during the war? Were you in one place long enough for that?"

"There wasn't any getting to know. It was a prostitute lady, and it was just once for a couple of minutes."

The color deepened across his face, and Sarah's spirits lifted. There wasn't a girl he cared about somewhere. Then the rest of what he'd said hit her.

A couple of minutes? Wouldn't it take a couple of minutes just to find out how much and pay one of those women?

She had trouble finding a way to ask more. "If it was just once, then that was the first time you ever.... How did you—know?"

"Soldiers talk, so I kind of knew what to expect, and she just grabbed hold of me and made it happen."

He caught Sarah's glance at the crotch of his trousers and flushed darker, even though he grinned at her. "Exactly. Like a handle."

Heat rose in Sarah's own cheeks, although he had to be teasing her. Didn't he? "She didn't give you any instructions at all?"

"The only instruction she gave me was 'hurry up.'"

"Hurry up," Sarah blurted, "but I wanted...."

Remembering what he'd said about wanting, she didn't go on until Matt said, "Wanted what?"

"Well, I was thinking next time we could try—slower?"

"There isn't going to be a next time. I'm not hurting you like that again."

"It won't ever be like that again. Aunt Lucy said...."

"Maybe your Aunt Lucy doesn't know everything. Maybe she's wrong. I'm not doing that to you again."

"I think she did know, about this anyway. She was the family scandal. If my father could have kept me from ever meeting her, he would have, but she visited sometimes when he wasn't there. She was my mother's oldest sister, and Mother never could tell her no. She even let me visit with her, and when I got older I went out shopping with her and then we'd go to a restaurant and talk over a meal."

"What made her a scandal?"

"She was a suffragette. She never married, and she had men friends. She died last year."

Sarah heard the thickness in her own voice as she said this and expected an admonition not to puddle up. Instead Matt said, "I'm sorry."

"Me too. She would have liked you."

"No wonder she was the family scandal. She had no sense."

Sarah watched him apportion the cooked meat, knowing that he would give her the bigger share and knowing that arguing with him about it was futile.

Further discussion on this new subject wasn't going to work right now either. No matter what he said about hard-headed Yankees, Matt Slade could out-stubborn her any day. Perhaps by the time the soreness between her legs passed, he'd be more amenable to— suggestion.

MATT HAD NEVER loved anyone before. Well, yes, he had, but what a boy felt for his family wasn't the same kind of love at all. For that matter, what he felt for some of the men he'd gone through the war with was pretty strong, like the way you'd love a brother maybe, although he'd no more say it than they would.

In spite of knowing he'd never get to sleep today, Matt lay still, his hat over his face, and pretended. Resting was as good a way as any to stop Sarah's questions about things they shouldn't be talking about.

Of course he shouldn't be thinking about her this way either. He shouldn't be *feeling* about her this way, but he had lost that war weeks ago. Loving her wasn't at all the way Matt had thought loving a woman would be.

He'd known about the wanting and even the getting, but not about the intensity like an artillery explosion right inside that just blew away all the careful control he'd been hanging onto. And something about that had been wrong, more wrong even than the tears and blood he wanted to believe really were because of that maiden thing.

Any woman as beautiful as Sarah could provoke that kind of wanting. The loving came from that and all the other things—the determination that kept her walking through knee deep water even when she was gasping with the effort, the courage to hit out at him after the trees even though she was still afraid, the way she tried to do her share whether it was picking up buffalo chips for a fire or cutting up a snake, the way she laughed when he teased her.

And of course today. Even if she felt things she never would except for being alone with him so long, the way she caressed his face and let him know she was willing to let him....

Something had been wrong there, though, something he couldn't quite figure out. That thing she'd said about slower bothered him. Everything he knew was that ladies let men do that to them when they were married because it was part of being married and they knew men had needs, which would be why Sarah.... But other than that you had to pay a prostitute to let you do that, and that prostitute lady sure didn't want slower. So why would Sarah say that? Slower would take longer....

Thinking about it was about to have an obvious effect on his body. He shifted onto his side, his back toward Sarah, as if turning in his sleep. His sleeve pulled out of her grasp, and he waited until he felt her take hold again before taking his thoughts in a different direction.

Her Yankee must know something was wrong by now. Maybe someone had found the bodies, even way north like they'd been. If the Yankee knew Broderick's men had been wiped out and that Sarah's body wasn't among them, he'd be crazed with fear for her, thinking the Comanches had her.

Maybe no one knew anything except that Broderick was late, lost, but the Yankee would still worry himself sick over that. He must love her just as much. Any man who got to know Sarah would love her, and the Yankee major could give her the life she should have.

Still the thing about that Yankee that Matt couldn't quite get by was why he had let Sarah come to Texas alone except for a couple of other ladies. Why hadn't he married her back East and brought her out here himself and kept her safe? A Yankee major couldn't be as green and stupid as Broderick, could he? He fell asleep worrying about it.

13

Two hours west of the creek, the land changed character. Sarah stumbled her way through the rocky, broken ground at a slower and slower pace. Holding Matt's hand over a particularly rough patch only proved she needed her hands free for balance. A sliver of light from the new moon left the landscape shadowed and eerie.

Matt showed no sign of impatience, but Sarah hated being the cause of the crawling pace. Trying to hurry on a downslope of unstable shale proved her undoing. A rock she judged as solid enough to hold her weight gave way, and her right foot slid sideways into a hole. She fell in a heap, unable to stifle a cry of pain as her ankle twisted. Matt had hold of her in seconds, pulling her up, and breaking the nighttime silence in a low voice himself.

"What's wrong? Are you all right?"

"I slid and my ankle turned. I think—I think it's bad." Standing on her left leg only, she tentatively touched her right foot to the ground. Pain shot up past the knee, and she fell against Matt.

"Which ankle. Show me."

Matt helped her down. She sat with her legs straight out and whispered. "Right."

As he ran his hands over the ankle, exploring, Sarah couldn't help saying more. "I'm sorry. Matt, I'm so sorry. Just leave me here with some water. You can get to the fort by yourself in no time, and you can send someone back for me. You can...."

His hand over her mouth stopped her. "No more of that. You keep quiet while I figure out what we can do."

After a little more probing of the rapidly swelling ankle, Matt pulled her belt off and wrapped it in a tight spiral up the ankle. Gritting her teeth, Sarah managed not to moan or scream. He cut a piece from the rope still in the knapsack and tied it around her waist to hold her trousers on. When he grabbed her arms as if to help her up again. Sarah tried to shake him off.

"We can't go on like this," she whispered. "You can't carry me, and I can't walk."

"We're not going on. We're going back. We've only come a couple of hours, and we know there's water back there. You're going to lean on me, you're going to hop, you're going to use that leg as much as you have to, and if it hurts, you're going to think about something else and keep going. Now be quiet and let's go."

Before they'd traveled ten feet, Sarah wanted to beg him to shoot her. No, a sound like a gunshot carried for miles, but he could cut her throat couldn't he? Hopping meant using the right leg a little for balance, and the pain stabbed through the joint like a hot poker. She ground her teeth until her molars ached then switched to biting her lips, tasted blood and bit down harder. Nothing stopped small sounds from escaping occasionally, but somehow she managed to keep from moaning, or screaming, or cursing.

Cursing, that would be good. Sarah called to mind every word her father or brothers ever used when they thought no females could hear. Then she started on words Broderick's men had let loose now and then. That's when Broderick himself spoke in her pain-filled mind. *"You stupid little bitch."*

For once, instead of making her feel small and cowardly, the thought made her angry. Where did Broderick get the nerve to criticize? He never had a hot poker in his ankle. He took the easy way out. Broderick never endured Matt Slade forcing him to walk over miles of ugly *damn* Texas. If Broderick wanted to offer an opinion, he should have stayed alive long enough to find out what a royal *bastard* Matt Slade could be.

In fact Broderick should have stayed alive long enough to hear what Matt thought about him in detail. Matt considered Broderick a green, stupid *son of a bitch* who led his men into a trap and let them get drunk. Except, of course, that Matt couldn't say it that way because of soap. She could say it. *Son of a bitch!*

Every time Matt stopped, eased her to the ground and sat beside her to rest, Sarah grabbed a canteen and guzzled. After all, the reason for all this torture was water, going back to water. No need for conservative little sips. She considered pouring a whole canteen right over her sweaty head but decided not to bother. Stupid *damn* canteen.

The rosy hues of dawn had faded to full daylight when the sparse line of trees and bushes that marked the course of the stream appeared in the distance.

Matt kept right on pulling, pushing and half-carrying her until they reached a large clump of bushes. He unloaded the canteens and knapsack beside her.

"You hunker down as best you can. I'll be back in a minute."

Damn him. Yes, she'd told him to leave her, but she'd meant really leave her, not leave her alone here for a minute that wouldn't be a minute. What if the Comanches came? What if…. She checked the bushes for snakes and hunkered down.

Looking around, Sarah realized that even though this had to be the same creek they'd left earlier that night, they'd come back to it at a place where it ran through the same rock covered, broken ground that had caused her fall. The hills on this side of the creek were steep, littered with flat rocks that would slide right out from underfoot in exactly the way that had happened to her. The narrow streambed cut into the land.

Reaching the stream at a different place didn't surprise her. One of the things Matt kept in his pocket was a compass, but Sarah knew most of the time he used the stars to stay on course. Returning to the stream at all while dragging and carrying her had to be some kind of miracle. *The son of a bitch!*

Half asleep, worn out by pain, effort and fear, Sarah found no comfort in Matt's words when he returned.

"I found a good place. A really good place. We just have to get you up there. Come on."

He wanted her to climb an impossible hill, too steep, too rocky, impossible. Except that he made her sit down and dragged her up it backwards. Of course he didn't care what the stones and thorny bushes did to her trousers or her backside. *Damn him, damn him, damn him!*

It *was* a good place. High on a rocky hill right above the stream, a small cluster of stunted trees screened a cavity. Less than a cave, the hollow still provided a hidden place with some room to move around and views to the north, west and east that extended for miles. Warning from the south would come from the sound of sliding rock. The morning sun didn't reach into the deepest part of the hollow, and the afternoon sun wouldn't either.

Matt unwound the belt from her ankle, pulled off her shoe and stockings. Red and purple covered the swollen mess and streaked up toward her knee. Sarah felt despair. This couldn't be a sprain. Her ankle must be broken, and broken would mean many weeks to heal.

"Oh, Matt, I'm sorry. I'm so sorry. Please, please. This is a good place. Leave me here and go get help. I'll be fine here, and we have to be close to the fort now. You said so yourself. I'm so sorry. I know you're already worried about water, and this makes it impossible. It's going to be weeks before I can walk. I'm so sorry."

Sometimes Sarah had wondered what it would take to make him angry, what his temper was like. She didn't like finding out.

He stopped the gentle probing of her ankle and gave her a look made frightening by the narrowed eyes, tight, hard lines of his face and set of his mouth. "One thing you've never been through all this is a whiner, Boston. I never expected it, and you'd better quit it. If you've got nothing else to say, you just shut up and don't say anything at all."

"I'm not whining," she protested. "I'm trying to tell you I'm sorry I...."

He grabbed her shoulder and shook, "One sorry is manners. Two is too many. A whole bunch is whining. So you quit it right now or so help me I'll stuff one of these socks in your mouth."

Sarah cringed away. She was never going to speak to him again.

MATT HAD NEVER BEEN SO scared before. Well, maybe a few times in battle and in the hidey-hole with the Comanches stomping around overhead. Making her walk on that ankle had most likely done damage that would take weeks to heal if it ever did heal right. But what else could he do, sit down beside her, dry up and blow away knowing water was only hours away?

Matt got busy moving rocks from the back of the hollow toward the front, leveling things off a little to make a better floor. He'd checked for snakes when he first found the place. Uncovering a tarantula under one of the rocks, he smashed it with grim satisfaction. Right now he'd like to smash a lot of things. He shouldn't have yelled at her like that. She sat right where he'd put her, white faced with pain and fear and working at not crying.

He'd seen men with wounds that should never have killed them die during the war. They died because they gave up, didn't want to make the effort to live. If being mad at him kept Boston from that, good. Except she didn't look mad. The dark blue eyes took up about half her face, and she looked miserable and exhausted.

He finished leveling the ground as best he could and spread the ponchos down. The ragged edge of the one he'd cut short for Sarah caught his eye. That unraveled stretchy stuff could be downright useful. He stuffed a long rubbery strip in his pocket then spread both blankets on top of the ponchos and folded a knapsack for a pillow.

"You move over here, lie down and get some sleep." Sarah didn't look at him, much less say a word, but she wiggled onto the blankets and turned her back to him. He thought about trying to talk to her but decided to leave well enough alone.

"I'm going to see what I can find to eat. I'll be back in a while."

Her silence told him not to hurry.

ONCE MATT LEFT, Sarah let go and wept. He was the least sympathetic, meanest human being in the world, entirely lacking in the most elementary compassion. She cried until exhaustion overtook anger, fear and even pain, blew her nose on a leftover piece of chemise, closed her eyes and slept.

The clatter of sliding rocks woke her. Her heart didn't slow until Matt appeared. The sun, low in the west, told her she'd slept most of the day and Matt had been gone all those hours. He carried a rabbit and more nasty looking green stuff. Her stomach contracted sharply.

She sat up but refused to look at him.

"Feeling better?"

She wasn't speaking to him either.

He left the makings of a fire, crouched down beside her, and took her hand. "Listen to me, Boston. This is a good place. If it takes a week before you can walk or if it takes six weeks, we're fine here, and maybe it won't hurt if we get some rest and enough to eat for a while. This is my fault. When we hit that rough ground, I should have stopped. I've been thinking for days maybe it's time to give up walking at night, and I didn't do it, and it was a mistake. There's no use fussing over it. We're both doing the best we can, and we're beating the odds so far."

"I wasn't whining."

"Yes, you were."

"I wasn...."

He kissed her then. A daydream kind of kiss, gentle and loving, and when his mouth left hers, his eyes were full of humor again. "So how are you feeling?"

"Good." A whole lot better than just a minute ago, in fact. A stomach full of rabbit might just make life perfect.

14

DEEP INSIDE SARAH, THE girl who grew up in the large house in Boston with servants doing anything that qualified as work marveled. How could she revel in this life? Yet she did. Matt left her alone for hours every day while he hunted, hunted quite successfully with a slingshot made with rubber from the poncho. Hunger no longer gnawed day and night in her belly, and fatigue didn't slow every motion.

Matt used the stream as a roadway to reach areas at a distance to hunt without leaving tracks. He built a fish trap with thin branches from streamside trees and wire from the knapsack and left it in the stream. After several disappointing days, the trap caught two small sunfish. The tiny fillets from those fish tasted better than anything the Hammond cook ever produced in Boston.

Sarah watched from her lofty perch while Matt hunted, but that still left a lot of time to think, and she thought of many more things she wanted to know.

"Why did you only go to that prostitute once. Didn't you like it?"

"I liked it fine, but afterwards I found out some things that put me off. Things ladies don't need to know about."

"I told you I'm a fallen woman now. Perhaps I do need to know those things. Tell me."

"No."

It took her two days of persistent sneaking up on the subject and asking again before he gave in. "You're going to be sorry."

"No, I'm not. Tell me."

"A couple of days after I saw that prostitute lady...."

"Prostitutes aren't ladies."

"Maybe not, but there's no reason to talk mean about them. They're just getting by the best they can like everybody else."

A man who had a less generous attitude toward prostitutes might have a less generous attitude toward fallen women. Sarah said, "A couple of days after you saw that prostitute lady, what happened."

"Well, you know, in a war things are—there's not much privacy. Kind of like you and me here. So I was at the sinks, and there was this fellow near me, and he was moaning and crying, and all but falling down, and I couldn't help but look at him, and I saw...."

"Saw what?" Sarah said, hanging on every word.

"His male parts looked as bad as your ankle ever did. Red and purple and swollen with this yellow stuff leaking out. Seeing it made me half sick. So I went over and said come on, I'll help you to the surgeon, and he went crazy. Said he'd shoot himself first and all sorts of crazy things, so I left him be. It's true those surgeons figured the way to fix anything was to cut it off. The only time I was wounded I got one of the other fellows to cut the ball out and never let on."

"Is that what the scar is?" She touched the place on his chest.

"It is. It didn't go too deep, and it healed up fine."

"They couldn't have cut your chest off," Sarah pointed out.

"They might have tried. I wasn't taking any chances."

"So why did seeing that man make you not go back to the prostitute?"

"Because when I told what I'd seen, some of the older men said that fellow had a disease you get from those ladies. If they have the disease, you get it when you.... You know."

Sarah nodded. For once she did know.

"And if you get it, you give it to any lady you.... Well, getting that would mean you couldn't ever go near a lady again, even after you got past the moaning and screaming part."

"Until you were well again."

"You don't get well. The surgeons do awful things to you so you can pass water without all that fussing, but there's no cure. It's a kind of pox, and if you get it, you've got it till it rots your insides out and kills you. They said sometimes at first when you get it, it's not as bad as what I saw. It starts out with just a sore or a rash. I never got any sores or rashes, but I figured doing that again would be a bad gamble. Any time we camped near where those kind of ladies were doing business, half of the army went to see them. No matter how much I liked it, I decided I could just keep taking care of myself like I'd been doing."

"What do you mean taking care of yourself?"

"Forget I said that. You never mind."

He moved away from her to the edge of their space, sat down as if keeping watch, although the sun had disappeared hours before.

Sarah stared at his back thoughtfully. Trying to worm it out of him now would make him dig in harder, but tomorrow, or the next day, she would pry the information loose. Not only that, but all this rest and food had her eager to try—what had Aunt Lucy called it? When she described the mechanics she had called it sexual congress, but when she talked about the pleasure of doing that with the right man she referred to lovemaking. That sounded better. With all this time on their hands, why not practice sexual congress and figure out how it became making love?

To Sarah's surprise it took three days to wear Matt down. They were relaxing as they did after meals, Matt leaning back against the side of the hill, Sarah prone on the blankets with her bare feet elevated in his lap.

Matt no longer wore his shirt or undershirt from the time he bathed in the creek and shaved until night brought some relief from the heat. They were turning into Indians themselves, he'd remarked, brown and half naked most of the time, but he didn't seem too upset about it, and Sarah liked it. She liked looking at his bare chest and back and liked not having her feet, ankles, and calves always hot and itchy under the layers of heavy stockings.

Of course, *he* got to cool himself off in the creek every day. *She* had to be satisfied with rubbing herself down with water from the canteens.

"Push against my hand," he said.

Sarah pushed her right foot against his hand. "It's better than yesterday," she said. "I can put my weight on it when I stand, but walking is still pretty bad."

"Stay off it."

"I need to try a little now and then to see how it's doing," Sarah said. "So how do you take care of yourself?"

"I'm starting to think those poor Yankees should have won the war in '63."

"It would have saved a lot of misery. Tell me."

He sighed and gave in. "There are ways men can—rub themselves that—provide relief."

Sarah glanced at the place that must need rubbing then met his eyes. "You mean you don't need a woman?"

"It's not as good. It's just better than nothing."

"Show me."

"No."

"Why not? We've already done that, and you said yourself we have no privacy being together like this."

"I'm not doing that to you again."

"I know that," Sarah said reasonably. "We're talking about something different now, aren't we? Perhaps it's something I should know."

"You already know more than any lady should and don't start with that fallen woman story again. The only place anybody would ever figure you fell from was the sky, maybe an angel pushed out of Heaven for asking too many questions."

Sarah laughed. "There is not one single person in this world you would ever convince I'm angelic. What if we were married, and I was sick and we couldn't do, you know, married things. I'd need to know what to do."

"You wouldn't need to do anything. It's not like a man can't do without for a while. Your Yankee probably has a strong character and never does sinful things like that."

Sarah didn't care in the slightest what Carter did or didn't do. "Is it a sinful thing?"

"Mrs. Stolfelz sure said so. According to her a fellow wouldn't just go to hell, he'd go blind right here in this world first. Of course I question that since I can still see pretty good." He grinned at her.

"Did she beat you for it?"

"She never caught me at it, but the boy she did catch.... She didn't beat him. She got Reverend Stolfelz to do it. It was the only time he ever hit any of us, and he used his belt, and it was bad."

"I really do hope those people burn in hell."

"Boston."

"Show me."

"No."

Her ankle was enough better that she could pull her legs in and crawl beside him. She cupped both hands along the sides of his face. "Show me, or I'll ask you every five minutes from now until you give in or, or stuff a sock in my mouth."

"Are you going to cry uncle when you realize you're pushing for something you don't want after all?"

"If you're right, I will cry uncle, but you're wrong."

They were both breathing hard, their eyes locked on each other. Sarah knew she had won even before he began unbuttoning his trousers.

The glimpses of his body she had stolen one time or another had given her expectations of what she would see. She had felt but not seen his fully erect organ in their previous coupling. What she saw now made her gasp and look up at him.

"Are all men like that?"

The devil was in his eyes now. "Only when some pesky Yankee is teasing them."

She reached out and touched, then yanked back her hand. "The skin is so soft. I didn't expect...." She laid her palm flat on his chest. "I thought your skin would be the same everywhere, like this, but I suppose it's different here too." As she spoke, she ran a finger around one flat nipple, surprised when it tightened and hardened and he made a sound deep in his throat.

"Have mercy, Sarah. The way you're torturing me, if the Comanches had got ahold of you, they'd have made you a lady chief by now."

She smiled at him, feeling wicked and powerful and enjoying the feeling. "I don't want to torture you. I want to make you feel good. Show me."

He took her hand in his and wrapped it around that part of him, pressing until she was holding him firmly. "Uncle?"

"No," she whispered.

He began to move her hand then let go as she tightened her grip and experimented with the rhythm and pressure. She watched what happened in awe. "Matt, I want that to happen inside me. That's supposed to happen inside me, isn't it?"

His breathing was slowing, and he looked... easier, which wasn't at all how Sarah felt.

"It's sure not supposed to happen like it just did. The only comfort is we'll be roasting side by side in hell for it."

The laughter in his voice belied any fears about fire and brimstone, and Sarah had long ago decided that God would understand. God simply could not be angry with her for loving Matt Slade.

"Matt, I want...."

"Ah, Sarah, you are the wanting-est woman." He touched her face in that same way he had once before then surprised her by pushing her back on the blankets. He pulled off her shirt without popping buttons since there were none left to pop, then her trousers and drawers. "Now maybe it's time for what I want, and I always did want to have a close look at what ladies hide in private places."

She hadn't thought about how it would feel. Had he felt like this, more naked than naked? Closing her eyes, unable to watch him, she felt his hands on her breasts. He ran a finger around her nipple the same way she had his, and it had the same effect on her, even to bringing a low moan from her. He did the same thing to the other nipple, then ran his hand down her stomach to her inner thighs, pushing them apart.

He was gentle, but still she tried to close her legs when he parted her flesh and his fingers probed in places she had hardly ever touched herself.

"Matt! Oh, that felt, that felt—good."

Her thighs parted again without conscious thought. She opened her eyes to see him looking at her, no longer relaxed but intense.

"There?"

Sarah couldn't answer, only whimper with pleasure. He experimented, rubbing, pressing, pulling. Somewhere in her still functioning mind, the sounds coming from her throat mortified her, but every other part of her gladly abandoned itself to the pleasure. His fingers probed deeper, right into the core of her, even as he kept stroking that first place he'd found, his hand moving with the rhythm he had helped her use on him.

Sarah came undone.

When it was over, he stretched beside her on the blanket. She understood now how he had looked afterwards, the feeling of utter satisfaction, but she was embarrassed as she'd never been before. "If I say I'm sorry for being so noisy, are you going to accuse me of whining again?"

"You better not be sorry. That sounded liked music to me."

She risked looking at him. His expression had her once again half expecting him to say, "There," in a self-satisfied tone.

She said, "You're pretty pleased with yourself, aren't you?"

"I am. I figure I got that slow enough for you."

Sarah couldn't help herself. She laughed, and then so did Matt until they were both holding their sides and rolling and then holding each other. The satisfaction melted away and the wanting returned.

"Matt."

"No. I'm not doing that to you again. Leave me alone for a few minutes, and we'll both calm down."

He pulled away and sat up.

"But it would be all right this time. You know it would. It would be good."

"I don't know that, and hurting you again would spoil what just happened. You made me feel good, and I made you feel good. That's enough."

No, it wasn't. He sat in the same way he had at the beginning, his back against the hillside, legs stretched out in front of him, bent slightly at the knee. Except he was naked now and fully aroused, his head back, eyes closed, shutting her out and ignoring her.

Studying him gave Sarah an idea. Why waste three days, or more, convincing him he was wrong? If she could move quickly and smoothly enough, she could do that right now. She raised up on her knees, put all her weight on one and swung the other bent leg up and over, lowering herself on him, at the last moment using her hand to guide him into her.

Hard hands on her waist stopped her before she had captured more than the tip of him. She smiled into narrowed, pale blue eyes.

"See? I told you it would be fine."

For a second she thought he would push her away, but he loosened his hold, and she sank slowly down over him. His body filled hers, without pain this time.

At last Sarah understood her own aching desire. Without knowing or understanding, all the wanting came down to this. More than touching, more than being touched, she wanted to have him like this, to hold him like this.

When she tried to move, to start the rhythm, pain shot through her ankle. She feared he would use that as an excuse to stop her.

Instead his hands slipped around to her back. He pulled her forward, then rolled them both over without breaking their connection until she was under him.

He held himself above her on his forearms, still looking at her with that narrow-eyed intensity, his eyes darker now in the shadows with the light behind him. She pushed her hips up, dug her fingers into his back, tried to make him give what she wanted without speaking the words. Matt did speak. His voice, barely a breath across her lips, vibrated through her.

"Sing, Sarah. Sing my name, Sarah."

He moved then, and Sarah sang.

15

EACH DAY SARAH'S ANKLE hurt less and bore more of her weight without pain. Each day she grew less eager to leave their primitive existence and rejoin the civilized world. Perhaps she worried when Matt left and went hunting, but every other waking moment brought one kind of pleasure or another.

Full bellies and enough water meant lots of energy for hours of making love. Sarah even convinced herself she saw a thin layer of flesh returning under the skin over her ribs and Matt's. Every evening they sat shoulder to shoulder and watched the sunset put on a show.

A brief thunderstorm that swept over them one afternoon put on the best show of all when it left a rainbow in its wake. The colors started as a mere hint in the sky then strengthened until they shimmered, strong and true.

"Does it make you think of pots of gold?" Sarah asked.

"No, it makes me think of magic," Matt said. "I wish there was some way to grab hold and pull it out of the sky. If I could wrap you up in that rainbow, you'd be safe no matter what because it would be magic."

"We'd have to cut it in two. I don't want magic unless you have it too."

"I'd look pretty foolish wrapped in a rainbow."

"Maybe we could make you an under vest out of it and nobody would know but me."

"You can sew rainbows?"

Sarah laughed. "All the sewing I can do is absolutely useless, like embroidering pillowcases, but I'll learn." She kissed his shoulder and leaned against him. "I'll learn, and we'll both wear rainbows and be safe."

Most of those evenings they shared stories about their lives. Matt told about the trading and banter that went back and forth between Union and Rebel lines, about the tedium of weeks in camp and passing the time playing baseball and cards, about the cavalrymen who hadn't believed a Texan who said he'd never been on a horse.

What Sarah had to pry out of him was the truth about anything bad, the sickness and hunger, the fighting he'd seen and the battles he'd been in. When she did coax him into telling about the fighting, he put a sugar coating so thick on what he told her that it bore little resemblance to the newspaper stories she had studied with her family.

In Matt's version Antietam—Sharpsburg the Rebels called it—sounded like a picnic where there had been some gunfire in the background. Sarah clearly remembered what the newspapers blared in their headlines and detailed in stories. Antietam, a one-day battle with casualties estimated at 17,000 men, stood out in her mind because after that day Lincoln issued his Emancipation Proclamation and her brothers enlisted. The Texas Brigade fought in a cornfield in the morning, and in the afternoon, when another general asked John Bell Hood where his men were, he replied, "Dead on the field."

Her own life had been so safe and dull in comparison to Matt's, Sarah now saw it as pathetic, but Matt's curiosity was endless. She gritted her teeth and told him the truth, even, when he asked again, the truth about Carter Macauley.

"I lied when you asked before. I was embarrassed to admit I never loved him. My parents were so careful about whom I could meet. I thought he was the best I'd ever do."

"But he loves you."

"No, he doesn't. He never even pretended. He wanted a wife from a certain background, and I qualified, and my parents liked him, so we decided to marry. There are lots of people who marry for practical reasons, not for love."

Matt frowned at her. "But after he got to know you, he must have started to love you. Maybe he just never said anything."

How could she convince him? "Do you think if Lieutenant Broderick and I were the ones who survived the Comanche attack, he would have come to love me?"

That brought a grin. "There's no way to imagine that poor fool surviving long enough to get to know somebody, but Macauley's smarter than that, isn't he? He made it through the war."

Suppressing the urge to do some sugar coating of her own, Sarah admitted the truth. "He spent the war in Washington working in the War Department. His family is influential, and they arranged it."

"Good for him."

"Don't you ever think badly of anyone for anything?"

"I do. I thought a whole lot of bad things about Hank and Barney, and I told you how I feel about Broderick. I'm not feeling too fond of Comanches at the moment either."

"Well, Comanches are the reason Carter stayed in the army. He wants to run for office, for Congress, and he's afraid of being called a Sunday soldier, so he thinks a couple of years fighting Indians will fix that."

"So you marry him and maybe you'll end up the wife of the president."

"I'm not going to marry him. He wouldn't have me now anyway."

"Sure he would. Nobody will hold what happened out here against you."

Yes, they would. Everybody except Matt himself would.

He said, "So why didn't you get married back East and come out here with him? Even if he never led a battle charge, he could keep you safe a lot better than Broderick."

"I told you. He wants a wife as pure as driven snow. My parents had only just announced our engagement when he got his orders, and he was afraid that if we married immediately and I traveled with him, someone would think there was a reason for us to get married so quickly, a reason other than his orders."

"What kind of a reason?"

"Oh, something like the two of us getting alone and doing the kind of thing you and I are doing. One of the reasons he wanted to marry me in the first place was that my parents would never allow me to be in a compromising situation. I was hardly ever out of their sight and alone with Carter even after we were engaged, but he was so sure marrying quickly would be scandalous, he convinced my parents. Then he found out Mrs. Royer and Mrs. Lowell were traveling out here to join their husbands. My mother cried herself sick. I'm not sure she ever believed what Carter said, but she went along with him and my father in the end. Nobody listened to me, thank goodness."

Matt tipped his head and studied her for a moment, and she thought he might ask her more, but he didn't.

After days and nights that were pure magic even without a rainbow wrapping, Sarah fought a temptation to malinger and steal more time. Only she couldn't bring herself to lie to Matt when walking no longer hurt.

The first time she slid down the hill on her bottom and walked for a while on level ground, her ankle swelled afterward. By the third day there was no swelling.

"Tomorrow?" she asked.

Matt nodded. "First light. I'm going to go back down now. I'll pull the fish trap, and if it's empty, see about a ground squirrel or two."

Her heart quickened as it always did when he left. She was afraid for him and afraid for herself, and she studied the horizon intently. When a tiny smudge appeared in the east, she stared for long seconds before accepting it as real and reacting.

"Matt! Matt!" Waving at him wildly, she plunged part way down the hill toward him. He never looked to see what had excited her. He yanked the fish trap out of the water and ran, his long legs covering ground faster than Sarah imagined possible. Pushing her back behind cover before scanning the horizon himself, he squinted at the dust cloud moving steadily toward them.

"Tell me it's a cavalry patrol," Sarah said, wanting it to be true.

"I don't think so, and it doesn't look like enough dust for a war party either."

"Have they seen us?"

"Most likely not."

"We've left tracks all over, haven't we?"

"Only on this side of the creek, and the ground's hard and rocky. Be patient, Boston. We're going to find out soon enough."

She didn't want to be patient. She wanted to *know*, and she wanted that dust cloud to be hiding something good. If it couldn't be a cavalry patrol, perhaps it could be buffalo hunters. Friendly buffalo hunters.

Horses and riders materialized in the cloud. Three horses, three riders, and a fourth horse, no a mule, with a pack. One of the riders was a Comanche, but the others—something about the others looked familiar. Jake and Alvaro. "What are they doing here?" she whispered.

"Looking for us."

"But why here? In all of Texas, why here?"

"Most likely that Comanche or one of his friends saw some sign of us. Calm down. They're not acting like they know we're here."

How could she calm down? Her heart pounded like a drum. The men stopped right below their hill but on the far side of the creek and started talking. The Indian kept gesturing downstream.

Yes. Go there. Go.

In the end the men did move downstream, but only a few hundred feet. There, they dismounted and set up camp. Sarah watched and wanted to weep. "We're trapped here, aren't we? And they're going to find us sooner or later."

She glanced at Matt, surprised to see the same wolfish look on his face he had worn weeks ago firing a rifle at the Comanches.

"What are you thinking?"

"I'm thinking this is a good defensive position. I'm thinking if they start up this hill the thing to do is let them get close and do as much damage as I can with five bullets. I'm thinking if I can kill or even badly wound one of them, I could get his gun and have enough ammunition to make them sorry they came looking."

His expression changed then to one that made her heart ache. "I've got to tell you honest, Sarah, I'm not sure I have the strength to shoot you. Shooting them isn't a problem."

"You'd only do it if they find us?"

"Only if they start up this hill and get close. If they never figure out we're here, that's best. But you tell me what you want, because if we try and fail, they'll kill me, but they won't kill you."

The thought of living if Matt died was beyond her. The kind of life wouldn't even matter. "Can I have the knife?"

"You can."

The smile he gave her as he said that almost made enduring the fear worthwhile.

IN THE MORNING, THE GUIDES and their Indian companion saddled their horses and rode upstream, leaving the mule behind braying in its hobbles and the camp set up.

"They've gone looking for us, haven't they?" Sarah said.

"They have, and they're not going to find us wherever they're going," Matt said, "but if they keep us hiding up here, they may starve us to death. You stay here. I'll be back."

He picked up one of the knapsacks, emptied it of everything but the tin cans, slung it over his shoulder and the empty canteens around his neck.

"No! You can't go hunting when they're down there. We can do without food for a day or two. Matt!"

She wasted a few more words on empty space because he was gone, not gone hunting but gone scavenging right in the enemy camp.

By the time he returned, Sarah had worked herself into a frenzy. "I can't believe you did that. They'll see your tracks. They'll know what you did."

"No, they won't. I got right to the camp staying in the stream, and the way the wind is blowing, everything's going to be all stirred around by the time they get back. Here, look what I've got."

Cooked beans overflowed the cans, and he also had dried fruit and a chunk of burned cornbread. Bread! The sight of the cornbread stopped Sarah's arguments dead. She watched eagerly as he scraped off the char.

"Won't they miss this?" she asked.

"I didn't take all of anything, and if they're leaving it sitting like that they ought to be expecting coyotes to help themselves."

Sarah tore into her share of the cornbread. Finished with that, she started on beans in a more ladylike fashion, thought about berating Matt some more and kissed him instead.

For three days, the hunters below unwittingly fed their prey above. On the fourth day, they packed up and rode off to the south.

"I can't believe they didn't find any sign of us," Sarah said.

"They most likely did, but they didn't find anything fresh enough to make them look here. Let's hope what they found was so old they think we're already tucked up at the fort, and they'd better be heading for Mexico as fast as they can."

"I wish you could have shot them. I wish *I* could have shot them."

"It wouldn't keep me awake nights," Matt said. "Let's hope we can get the army to do it for us."

The next morning they slid down the hill for the last time and headed west.

16

SARAH HAD BEEN PROUD of herself for learning to ignore hunger. What a small, unimportant accomplishment that turned out to be. Hunger was nothing; thirst everything. Thirst could not be ignored. Every labored breath dragged hot air across her dried out nasal passages. Her swollen throat hurt with every swallow, yet the cotton in her mouth forced her to keep swallowing. Her cracked lips bled. Her eyes grated in their sockets, and she could no longer trust that anything she saw dancing in the distance was real.

Matt let go of her hand and put his arm around her. The canteens had been empty for days, and the land around them looked as if rain never fell. Yesterday the heat had been dreadful. Today must be cooler because she no longer sweated. Yesterday the grim, worried look on Matt's face frightened her. Today she no longer felt afraid or worried.

Still, she had to keep walking so that Matt didn't waste his strength helping her, carrying her. Doing that wasn't so hard. When her vision blurred, she could hear him, follow his voice. When she stumbled, he steadied her. There would be water soon. Matt knew how to get fat girls up trees. He knew how to get skinny girls across miles and miles of Texas. He knew how to get clumsy girls to safety on one leg. He could find water. He could. He would.

MATT HAD NEVER FELT despair before. Through all the bad times he always believed there was the chance of something better ahead. Now he saw his life as a long chain of loss. Losing his family. Losing the war. Losing the job and start on a better future. And totally and absolutely unbearable, losing Sarah.

Matt sat on the hard, dry ground and held her. How had he not noticed how small she'd become, all skin and bones? She had been drifting in and out of consciousness for hours now, no longer responding to his voice or touch.

He took no comfort from the knowledge he wouldn't outlive her by more than a few days. What strength he had left was fading, his vision wavering. On his last attempt he had carried her less than a hundred feet before the slight grade of the hill brought him to his knees. Maybe right here was as good a place to stop and admit defeat as any.

Then again, maybe this would be the hill that hid the sight of a road or even the fort, and anything was better than sitting thinking about how his mistakes had brought them here. He lurched to his feet, half lifted and half dragged Sarah up the rest of the hill before sinking down and looking to the west.

His traitorous eyes picked out a moving dust cloud in the distance. If his throat and tongue weren't so swollen he might have laughed. Seeing visions happened near the end, and this dust cloud was a vision from the war years, metal flashing and blue uniforms showing through brown haze.

Yet he wanted to believe, and wanting to believe aroused all the old feelings toward Yankees. The dust cloud stopped, churned around and started toward him. Matt pulled the gun from the holster, pushed it into the back of the waistband of Sarah's trousers and made sure her shirt hung over it. Then he grabbed everything he could from his pockets, shoved it all deep into hers and stuffed the dirty rags of their handkerchiefs on top.

As the cavalry surrounded them, he held Sarah in his arms, her head on his shoulder. The well fed, plumped up cavalrymen in blue looked down on him with hard eyes, and he didn't care. Nothing mattered except whether they could save Sarah.

17

"HUSH, SARAH, HUSH. You're safe now."

Hearing a voice other than Matt's surprised Sarah so much she opened her eyes. The stranger's strong resemblance to Lydia Lowell startled her so much she stopped struggling and let the woman press her back in the bed.

"Who are you?" she croaked.

The woman's calm manner and soothing voice banished the resemblance to Mrs. Lowell. She said, "I'm Mrs. Jenny Edler. My husband is Lieutenant J.T. Edler, and you're going to be staying here with us until you feel better."

Sarah examined the almost bare white room, and Mrs. Edler laughed.

"No one gets extravagant quarters at Fort Grissom, and lieutenants most certainly do not. This is our spare bedroom, and even if we had better furniture, it wouldn't be impressive would it? Now, here, let's see if this doesn't help your throat."

Mrs. Edler poured water from the pitcher on the bedside table, but before she offered the glass, Sarah said, "Where's Matt?"

The other woman kept her eyes on the glass as if it were so full it might spill. It was not. "He's being taken care of in another place."

"I want to go there. I want to see him."

"Then you need to get better because until then you can't go anywhere." Mrs. Edler said. "Doctor's orders are for you to stay in bed and eat and drink as much as you can until you're much, much stronger."

"He can come here. I need to see him. I need to know he's all right."

"He needs to recover also, although I understand he's going to be fine. You're both going to be fine, so you need to concentrate on your own recovery."

Sarah didn't like it and wanted to fuss but didn't have the strength. She fell asleep in the middle of marshaling her arguments.

Over the next days, Mrs. Edler became Jenny. The doctor and Lieutenant J.T. Edler also put in appearances, and each one of them turned aside questions about Matt with the same empty platitudes. Lieutenant Edler questioned Sarah about the Comanche attack and what happened before and after. He even took notes, but he told her nothing except that Matt was recovering somewhere else and she couldn't go to him and he couldn't come to her.

Every visit left her exhausted and frustrated. If only she had refused to talk to any of them until they let her see Matt!

On the morning of her third day back among the living, Sarah triumphantly, if shakily, walked to the dining room, sat in a chair and ate breakfast with the Edlers. In bed again, before giving in to the urge to take a nap, she told herself, *tomorrow I will find Matt. Tomorrow I will be strong enough to go wherever he is.*

SARAH WOKE TO THE sound of voices in the parlor. Jenny Edler and a man. Something about the male voice plucked at her memory, and as the conversation stopped, she identified Carter Macauley's baritone. Boots clomped on wood floors. He entered the room without knocking or calling out.

From her position in the bed, Carter loomed larger than she remembered. Black hair slicked back off his high forehead and clean-shaven cheeks above his beard and mustache allowed a great deal of angry red skin to show. His dark eyes blazed with an emotion that made her pull the covers up higher and press back in the bed.

Before Sarah worked her throat enough to say anything, Carter spoke. "You slut."

The word was foreign to Sarah, but the hate in his expression defined it. She managed, "Carter, I'm sorry, I...."

"Shut up, you whore. You were out there spreading your legs for that Rebel trash for months. Months! Did you think after that you could come crawling out of that desert half naked and show my men exactly what you gave that grayback son of a bitch in order to save yourself and just apologize?"

"Don't you talk about Matt like that! Of course, I didn't think we'd marry after everything that happened. I know...."

"Shut up! I'll talk about him any goddamn way I want. If they won't hang him, I'll see him in prison for the rest of his worthless, miserable life, and you, you...."

Recognizing the madness glittering in his eyes, Sarah shrank back against the pillows but couldn't get away. His hands closed around her throat, shutting off her air and any chance to cry out.

Sarah tried to pull his hands off, scratched and hit at him without effect. As she thrashed desperately, her hand knocked against the empty water pitcher on the bedside table. She reached, grabbed and smashed it against the side of his head.

His hands loosened for only a moment, then tightened again. What made him let go and take a step back from the bed, was a calm voice from the doorway.

"Oh, I'm so sorry. I must have left that pitcher too close to the table edge," Jenny Edler said. "Let me pick up those pieces, and then perhaps you'd like some refreshment, Major? I can have tea or coffee in moments, and I baked yesterday."

"No, thank you, Mrs. Edler. I believe I've said everything to Miss Hammond I need to. I can see myself out."

"I would never let you do that, Major. I'll walk with you."

The two of them left. Sarah sank back against the pillows, panting. Her throat burned worse than it had for days, a different pain and different burn. She shook from head to toe as badly as after seeing the Comanches.

The sound of the door opening and closing came, then Jenny returned.

"I can't believe what I saw. Are you all right?"

Unable to speak, Sarah nodded.

"Let me look at you."

Jenny's cool fingers felt good on Sarah's neck. "The bruises are starting to show already. I can't believe.... I'll get the doctor."

Sarah held Jenny's arm and managed to speak in a hoarse whisper, "No. The doctor can't do anything. Don't leave me alone. You saved my life."

"He couldn't have meant to kill you. He lost control for a moment is all."

"He did mean to kill me, and he wants to kill Matt, so you're going to tell me what he's done to Matt. You will tell me, or I'll never let you go."

"I can't tell you. The doctor said not to tell you anything that would upset you until you're stronger."

"I'm already upset!"

If her voice worked properly, Sarah would have screamed. "Do you think not knowing is easier than knowing?"

"No." Jenny sighed. "No, I don't. Let go of me, and let me get this mess on the floor cleaned up. I'll make us some tea with honey. It will soothe your throat and help me calm down. Then I'll tell you. I promise."

Sarah let go reluctantly, afraid Jenny might leave and not come back, but the other woman kept her word.

"The same patrol that found you came across two men a week or so earlier. Those men said they had been with Lieutenant Broderick for a while, but then they parted company. They seemed very surprised that he and his men were missing, and they described everyone in the party. Of course they mentioned the bounty hunters—and Mr. Slade."

Jake and Alvaro! "They're the ones who led us into the trap," Sarah said.

"Yes. Everyone knows that now, but at the time there was no reason to disbelieve them, and they said Mr. Slade was the killer of the Dingess family. He fit the general description, so when you were found, and he admitted he was Matthew Slade, they put him in the guardhouse."

"That's where he is?" Sarah said, horrified.

"No. It turns out the real killer was caught sometime ago. He was identified by the man who survived the attack, the uncle, and he had things he'd stolen from the family with him. He was tried, convicted and hanged weeks before you were found."

"Then why...."

Jenny made a show of refilling their cups, stirring in more honey, and taking a sip before answering. "Sarah, I shouldn't say this to you, but considering what happened here today, I will tell you. In spite of everything you've been through, you are extremely fortunate that you will not be marrying Major Macauley. He is not a nice man."

Sarah smiled at the gentle phrasing. "You must know you aren't telling me a secret."

"No, after what happened.... Well, you can understand when I tell you he is heartily disliked by the men, and while I believe most of them are sympathetic to you and even to Mr. Slade, they have lost no opportunity to embarrass Major Macauley over the condition in which you were found."

"Oh." Sarah remembered the tears in her trousers, the way the buttonless opening in the neck of her huge shirt would fall almost over one shoulder, exposing most of her chest. "And he was already all but obsessive about propriety and, and *righteousness* before this happened."

"Yes, and he blames you and Mr. Slade for his humiliation and wants to make you pay."

"But you said everyone knows Matt didn't kill those people."

"They do, but you understand Colonel Royer is the senior officer here. He and Lieutenant Lowell are grieving their losses too, and Major Macauley convinced them that...."

Jenny's reluctance to tell the rest of the story made Sarah half afraid to hear it, but if everyone knew Matt didn't kill those people, what could be so bad?

"Convinced them that what?" Sarah asked.

"Convinced them that the reason Mr. Slade saved you instead of either of their wives is that you, you offered yourself...."

"Mrs. Lowell died right at the beginning of the attack. There was no question of saving her," Sarah said.

"Yes, once you could tell us what happened and what you told us matched what Mr. Slade said, Lieutenant Lowell accepted that Mr. Slade had nothing to do with Mrs. Lowell's death. He takes comfort from knowing that she died early in the attack without suffering."

Afraid Jenny would see the truth in her eyes, Sarah looked down and sipped at her tea.

Not without suffering. You'll never know how frightened she was, how long it took her to die.

Unaware, Jenny continued. "However, Colonel Royer still believes that his wife could have been saved except that you—made sure you were the one."

The fact that Jenny couldn't say it made the outrageous accusation clear. Hardly able to credit it, Sarah said, "They think that with Comanches attacking and people bleeding and dying, instead of huddling on the floor in a terrified heap, I somehow charmed Matt into saving me instead of someone else? I was the only one left alive by the time he was awake enough to get off the floor. Barney Webb almost killed him."

"I understand how it was, and I believe you, but Major Macauley doesn't want to believe you. He wants to believe something ugly of you and of Mr. Slade, and Colonel Royer is allowing him to act on his feelings. You understand Texas has not yet ratified a new constitution and rejoined the Union. Federal authorities are still in charge of everything here."

"What have they done?" Sarah whispered, "What have they done to Matt?"

"They've charged him with several crimes. He was wearing a cavalryman's clothes, and he had things in a knapsack that belonged to the dead."

"*I* was wearing clothes from one of the dead soldiers. *I* ate the food we took, and *I* used the things we took. Are they charging me with crimes?"

"You are not an unreconstructed Rebel," Jenny said.

"Matt's not an unreconstructed Rebel. He took the loyalty oath before they paroled him at Appomattox."

"Then I'm sure that will come out at the trial, but no one believes you were responsible for anything that happened."

"I certainly wasn't responsible for anything constructive. Matt not only almost died because he saved me, now he's in jail because of me," Sarah said bitterly. "If Colonel Royer and Carter believe I'm a slut and a whore and Mrs. Royer died because of me, why aren't they charging me with murder?"

"Don't speak those words. I don't think they really believe those things. Major Macauley is humiliated and angry, and Colonel Royer is grieving. They know you did what you had to in order to survive. What happened out there is best forgotten."

Sarah stared at Jenny in astonishment. "I'm not forgetting a minute of what happened. I love him, and I'm not going to let Carter Macauley or anyone else punish him for saving my life and loving me back. Where is he, and how do I get there?"

Jenny shook her head as if she couldn't believe Sarah's words. "He's in jail in the closest town to here. Charon. There will be a trial, and if Mr. Slade did nothing wrong, he will be free. You aren't going anywhere until you're stronger."

Soon after that, Jenny left so that Sarah could get some rest, but Sarah stayed awake for some time. Strong or not, she was going to find a way to get to Charon as fast as possible.

VOICES WOKE SARAH LATE that afternoon, Lieutenant Edler low and reasoning, Jenny Edler high and distressed. Before she could decide what to do, the front door slammed and silence descended. Sarah lay awake, worrying, watching the light from the room's single window fade as afternoon turned to evening.

The door sounded again, more agitated voices, then Jenny came into the room, lit the bedside lamp and started fussing in an uncharacteristic manner. She plumped the pillows, helped Sarah sit up and wrapped her in a bed jacket several sizes too large.

What was going on? Every nerve in Sarah's body quivered with anxiety. Jenny sat on the edge of the bed and called to her husband. Except for the one time he had questioned her about the Comanche attack, Lieutenant Edler had never set foot in this room.

"May I look at the evidence of what happened here today, Miss Hammond?" he inquired formally.

Edler was an ordinary looking man of average height with light brown hair and mustache and blue-gray eyes. Like every other person she saw these days, he looked overfed and soft to Sarah. Everyone except Carter. He had looked overfed but certainly not soft.

Edler's expression didn't change as he examined the bruises on her throat from a respectful distance. He lowered himself into the bedside chair and leaned forward.

"You know that as an army officer, I've sworn an oath."

Sarah nodded, wondering what this was leading up to.

"Major Macauley and Colonel Royer are my superior officers, and today I received orders. Orders that concern you."

Sarah's pulse quickened even more, and she shivered. No orders that Carter gave concerning her could be good.

"The orders are that since you no longer have any reason to be at the fort, my wife and I are to stop 'harboring' you. Of course, the assumption is you have no money. We are to take you to where the—laundresses work at the fort and leave you there to earn your way."

Sarah stared at him, without understanding. "I don't have any money, but I don't think I could do laundry yet. I feel better every day, but...."

Her voice tapered off as she remembered some of the things Matt had told her about army life. About the camps. "Prostitutes. He wants you to take me to where the prostitutes work. That's ridiculous. You know my parents will send me funds. I won't go. I won't do that." Fear and the beginning of hysteria caused Sarah's voice to rise.

"Hush, Sarah, hush," Jenny said, patting her hand. "You're right. You're not going there."

"But I don't have any money, and you said he has to obey orders. Your husband has to obey orders." Sarah couldn't bring herself to look at Edler again.

"Yes, he does, but I am not in the army, and I'm not obeying those orders, and as a matter of fact, you do have some resources." As she spoke, Jenny opened the drawer in the bedside table and took out three things, a pistol, a wad of bills, and a twisted handkerchief with a knot tied in it.

The sight calmed Sarah a little. "That's my—Carter's ring in the handkerchief. I put that in my pocket so long ago I forgot it. But the other things, that's Matt's gun and his money. How did you get them?"

"The gun was in your trousers and the money and ring were in your pockets."

Why would he do that? Why would Matt do that? Because he knew, that's why. Because he knew the soldiers would take the money and gun away from him and that she might need them.

"Will you give the ring back to Major Macauley for me? I don't want to see him again," Sarah said.

"No! I will not give it back to him, and neither will you," Jenny said with a surprising display of temperament. "You may need what you can sell that ring for soon, and you're going to have it. Listen to me. No one in this garrison will take you to Charon or anywhere else. They've all been forbidden to help you. And the civilian freighters have been told if they help you, they won't do business with the army again."

Sarah stared at the other woman, lightheaded with fear, and then she caught hold of herself. Matt had given her his money and his gun so that she wouldn't be helpless. He wouldn't approve of dissolving into a whimpering heap any more than crying.

"If you will give me back the rags I came in, I'll leave now," she said throwing the covers off. "I walked across a lot of Texas with Matt, and I can walk to Charon by myself if I have to."

"I burned those things, and you get right back in that bed and stop being silly. I told you, I am not obliged to take orders from Major Macauley, and I spent the afternoon talking to some of the other wives, and then I went down by the corrals and talked to the freighters myself."

Jenny met her husband's eyes. "Do you want to hear this?"

"Yes, I do, but you're right that I shouldn't." Edler got to his feet slowly. "Be careful, Miss Hammond. Major Macauley has chosen to take everything that happened as a personal insult, and he wants vengeance. My wife may be able to help you now, but you won't be safe until you're back in Boston."

Sarah said a polite goodbye and didn't correct the lieutenant. When he was gone, she said, "I'm not going back to Boston."

Jenny smiled, disbelief on her face. "Time will tell, Sarah. Now we'd better get busy. We have to have you outfitted and ready to travel before first light. Some of the other wives are going to be here in a little while. They've agreed to bring what they can and to help alter some dresses for you."

"But you said no one will take me anywhere."

"No, we said the freighters have been told that if they did take you, they wouldn't get any more army business. It seems several of the freighters were Rebels themselves and find the prospect of defeating a Yankee once more appealing. You're going to hide in a freight wagon leaving here first thing in the morning, and the driver acted insulted when I told him you would pay. If you need help once you're in Charon, I suggest you look for others like him."

"Thank you," Sarah whispered.

"I wish I could do more. Jim was right to tell you to be careful."

Sarah nodded. The last trouble-free day seemed in the distant past, and since it had been a day before she knew Matt, she didn't want to go back.

18

"I'LL WAIT FOR YOU," the big man standing beside her in the dark said harshly.

"Please don't do that," Sarah said. "What I need to talk to Mr. Payne about is going to take hours, and I'm sure he will escort me back when we're done."

Following Jenny Edler's advice to seek help from Confederate veterans, Sarah had asked the freighters for help. They introduced her to George Sudkamp and his friends in her first hours in Charon. The motley group of ex-Rebels considered a Yankee in trouble cause for celebration, but as a Yankee that one of General Hood's men cared about, Sarah got grudging help.

The men found her a place to stay, provided her an escort that brooked no disrespect when she went out, and taught her how to clean and shoot Matt's pistol, just in case. The brusque way they spoke and acted even as they helped didn't bother Sarah because she agreed with them. Matt was in this trouble because of her.

"I'll wait."

"Thank you." Sarah didn't argue further. She crossed the street and knocked on the front door of the small frame house where Curtis Payne, the lawyer supposedly defending Matt, lived.

The gray-haired woman who answered the door had the air of a sparrow, all bright eyes and interest. "So you are Miss Sarah Hammond. Come in, come in. My husband is in his study, and I'm sure he'll be pleased to meet you."

Mrs. Payne's tone said she knew the lengths to which her husband had gone to avoid Sarah. The mischief in her smile said she looked forward to seeing him cornered.

Payne's study mirrored that of Sarah's own father. A lump of homesickness rose in her throat at the sight. Bookshelves lined one wall. The huge desk covered with messy heaps of paper dominated a room mysterious with shadows in the lamplight. Wisps of smoke swirled from the cigar Payne dropped in a heavy glass ashtray as he got to his feet.

The lawyer didn't waste time on pleasantries after his wife made introductions. "I'm sorry, Miss Hammond," he said, "but I cannot see you, cannot speak with you. Mr. Tembley is calling you as his witness."

"I don't want to be his witness. I want to be Matt's witness."

"That's not possible. Mr. Tembley has called you, and I cannot speak with a witness who is being called by the prosecution."

Sarah studied Payne. Silver haired and more overfed than most, he stood behind his big desk in his cozy study, the picture of a man who lived a secure, comfortable life. Not only had he not helped Matt, he was one of those trying to keep her from helping.

"So you're part of it. How much did Major Macauley pay you? Or did you do it to curry favor with the army? Are they in a position to send business your way?"

Mrs. Payne gasped, her attitude changing in a flash. She grabbed Sarah's arm hard and pulled her toward the door. "I beg your pardon. No matter how upset you may be, you have no right to speak to my husband like that. He has always done his best for any client, even an ungrateful, stubborn charity case like Mr. Slade."

Sarah jerked her arm free. "He got Matt to say he's guilty when he's not. He's not guilty of anything, and everyone knows it."

Payne said, "Miss Hammond, even though I cannot make things be the way you wish they were, I can tell you that I all but begged Mr. Slade not to enter that plea. He wouldn't listen to a word I said. All he cares about is protecting you and that means keeping you from testifying under oath. The only way I failed Mr. Slade is in not foreseeing that if he did plead guilty, Major Macauley would simply insist on a sentencing hearing where you could be called as a character witness. I'm afraid I didn't understand the intensity of Major Macauley's feelings at the time."

"I know that Major Macauley is doing this to Matt because of me. Are you saying that they used me to make him plead guilty to these ridiculous charges?"

"I am talking about the fact that Mr. Slade would build his own gallows and thrust his neck into the noose willingly if it would keep you from having to testify at a trial, and by pleading guilty to the charges, he intended to accomplish that. Where I failed him was in not seeing that Major Macauley can and will accomplish *his* purpose at a sentencing hearing instead of a trial."

"Then take back the guilty plea." Sarah had come here to beg or bribe Payne to do just that.

"I cannot take it back. Mr. Slade cannot take it back. The judge has accepted the plea, and the day after tomorrow there will be a sentencing hearing, and in truth I'm not sure the outcome would be any different at a trial. No one who served the Confederacy in any capacity can serve on a jury. The judge is from Illinois, and he lost a son in the war. He is going to accept Mr. Tembley's recommendation as to sentencing, and Mr. Slade will spend the next ten years in prison."

That couldn't be true. It could not be true. A wave of dizziness swept over Sarah, and she swayed on her feet. Mrs. Payne took hold of Sarah's arm again, gently this time, and guided her into one of the leather chairs facing the desk.

"Since my husband shouldn't be talking to you, we certainly can't have you fainting right here at our feet. While you and Curtis work out what you can't talk about, I'll make us all some tea."

After his wife left the room, he said, "I'm sorry, Miss Hammond."

He did look sorry. Sarah said, "They can't, not even Cart... Major Macauley can do that to him. No one can really think it was a crime for us to take those clothes or eat that food. Even the other things. We needed those things to survive. The dead would have given them to us gladly and so would their families. I have Matt's money. I can give you whatever it takes to pay for what we took."

Payne sighed and sank down into his chair. "They won't take payment. They're out for blood. Right and wrong, law and justice have nothing to do with it. You're right. If one of the families wanted Mr. Slade prosecuted on charges like this, they'd be laughed out of court, and if for some reason they weren't and he pled guilty, he'd likely spend a month or so in jail right here in Charon and that would be the end of it. But those uniforms were U.S. Army issue, and no one in the South can afford to laugh at the army these days. Everyone involved knows this is vengeance, just plain vengeance."

"Because of me," Sarah whispered.

Payne looked down at his desk and rubbed his forehead. His wife's return spared him from having to answer. She poured tea for them all.

Without asking, she stirred several lumps of sugar into the cup she gave Sarah. Mrs. Payne didn't relax until Sarah agreed to a slice of gingerbread cake.

"Everyone is trying to fatten me up," Sarah said, forcing a smile. "They don't know all my life my problem has been very much the opposite of being too thin. It won't be long before people are calling me plump again."

Mrs. Payne looked her over carefully. "You won't be in any danger of that for quite a while. Now, my husband may not want to give you legal advice, but I would like to hear your story. Suppose we sit here and have our tea and you tell us what happened."

Payne stopped stirring his tea. "Millie...."

"Oh, hush, Curtis. If you don't want to hear it, you can leave. I'm not passing up a chance like this."

The resigned way Payne settled back in his chair indicated this kind of exchange was not uncommon. Sarah sipped her tea, nibbled on her gingerbread and told the story.

When she was finished, Mrs. Payne said, "Oh, my. How remarkable. I do believe I would pay to hear a story such as that, and of course your Mr. Slade didn't tell Curtis half of it, did he dear?"

Payne gave his wife an amused look. "No. He answered the army's questions at Fort Grissom, but they refused to share anything with me, and all Slade is interested in is protecting you, Miss Hammond.

"But he doesn't need to protect me," Sarah protested. "I'm willing to tell the story in court. How can anyone think I'll say anything that will hurt Matt? Why can't I testify for him?"

"You can't testify for him because Mr. Tembley is the one who is calling you, and I didn't call you because Mr. Slade wouldn't let me."

"But it doesn't matter who is asking the questions. They can't make me say anything bad about Matt or his character."

Payne toyed with his empty cup. "I will give you this much advice, Miss Hammond. When Mr. Tembley starts questioning you, you would be well advised to tell him you were hysterical with fear from the moment the Comanches attacked until you passed into delirium just before the army found you. Tell him even trying to remember makes you ill and being in court has you light-headed, afraid of fainting and unable to remember anything. Keep repeating that no matter what he asks."

"Why would I do that?" Sarah asked turning to Mrs. Payne. "You heard what happened. Would you send Matt to prison after hearing what I had to say?"

"No, dear, I wouldn't."

"See?" Sarah said to Payne. "I'll tell them what really happened, and they'll let Matt go."

Payne exchanged a look with his wife, who stood and gathered the cups and plates onto the tray. After patting Sarah on the shoulder, she picked up the tray and left.

Payne leaned forward in his chair. "Listen to me, Miss Hammond. Nothing is going to change things. Mr. Slade is going to prison for ten years. The pressure being brought on everyone involved in this case is enormous. If Major Macauley thought he could get away with dictating an execution or a life sentence, he would do it, but ten years is as far as he dares push things. His feelings about you are equally as vindictive. He wants you testifying under oath as to what happened between you and Slade because it will ruin you. Slade will be out of prison in ten years, but you will be branded for life."

Sarah looked into the man's eyes and saw knowledge there. Still she asked, "Are you so sure about what happened between us?"

"Everyone is sure, but knowing is one thing. Having it spoken in court is quite another. Mr. Slade is desperate to keep this from happening to you. He can't save himself. Let him save you."

"I don't believe you. There has to be a way to help him."

Payne slapped his hand on the surface of the desk, and Sarah jumped. "Pretend you are under oath and I am Mr. Tembley. You are required to answer my questions truthfully. Now, tell me, Miss Hammond, did Mr. Slade have carnal knowledge of you?"

Sarah couldn't believe her ears. No one would ask such a thing outright like that, would they?

Payne wasn't through. "Were you willing, or did he force you? Where did this happen the first time? Did he promise to marry you as inducement?"

Mrs. Payne bustled back into the room with a fresh pot of tea. "Now have you two got everything all worked out?"

Sarah had mastered her shock. She straightened in her chair. "Yes, Mrs. Payne. It seems your husband has decided to talk to me about legal matters after all. He's about to give me lessons in what I will be asked when I testify and the best way to answer. Isn't that right, Mr. Payne?"

The lawyer gave her the same resigned look he'd directed at his wife earlier. "It seems that it is, Miss Hammond, and since we only have tonight, we better begin."

The clock on Payne's desk chimed six times before he gave any sign of satisfaction with Sarah's answers to his questions. She felt brutalized.

The lawyer leaned back in his chair and said, "That's the best I can do, Miss Hammond. My wife and I will deny this meeting ever took place, and I beg you to reconsider. Nothing is going to make any difference, and you will do yourself great harm."

Over the last hours, exactly how much harm she would have to do herself had become only too clear. The knowledge made no difference in her determination to do it.

"Thank you, Mr. Payne," she said. "They won't let me see him, you know. They turn me away from the jail every day. I don't suppose you can do anything about that."

She expected his tired headshake. Getting to her feet, she fumbled in her pocket for Matt's money. "I want you to make sure Matt has a bath and shave and decent clothes for court."

"I doubt he'll let me spend a cent of that for such things."

"Yes, he will. You tell him he'd better not embarrass me by walking into that courtroom dirty and ragged."

Payne smiled at her words and accepted several of the bills.

Sarah turned to go, then turned back. "And Mr. Payne, you tell him there's no use fussing over this. He can't change it. You tell him I said that too."

19

WALLS BUILT OF NATIVE stone gave the Charon courthouse an air of authority in spite of its small size and lack of amenities. The judge sat behind a wood table. An empty chair at one end of the table awaited witnesses. Sarah glimpsed half a dozen men in chairs facing the judge, Matt and Curtis Payne among them. Everyone else had to stand.

A line of men in blue uniforms stood right behind Matt and the lawyers. Sarah recognized Carter and Lieutenant Edler. From this distance she could not identify rank insignia but knew one of the other officers would be Colonel Royer, here to see justice for his wife. How did Edler and the others feel, she wondered, following orders to attend, knowing the only purpose was to intimidate?

Sarah had argued against the bulwark George Sudkamp and his friends formed around her as she entered the courthouse. Now, as Carter Macauley turned and swept her from head to toe with a contemptuous glare, only the stolid presence of the Rebels kept her from running back out to the street.

She had to ignore him, she reminded herself. She had to concentrate on Matt and pretend Carter Macauley didn't exist. "Can you get me closer to the front?" she whispered to Sudkamp. "I want to see Matt, to talk to him." She wanted more than that. She wanted to hold and be held. She wanted to kiss and be kissed. She wanted....

"No." Sudkamp rocked back on his heels, as immovable as a mountain.

He and his friends had her locked in position in the crowd where she could barely catch sight of the back of Matt's head, although she noted with satisfaction that his hair was clean and freshly shorn and the little bit of shirt she could see was white.

She could hear even less than she could see. Male voices droned, an occasional word floated back, but never an entire phrase.

Intent on keeping Matt in sight through the shifting bodies of the crowd, Sarah didn't register the first call of her own name. The second time "Sarah Hammond" echoed through the room, Sudkamp and his friends began pushing forward en masse, but the crowd quieted and a path opened through the throng as every person turned to stare at her. Sarah walked to the front of the room alone, the heels of her new shoes clicking loudly on the board floor.

After swearing to tell the truth, Sarah took her seat at the end of the judge's table and looked toward Matt, eager to see his face for the first time in weeks. He sat with head bowed, his face hidden, and he wore handcuffs again she saw angrily. As if he really had murdered someone, instead of....

John Tembley rose and approached, blocking her view of Matt. Sarah dragged her eyes to the lawyer who planned to make her say things that would justify sending Matt to prison for years. She had to stay alert and use Curtis Payne's lessons and her own plan, the things she had practiced over and over yesterday.

With that thought in mind, Sarah adjusted herself on the chair and inside Jenny Edler's too large blue dress in the way she knew best emphasized her skeletal condition. She widened her eyes, bit her lower lip, and gave first Tembley, then Judge William Carnott, a quick glance filled with anxiety.

At least Curtis Payne's appearance suited his calling, she thought. Tembley's didn't. Young, blond and thin, he probably considered himself handsome. Sarah decided he looked like a hungry coyote pretending to be a well fed dog.

He gave a coyote smile and began asking her gentle questions about her background, why she had traveled to Texas and come to be escorted by Lieutenant Broderick and his men.

He moved on to the civilians in the group, to the Webbs and Matt. Sarah showed him how well he was winning her over by relaxing in the chair, smiling back at him, and watched him swell with confidence.

He moved on to the Comanche attack. "Now, Miss Hammond, you and Mrs. Royer and Mrs. Lowell all slept inside the house, is that right?"

"And Lieutenant Broderick, yes."

Sarah saw surprise flare in his eyes, but he didn't pursue Broderick's presence in the house.

"How did Mr. Slade come to be in the house?"

"Mr. Webb, Mr. Barney Webb, came running into the house, and he pulled Mr. Slade with him by the handcuffs."

"I understand Mrs. Lowell was shot and died early in the attack. Would you describe the circumstances of her death?"

"Soldiers came running inside, one of them carrying another, and then Mr. Webb and Mr. Slade came in. Mrs. Lowell was standing across from the open door, and she was shot."

"Fatally shot?"

"Yes."

Sarah saw no reason to describe Lydia Lowell's death with her husband sitting right there unless Tembley asked far more specific questions. He didn't.

"But Mrs. Royer was alive when Mr. Slade discovered the hole in the floor, wasn't she?"

Sarah dabbed at an eye with her handkerchief, and a tear rolled down her cheek. "No. Mr. Webb hit Mr. Slade in the head with his rifle early in the attack. Mr. Slade was unconscious on the floor all that time. I saw him move a little, but he didn't get up until after Lieutenant Broderick shot Mrs. Royer and himself."

"But Lieutenant Broderick didn't shoot you, did he Miss Hammond? Was he derelict in his duty?"

Sarah used her handkerchief again. Tears fell. Behind Tembley she saw Matt, head up now, studying her with his head tipped in that familiar way. She ached to really look back, drink in the sight of him, and didn't dare.

She mopped up and avoided Tembley's eyes. Curtis Payne had warned her against saying or even hinting at anything but praise for Broderick. "No, Lieutenant Broderick was very brave, but I...." She threw a frantic, helpless look at the judge. "I told him no and crawled into the fireplace to get away."

"Why did you do that?"

"Because he didn't say anything, and I didn't understand about the Comanches." Sarah shuddered and whispered. "I didn't understand what they—what they do to captives." She straightened in the chair and continued in a clear voice, "I'm sure he thought I knew from the other women, but I didn't, and when he shot Mrs. Royer and then pointed the gun at me, I panicked, and I crawled into the fireplace and hid."

Sarah hunched over in the chair with her arms crossed defensively over what little was left of her breasts and made sure the judge got the full effect of her pitiful expression.

"Let's give Miss Hammond a moment to collect herself," the judge said. "And perhaps some water, Miss Hammond?"

Sarah dabbed at her eyes, gave the judge a tremulous smile and a soft, "Thank you." Over her handkerchief she saw Payne holding Matt's arm as if to keep him in the chair and talking fast. Matt gave no sign of listening to the lawyer and every sign of knowing exactly what she was up to and wanting her to stop. She smiled at him as reassuringly as she knew how and prayed that Payne would succeed in keeping Matt in that chair and quiet.

After sipping her water and wiping away a few more tears, Sarah turned her brave face toward the judge. "I'm ready to go on now."

He gestured to Tembley, who was more than ready to continue. "So you are telling us that Lieutenant Broderick killed Mrs. Royer and turned the gun toward you but did not pursue you when you crawled inside the fireplace to get away from him?"

Delighted that Tembley had accepted her hint that the fireplace was so cavernous Lieutenant Broderick couldn't dig her out, Sarah bit her lip again to keep from showing anything but sorrow. "Yes."

"And that left you and Mr. Slade as the only ones alive in the house."

"Yes."

"And Mr. Slade did manage to pull you out of the fireplace and into the hole in the floor he found."

"Yes."

"How big was this hole, Miss Hammond?"

Sarah looked at the lawyer in genuine confusion. "I don't know measurements. It was small. It made me think of a coffin."

"So you and Mr. Slade were in intimate contact in that hole."

Ahh, so that was what he was up to. Sarah treated the judge to her anxious face. "Yes, it was intimate. He had to keep his hand across my mouth to stop my whimpering, and he had the barrel of the pistol under my chin so he could kill me quickly if they found us."

Tembley regarded her with more caution than previously. "So the Indians left, and you and Mr. Slade got out of that hole, and he robbed the dead."

"No."

"No? Are you saying that Mr. Slade did not take clothing and other items from the dead?"

"I'm saying we both took the things we needed to survive. If you want to call it robbing the dead, then we both robbed the dead. Do you want to arrest me?"

Sarah pushed up her dress sleeves and held out her arms dramatically as if ready for handcuffs. Presented like that, her wrists looked like matchsticks.

Tembley ignored her theatrical gesture. "Did Mr. Slade ever mention the expression 'to impress into service,' Miss Hammond?"

Sarah took enough time to be sure everyone understood she was trying to remember. "No. I read that term in the newspapers. That's when the government, the army, took property from civilians without paying for it, like horses for the cavalry."

Tembley didn't like that answer, but he pressed on.

"What about the expression 'administer the estate' of a dead soldier, Miss Hammond. Do you know what that means?

"Yes," Sarah admitted. "That's when soldiers take ammunition and supplies from others who were killed."

"Did Mr. Slade ever admit doing that to you?"

Sarah knew she had to give Tembley this one, and so she did. "Yes. He said he probably got more food from haversacks of the dead than from the Confederate Commissary."

Satisfaction spread across the young lawyer's face.

"And what about 'bummer,' Miss Hammond. Do you know that term? Did Mr. Slade admit to you that he had ever acted as a bummer?"

"No," Sarah said with conviction. "Mr. Slade made it clear he spent his entire service in the ranks of the Fourth Texas Infantry Regiment. Bummers were foragers turned loose on the countryside who stole anything they could, like General Sherman's men on their march from Atlanta to the sea."

A man yelled from the back of the courtroom, "You tell that carpetbagging son of a bitch, lady! You tell him who the robbers were!"

The judge stared angrily into the crowd, banged his gavel and threatened to throw anyone who disrupted the proceedings in jail on the spot, but there was no way to tell who had done the yelling. When the judge gestured to Tembley to continue, the lawyer abandoned his questions about bummers and foraging.

He said, "Now, Miss Hammond. I understand you were in night clothes when the attack started, but Mr. Slade was wearing perfectly serviceable clothes of his own, wasn't he? He didn't need to steal clothing from dead United States cavalrymen, did he?"

"We were both soaked with excrement. We both had to have clean clothes. As Mr. Slade said, the Comanches would find us with their noses if we didn't get clean."

With considerable effort, Sarah hid any trace of satisfaction at the effect her words had on Tembley, who seemed unable to process what he had just heard.

"Miss Hammond."

Sarah swiveled toward the judge and gave him a timid smile. Swarthy, bald and heavy set, Carnott's appearance really did intimidate her. She clung to the memory of Curtis Payne's description of the judge as a decent man.

He said, "Why don't you just tell us what happened from this point on, Miss Hammond. Then Mr. Tembley or I will ask you any specific questions for clarification when you've finished."

Permission to tell the story was her first goal, one that Payne had been sure she couldn't achieve.

Sarah took another sip of water, waited for the urge to give a triumphant yell to pass, and told Judge Carnott her story in words she hoped would play on every sympathetic nerve the man had in him.

When she finished the story, a sound like a collective sigh ran through the courtroom, which had gone quiet as a church while she talked. Tembley hurried to break the spell.

"That's a pretty story, Miss Hammond. At what point in this tale did Mr. Slade seduce you?"

"He didn't."

"I remind you that you are under oath, Miss Hammond, and that your behavior after you were rescued by the cavalry made it clear that you and Mr. Slade had been intimate. When did he seduce you?"

"He didn't. I seduced him."

A Rebel yell reverberated from the back of the courtroom.

Judge Carnott banged his gavel and called for order, but a scuffle broke out that didn't stop until Colonel Royer sent several of the cavalry officers into the crowd. After they shoved several resisting men out through the door and slammed it behind them, the crowd quieted.

The interruption exposed the first cracks in Tembley's composure. "*Miss* Hammond, do you seriously expect anyone here to believe that a young woman from your background, in the circumstances in which you found yourself, would seduce someone like Mr. Slade?"

For a second Sarah forgot her purpose and matched his temper. "What exactly do you mean by that, Mr. Tembley? 'Someone like Mr. Slade?'"

He leaned in toward her. "You know perfectly well what I mean, *Miss* Hammond. A drifter, Secessionist trash."

Judge Carnott's angry reprimand saved Sarah from herself. He snapped, "Mr. Tembley, if you use language like that in my court again, you will find yourself charged with contempt. Miss Hammond has answered your question. Are you through?"

"I beg your pardon and your indulgence, Your Honor. I have a few more questions."

The judge gave a curt nod, and Tembley turned back to Sarah.

"When did this seduction occur, Miss Hammond?"

"After we saw the Comanches. I knew I loved him and suspected he felt the same."

"Did he promise to marry you?"

"We talked about it, but no, no promises."

"What did Mr. Slade tell you about himself? For instance, did he dazzle you with stories of how he was a war hero?"

Sarah told Tembley what Matt had to say about heroes, and she watched the coyote slink away, leaving a worried young man behind. Then it was over. Curtis Payne declined to question her. Sarah left the witness chair and started for Matt almost at a run, hoping no one could stop her before she reached him, but a big man with a badge stepped in her way.

Accepting defeat, she redirected her steps toward George Sudkamp, only to feel someone plucking at her sleeve.

"Whore!"

A gobbet of spit spattered her cheek and dripped onto the neck of her dress. Sarah heard a commotion behind her and whirled to see Matt, already over the back of his chair, through the line of army officers and bulling his way through the crowd toward her. The men in blue uniforms were right behind him, then on him, two of them restraining him, another plowing a fist into his stomach.

"Matt!" Sarah screamed, trying to get through the bodies closing in around her. She got nowhere. George Sudkamp reached her, picked her up and carried her, hitting, kicking and screaming, out of the courthouse.

When Sudkamp put her down outside, Sarah said, "Damn you."

"Maybe so," the big man said, "but if you stayed in there you'd make it worse for him and worse for you. Hit me if you want."

She did want to hit him, but his words changed her mind. "I'm sorry. You're right, but it's so hard to see him right there and still not be able to even...."

"I know. They got you two locked up good, but you don't have to play into their hands. Here, use this and wipe yourself off."

Sarah took the big handkerchief and wiped the spit off. "I'll wash this and give it back tomorrow," she said.

"Don't bother. Throw it in the trash. What is it you've got on your own hanky anyway?"

Sarah looked up with concern. "What makes you think I have something on my handkerchief?"

"You ain't much of a weeper, but you had those tears falling like rain in there, and they seemed to come at the best of times, right after you wiped your eyes."

"No one was supposed to know. Do you think the judge could tell? Did I overdo it?" Sarah said, suddenly sick with worry.

"Nah, you had that carpetbagger judge wrapped around your little finger. Maybe the lawyers wondered, and Slade sure knew, but the judge—you did fine there. What did you use?"

"I soaked a corner in tobacco juice. The problem was hiding the stain."

For the first time since she'd met him, Sudkamp smiled at her. "I suppose you used that mirror you wanted yesterday to practice them looks."

Sarah smiled back. "Yes, I did. I'm already good at what Matt calls my pitiful look, but I had to work on the others."

Sudkamp threw his head back and laughed, and Sarah laughed with him, but inside she kept worrying. Was he right? Had she really won the judge over?

THE HONORABLE WILLIAM Carnott used a room at the back of the saloon for an office since the new courthouse didn't have such a convenience. The arrangement had its advantages. He picked up a bottle of whiskey and three glasses at the bar and ordered one of the men there to round up Curtis Payne and John Tembley.

Sinking into one the chairs with a groan, he poured himself a double. Coming down here and overseeing the reestablishment of real law in Texas had sounded like an adventure when he was offered the appointment. So what if the natives looked at him with more contempt than respect and called him a carpetbagger? He'd come here with every intention of upholding the law to the best of his ability, and right now he heartily wished he'd stayed in Illinois.

Payne and Tembley showed up together and sat on the other side of the table, looking more like partners than adversaries. Carnott regarded them with suspicion.

"So which one of you is going to tell me why we're sending that boy to prison instead of pinning a medal on him?"

The two lawyers sat like statues and said nothing.

Carnott leaned forward and barked, "One of you sons of bitches start talking, right now!"

Tembley finally said, "He stole from the army, and they want him to pay."

"Horse shit. Can you do better?" The judge pointed at Payne with his glass.

Payne said, "The girl came to Texas to marry Major Macauley. When they were rescued by a cavalry patrol, they were both ragged and filthy as you'd expect, but Miss Hammond's clothing was much more ragged. One grinning young cavalryman told me the trousers she had on looked as if they'd been dragged through cactus for miles. Every man in that patrol got a good look at a lot of female flesh. Probably worse from Macauley's point of view, as soon as they got a little water down her she started babbling about Slade. Babbling about how much she loved him and all the ways she would prove it as soon as they were saved."

Payne's voice died away as if he couldn't bring himself to say more, and Carnott had mercy on him. "We get the idea. So that's what set the major off on this vendetta?"

"In part. According to my informant, the troops also rubbed salt in his wounds. Evidently they're less than fond of the major, and they went so far as to come up with a little ditty about it that they made sure he heard them singing as often as possible."

Payne cleared his throat and chanted:

> "Fiancée, fiancée.
> Reb poked her
> Three times today."

Carnott grunted and threw Tembley a look that wiped the smirk right off the young lawyer's face. "And that's why I've been threatened by some jackass claiming to be a 'representative' of the army? And that's why I'm expected to send that boy away for what should be the best years of his life, the years he'd be marrying that girl and starting a family?"

"Yes, sir," Payne said.

"You been threatened?" the judge asked.

"No, sir, but there was no reason to threaten me. Major Macauley thought he had things fixed so the girl couldn't get out of Fort Grissom. In fact the good major intended her to have to resort to the cribs there. Without her as a witness, convicting Slade would be guaranteed, and when she showed up here after all, Slade thought he could keep them from asking her about him under oath by pleading guilty."

"And you didn't tell him different."

"To my shame, I didn't."

Carnott grunted, refilled his own glass, poured into the other two and shoved them across the table. "What about you?" he said to Tembley. "You get threatened?"

"Yes."

"They tell you exactly how you'd be sorry if that boy walked out of here a free man?"

"I couldn't testify to a specific threat in court, but if you let him go, I'll be on my way back to New York tonight."

Carnott nodded. "Same here, but you don't have to worry. I don't have the kind of courage it would take to let him go."

Tembley sagged with relief. Payne's expression didn't change. Carnott said, "I don't have the courage and yet I owe that boy. You know why I owe him?"

The other men shook their heads. Ignoring them, Carnott stared into his glass. "My son Walter died in the war, not in some battle you read about in the papers, not giving his all for the Union. He was artillery, and a shell exploded next to him, just an accident, and then you asked that girl if Slade claimed to be a hero."

Carnott took a large swallow of whiskey, struggling to control his emotions. "And what she told you.... I think of what that boy saw, what he did, and that's all he had to say about it. 'Hero, straggler and ordinary soldier, they all died just as dead, and they all got buried just as deep.' He's right, you know. It doesn't make a damn bit of difference how any of them died. They're all just as dead."

The judge tossed down the rest of his drink and looked at the lawyers again. "Get out of here, you two. I can't stand the sight of you, and I can't stand myself."

SARAH SAT ON THE wooden walk where she had collapsed, rocking back and forth, weeping real tears. Sudkamp and his friends stood guard in a loose circle around her, awkward and uncomfortable, with no idea what to do.

"You should be dancing in the street, not crying."

Through a blur of tears, Sarah saw Curtis Payne standing over her. "Dancing," she said bitterly. "I should be dancing when they're sending Matt to prison for three years because of me. You know that's the real reason. You know it."

With a grunt, Payne lowered himself to sit beside her and took her hand.

"Aren't you afraid to be seen with me?" Sarah said.

"Not now. It's over and no one can fault me for comforting a friend of my client. Listen to me, Miss Hammond. You have accomplished something I swore couldn't be done. Three years is a very different proposition than ten. The judge talked to Tembley and me during the recess, and he actually said we should be pinning a medal on Mr. Slade. You would have succeeded outright except that the judge has been threatened, and he's afraid. He defied Macauley and Royer as much as he dared, and he's going to pay a price for it, but he did defy them, and you're the one that made him do it. You should be proud."

Proud. Sarah couldn't imagine ever feeling proud of anything again. Certainly not anything that happened in Charon. "Where will they send him?" she asked.

"The state prison in Hartsville. You need to go home now, Miss Hammond. Go back to Boston and let your family help you recover from this."

Sarah stared at the lawyer. "Thank you for your help, Mr. Payne," she said formally.

He grunted again as he pushed to his feet. "It's been an honor knowing you, Miss Hammond. Good luck to you."

As soon as he was gone, Sarah stood up too. "How do I get to Hartsville?" she asked Sudkamp.

20

From the moment the cavalry patrol found them, Matt had gulped down any liquid and wolfed down any food offered. Now the supper the pimply young deputy had delivered sat untouched on the narrow cot at the back of his cell, and Matt paced back and forth across the small bit of open floor available.

Three steps, turn. Three steps, turn.

He used the motion to fight the urge to throw anything not tied down, smash anything smashable, tear anything tearable.

Jubilant over the result of today's court hearing, Curtis Payne had gone on and on about Sarah's performance. Matt scarcely stayed polite until the lawyer left. Three years instead of ten. Sure he understood the reason for celebration. He had been in the army four years. He had suffered Mrs. Stolfelz' reign of terror that long. Ten years stretched so far in the future he couldn't imagine how it would be, how *he* would be when it was over. But three years. Most likely he could survive three years of anything.

The thought that had him half crazed was the price Sarah paid to buy him those years of his life. Seeing her today shocked him. When he saw Sarah in his mind, he saw her marching off to get her own clothes in her filthy night dress, saw her smiling at him over meals of snake or crawdads, saw her laughing when he kissed her in ticklish places. The memories of the ghostly girl he'd held at the end had faded away—until today. She looked as terrible in the courtroom as the last time he saw her. Well, maybe not quite. She wasn't fading in and out of consciousness today but wide awake and playing that judge like a fish on a line.

He stopped pacing and rested his head against the bars of the cell. What would happen to her? She couldn't have much of the money left. Her family would send more. Maybe they already had. They'd send enough that she could get back to Boston.

Then what? Were her folks wealthy and powerful enough to fix what had happened to her? What he had done to her? From everything she ever told him, they were rigid in their righteousness. That wouldn't matter, would it? She was their daughter. Matt started pacing again.

Three steps, turn. Three steps, turn.

He tried to picture getting out of prison, traveling to Boston, finding a big, three-story house in the Yankee city, tried to imagine walking to the front door of such a house and knocking, telling the servant who came to the door he wanted—needed—to see Miss Hammond. No picture came. Even ignoring the problem of how to get there, he knew a door like that would never open for him.

For a little while he'd let himself believe he and Sarah had a future, that he could build a decent life with her, take care of her. The moment they were no longer alone, the truth he'd always known shoved its way back out of the place in his heart where he'd tried to hide it. Today made it even more clear—all he'd brought her by loving her was the horror of laying herself bare before all those people in the courthouse, being spit on and called names she should never hear.

Three steps, turn. Three steps, turn.

The sound of the door to the sheriff's office opening brought him to a halt. The sight of Major Carter Macauley and Lieutenant J.T. Edler following the young deputy through the door brought him to attention.

Edler had commanded the patrol that found Sarah and Matt. The lieutenant hadn't been friendly, but he had controlled his troopers and been fair in his way. Tonight he looked like a different man, his eyes darting from side, a film of perspiration on his upper lip. Maybe the presence of a superior officer always had that effect on him, but Matt reckoned it didn't.

Curtis Payne had disabused Matt of any notion that Major Carter Macauley felt so much as a shred of understanding or forgiveness toward Sarah. The times Matt had glimpsed Macauley in the court-room today, staring at Sarah with furious contempt, drove the lawyer's words home.

Macauley's attitude now was different, jovial, with an underlying air of excitement gleaming in his dark eyes. Even before Matt saw the handcuffs in the deputy's hands, the hair at the back of his neck rose. The boy shouldn't have a badge, but his father, the sheriff, had some notion the job was going to make a man of his timid son.

Matt knew better than to resist, but he tried reasoning with the boy. "You don't need those, Ben. I'm already locked up. These officers can talk to me just fine through the bars."

Ben hesitated, and Macauley pulled the keys out of the boy's hand and unlocked the cell door himself.

Once close, Ben whispered, "Come on, Matt. You know I've got to do what they say. The major wants these on."

Reluctantly, Matt held out his arms. Every survival instinct screamed at him to fight or to run, but there was no way to fight and nowhere to go.

Even so, when Ben closed one cuff over his left wrist, then ran the chain through the bars behind him, Matt tried to twist away, but Macauley closed in on him, using his greater weight to shove him back against the bars, helping Ben pull his right arm back and close the cuff around the wrist. His work done, Ben slunk away.

Macauley strutted back and forth in the same small area Matt had been pacing, working himself up to whatever he'd come here for. Matt glanced at Edler, sensing that nothing but the lieutenant's presence stood between him and disaster.

As if he heard Matt's thought, Macauley said, "Wait outside for me while I talk to Mr. Slade, Lieutenant."

Edler met Matt's eyes for second, hesitating.

"That's an order, Lieutenant!" Macauley snarled.

Edler turned and left, closing the door quietly behind him.

Matt faced Macauley, suddenly sure his chances of surviving until morning were less than they had been when the Comanches raged outside the homestead and he had not yet found the hidey hole.

Macauley stalked back and forth for another few moments before stopping in front of Matt. The strange smile disappeared; only the hate showed. "I suppose you think I should be grateful that you showed her for the whore she is before I married her, don't you?"

Macauley had been smart to insist on the cuffs. Matt pulled futilely against iron. "You know that's not the way it was, Major. You were right to want to marry her. She's special, and you know it, but we were alone out there, and I was all she had. She just...."

"Shut up, you son of a bitch. Shut up!" Macauley leaned in so close Matt smelled the liquor on his breath. "She's a slut and a whore."

Matt crouched slightly to get as much slack as possible then head butted Macauley with all his strength. The man fell backwards against the bed, lay still for a moment, then got up shaking his head. "You stupid son of a bitch. You're going to make this a pleasure, aren't you? But first you're going to hear what I have to say about Sarah the slut. Why the hell didn't you save Royer's bitch of a wife and let the Comanches have Sarah? I could mourn, and she could spread herself out for every one of them as quick as for you. It doesn't make any difference for her. She's going to spend the rest of her life on her back or her knees for any man stupid enough to pay a couple of dollars for her."

"Her family...."

Macauley threw his head back and brayed coarse laughter. "Her family, her fine, upright family that breeds like rabbits isn't going to give her a dime or the time of day."

"They will. They'll help her," Matt said, fear twisting in his gut. "She's their daughter, and even if you can't understand how it was, they will. They'll know...."

"What they'll know is what they'll read in the newspaper I sent them with my letter expressing extreme regret over the moral degeneracy of their daughter. It's a special edition of a newspaper I had printed just for them and right on the front page is the story of how Miss Sarah Hammond let her traveling companions die and saved herself from Comanches by whoring for a Rebel killer and helping him escape justice."

"That's not...."

"Oh, yes. It must be the truth. It's right there in the newspaper. Maybe they have it already. If you think family feeling will override the Hammond reaction to that kind of disgrace, you're even stupider than I think you are, and I think you're stupid, you miserable son of a bitch!"

Macauley's last words were almost a scream. Matt saw the blow coming, tried to roll away from it, but the back of his head smashed into the bars behind him so hard the pain blended with the fire streaking through his left eye and cheekbone. The second blow turned the world a bright red studded with starbursts of orange and yellow. The third brought the mercy of blackness.

J.T. Edler stared out the window of his second-story hotel room at the dark street below trying to convince himself that nothing out of the ordinary had happened at the jail. No cowardice could be imputed to a lieutenant who obeyed a direct order from a major. The alternative was court martial and disgrace.

He wanted to put it all out of his mind, go to bed and forget the whole sorry saga. Sarah would give up and go back to Boston. Slade would be transported to Hartsville. With the two of them gone, life at Fort Grissom would return to routine, and Macauley would learn to live with what had happened. With his ambitions, he'd be gone in a year or so anyway, transferred, or out of the army altogether.

Edler sat on the bed, started to pull a boot off, then stopped, unable to conquer his misgivings. The same sick, guilty feeling that had swept through him as he accompanied Macauley to the jail rose again.

If only he hadn't seen the bruises on Sarah's neck, heard the certainty in Jenny's voice when she described how she'd walked in on Macauley strangling that sick, starved skeleton of a girl. If only he didn't know the extent of Macauley's vengeful obsession with how Sarah and Slade had disgraced him, dishonored his name.

Macauley had stayed in the cell with Slade for a long time tonight. When he came out, he closed the door behind him with a calmness in stark contrast to his earlier attitude. Then he told that fool of a deputy to leave Slade alone until morning. And would he have even given the deputy the keys back if the boy hadn't asked?

Standing there with his arms chained behind him all night would be damned uncomfortable, but the sheriff had the stones his son didn't. Once he got back, he'd release Slade. Along with all the useless nattering the boy deputy had done while they waited for Macauley to finish with Slade, he'd said that his father would be back for supper.

Edler knew Macauley wanted to kill Slade, even understood the desire on some level. If that had happened to Jenny—but no matter what he wanted to do, the major wasn't crazed enough to strangle Slade right there in the jail with witnesses to the fact he'd been alone with the man.

Still, Edler couldn't forget the strange way Macauley had behaved tonight, as excited on the way to the jail as a man on the way to a banquet in his honor, as calm as if he'd taken laudanum after he'd talked to Slade.

To hell with it. Edler stomped his foot back down into the boot. His own wife had the courage to defy both Macauley and Royer and get Sarah out of Fort Grissom and to Charon. He could at least force that gutless boy deputy to take the cuffs off Slade.

The deputy was locking the sheriff's office and leaving for the night when Edler approached. "I thought you said your father would be back tonight."

"Well, he ain't, and when he's this late it means he stopped by Mrs. Barrow's. You know."

Edler didn't know and didn't care whether Mrs. Barrow was the local madam or a widow the sheriff fancied. "Did you take the handcuffs off Slade?"

"Not me. I did exactly what you said. I left him alone."

"I didn't.... We've changed our minds. Let's let him loose and then you can lock up for the night."

"You sure?" the deputy said. "He's tough, you know. He can stand the gaff."

"I'm sure," Edler said, putting an arm around the boy. "You get the keys. It will only take a minute."

Edler carried the lantern and walked back to the cell ahead of the reluctant deputy. What he saw hanging from the bars of the cell made him drop the lantern and run. The cell door was locked.

"Bring the keys. Bring the keys. Damn it," he bellowed at the deputy.

The boy stood there, unmoving and starting to make sounds like a wounded animal.

"My pa will kill me. He'll kill me."

Edler went back, grabbed the boy by the front of his shirt, and shook him. "The keys. Where are the keys?"

The boy held out the iron ring of keys, still keening. Edler took the keys, then slapped the youngster across the face hard. "You shut up and come help me. Hear me? You shut up and come help."

He started to hit the boy again and stopped himself. No use taking his guilt and fear out on the boy.

With the deputy silenced, the terrible sounds of Slade's labored breathing gave evidence he was alive. Alive but unconscious, thank God. Edler held Slade as the deputy unlocked the cuffs, surprised to find that even though Slade was much taller, he could easily lift the thin body.

"Where's the doctor in this town?" he asked.

"Up the street. It's way up by the livery. We need a wagon or something."

"No, we don't. You lead the way, and I'll carry him."

Edler followed the deputy out into the night, the bones of the man he carried digging into his shoulder, blood dripping onto the back of his shirt.

HOURS LATER EDLER RETURNED to the hotel, the bottle of whiskey he'd stopped at the saloon to buy dangling from one hand. He turned at the top of the stairs toward his room and stopped in his tracks. Major Carter Macauley sat in a chair blocking the door to the hotel room. As soon as the major spoke, Edler realized Macauley was drunk, very drunk. In fact he was almost as drunk as Edler planned to get before morning.

"You couldn't mind your own business, could you?" Macauley slurred. "You and that interfering wife of yours got Sarah the slut out of the fort too, didn't you?"

Edler said nothing. Macauley didn't seem to notice.

"It doesn't matter. However much money you scraped up and gave her, she'll run out soon and be whoring the way she deserves. I fixed her family, you know. Sarah the whore will be whoring." He laughed then seemed to sober. "So is the whore-maker still alive?"

The dark eyes bored in on Edler, demanding an answer this time.

"Yes, sir."

"It doesn't matter. Women won't be standing in line to roll on their backs for him ever again, will they?"

"No, sir."

"What are you looking at? I see the way you're looking at me. What are you looking at?"

"Your hand, sir. I'm wondering how you got the blood off your hand and your ring."

Macauley laughed again.

"His dinner was sitting right there with a cup of water and a napkin all ready for me. I didn't think about that on the way there. All I thought about was how to kill him."

He tipped the chair back against the room door. "You're not looking at my hand. You're looking at me. You're thinking about Colonel Royer and you're thinking about the sheriff. You think they'll do anything to me over that Rebel?"

Macauley thumped the chair back down on its front legs and lurched up, looming over Edler. "Let me tell you something, lieutenant. For a few dollars, that sheriff would take Slade's body out the back door and bury him without a word. Just one more dead Rebel that never got over all that starving. And now? Now all that sheriff's going to worry about is making sure nobody finds out what happened in his jail."

"Yes, sir."

"I destroyed them. I destroyed them both, and none of your pathetic little efforts made any difference at all."

"No, sir."

"Get out of my way."

Edler stepped aside and watched Macauley stagger down the hall.

After the major disappeared around the corner, Edler unlocked the door to the room and carried the chair inside with him. He put the chair down, sank into it and twisted the cork out of the whiskey bottle. The first gulp burned all the way down; the second not so much. Neither one dimmed the memory of the doctor forcing him to wash up and help work on Slade, of the doctor cutting a hole in Slade's throat and inserting a tube so he could get air, of the crunching sound the shoulder bones made when they finally went back in the socket.

Edler took another swallow of the cheap whiskey. Sooner or later the alcohol would bring oblivion and erase his guilt, and when it stopped working, he'd drink more.

21

FOR THE THIRD AFTERNOON in a row, Sarah stood and stared at the big white house at the edge of the town of Flowers. In spite of the pretty name, Flowers had proved as inhospitable as Hartsville. Not only had the prison guards in Hartsville refused to let her see Matt, they had not turned her away with the respect or regret of the sheriff in Charon. Sarah's mind skittered past the memory of her experience at the Hartsville prison.

In part she understood the attitude of the citizenry of Hartsville. Sarah wasn't the only woman in the town because of one of the imprisoned men, or the only one desperately looking for any employment that would allow her to stay. Many of the shop owners and tradesmen she talked to were out of sympathy and rude. The few who tried to help all gave the same advice—try another town. Thus, Flowers.

Except that word about Sarah Hammond had spread through the town somehow. Few people would speak to her. Those that did all said the same thing in terms that ranged from indifferent to malicious: go see Kate Pell at the brothel at the edge of town. More than once Sarah gave thanks for George Sudkamp's lessons with the pistol, but if Flowers had residents like Sudkamp, she could not find them.

A letter from home had finally pushed Sarah into taking everyone's advice. The long-awaited letter consisted of only five words scrawled across the page in her father's strong hand. He had signed his full name beneath those devastating words. "I have no daughter

Sarah. John Emory Hammond." Sarah saw Carter's signature as clearly as her father's.

Thousands of miles from home, trying to stretch the few dollars left of Matt's money by eating only once a day again, Sarah wept over that letter until it turned into a sodden mess. Blinking away more tears, she refocused on the white house.

Deciding to visit the brothel had been hard enough. After much deliberation she settled on early afternoon as the best time, but for the past two days she had been unable to find the courage to cross the road and knock on the door. The house didn't look like a den of iniquity. In fact it looked more prosperous and better maintained than most in town.

No scantily clad women hung from the railing of the porch around the second story. No line of men snaked around the place, although in the time she'd stood and watched, several had ridden around the back of the house and disappeared.

The first day Sarah all but ran back to town when that happened. Yesterday she merely stepped behind a clump of bushes until the man was out of sight.

Today was the day. Sarah stiffened her spine, raised her chin and walked across the road. The plump young woman who answered the door matched Sarah's idea of what a prostitute should look like exactly. Her dress was a ghastly combination of purples and pinks, and the low cut bodice showed breasts pushed up and together like mounds of, of.... Sarah's imagination failed her.

"So you got up your nerve, did you," the girl said with amusement, looking Sarah over from head to toe in a way only men had ever done before. "Come on in."

"I would like to talk to Miss Pell," Sarah said. "If I should make an appointment for another time, I will do that."

"Nah, we're not letting you off the hook that easy. Follow me. I'm Lily."

Sarah didn't answer. She followed the girl's twitching hips through rooms that shrieked *whorehouse* in red paint and gilded furniture even to a first-time visitor like Sarah. Nothing changed in the stairwells as they climbed to the third floor. Heart pounding, Sarah waited while Lily knocked on a plain white door, stuck her head in and told someone inside who had come calling.

When the girl stood aside, Sarah walked into a room as different as possible from the tasteless extravagance downstairs. Perhaps the screens dividing the room hid something bawdy, but everything visible was done in pale rose and gray. Kate Pell sat behind a desk as large as Curtis Payne's, but much neater. Dark of hair, smooth of skin, the woman appraised Sarah with cynical green eyes and gestured to the chair beside her desk.

"What can I do for you today, Miss Hammond?"

For a moment, Sarah couldn't think what to say, how to start. At last she said, "I believe you know about me."

"Of course, Flowers is as rife with gossip as any place in Texas."

"Then you know that my—the man I'm going to marry is in prison in Hartsville for three years. I searched for employment there, and then I came here hoping to find a way to support myself. My funds are low, and everyone in town keeps telling me to come to you. I need work, Miss Pell, and wondered if in an establishment as large as this you need help to do the kind of work I could do— laundry, cooking, sewing, cleaning. I'm willing to do any of those things."

A small, cold smile played across the madam's lips. "I have people who do all those things for me, Miss Hammond. The one thing I could hire you to do is the thing you think you're too good to do. Why don't you come back when you realize you're going to have to lower yourself to my level."

Hoping for work here had been stupid, Sarah realized. She caught herself slumping in disappointment and squared her shoulders, lifted her chin.

"Thank you for seeing me without notice like this, Miss Pell. I apologize for wasting your time."

She stood and then couldn't stop herself saying, "I've lowered myself to gathering buffalo chips with my bare hands, to eating snake and rodents and eating them eagerly. If you know my story, you know that in the eyes of respectable people I am as much a whore as any woman you employ. But I cannot sell what I gave to someone else. My body is not mine to sell."

"That sounds very romantic, Miss Hammond, but the fact is every woman in this place, including me, is here because she was led down the garden path by a man who betrayed her and left her. There's nothing different about that part of your story."

"Matt didn't betray me," Sarah said fiercely. "He's in prison because of me. They invented charges, and they used me to get him to plead guilty, and they sent him away for years because of me."

"Miss Hammond."

Sarah's was halfway to the door when the words came.

"What do you plan to do?"

The woman's very coldness made Sarah smile at her. Little did Kate Pell know she was talking to someone who, when pressed, could climb trees.

"I'm not sure," Sarah said. "I have Matt's gun. I've thought about using it to rob someone. Or I could march out onto the prairie and try to get by. The truth is if I fooled you into hiring me as a cook you'd be sorry. I really can't cook anything except snakes, rabbits and ground squirrels, but if I can figure out how to catch them, I can cook them."

To her surprise, the madam smiled genuinely for the first time. "Your real story must put the rumors to shame, Miss Hammond. I usually have my cook, who can cook a great many things and cook them very well, prepare a meal about this time. Will you trade your story for a very good meal?"

Yes, I will, Sarah thought. *If even prostitutes want to fatten me up, why not?*

To Sarah's relief, the kitchen was also an ordinary room, and to her surprise, the madam introduced her to Clara, the cook, and then sat across from her at the big table in the center of the room. The cook tut-tutted over Sarah and busied herself setting out a feast of buttered bread, sliced ham, hard boiled eggs, puddings and pastries.

Sarah sipped at a large glass of fresh milk and smiled apologetically at Clara. "This is wonderful, but I can't seem to eat much at one time any more."

The madam had only very small portions on her own plate. "Unlike you I have to worry about my figure," she said. "Your stomach has shrunk is all. Eat what you can and by the time you've finished your story maybe you'll be ready for more."

Sarah swallowed a heavenly bite of fresh bread and ham. "When all this started, I had to worry about my figure also, although worrying never affected it in the least."

They ate in companionable silence, and when her stomach was full, Sarah started the story without prompting. Somehow, sitting in a brothel, talking to a prostitute and another woman who worked for her, what came out wasn't the censored version of events she had told Lieutenant Edler and Curtis Payne and his wife. She never considered dramatizing the way she had in the Charon courthouse.

Her audience was sympathetic. Working as she listened, Clara gave Sarah a little pat on the shoulder every time she walked by. As she talked, Sarah saw Kate Pell's expression softening. She made sympathetic sounds over the horrors of the Comanche attack and smiled at the story of climbing trees.

When Sarah told about her problems with Matt over her month-lies and their first sexual congress, all the madam's reserve dissolved. She laughed out loud.

"Oh, my, I can't believe it. Two virgins out on the prairie!" she said, laughing.

"Matt wasn't a virgin," Sarah said. "He...."

"Miss Hammond, believe me, a man who spent a few minutes with a whore who grabbed him and told him to hurry up was a virgin in every way that counts. You poor thing."

Sarah frowned at her. "I'm not a poor thing. I love him, and after we practiced, we got better at it."

Kate Pell leaned forward, her chin in her hand. "Tell me."

Sarah did. To her surprise, the madam didn't laugh again on hearing about what happened in the hollow in the hill. Instead, she shook her head in what looked like admiration. "If most married couples figured things out as well as you two, I'd be out of business."

"Really?" Sarah felt shy. "Sometimes I wondered if other people do those things. I mean I wanted to kiss him all over and to have him—but I wondered."

"Women who don't do those things end up as bitter old crones whose husbands spend time and money here. And while I'm grateful to them, I feel sorry for them and for their husbands."

Reassured, Sarah told the rest of it, all of it, including being turned away from the prison in Hartsville.

"That's not good," the madam said.

"No," Sarah whispered, "and I'm afraid to go there again."

"You need a gentleman to accompany you."

"Yes," Sarah agreed, not bothering to point out that she didn't know any gentlemen she could ask for escort.

She stood up and thanked both Clara and Kate Pell. "I need to get back to my room before dark."

The sounds of a piano and a mixture of male and female voices came from the front of the house, heightening Sarah's desire to be gone.

"Wait here a moment," the madam said. "I'll be right back, and I have something for you."

When she returned, Kate Pell handed Sarah an envelope. On the outside was written, "Jane Rodman."

"I've already spoken to Miss Rodman," Sarah said. "She doesn't need help."

"Be that as it may, I urge you to take her that note tomorrow and wait while she reads it. Good luck to you, Miss Hammond. It's been a pleasure meeting you."

Sarah thanked the other woman again and took her leave, unsure what she was thanking the madam for.

KATE PELL THREW HALF of the fabric samples spread out on her desk aside and stared at the remainder with dissatisfaction. The dressmaker would do without the order for a new traveling ensemble until she came up with better choices than these. Kate welcomed the distraction of a knock on the door. Lily stuck her head into the room, grinning.

"She's back. The skinny, scrawny one."

The strength of the wave of regret that passed over Kate surprised her. Foolish as it might be, she had really wanted this one to make it. Something about that stiff spine in the scrawny body had moved her to offer a meal. The way the girl relaxed in the kitchen and told such an extraordinary story without airs had won her over.

She sighed. "Send her in."

The sight of Miss Sarah Hammond told Kate the girl hadn't returned to admit defeat. In the week since her previous visit, Miss Hammond couldn't have put much flesh back on her small frame, but she looked stronger. Her cheeks had color, her eyes glowed, and her smile was contagious.

"I apologize for bothering you again like this, but today is my free day, and I so want to thank you. Thank you so much. Miss Rodman did give me a position helping in her restaurant after she read your note, and she let me clean out a storeroom in the back, so I can stay there, and there's always enough food."

"Is she paying you?" Kate asked.

"Yes. Not much, but do you know that men leave money on the table after they eat? Tips? Miss Rodman shares that with me, and since I'm no longer paying board or for food...." Sarah wound down and said more calmly. "It's wonderful. Thank you."

In Kate's opinion even with a thorough scrubbing, fresh coat of paint and new furniture, Jane Rodman's dingy little restaurant wouldn't qualify as "wonderful."

Fortunately for Jane the rough men who frequented the place didn't have a selection of better establishments to patronize. And if the job suited Miss Hammond, then Kate had paid a fair price for the incredibly entertaining story of a Comanche attack, first love on the prairie and a court hearing in Charon.

"I'm glad it's working out for you," she said. "I wasn't sure you were strong enough to do work like that."

"It is hard, but every day is better. All that food, and I'm not limited to just three meals I can't finish. I'm grazing all day long like a sheep. Pretty soon people will be saying I have a pretty face, but it's such a shame I'm chubby."

"Not for a week or two," Kate said dryly.

Miss Hammond brought the hand she had hidden in her skirts out and put a small box tied with a yellow bow on Kate's desk.

"I told Lily I would leave this token of my appreciation for you," Miss Hammond said, "but she wanted me to come up and see you myself. It's only a small thing, but I wanted to give you something, something real."

Kate stared at the box in disbelief. Had another woman ever given her a gift of any kind for any reason? She touched the bow gently, ran a finger over the ribbon. "Shall I open it now?"

"Oh, yes, please do, but it's only...."

"I understand," Kate said. "It's only a token." Inside the box was a satin sachet, lavender of color and scent. "It's beautiful, Miss Hammond, and it's exactly the kind of sachet I use in my linens. Thank you."

Before the girl could take her leave, Kate said, "Would you like to stay and have tea with me? I'm expecting a friend shortly, Bradford

Denham, and I'd like you to meet him. I'm thinking we might prevail upon him to help you visit the prison again, visit more safely.

Miss Hammond's dark blue eyes widened until they dominated her thin face, and Kate laughed at her. "You are both right and wrong in what you're thinking. I own this place, and I don't see customers any more, but he and I are—friends."

Uncertainty, curiosity and something close to fear flickered across the girl's face, but in the end she met Kate's eyes and smiled. "I'd love to have tea with you, and I'm sure I'll like your friend."

Kate felt uncertain herself. The world was full of girls whose lives turned to hell because of foolish love and loyalty to a man who never deserved it. In the past, when girls like that turned up on Kate's doorstep, they ended up working for her on their backs or heading on down the road to work for someone else in the same way. She treated the girls who worked for her well but didn't waste much emotion on them. Hard years earning her own living on her back had left Kate with no charitable feelings for others in the same straights. She had already given this bundle of bones, upper crust manners and courage a considerable boost. Why the hell was she thinking of doing more?

Looking down at the untied yellow ribbon and satin sachet in its box on her desk, Kate knew she was going to do more. "Call me Kate," she said.

22

HOMESICKNESS TOOK MANY forms. Months ago Sarah had hidden the heartache of losing her family in a dark place in her mind that she refused to visit. She could not hide from the loss of home as a place.

In Texas fall did not mean trees sporting a riot of bright colors and crisp, cool weather. The cedar and live oak trees stayed green. Leaves died on the hardwood trees and fell, leaving branches bare in a pathetic, subdued imitation of real autumn.

With Christmas less than two weeks away, the weather remained so mild Sarah walked toward the brothel without even a shawl over her new gray wool dress.

Lily answered her knock and led her to the kitchen with a smile. "Wait till you hear what happened to Grace and me last night," she said happily.

Sarah sat at the table and listened to an outrageous story about a customer who couldn't do what he had paid to do with one girl and demanded to try another, then demanded a refund. Before the young prostitutes finished their richly embellished tale, Sarah's cheeks burned, but laughter bubbled up too.

The friendship these girls provided erased a lot of the loneliness of her long work days. Close to Sarah in age, Lily, Grace and the others competed each week to see who could shock Sarah the most with tales of their customers. Sometimes their stories evoked only shock, not laughter. This week was a good one, at least for Lily and Grace.

For months Sarah had come here on her free days. She visited with Lily and the other prostitutes, and she visited with Kate. Sarah regarded the girls as friends. Older and more serious, Kate Pell and Bradford Denham, had become something more than friends.

Usually Sarah passed time with Lily and the others until Kate arrived in the kitchen, ready for a late afternoon lunch. Today Sarah extracted herself from the crowd as soon as she could and made her way to Kate's aerie.

Kate smiled in greeting. "So what are you up to today? I've been thinking about a visit to the milliner. Would you like to come along?"

Sarah shook her head. "No, I'm…. I need advice."

"All right. Sit down and tell me what you need advice about."

Swallowing hard, Sarah said the words she had repeated in her head until they almost sounded real. "I'm going to have a baby."

Of all the reactions Sarah had worried about, she had never imagined that Kate would laugh at her.

"Oh, Sarah, my advice is to forget the thought. You'd have to be what, five months along by now, and you may no longer be a skeleton, but you barely have enough meat on your bones to look normal. Clara still wants to feed you every time she sees you."

Part of Sarah wanted to accept Kate's words as fact, but another part knew better. "There is some thickness. Here," Sarah said, running her hand over her stomach. "And I feel things inside, a fluttering."

The laughter left Kate's face. "When was the last time you had monthly courses?"

"That time with Matt. Before we—when we were—out there. I thought it was because I almost died. I thought it would start again when I was better."

Kate frowned. "That would explain a month or two, but once you were eating regularly—nothing these last months at all?"

"Nothing. Is there a way to find out for sure? I mean it's hard to believe. We were starving, and at the end—Matt was stronger than I was, but we were dying. If there is a baby, will it be all right?"

"A baby would explain why you were in worse shape than he was," Kate said bitterly. "You say he gave you most of the food, and men need more. Babies are like parasites. They suck what they need out of you, and you get the leavings."

The harshness of Kate's words dismayed Sarah, but she said nothing.

"Well, I suppose the first thing to do is find out what we're dealing with." Kate walked over to the bell pull and gave it a yank. When Clara appeared, she said, "Bring us some tea, would you Clara, and get hold of Dr. McDaniels. Tell him I need him. Now."

Clara ducked out of the room, and Sarah looked at Kate anxiously. "A doctor? What will he do?"

"He'll examine you, and he'll talk to you, and he'll give us an opinion, which may not be worth what he'll charge for it, but it's probably better than what you and I will come up with sitting here and guessing."

By the time Kate and Sarah were through pretending to drink their tea, the doctor arrived. Sarah looked at the portly older man who smelled of cigars and hair pomade and had to stop herself from reacting to him the way she had to Broderick with his pistol.

Kate gave her a knowing look and said, "I'll just stay and keep Sarah company."

Hanging on to Kate's hand got Sarah through the examination without giving way to the panic.

"No doubt about it," the doctor said. "So far as I can tell that baby's healthy as a horse. It's turning somersaults in there."

Something fierce swept through Sarah, and tears welled. No puddling up, she thought to herself, suppressing the urge to laugh.

Kate and the doctor talked in low tones. Sarah heard Kate say, "Just put it on my bill."

"Oh, no," Sarah said. "I'll pay you myself, thank you, doctor."

The doctor directed his last words as he left to Kate, and at first Sarah didn't understand them. "You can't handle this in your usual way, Kate. She's way too far along, and with that history, she may not be strong enough for surgery anyway. I won't do it, and don't you even think about getting someone else to do it."

"I'll do what I damn well think is best," Kate said with real venom in her voice. "You've said your piece, now get out."

As the door closed behind the doctor, Kate turned to Sarah. "Much as I hate to admit it, the old fool is right. We can't just get rid of it. I know of a place you can go, and when it's born the people there will take care of it. They find homes for babies like this. You'll have to have it, but it will be all right in the end."

*Get **rid** of it? Get **rid** of her baby? Get **rid** of Matt's baby?*

Sarah rose to her feet, outraged. "I'm not getting rid of my baby. I'm not giving my baby away. *I am **not** getting rid of my baby!*"

Kate didn't hide her feelings. "Give up that romantic silliness, Sarah. You know by now that Slade sat in that courtroom and watched you strip yourself naked to try to keep him out of prison and decided you were a whore he didn't want any part of just like all the rest of them did. He isn't going to get out of prison and marry you, and he couldn't take care of you if he did. He won't be out for years anyway. Do you think Jane's going to let you work for her with a baby strapped to your back like some squaw? Or do you think maybe you can leave it with family while you work? Maybe now that you're going to have a bastard your family will take you back?"

The truth of those words hurt, but not enough to change Sarah's mind. "I've managed up till now. If I can't have Matt, at least I can have his child. I'm sorry I bothered you with this problem. I won't do it again."

With that, she headed for the door.

Kate wasn't done. "You managed because I helped you. If I hadn't told Jane to hire you, you'd be downstairs with Lily and the others right now."

Turning, Sarah said, "If you hadn't helped me, I'd be somewhere else doing something else, but I wouldn't be downstairs here, and we both know it. Thank you for that help. And goodbye."

Sarah closed the door firmly behind her and walked down the stairs steadily. She made excuses to Lily and the girls for leaving so early and headed back to her storeroom home with her back straight and her chin up. Not a single tear fell until she was alone. Her Aunt Lucy would have been proud of her.

VERY FEW PEOPLE KNEW that Sarah lived in the back of the restaurant. Having Matt's gun gave her some sense of security, but she had no illusions about the limits of her ability to defend herself. So the sound of knocking on the restaurant's front door long after closing had Sarah clutching the pistol in both hands and tiptoeing to peek through the front window.

Bradford Denham stood outside. He knocked a second time before Sarah unlocked the door and let him in. A man in her small bedroom was unthinkable. Sarah gestured toward one of the tables, one of many spooky shadows in the dark room.

When Sarah first met Brad Denham, the wedding ring on his hand offended her. As she learned more and more of his story, she abandoned her prejudices.

Brad loved his wife, loved her enough that when she first became ill with a debilitating sickness that no local doctor could diagnose or alleviate, he had taken her to specialists all over the country and then to Europe looking for answers. No one could give him any, and Myra Denham slowly lost her ability to walk and then to perform even the simplest tasks for herself.

Brad's businesses required him to travel throughout the Western United States several times a year, but he stayed home as much as possible now, even though hired nurses cared for Myra round the clock.

Sometimes Sarah saw an expression on Brad's face that she recognized as guilt, guilt for seeking not only the pleasure his wife could no longer give him elsewhere, but companionship and solace.

If she were like Myra and Matt were like Brad, how would she feel, Sarah wondered. She answered that question differently in her own mind every time she asked it. Like everyone, Sarah realized, Brad suffered for his sins. He loved his wife, and guilt plagued him. He loved Kate and could do nothing about it.

Sarah and Brad sat in silence in the shadowy room for a while before he said, "You know why I'm here."

"Yes," Sarah admitted. "But you're wasting your time. I'm not giving away my baby, and I'm not forgiving Kate for acting as if my baby, Matt's baby, is something to *get rid of*."

"Sarah, just for a moment, try to put your anger aside and put yourself in Kate's shoes. In some ways her life has been similar to yours. She came from a good family, and she fell in love with a man who—didn't marry her. One of the reasons she's taken to you the way she has, I think, is that she sees herself in you, herself if she had struggled down a different path than the one she chose. She wants you to make it, to end up with a good life that makes it all worthwhile, and she knows that a baby is going to make that impossible."

"*Getting rid of* my baby is what's impossible. I'll manage somehow."

"How? Even if you can work here until the day the baby comes, how do you see yourself getting by afterwards? Once you're on your feet again, maybe you can work, but who is going to care for this baby?"

Sarah stood. "Wait here. I have something to show you."

She went to her room, dug the engagement ring from its hiding place, brought it back to the table and struck a match so that the facets in the big diamond caught the light and glittered for a moment and the emeralds glowed.

As she shook the match out, Sarah said, "I know that no one here in Flowers would give me more than a few dollars for it, but it would bring enough to live on for a while if I could get a fair price, wouldn't it?"

Brad took the ring from her and walked to the door, examined the ring in the moonlight then with another match. He didn't speak until he sat across from her again.

"Macauley's?"

"Yes. No one ever asked me about it, and Mrs. Edler refused to give it back to him. She said I should keep it."

"Your Mrs. Edler had a strong sense of justice, didn't she? Yes. If those stones are real and if you're frugal, you might be able to live for a year off of what that will bring in Denver or Kansas City. Would you like me to see what I can get for it the next time I travel?"

"I planned to ask you before—before Kate got.... I'll pay a commission, of course."

"Don't be silly. The only commission I want is that you think it over, and if you can't find it in your heart to forgive her, at least try to understand, and maybe, accept."

Sarah lowered her head and rubbed her temples. "Perhaps. I don't want to hear any more of the kind of thing she said today."

"I don't think you have to worry about that. I bet you both avoid the subject until you trip over it from now on, but I'm going to make some suggestions myself. You can get angry at me if you want to, but I hope you'll listen and think about it."

"I'm not going to...."

"Just hear me out," Brad interrupted. "You don't have to make any decisions tonight anyway, so listen and think it over before you tell me to go to hell. You can probably keep working here until I get the ring sold. Once you have that money, you can live off that until after the baby comes and for a while after, but you'll need to find a way to support yourself again eventually. I have some friends in San Antonio who are childless."

"No. I am *not*...."

"Sshh. Listen. Yes, John and Evelyn Reynolds would love to adopt a child from a young woman like you, but I'm not saying you have to give them your baby. The fact is, though, that they are wealthy people and they employ more servants than anyone needs. I think I can talk them into employing you and letting you keep your baby with you. Yes, they would be hoping you would let them adopt the child, but you would be under no obligation. And if you do find that trying to raise a child on your own is more than you can manage, you would at least have the choice. There's nothing wrong with leaving yourself choices."

"You think Kate's right, don't you?" Sarah asked angrily. "You think that once I have the baby, I'll find it's too difficult and take an easy way out."

She thought she heard Brad sigh. "I wouldn't want to bet against either one of you, Sarah, and I'm not going to. I'm offering you what seems like a reasonable solution to me. What you do is up to you, and as I said, you don't have to decide tonight. I hope you won't. I hope you think about it for a while."

"And what did you mean when you said they'd like to adopt a child from a mother like me?" Sarah said tartly. "They'd only want a child from a fallen woman if the woman fell from a lofty perch?"

"Yes, I'm afraid that's exactly what I mean."

"And if they knew Matt was the father? Would they be willing to let a slut and a whore live in their house with her bastard in hopes of stealing her child if they knew Matt was the father?"

Brad's chuckle at that was unmistakable. "I'll tell them about young Mr. Slade myself, Sarah. One of General Hood's men whose own father was one of the heroes who fought Santa Ana? By the time I'm through, they'll be casting bronze statues." He got to his feet. "And no one is going to steal your child. The decision is yours. I give you my word."

After he left, Sarah locked the door, leaned against it and closed her eyes. "Life really does get ugly sometimes," she whispered.

Convict and Whore

1870 – 1874

23

FOR THE FIRST TIME in three years, a door slammed and locked Matt out, not in. He walked away from the prison without looking back, sweat soaking him from head to toe in the first hundred feet. The humid heat of the early fall day had less to do with his condition than raw nerves. For weeks other inmates had been taunting, stirring the caldron of his mixed feelings about freedom.

"Hey, Slade, you know the first thing you do when you get out? Steal a horse."

"Aw, no, the first thing you do is steal cash. Then you buy the horse."

"Hell, that ain't right. First you steal a gun, so you can steal everything else after."

"First thing I'm going to do is see a whore."

"Slade's problem is when the whore sees him. She'll run so fast jackrabbits will die of envy."

He had no recollection of the trip to the prison or the first days there. Heavy doses of laudanum had wiped out memory along with pain. Today he found out that whatever else happened back then, he had been brought to the prison in the clothes Curtis Payne bought for the courtroom in Charon.

The guards enjoyed watching him squeeze into those clothes. Old bloodstains covered half the once white shirt, which fit so tight if he brought his arms forward it would rip from shoulders to waist. The trousers were no better, worse most likely, because if those seams gave way the law would be after him right quick. At least his boots fit, and maybe the soles would stay half attached to the uppers for a few more miles.

After three years of hard labor, the guards handed him three dollars to start a new life. New boots were out of the question. Maybe he could stretch three dollars over the cost of a shirt and trousers, but after that?

Matt shrugged without breaking stride.

He walked into the town, looking for a shop that would sell cheap, ready-made clothes.

Matt didn't pay much attention to the couple who left the shade of the hotel porch and crossed the street toward him. The only people in town he would know or who would know him worked at the prison, and the prosperous looking pair definitely did not fall in that category.

When the couple stopped in front of him, blocking his way, Matt got ready to tell them he didn't know the town well enough to give them directions or any other information.

"Excuse me," the man said, "but are you from the prison?"

The answer to that was so obvious that this stranger was either carrying politeness to new extremes, or afraid, and that was a sobering thought.

"I just got out," he admitted.

"Would you know of another man scheduled to be released today? His name is Slade, Matthew Slade."

Those words got Matt's full attention. He stopped squinting down the street and examined the couple closely. Average height, heavy set, the man wore a fancy suit and thick gold wedding ring that spoke of wealth.

The elegant woman whose gloved hand rested on his arm looked like a good match, although her dark beauty and a hardness in her expression reminded Matt of Sourpuss.

Ignoring a painful spasm of his stomach muscles, Matt met the man's polite gaze. These people were looking for him, and they had a notion of what he was supposed to look like.

"You could say I know him. I'm Slade."

Both faces registered shock. The woman's grip on the man's arm tightened. Matt faced them silently and counted the thud of his own heartbeats. At one hundred and seven, the man moved, pulled a thick envelope out of the inner breast pocket of his suit and held it out. His speech was formal, rehearsed maybe.

"My name is Bradford Denham, and this is Kate Pell. We are friends of Sarah Hammond, and we promised Miss Hammond we would meet you here and see that you received this."

Matt made no move to take the envelope, and Denham gave a polite smile. "I can't make you take it, but we did promise. Miss Hammond says this belongs to you. Will you relieve us of our obligation? We would also like to speak with you on Miss Hammond's behalf."

Matt reached out, raised his hand and closed it on the smooth paper. Had Sarah touched it? He stepped around the couple and continued on toward the business section of the town.

He didn't tear open the envelope until he was out of the couple's sight inside a dry goods store. The envelope contained a wad of green notes but no letter. *Had he really expected one?*

Staring at the money, Matt stifled an urge to throw it at the clerk and walk out. *No use being stupid.* He examined the unfamiliar pieces of paper. Two hundred dollars. More than he'd ever had, more than he'd given Sarah at the end. These must be the new notes the Yankees issued. They were supposed to be easier to spend than the variety of paper money circulating before the war.

Matt decided to find out about Yankee greenbacks for himself.

BRAD HAD REGISTERED MR. and Mrs. Denham into the most luxurious room of the hotel. That meant besides the standard bed and washstand in the other rooms, a worn rug covered part of the floor and two uncomfortable upholstered chairs sat near the door. The chairs, rug and heavy drapes were all varying shades of faded maroon.

Kate hated the room, hated the hotel and hated the town. What she hated most of all was herself. From the moment she and Brad returned to the room after the encounter with Matt Slade, she kept watch out the window, staring down the street, worrying at the sheer white curtain and reporting on Slade's progress through the stores of the town to Brad.

"I can't believe it. First he's in and out of every damn store in this town. He must be spending that money by the nickel. And now he's been in that bath house for how long?"

With a heavy sigh, Brad pulled his watch from his vest pocket and answered, "Not quite an hour. It's really not that...."

"It is too! A man could soak his skin off in an hour. What the hell's the matter with him? The way he walked away. No matter what, he should have at least asked if she's all right."

"Kate, Kate. I'm as fond of Sarah as you are, and I'm feeling just as guilty about the ugly things I've said and even uglier things I've thought about that man these last years. We've found the explanation for the unexplainable, haven't we?"

"Yes," Kate whispered. "And the terrible thing is it wouldn't make any difference to Sarah, but it does make a difference doesn't it? His chances of making a decent living are less now than they were before, and I'm not telling him about Laurie."

"Are you sure? You know Sarah will never forgive you. Are you going to lie to her?"

"No, I'm not going to lie. I'm going to tell her exactly what happened. We gave him the money, and he walked away and didn't give us a chance to tell him anything."

"That won't work, and you know it. Sarah would expect us to shout it at his back if necessary."

"Sarah knows me well enough to know I'm not shouting anything at anyone's back," Kate said angrily.

Brad just looked at her.

"I want her to have a good life. Is that evil of me? And now that she's given in and bought a wedding ring and is telling people she's a widow, all she has to do is give up her obsession with Slade, and she can have a good life. She's a pretty woman. All she has to do is encourage someone suitable."

"She doesn't want suitable. She wants Slade."

"Well, she's not getting him. He walked away without even asking about her."

Kate had never turned completely from the window, and she caught sight of her quarry again. "There he is! Oh, I can't believe it. He shaved! Why would he do that?"

Brad came over to the window at last, put one hand on her shoulder and looked down with her. "Sarah said he hated a beard. It didn't really hide the damage, you know. He may as well feel comfortable."

Kate moaned softly, turned from the window, and threw herself on the bed. "He's coming here, damn it. Damn him."

"He might be coming here only to get a room for the night, or to eat."

"You know he's not. He's coming here, and he's going to make me decide all over again. Are you going to tell him?"

Brad shook his head. "You decide. Just make sure you're willing to bear the consequences."

"Maybe he would walk away if we told him. Maybe he would, and it would be the truth and Sarah would have to live with it."

A hard knock sounded on the door, and Kate flinched. After a sharp glance at her, Brad moved to answer the door, but Kate went back to the window, standing this time with her back to it, facing the room.

With considerable justification, Kate Pell prided herself on her knowledge of men, but try though she might, she could find little resemblance between the man who walked into the hotel room and the man Sarah had described to her.

All right, his hair was dark brown, but in this light there was no hint of red in the freshly cut thick sable. And his intense gaze was an unusual brilliant pale blue but from only his right eye. A black patch took the place of his left eye. The patch rested against a lump at the bottom edge of the eye socket.

His cheekbone had been broken, as had his nose, and maybe, Kate thought, his jaw. A fine white scar ran through his eyebrow. More of the fine lines traced across the cheekbone and cheek. Someone had stitched him up with great care, but nothing could repair so much damage.

More than Slade's face had changed. Close now, Kate confirmed the opinion she had formed watching him move up and down the street all afternoon. All men matured in the years after twenty-two, but three years of constant labor had turned Sarah's lanky young lover into a subtly powerful male animal.

The new blue chambray shirt and wool trousers didn't reveal his body the way the too tight clothing bought for the starved boy-man of the courtroom had, but even now his overall silhouette was long-legged and trim. His shoulders tapered noticeably first to the rib cage, then to the narrow waist and slim hips. Men who moved in that easy way did it because smooth muscle layered the bone structure.

Slade shook his head at Brad's offer of a seat. He stood by the door, tense and obviously unwilling to start the conversation. When he did speak, the words slapped Kate right in the face.

"Is Sarah a whore?"

The deep, harsh voice hit as hard as the words, and Kate lashed back with all her own pent up anger. "I thought I looked as respectable as hell today. What exactly tipped you off? Is it a smell only the righteous smell, or have I got a scarlet A on me somewhere I haven't noticed?"

Before she finished hurling the words at him, Kate recognized her mistake in the surprise of Slade's expression. She spun back to face the window. Behind her she could hear Brad, calmly straightening things out.

"I think we're all misunderstanding each other here. First of all, no, Sarah is not and never has been a prostitute. What makes you even ask?"

"She just said...."

"It's Sarah we're talking about, isn't it?"

"How else could Sarah get two hundred dollars? There's no way...."

Raising his voice as he interrupted, Brad said, "As a matter of fact, she sold Macauley's ring. I acted as agent on her behalf and got her a very good price. Considering what he did to you both, there's justice in that, isn't there? If you will please sit down, I will tell you how Kate and I came to know Sarah."

Kate listened to Brad tell the story, at least as much of the story as she wanted Slade to know.

By the time he finished, Kate was in control again. When she turned around, Slade said, "Ma'am, I never meant to—I mean, I didn't know...."

"I saw my mistake as I spoke. It's stupid to be sensitive because I'm playing at respectability today, isn't it? What made you ask that right away? You know what kind of family she comes from. Why not assume the money came from her family?"

Slade turned the new black hat on his knees around and around. "Macauley told me what he did to her family. He said he fixed it so she'd have to sell herself or starve. Then they brought a fellow into the prison who said he saw her, working as a waitress somewhere and looking all right. I was afraid to believe him, but I had to, or go crazy."

Kate exchanged a quick glance with Brad, who asked, "What did he tell the Hammonds?"

The flame of Kate's anger burned brighter than ever as she listened to what Carter Macauley had done to assure that Sarah would get no help from her family.

"That son of a bitch!" Neither of the men disagreed with her. More calmly, she added, "It will help Sarah to know that. She always said her family would never abandon her because of what happened, and she couldn't accept that they'd simply believe whatever Macauley told them. A newspaper for evidence! Damn him!"

Studying Slade more carefully, Kate realized something else, something even more disturbing than the lies Macauley had made the Hammond family believe. "If he told you that himself, you saw him. He did that to you, didn't he?"

The pale blue gaze drilled right into her. "I wouldn't want Sarah thinking that, Miss Pell. In fact I'd appreciate it if you don't tell her about it."

Kate felt a wave of vindication. She wasn't cheating him out of anything. He didn't want to see Sarah, didn't want her to see him.

Brad, damn him, asked outright. "Don't you want to see her?"

"Wanting makes no never mind. She only knew me a few months, and it cost her everything. That's what knowing me got her, and all it ever would." Slade's voice was too carefully expressionless. "There are a lot of good men who will take one look and know how lucky they would be to have her, and every one of them will be better for her than me."

He stood and walked to the door. For just a moment, Kate saw only the unscarred side of his face, and there was the man Sarah had described so often and with so much love. Before she could decide what to say, if she wanted to say anything, he was gone.

Kate couldn't remember the last time she cried, and she didn't now, but she sat on the bed wishing. Tears might dissolve the lump in the back of her throat. When Brad sat beside her and took her in his arms she buried her face against his shoulder.

"I hated him, you know. Ever since the first time she came back from the prison looking so *desolate*, I hated him."

Brad tightened his hold, kissed her cheek. "You don't have to tell me. I believed exactly what you did, and despised him in exactly the same way."

"He still loves her."

"Yes, he does."

"Sarah's right. If he knew about Laurie, he'd go to her."

"Yes, he would."

"I don't care," Kate said passionately. "He's going to have enough trouble taking care of himself. I want something better for Sarah, something better for Laurie. And now she's going to have it. She'll give up this insane romantic foolishness and marry the kind of husband she should have."

"I hope so," Brad said heavily. "I really hope so."

24

MERE WORDS ON PAPER should never be able to cause this kind of pain. Sarah's hand shook so violently the words on the letter from Kate jumped and twisted. She dropped the paper onto the bed, where it sat unmoving and legible again. The words were the same. The meaning was the same.

Her father's letter disowning her had hurt so much Sarah erased the words with her tears. Reaching out, she touched the small figure asleep on the bed. Laurie. Her daughter. Matt's daughter. The daughter Kate had not told him he had. A deep moan escaped from her throat, and Sarah struggled for control. Falling apart would not only wake Laurie, it would frighten her.

The fault was her own for trusting Kate to see Matt, to tell him. Yes, Laurie had spiked a fever the day Sarah planned to leave for Hartsville herself, but she should have done something other than send Kate a frantic telegram asking her to meet Matt. She should have…. A single tear slipped across her cheek. Even now no alternative came to mind.

In the letter Kate claimed that Matt said he didn't want to see her, that he turned and walked away. Sarah didn't want to believe it. Didn't want to, and even if she did, didn't care. Kate should have said the words, should have said, *You have a daughter.* Why didn't she? Why didn't she? *Because she wants you to marry someone else,* a small voice inside said. *You know that. She wants you to marry someone like Brad.*

Sarah left her room and knocked on the door across the hall.

Juana's round brown face showed a wariness as she answered the door that Sarah understood well. Even though their work was done for the day, maids never enjoyed freedom from random requests from their employers.

"Would you watch Laurie for me for a few minutes?" Sarah asked. "She's asleep and shouldn't awaken in the time I'm gone. I'll only be a short while."

Juana agreed readily enough, and Sarah headed out of the servants' quarters to talk to her employers. Intent only on her purpose, she passed through the spacious rooms of the lovely, Spanish-style house with none of her usual appreciation. John and Evelyn Reynolds were exactly where she expected, in a small sitting room at the heart of the house.

After two years of working for the Reynolds and living in their home, Sarah had come to like the couple, but never to trust them. True to Brad's promise, they never pushed her to let them adopt Laurie. They behaved like loving grandparents. Yet something in the way Evelyn Reynolds held Laurie whenever she had the chance assured that Sarah never once considered leaving her sick daughter with the woman and traveling to Hartsville to see Matt, to force him to see her.

Envisioning the Reynolds bundling Laurie into one of their expensive carriages and using their wealth to disappear with Laurie was all too easy. Sarah never voiced her suspicions to Brad or Kate, knowing they would denigrate the idea, but she also never left the Reynolds' house without Laurie in her arms. Not once.

John looked up from his newspaper and saw her before she could knock.

"Come in, Sarah, come in. What can we do for you this evening?"

Nothing would make this easier on anyone. Sarah came straight to the point. "I'm sorry, Mr. Reynolds, Mrs. Reynolds, but I've come to give you notice. I'll be leaving as soon as I can make arrangements."

"No!" Evelyn leapt to her feet. "You can't."

"I'm sorry, Mrs. Reynolds. Yes, I can, and I am." Sarah started to leave the room, but John's voice stopped her.

"I received a letter from Brad Denham today. He warned me you might do something foolish."

Sarah gave her employer a hard look. "How nice of him to tell you my business. You can reply and congratulate him on his foresight."

She left the room almost at a run and barely managed to thank Juana in normal tones and send her off. Dragging her bags, her carpetbags, out from beneath the bed, Sarah packed quickly. Perhaps she was being too careful, but it was time to hunker down.

25

Fall 1870, Texas

DUST MOTES DANCED in the afternoon sun slanting through the windows of the saloon. Two drunks sagged over their table in silence; two whores whispered and giggled at the end of the bar.

He should have waited a few more hours to come here, Matt thought, but then where else did he have to be? Outfitting himself with a horse, a good plain horse, and enough equipment to survive the life he faced now had left precious little of Sarah's money. Last night, playing poker with care, he had almost doubled that small amount. After tucking his winnings away safe in one pocket, he'd left his original stake loose in another to try again.

Matt sipped his whiskey and stared at the solitaire pattern before him without much interest. No matter how things went tonight, he'd move on in the morning. Sure, the one-legged veteran at the livery stable had given him a week's work building a new corral and repairing the old ones, but he had finished the last of the job before noon today.

In the weeks since his release, no one in any of the towns where he'd stopped had offered more than temporary work. Few could pay cash. Most times a day's labor brought only meals and a place to stay. The stable job had been better, feed for the horse and a few dollars.

Boots sounded heavy on the wooden walk outside, and the door slapped open. Two men stopped in the doorway and examined the room before coming all the way inside. Their caution marked them as strangers to the town. Gunbelts slung low around narrow hips and so much arrogance the room buzzed with it marked them as dangerous. The Anglo strode to the bar, got a bottle and two glasses while the Mexican continued scrutinizing the room and everyone in it.

Matt debated whether to sit tight or pick up his cards and leave. Before he made up his mind, the gunmen walked straight to his table and sat down as if they'd been invited. The Anglo thumped down the empty glasses, filled them and topped Matt's glass.

If they wanted him to take offense, they'd have to try another approach. Matt took a polite sip, tipped the glass to each of the men in turn and waited.

"Beau Taney," said the Anglo. He nodded toward the Mexican. "Roddy Rodriguez."

"Jaime Francisco Rodriguez y Candelaria," said the Mexican icily. "Matt Slade."

Taney was blond under the trail dust, beard stubble glinting gold in the afternoon light. In spite of the layer of dust, old stains and frayed cuffs, the material and fit of his clothes said they hadn't come off the shelf of a general store. What did it say about a man that he bought things like that and then didn't take care of them?

A button missing at the neck of the shirt caught Matt's eye, and the memory of another shirt with all the buttons missing filled his mind. Because he had ripped the buttons off that other shirt, it gaped open and slipped around on Sarah's small frame, and the Yankee soldiers stared at her and grinned at each other....

He yanked himself away from the recollection of past danger to the reality of present danger.

"You like solitaire, or are you looking for a real game?" Taney said.

"I'm hoping to get in a game later, but I need low stakes. Dollar limit," Real luck would be these two leaving because they were unwilling to play for small sums.

"Roddy and I can oblige. Go ahead and deal."

Matt shrugged, gathered up the cards and shuffled. Taney played to win but had too much faith in his own luck and no patience. Rodriguez barely looked at his cards and threw in each hand wordlessly as soon as possible, yet when he dealt, he handled the cards with expertise.

At first sight, Matt had lumped the two together. The longer they played, the more he saw that they had nothing in common but the arrogance and guns.

A slim blade of a man, Rodriguez emphasized his own darkness by the black he wore from head to toe. He controlled every word and motion as if only in that way could he control the anger that burned in his eyes. He spoke in such a formal manner that Matt figured the Mexican had not learned English until he was more than half grown, and he had learned it from a fancy teacher, not from regular folks.

Taney on the other hand spoke in the soft drawl of somewhere far east of Texas. He affected an easy affability, but the coldness in his gray eyes gave that the lie. After the second time he leaned forward and rolled his broad, heavily muscled shoulders when trying a bluff, Matt knew the move was purposeful. Taney was used to intimidating others and good at it.

The whiskey bottle was more than half gone when one of the whores came over and tried to lure Taney away from the game. He brushed her off with contempt.

Undeterred, she winked at Matt. "Changed your mind, sugar?" she purred.

A headshake sent the girl trolling for business elsewhere. She never looked at Rodriguez. Something close to triumph flashed across the gunman's narrow face, and Matt saw that the Mexican used such sleights to feed his anger.

The saloon filled with the night's customers and the sounds of their talk and laughter. Matt concentrated on winning and now and then on losing. Over the next hours, he more than doubled his stake, all with Taney's money. And of course as soon as Matt decided to lose a couple of hands and get out of the game any way he could, Taney decided to get sociable.

"You get hurt like that in the war?" he said.

"No, after."

"What happened?"

Matt shrugged. "Lost a bad fight."

Taney grunted and went back to the subject of the war. "You didn't sit it out, did you?"

"I'm not that smart. Fourth Texas."

"Third Alabama. Cavalry."

Matt couldn't suppress a smile, and Taney didn't like it. The gray eyes turned colder. "You one of those foot soldiers that think cavalry fought less war?"

Oh, hell! Matt took a large swallow of whiskey to chase the soap taste. "No, as a matter of fact, when Jeb Stuart's boys heard about a Texan who'd never been on a horse, they spent some time one winter remedying the situation and laughing themselves sick. I'm right fond of cavalry, so long as it's not Yankee cavalry," Matt said, surprised to hear the bitterness in his own last words.

"Those shackle scars on your wrists?"

Questions that personal were a good way to start a fight anywhere in Texas, but Matt didn't care enough to take offense. "They are. I got out of Hartsville last month."

"What were you in for?"

"Yankees said I stole some things."

"Did you?"

"I administered the estates of some Yankees after a Comanche attack."

Taney laughed out loud, the coldness gone. "Do you do everything the way you play poker, careful, and to win?"

"I try. Poker seems to be the only thing it works for."

"The man at the livery says you're looking for work."

That's what all this was about?

"I am. What kind of work would we be talking about?" Matt asked cautiously.

"Soldiering. Only for decent pay. We hire out to handle trouble that gentler citizens don't want to handle for themselves."

Since the war men like Taney and Rodriguez had roamed over the West, hunting alone or in wolf packs. Matt had never considered joining them. He said, "I don't believe I have the skills to work for you, Mr. Taney. The look of me is giving you a false impression. I don't even own a handgun. I gave the one I brought back from the war to a friend."

"You've soldiered before. That's all it is. How about that Yellow Boy? Can you use that?" Taney gestured at the Winchester leaning in the corner.

Matt was still not over the wonder of owning such a thing. He reached over, picked it up, and laid it on the table with care. The brass frame that gave the rifle its nickname gleamed. "I can use this," Matt admitted. "I've been wanting a repeating rifle ever since the first time I saw one. I looked to buy a Spencer like the Yankees had, but the gunsmith told me this is better, and I do believe it may be."

"Well, if you're interested in the job, be at the livery in the morning. No earlier than nine. There are five of us, and the others are doing too much whoring and drinking tonight to be ready earlier. I'll take you on for the next job, and we'll see if you can use a pistol. If not, no harm done. The pay's a hundred a month, but only when we're working."

"A hundred a month!" The incredulous words slipped out before Matt could stop them.

"Not enough?"

"Enough? I never made a hundred dollars in six months, maybe even a year."

"Well, if you want to try it, show up in the morning."

Matt scooped up his winnings. This had to be as good a time to leave as any. He got to his feet and so did the other men. Taney held out a hand, and they shook. Rodriguez hooked his thumbs in his belt and glowered.

At his camp outside of town, Matt cooked supper over a small fire then bedded down. He lay in his blankets staring at the sky as he did every night, fighting visions of eyes that same mysterious dark blue. Mind-numbing physical labor filled the days in prison, and sleep came easy. Since he'd been out, memories and regrets made each night a torture. The rest of his life stretched before him, clear in his mind, a long empty road he didn't want to travel.

And he didn't want to take up with hard men who sucked a living out of other folks' troubles either, but what else could he do? People looked at him, then looked away fast, but not so fast he couldn't see the fear. Drifting from town to town looking for work didn't have much to recommend it either.

A hundred dollars a month. Even if he only gave it a try for a couple of months and it didn't work out, he could send Sarah the money back. Sarah. She had made her choice, made it achingly clear, and she was right. When something was impossible you gave up on it and did something else.

She would find a husband, like that Denham maybe. Only married to Sarah he wouldn't be spending time with another woman. No man would. And for him—a job as a hired gun with men whose shabbiness took second place only to their arrogance? Well, he had a whole sleepless night stretching before him to think about it.

In the morning Matt waited at the stable long enough to fight waves of second thoughts before any of the gunmen showed up. Quick introductions proved only that none of the others liked having Matt along any more than Rodriguez did. But something about the casual way Taney thanked the crippled stableman for extra grooming on the horses and flipped him a silver dollar gave Matt a sliver of hope.

26

Late fall, 1870

TWO MONTHS AFTER joining Taney's outfit, Matt had developed a pretty good understanding of the men he had joined. Ward Carson was a sadistic brute and bully. Matt avoided him as much as possible. Young Vic Linear, thin, dark and intense, and Whitey Bascomb, named by his almost albino coloring, had aligned themselves with Carson within the group.

Beauregard Emmett Taney wasn't all that much older than Matt, but he had finished the war as a captain. For Beau, the South's surrender was only the first tragedy. The childhood sweetheart he married shortly before the war and the son he never saw died of fever only months before he made it home. Beau returned to his family's Alabama plantation to find the brother who had dodged service running the place and not wanting help.

The lifestyle he fought to preserve was as lost as his family, so Beau drifted west and coped with loss and anger by going crazy now and then. The first time Matt witnessed one of Beau's insane fits, astonishment kept him from reacting. The man acted like a mean drunk without touching a drop, and the anger all erupted in violence. He wanted to kill anything that moved, and Roddy handled it by slowly, carefully channeling the violence from people to things.

So the craziness always caused massive amounts of property damage, which Roddy simply paid for. Even if you figured Beau and Roddy were each keeping say three times as much money as what Beau paid Matt, they had to be constantly broke.

Roddy now, Roddy was only insane if overbearing pride carried to extremes was insanity. Born near San Antonio, he had been fourteen when he watched Anglos steal land that had been in his family for generations by killing his whole family. Left for dead himself, Roddy spent a long recovery honing skills with gun and knife, then hunted down the killers of his family like rabid dogs.

To Matt's way of thinking, Roddy now teetered on the edge of turning into a killer as amoral as those he had hunted. He hated those who called him a foreigner in his own land with a single-minded proud fury.

The two men used all the self-control either had to keep the antagonistic feelings between them at a level where they never exploded. They needed each other to survive, but the prejudice bred into each formed a solid wall between them, and each carefully maintained his side.

Beau Taney, once heir to a slave dependent Alabama plantation, kept Jaime Rodriguez from getting killed or hung over his reaction to any slight, real or imagined.

Jaime Rodriguez, who practiced no religion but believed anything not Spanish and Catholic was barbaric, deflected Beau Taney's madness enough that it only kept him broke, didn't get him killed or hung.

Maybe Matt understood these two so well because he was like them, trying to find a way to bear a loss so terrible there seemed no way to build another life around so hollow a center. Wasn't pain supposed to lessen with time? How could it hurt the same today as yesterday and all the yesterdays right back to the Charon courthouse?

Of course, understanding the men he had thrown in with was not going to make this gun fighting business work out. Matt had some real problems with it. First of all, it really was a lot like soldiering. They spent most of the time waiting, being ready for something to happen. The other men passed the time playing cards, telling tall tales, cleaning weapons, practicing with them, and just plain sitting around.

But here on this ranch, there was plenty of work, and Matt knew all the advantages of a body so tired it pulled the mind right along with it into dream-free sleep every night. When he volunteered his help to the foreman of the regular crew, the man looked skeptical but told him if he really meant it he could start with postholes.

Digging postholes hardly qualified as work to someone used to what a judge meant by "years at hard labor," but that night Beau cornered Matt and lectured him on the proper attitude for a gunman.

"It doesn't matter if you're the best rifleman in the whole damn state if you're acting like some grubby cowhand," Beau said. "We get paid to shoot things, not to dig holes, and you can't use a gun worth a damn if your hands are covered with cuts and callouses. So you quit the damn digging, hear me?"

Matt thought it over and decided only part of that made sense. The next morning he rode to town, bought several pairs of work gloves, came back and returned to the postholes. Beau's expression could have scared the devil, but he said no more. In part, Matt thought, because Beau realized that when this job ended, Matt would have to find something else to do.

Beau had insisted on a Smith & Wesson pistol. According to him the Colt was unwieldy, and he had objections to guns from every other manufacturer. The other men carried some of those deficient weapons, but Matt said nothing. Learning to draw the weapon presented no problem. He never had trouble with that sort of thing, and the fast, fluid motion came easy to him. Hitting anything with the gun in hand didn't. In sharp contrast, his skill with a rifle hadn't deserted him. He had better speed and more accuracy than anyone on the ranch with the long gun.

Beau's disbelief, Carson's contempt, and Roddy's relief, not to mention his own frustration, had stopped Matt from even working with the pistol. Until today. Yesterday the cowhands tried to show him how to throw a rope, and he couldn't place a loop on a cow any better than a bullet in a target. Lying awake last night, worrying about it, he had fastened on an idea.

So today he had come alone to this gully with several boxes of bullets and a determination to find a solution to the problem.

As morning turned to afternoon, Matt's arm grew sore, his eye and lungs burned from gun smoke, and his ears rang from the steady sound of shots, but before the light faded he proved his idea to his own satisfaction.

That night, Beau asked, "You making any progress?"

Matt shook his head. He didn't want an audience or an impatient instructor until he had a handle on the problem.

The next night, Beau said, "They didn't use that much ammunition at Gettysburg."

Matt shot him a hard look. "That tells me you weren't there."

Beau shrugged, "No, but I bet I'm not exaggerating much either."

The third day, Matt turned from his targets to find all five gunmen standing in a line behind him. Not one looked pleased. He reloaded, just five bullets this time, leaving an empty chamber under the hammer to signal he was done for the day.

"It looks to me like you've made some progress." Beau's voice had the exaggerated drawl he used for emphasis.

"You could say I've got the beast by the tail. He's sure not broke yet." Matt grinned in a friendly fashion, knowing Beau's game and refusing to play.

"What made the difference?"

"Can't seem to judge distance too well with one eye, so I studied on it till I figured out how to allow for it. I'll never drill a tossed coin like you, but I'll stop a man, I reckon."

"I reckon you will." Beau shifted into full fighting stance, legs slightly spraddled, right hand near his gun, and he was using those cold eyes to full effect.

Matt hooked his own thumbs in his belt and waited. Craziness aside, Beau was too used to getting his own way with this kind of behavior.

"A lot of men hire out who can't use a pistol that well," Beau said, "but I'll tell you right now, nobody rides with me and spends his time digging cows out of mud or digging anything else except an occasional grave."

"You said right off we'd just give it a try for the one job." Matt met the icy stare steadily. "I'm willing to call it quits right now if that's what you want. I can't sit around day after day till my rump's sore from the abuse. When the fighting starts, I'll be there, but I need to keep busy, and I like learning new things."

Matt widened his grin to full force. "The look of me is enough to scare folks without trying anyway. It's handsome devils like you and Roddy have to work so hard at looking mean."

One of Beau's problems was that he had no sense of humor about himself. Of course, a man might develop a bit of that if someone kept prodding. Matt prodded. "Take that look on your face right now. That might give a smart man the shakes."

Beau didn't relax at all, and now Roddy tensed, ready to back Beau all the way.

"Smart men," Beau said, "walk real careful when they can tell they're starting to rile me."

"That must be why you don't hire smart men. You get Texans like me and Roddy, and then we aren't watching our feet all the time."

Walking through the line of men, heading back for the bunkhouse, Matt saw blank astonishment on all five faces. As he climbed out of the gully, laughter roared from behind him. It sounded like Roddy.

27

"GOOD NIGHT, MR. DOLAN. I'll see you in the morning," Sarah said.

"Hmph. Yes, eight o'clock. Sharp."

Sarah nodded, pulled her shawl tight around her shoulders and left the general store. In the six months she had worked for Mr. Dolan, she had never been late for work. Not once. And every evening when she said good night, he behaved as if she were chronically tardy.

As Sarah walked through the small town of Heber, she studied the flat grasslands beyond the town. This part of Texas had none of the charm of the hill country around Flowers. Her New England bred eyes longed for trees, hills and color. The coming spring would not be green enough or wet enough. Fall gave relief from the unholy heat of summer, but nothing more. Winter? March should bring signs of spring, but this bleak winter stretched on and on.

Perhaps the next time she and Laurie moved on, they should travel north. Surprised at the direction of her own thoughts, Sarah shook her head. Leaving Heber was no longer an option.

Her steps quickened and heart lightened as she approached Maud Branson's small house. A knock on the door brought the sound of a happy squeal. Three-year-old Laurie opened the door, and Sarah leaned down for an enthusiastic hug and kiss.

"Mama, Mama, I helped with the laundry. I stirred and stirred. Like this."

Sarah laughed as Laurie demonstrated the stirring motion.

Maud Branson's voice came from the next room. "Come in and warm up, Sarah. I'll make us coffee, and you can tell me about your day."

Maud made some version of that offer once every week on the day she expected payment for watching Laurie while Sarah worked, and Sarah always accepted and played out her part in the social charade. Knowing the routine, Laurie went back to where Maud's son and daughter debated the best way to construct a tower out of blocks of wood.

Sarah watched for a moment to make sure the children were getting along, then walked into the kitchen, folded her shawl over the back of a chair and sat down. Taking the proper sum from her reticule, she slipped the bills under the sugar bowl in the center of the table.

The kitchen was in its usual state of disarray. Widowed shortly after the birth of her second child, Maud eked out a living taking in laundry and doing sewing. The extra money for taking care of Laurie six days a week made her life easier, and Sarah's harder.

Maud poured two cups of coffee and sat down with a heavy sigh. "So how is it going for you, Sarah?"

"The same as ever. It's not as if he's going to change at his age." Sipping at her black coffee, Sarah studied the other woman. Her own experience over the last years had convinced Sarah that exhausting physical labor kept extra flesh off a body. Maud's thick waist and second chin challenged that belief, and every week Sarah searched for an answer to the puzzle. Watching Maud stir several spoonfuls of sugar into her coffee and then add enough cream to turn it almost white made her wonder.

"Did you ask him about a wage increase?" Maud said.

Guiltily, Sarah pulled her thoughts away from Maud's figure. "He said he'd consider it after a year."

"Ha. There's no one else in town desperate enough to work for him. Tell him either he pays more or you'll quit."

"Perhaps I will," Sarah said, finishing her coffee quickly and getting to her feet. "Right now Laurie and I need to get back to the boarding house and wash up for dinner. Thank you for the coffee."

Sarah bundled Laurie up for the walk back to the boarding house, thinking how she should never have shared her financial worries with Maud. Except another unplanned expense or two would leave her unable to pay the woman to watch Laurie, and warning her seemed fair. Last fall Dolan's offer of a position clerking in his store had seemed great good fortune. He offered a wage much higher than she had earned before, and he agreed that Laurie could spend the days in the store so long as Sarah fulfilled her duties.

In all honesty, Sarah couldn't claim Dolan lied. He never reneged on his agreement to have Laurie in the store. Instead he complained about the child ceaselessly and carped at her over every childish noise or action. By the end of the first week, Sarah knew she didn't want Laurie around the curmudgeon one day longer than necessary.

But after paying Maud and paying for the boarding house, Sarah's wages barely covered necessities. Any extras she or Laurie needed meant dipping into the ring money, and the ring money had dwindled down to a few dollars.

"Are you tired, Mama?"

Sarah looked down into the small face and felt her fatigue lessen. Meeting Laurie for the first time, people often remarked how much she looked like her mother, but when Sarah looked at her daughter, she saw blue eyes that paled a little more each year and a familiar taper to the jaw line, and she remembered—and rejoiced.

"Yes, I am a little. Not too much for us to work on your doll's new dress after dinner. How about you? Are you tired after helping with the laundry?"

"Yes, I am a little," Laurie said, face solemn, eyes dancing. Sarah laughed. Laurie giggled and ran ahead.

Still smiling, Sarah followed Laurie inside the shabby, two-story house she couldn't bring herself to call home. Her landlady, Clara Wolcott, appeared before they reached the stairs.

"Mrs. Hammond, you have a visitor." Her voice fell to a whisper. "He's waiting in the parlor if you want to freshen up before seeing him. I'll watch Laurie."

Sarah's heart leapt to her throat. "Did he give you his name?"

"Denham. Mr. Bradford Denham."

Tears of disappointment pricked at Sarah's eyes. She blinked them away. "Yes, I think we will wash and change for dinner before I meet with Mr. Denham, and Laurie would love to help you in the kitchen. Thank you."

Sarah changed to her best dress, a wine wool challis she had rescued from Evelyn Reynolds' discards. A stain on the hem had been the only blemish. Inches shorter, Sarah had rehemmed the skirt, taken in the bodice, and congratulated herself on the result.

Laurie's face fell at the sight of the dress. "Are we going to church?" she asked.

"No, sweetheart. I just thought it would be nice to dress up tonight." *And I'm wearing my Sunday best like armor.*

After settling Laurie in the kitchen with Mrs. Wolcott, Sarah marched toward the parlor. Paying the stage driver to mail a letter to John and Evelyn Reynolds from the farthest town on his route had been a waste, she reflected. Sending a letter to the Reynolds to let them know she and Laurie were resettled and fine had been a mistake that gave Brad the information he needed to find them. No use fussing over things she couldn't change.

She entered the parlor and shut the door quietly behind her. Brad rose to his feet and held out his hands. "You're looking lovely, Sarah. It's good to see you."

Sarah ignored the gesture and sat in a chair facing him. "It won't work this time, Brad. You've wasted your time tracking me down."

"Seeing that you're all right with my own eyes could never be a waste, and I have something for you, something that would prey on my conscience if I didn't get it to you."

He handed her an unsealed envelope. Sarah could see the bills inside at a glance. "What is this?"

"He sent the money back to Kate."

Sarah looked again and this time saw the piece of white paper in the envelope with the money. Holding her breath, she pulled it out and unfolded it. Two words: "For Sarah." She dropped the envelope in her lap and pressed the paper between the palms of her hands, trying to feel some essence of him. Nothing came but memories, and even so she wondered. Did he know? Did he somehow know she had been foolish and put herself in a corner and that the money would give her choices again?

"I'm sorry, Sarah," Brad said softly.

"Are you? If you could do it over would you do it differently?"

He sighed. "I don't know. Probably not. My problem is I can see both sides, and Kate has strong feelings."

"And you love her."

"And I love her. The thing I'd do differently is that I would lie to you. It's a weakness of mine, lying to women I care about to make life easier. Kate's feelings for you include a respect that wouldn't let her do that."

"Kate sees me as something I'm not. She wants me to lead the life she could have if she'd chosen a different path long ago."

"Yes, she does, but that also means she wants the best for you. Are you still too angry to even grant her that?"

"No," Sarah said. "I stopped being angry long ago. I think of the two of you often, you know. I think how much you helped me, how you gave him your own money that day and trusted me to pay you back, of how I only had that money in the first place because you got me such a good price for the ring. Perhaps I even forgive you, but there's something inside me, some cold, sad thing inside that isn't ever going to change. I don't trust you any more, and I don't trust her, and I never will. Nothing will ever be the same."

"Things never stay the same, Sarah. We stumble along and things keep changing." He pulled another envelope from his suit pocket. "If you've forgiven us, will you read this? Will you answer it?"

Sarah looked at the letter but didn't reach for it. "I will do that if you will tell me about that day. If you tell me every single detail about that day, I'll do that."

Brad's eyes shifted off to the right for a second then met hers again. She recognized his decision to lie. "Yes, I'll tell you about that day," he said agreeably. "I'll tell you everything I can remember."

Sarah took Kate's letter then. Even knowing Brad was going to lie about something, it was better than nothing. The lie would be just some small thing to protect Kate.

28

JAIME RODRIGUEZ LEANED back against the rough bole of a tree and looked over the campsite with satisfaction. A neat fire held off the darkness. A pile of extra firewood sat nearby. The gurgle of the small stream hidden by thickets of brush provided soothing background music for the last of the showy sunset fading in the western sky. Cool fall weather meant no mosquitoes, even in this part of Kansas.

Beau relaxed against another tree, puffing away on a cigar. "Where's Carson?" he asked.

"He, Vic and Whitey rode upstream. He said they would look for a farmhouse where we can get breakfast."

Beau gave a small grunt. Nothing cooked over their fire could compare to a real breakfast—stacks of hotcakes, fresh butter and syrup, bacon, even sausage maybe—served by some farm wife who would be happy to do the cooking in return for ready cash.

"Slade?"

That question meant Beau was hungry. A fair cook, Slade was, of course, willing to do the extra work. The fire, the pile of wood— all Slade's doing.

"Horse." The one word said it all. The incredibly plain horse, so appropriately named "Sam," was a continual sore point, and only one example of Slade's aggravating ways.

Roddy wondered, as he had at least a hundred times in the past year, why Beau put up with the man, and he answered himself as he had the same hundred times. Beau liked Slade. In fact Roddy had given up trying to keep aloof from the scarred man. *Texans like me and Roddy.*

He rolled a cigarette, thinking it over. At the first sight of Slade, a strong premonition of trouble had crawled up his spine. After a year riding with the man, Roddy had almost decided his instincts were wrong for once.

Imagining Slade bringing disaster down on them took some doing. Easygoing to a fault, the scarred man poked fun at anything and everything, including himself. Steady, careful and no glory hunter, he also lived up to all Beau's predictions of a first-class fighting man.

Of course, on the negative side, Slade had proved to be the most hard-headed, independent human being Roddy had ever run across. He made Beau look flexible. You could talk yourself blue in the face and predict dire consequences. Slade never argued, never even said he disagreed. He listened thoughtfully and then went and did what he damn well pleased.

Take the horse, for example. These days railroads ran all over the country. Whether the next job was a hundred miles away or five hundred, riding to the nearest train station, selling the horses and buying more at the other end simplified travel. Not Slade. When they rode the rails, so did that damned horse. Admittedly, after you got by the washed out muddy chestnut color, the gelding was a good one, but there were other good horses.

So here they sat, hungry and waiting for something to eat while Slade babied that horse. The thing got rubbed down at night, curried and brushed in the morning, picketed on grass for hours in a camp like this, offered water every time it walked a mile and fed grain every day of its pampered life.

Carson's voice interrupted Roddy's musings. As the big man appeared out of the brush near the creek, Roddy ground out his cigarette viciously. Here was trouble, and not of Slade's making.

Matt strolled from the grassy spot where he had picketed Sam toward the campfire. The night air was invigorating after a long day in the saddle, and he felt far closer than usual to at peace with the world and his own place in it.

The feeling disappeared without a trace when he drew close enough to see what his fire illuminated. He stopped outside the circle of light, taking in what he could see and hear, what it meant, and what to do about it.

Ward Carson had a girl in his meaty grip. Probably not very big anyway, she looked frail held against the massive man's chest and belly. Loose dark hair contrasted starkly with her tear-stained, terrified white face. Except for sturdy shoes, she wore nightclothes. Carson had her robe pushed back to trap her arms and her night dress torn half off, exposing full breasts. A girl, yes, but woman enough for what Carson had in mind.

The big man stood across the fire from Beau and Roddy, holding his captive with one arm while the other hand squeezed a breast, pinched one pink nipple cruelly. The girl stood stiff and silent, already numbed by her hopeless situation and by the blow that had started a bruise darkening and swelling on one side of her face.

"Look what I found crawling around in the brush calling for somebody named Billy. Hope you fellas appreciate how generous I'm being," Carson gloated. "We brought her back to share. I'm first, since I caught her, but I told these two they'd have to wait for you, Beau. Then Roddy and that one-eyed bastard can flip a coin."

Matt knew the men he rode with pretty well. Beau Taney divided the women of the world into two simplistic categories, ladies and whores. By walking into the night dressed like that, this girl had put herself firmly in Beau's whore category, and his judgments were harsh and absolute. He would neither lower himself to participate in Carson's entertainment nor try to stop it. Carson hadn't dragged the girl to the fire to share, just to show off. Sure enough, Beau's indifferent words were what Matt expected.

"You drag her off somewhere far enough I don't have to hear you, and I don't have to hear her. I like women willing and a lot more skilled than that one's going to be."

Carson's laugh was ugly. "She's going to know some nice tricks by morning."

"You heard me, Ward. Out of my sight and out of my hearing. Now get."

After following the other two out of the brush, Whitey had stopped a short distance away, looking less than certain, but Vic hung right beside Carson, his eyes burning, lips slack and wet. He reached out and kneaded at a breast. Carson slapped him away.

"You wait till I'm done."

Matt also knew Roddy would not intervene. If the girl looked even vaguely Spanish, maybe, but Roddy would say what happened to stupid gringo girls who were stumbling around half-dressed where Ward Carson could find them didn't concern him.

Matt's mind filled with memories of another girl, of the only loss of innocence he had ever known, accompanied with pain and blood even though he had loved her so. Had loved her, still loved her. God help him.

He forced his attention back to the matter at hand. Almost against his will, he had developed considerable respect for Beau Taney and Jaime Rodriguez. He saw them as like himself, men struggling with lives they never planned or wanted.

At odds of five to one, he couldn't stop this himself. He had to find words to bring one or both these men back to something they'd turned away from years ago. Carson finished gloating, and time ran out.

Matt moved into the very last of the darkness outside the circle of firelight. "Let her go, Carson."

At the first word, Beau jumped to his feet, searching the night. "I told you before, Slade, I run this outfit. And I said he could have her. You keep your nose out of it."

"Are you really going to throw away everything you ever believed in?"

The unyielding expression on the other man's face told Matt his words made no difference even before Beau answered.

"You take a good look at what you're fussing over. She came sneaking out in the night dressed like that looking for a hard pecker, and she found herself three. It's just a lucky night for whores is all."

"You know better than that. What she most likely had in mind was a few kisses with some boy she's sweet on, and even if it turned to more, it's nothing to you. Virgin or whore, it's wrong the same."

Beau was through arguing. "You've got a hell of an edge out there in the dark, you bastard, but nowheres near enough. Either back off now or you won't be bothering me or anyone else ever again."

Roddy rose too, uncoiling like a deadly black snake. Beau spoke the truth. If this came to a fight, no edge gave Matt any chance at all. So he threw away the edge and walked into the firelight. Ignoring Carson and his apprentices, Matt tried to reach the only two who mattered.

"Trouble is, I don't believe you, you or Roddy, whatever he has to say. You're telling me a tall tale, and you're telling yourself a taller one. It's because life hasn't beaten the hope and dreams out of her you can't stand the sight of her. So you'll look the other way while her life gets ruined and tell yourself she deserves it. And when it's done, you won't feel better. You'll just be a smaller man carrying the same weight as before. Somehow I thought you cared more about what you lost."

Roddy pivoted to face Carson, most likely not even needing to see what Matt did flicker across Beau's face to know he was turning too.

"Let her go, Ward." Beau's voice was bitter but sure.

"Like hell. You know I can take that one-eyed son of a bitch."

"Maybe," Beau said evenly, "but you can't take me, and if you get lucky, Roddy will cut you to pieces before I hit the ground. Let her go."

Carson backed down, fury in every line of his face and body. He shoved the girl away. She fell at the edge of the fire, ignoring the flames as she fumbled to cover herself.

"I'm not riding with a man who backs off his word that easy," Carson sneered.

"I don't blame you for that. Good luck to you then," Beau said.

Carson showed surprise as he realized Beau expected him to leave. Still he blustered, "Damn right. You coming?"

With the last words Carson looked at Whitey and Vic. Vic nodded and started toward the horses, but after a long hesitation, Whitey gave the smallest of headshakes.

Matt caught Sam up, resaddled and took the girl home, putting her down close to the farmhouse, but not close enough for an angry father with a shotgun to make a mistake.

"Thank you." She gave him a quick hug and a kiss on the cheek before running into the darkness, her shadow blending into that of the house. Matt waited until he heard a door open and close, realizing then that he didn't know her name, never would.

Back at the camp, Matt busied himself with the supper no one else had bothered to start. Coffee and hot food were beginning to flavor the air, when Beau spoke. "You ever do that again, I'll kill you."

Matt studied the other man, considering. Maybe he could stave off the inevitable confrontation long enough it wouldn't be fatal when it came. Maybe. "I agree with you there. Once will have to be enough."

Matt thought he saw Roddy cross himself, but it had to be an illusion in the flickering firelight. Jaime Rodriguez was not a religious man.

29

November 1872, Heber, Texas

LIFE DID GET UGLY sometimes, but other times perverse would be a better description. Like now. Every other unmarried women in Heber seized any opportunity to attract attention from Jerome Mercer, widower, lawyer and self-described self-made success.

The moment Sarah recognized Mercer's interest, she hauled Jenny Edler's dresses out of storage. The sight of the two faded, baggy garments that had not yet been cut up for rags, patches or stuffed toys for Laurie stirred unpleasant memories. Wearing one to church took courage—and showed no sign of discouraging Mercer. Neither did pulling her hair straight back from her face into a tight, ugly knot at the back of her neck.

Last week, no polite excuse had kept Mercer from strolling beside her as she returned to the boarding house after church. Then he cadged an invitation to Sunday dinner from Mrs. Wolcott, who expected Sarah to pay for any dinner guest.

Rather than risk a repeat of that expensive misery, Sarah ignored the cold wind blowing from the gray November sky and sat on a bench in the churchyard. Laurie ran to join other children playing nearby.

Every muscle in Sarah's face ached with the effort of keeping a pleasant expression in place as she watched the children and did her best to ignore Mercer. She wrapped her shawl higher and tighter around her shoulders, partly because of the chill and partly as a barrier against the man sitting too close beside her.

Mercer caught her attention as he stopped droning on about his law business and real estate dealings and switched to personal matters.

"I understand you still have feelings for your husband, Mrs. Hammond. I still miss my wife, but we have to go on, don't we?"

Sarah said nothing. If he missed his wife so much, why was he pestering another woman less than a year after her death? The last time she even saw Matt was more than four years in the past. Some nights the hollow feeling inside became a pain so great she shook with it, wept with it, yet the thought of letting Jerome Mercer touch her the way a husband touched a wife brought bile to the back of her throat.

"The fact is I need a wife, and you need a husband and a father for Laurie."

"Laurie has a father," Sarah snapped without thinking. Hearing her own words, Sarah clamped her lips together too late.

"Excuse me," Mercer said, twisting on the bench to face her more squarely. "What exactly are you telling me, Mrs. Hammond?"

Her mind darted frantically from one possible explanation to another, but in the end, Sarah said, "Is it true, Mr. Mercer, that lawyers have an obligation of confidentiality to clients?

"Yes, it is," he said, studying her as if he'd never seen her before.

"How do I become a client of yours and consult you about my daughter's rights in regard to her father?"

"You pay me my hourly fee and describe the problem, and I give advice."

"I would like to do that then," Sarah whispered. "I have no money with me. If you would be so kind as to walk me back to the boarding house."

Wordlessly, Mercer rose and helped her up, his hand hard and possessive on her arm. Sarah cursed herself with all the words she had once used over a sprained ankle.

How could she have let her aggravation at this irritating man push her into making such a mistake, and what was she going to tell him?

At the boarding house, Mercer waited in the parlor while Sarah got more of Matt's money for the lawyer's "fee" than she thought reasonable. Then she told him the truth. Some of it. Most of it. He listened with a stony face, and when she stopped talking, said nothing but, "Miss Hammond," before walking out.

Sarah sat alone in the room shaking. Eventually the sounds of dinner preparations penetrated her trance. Retrieving Laurie from Clara Wolcott's care, she tried to calm herself. At least Mercer couldn't tell anyone else, and he wouldn't be ruining any more of her Sundays.

The next morning, Sarah readied herself and Laurie for the day still feeling vaguely uneasy about her dealings with Mercer. She walked Laurie to Maud Branson's where Maud's daughter answered the door and let Laurie in. Sarah called out a good morning to Maud before continuing on to Dolan's store.

Sarah was only halfway through the door into the store when Dolan blocked her way. "Whore," he said with venom. "Get out of my store, you harlot."

Too shocked to say anything until she was back outside with the door closed in her face, Sarah banged on the door with a fist. Dolan owed her money! Then the meaning of his words sank home, and she gathered up her skirts, and with heart pounding before she even started, flew back down the street to Maud Branson's.

Any inclination to knock politely on the Branson door dissolved when Sarah heard Laurie's high-pitched wail as she ran up the walk. Yanking open the front door, Sarah could hear Maud's voice raised in fury.

"You stop that crying, you little bastard!" The sound of a slap punctuated the cruel words, and Sarah got to the kitchen in time to see Laurie cringing away, both hands to her cheek.

Four inches taller and three stone heavier than Sarah, Maud's size meant nothing. Sarah grabbed chunks of Maud's hair with both hands, doubled her over backwards and threw her against the wall. Sarah smashed her fist into Maud's jaw the way a man would have. As the big woman slumped down the wall, Sarah snatched one of the irons from the stove and raised it high.

Before she could bring the murderous weapon down on Maud's unprotected head, she felt hard hands on her shoulders and heard the deep voice as if he were inches from her ear.

"Maybe they won't hang you, Boston, but who will look after my daughter when you're in jail?"

Sarah spun around, shaken right out of the killing rage, but there was no one else in the room except Laurie and Maud's children, all crying now. Frightened speechless, Maud huddled against the wall.

Many times in past years Sarah had heard Matt's voice, but it was always memories of things he once said, never anything like this. A trick of the mind, she told herself, just a self-protective trick of the mind.

The iron still in her hand, Sarah leaned over Maud. "You bitch. Nothing I ever did compares with hitting a little girl for something she doesn't even understand. If you ever get near my daughter again, I'll kill you."

Laurie was too big to carry these days, but Sarah managed it anyway. By the time they were in their room at the boarding house, Laurie's sobs had faded to hiccups.

Sarah wet a cloth in what was left of the morning wash water and soothed the traces of tears away.

Laurie asked, "Mama, am I a baster?"

Sarah never lied to her daughter. She always told Laurie as much as she thought a child could understand, and she didn't take the easy way out now.

"Yes, sweetheart, you are. Bastard is the word, but it's an ugly word people use when they want to be mean." Sarah tried to explain the concept but couldn't find words to make it clear to a little girl not yet four. To Sarah's relief, Laurie lost interest and fell asleep, worn out by the aftermath of pain and fear.

Hearing a soft tap on the door, Sarah stepped into the hall to talk to Clara Wolcott.

"I suppose you've had a difficult morning, Sarah."

Aware now that Mercer's ethics were non-existent and that he had spent all yesterday afternoon and evening sharing her secrets with the whole town, Sarah explained her difficult morning in a few terse sentences.

Clara made sympathetic sound. "I've been widowed myself for over ten years, and I'm not in a position to cast stones, but confiding in Jerome Mercer of all people...."

"He's an attorney! I paid him so I would be a client and he had an ethical obligation to keep my confidences."

Clara shook her head. "It's a hard way to learn the lesson, but let me tell you, no matter what anyone says, hell hath no fury like a *man* scorned."

Saying this Clara had a twinkle in her eye, but then she grew serious. "I hate to add to your troubles, but I have to live in this town."

"And you want me out of here right now," Sarah said.

"No," Clara reassured her. "I can put up with some pressure for a day or two, but the stage leaves town Thursday, and I think you better be on it."

"We're going to be."

"Yes. I think also, while you're still here, you should stay in your room with the door locked. I'll bring meals."

Sarah's surprise made the older woman add, "Mr. Mercer is on a crusade to arouse the town's indignation over how you have deceived them. You have your things ready early Thursday, and I'll get Joe to take them to the stage station for you. You take only what you can carry easily, and while you may hope I'm wrong, you be prepared to run a gauntlet."

At first, Sarah didn't want to believe Clara could be right, but she remembered the Charon courthouse all too well. After she thought over that memory, the names Dolan had called her and the sound of Maud slapping Laurie, she pulled Matt's pistol out from its hiding place, took down the tin box with the oil and rags and began the familiar cleaning ritual. Keeping enough of Matt's money for stage tickets in a pocket of her dress, she sewed the rest into the hem of Laurie's coat.

Early Thursday morning, Sarah loaded the pistol.

Prepared in every way she could imagine, Sarah gave Clara Wolcott her thanks and farewells, took Laurie by the hand, stepped out of the house into the dust of the empty street and started for the stage depot. She walked unmolested down Main Street but the unnatural quiet worried her. Where was everyone?

Turning the corner of Main on to First, she realized most of the people of the town must be out of sight as a way to avoid the mob who had responded to Mercer's call to action. Men stood on both sides of the street, forming the kind of jeering gauntlet Clara Wolcott had warned against.

Sarah stopped dead and glanced behind her, considering retreat, but two of Jerome Mercer's closest associates came up behind her.

"Slut!"

"Whore!"

Pulling Laurie tight against her side, the side away from the pistol, Sarah said "Hold on tight and keep your face in my skirts, sweetheart." She moved into the middle of the street and began the long walk.

By the time they reached the little building that served as the stage depot, Sarah's knees threatened to give way. Men stared inside through the doors and windows, and Mercer's friends who had closed off her retreat followed Sarah and Laurie inside.

Sarah knew the ticket agent, Lloyd Holthoff, well enough to exchange a few friendly words in Dolan's store or after church. Now the round, fleshy face sported the same ugly leer as all the others. He stayed seated behind his desk as Sarah approached, a deliberate insult.

The mob quieted, and Mercer pushed his way into the room, exchanging a conspiratorial glance with the ticket agent. Sarah saw that her ordeal was not over.

"What can I do for you today, *Miss* Hammond?"

"Two tickets, please," Sarah said with all the calm she could muster, "for my daughter and me to Santa Fe."

"I'm afraid I can't do that, *Miss* Hammond. You see this company doesn't let whores ride in its coaches."

Loud guffaws erupted from the other men. Encouraged, and enjoying himself, Holthoff leaned across the desk toward her. "I guess you'll just have to stay here in Heber and make your living here doing what you do best. Why you got, one, two, three—let's see, four customers here in the station right now."

Sarah played for time. "And what about my daughter, Mr. Holthoff? Surely you're not proposing that this commercial transaction take place in front of her?"

Holthoff's ugly sneer just widened. "You know what they say, like mother, like daughter."

Fear ebbed; anger surged. Sarah put a coy look on her face and moved around the desk, pulling Laurie with her. With the desk between them and the other men in the building, Sarah let go of

Laurie's hand, lifted the pistol free of her skirt and pointed it at the center of Holthoff's chest, holding it with both hands.

"Two tickets to Santa Fe, Mr. Holthoff."

"Who do you think you're fooling? That gun's bigger than you are, and you're shaking like a leaf." In spite of his brave words, Holthoff's expression changed to one of caution as he got to his feet.

The sound of the shot thundered in the little building, echoing and reverberating off the walls.

SARAH SETTLED HERSELF and Laurie inside the stagecoach, feeling absolutely drained, so exhausted sleep might be possible in spite of the loud noises of the moving vehicle and the jolting ride. A single fellow traveler was already in the coach, however, a man with slicked back hair and knowing eyes.

"I take it you're leaving town under less than auspicious circumstances."

In no mood for word games, Sarah said, "I was run out of town because they don't think my moral character is good enough for them."

"Maybe you need a protector."

"I don't need anything of the sort. I will do my own protecting."

"Forgive me if I doubt you, but a little thing like you surely could use a man like me."

The events in the stage station had shocked Laurie right out of her terror. "That other man said Mama was little too. That's when she shot him."

The man stared at Laurie in disbelief, then looked at Sarah, who raised her eyebrows and said nothing.

Proud of her mother and no longer very afraid of anything, Laurie continued. "He squealed like a pig and jumped around holding his ear." Laurie clutched her own ear and bounced up and down on the seat. "There was lots and lots of blood. And when Mama told the other men to get out, they ran. Mama didn't pay for our tickets. She says the bad man can pay for them on account of being so mean to us."

The man's astonishment changed to something else, then his lips twitched, and he pulled off his hat, bowing as best he could from his seated position.

"Ma'am I stand corrected. You most certainly do not need protecting, and no matter how small the package, there seems to be a great deal of lady inside."

With that settled, Sarah relaxed in her seat, although sleep was no longer a possibility until there were other passengers or this man got off. She had rinsed off the spit and bits of rotten vegetables thrown at her with water from a horse trough. As soon as the stage stopped for any length of time, she would get herself and Laurie into clean clothes.

In a few days they would cross the invisible line between the State of Texas and New Mexico Territory. Brad Denham visited Santa Fe often, and from him Sarah knew about the old city in the foothills of the Sangre de Cristo Mountains. Cooler summers and winters with real snow sounded good to her. Texas had never really wanted her, no more, in the end, than the Texan she must find a way to stop loving wanted her.

The time had come to leave Texas, leave the past and start a new life.

30

MATT STARED AT HIS cards without really seeing them, considering throwing the hand in and leaving. Spending a couple of days in Denver before heading for the next job had sounded good when Beau proposed it.

In fact Matt had been enjoying the poker game until a little while ago when one of the saloon girls dropped in his lap and wound around his neck. He'd pushed her away gently, hiding his distaste for smiling, painted lips under sad, lying eyes and his distaste for himself because of the short time he'd spent with her the night before.

Maybe a man would be better off never knowing how it was supposed to be. Then there wouldn't be the sick emptiness after, the anger over the paid for travesty. Never knowing how it could be, should be, would be better, except that not knowing would mean giving back the memories, cutting out of himself all that he most treasured.

Looking up, Matt caught sight of Beau and Roddy, and trouble, and put aside the old pain. Stiff, eyes wide and ringed with white, Beau resembled nothing so much as a maddened bull, pawing the ground and getting ready to charge. Roddy held him by the arm, talking fast. It wouldn't do any good, of course. These days Beau's true crazy spells flared up less and less frequently, but he still used this kind of wild temper whenever anyone bucked him.

And today Matt decided he'd had enough. Maybe because of his own black mood, or maybe because they'd just been walking soft around each other as long as they could, here was going to be the place, and now was going to be the time.

Beau stalked to the table, the tendons in his neck straining. "I want to talk to you. Now!"

Matt looked at Beau, looked at his hand, then folded the cards slowly. He needed a good opening to start this right. Beau was about his own height, but massive in the shoulders and more heavily muscled in the waist, hips and thighs. Of course, Beau avoided any physical activity that might produce fighting trim.

Matt got to his feet and started to walk away from the table, but Beau grabbed his arm, spinning him back around only a few feet from the other players, and making no effort to get out of hearing of the card players or anybody else.

"Nobody who rides with me plays cards with a nigra, much less a nigra wearing that goddamn hat!"

There had never been any doubt in Matt's mind what set Beau off. The faded hat in question had seen better days, but it was most definitely a Union kepi. Figuring the more frenzied Beau was the better, Matt glanced back at the table over his shoulder, as if to check to be sure that there was indeed a Negro who was indeed wearing a Union soldier's cap sitting there, then met Beau's crazed glare.

"I'm real sorry you feel that way," he said. "I reckon we're quits then."

Matt returned to his chair and picked up his cards with his left hand, aware that Roddy had managed to get Beau halfway back across the room only because Beau was rigid. His eyes showed more white than gray now, and Roddy was most definitely wasting effort. Beau jerked away, charged back over to the table and upended it with a crash on the players across from Matt.

"I've had all I can take from you. You think I picked you up off the ground when you got out of prison, taught you to shoot that goddamn gun and paid you more every month than your whole miserable life was ever worth, and you can just call it quits?"

Beau leaned over, his face only inches from Matt's. "You get yourself out in the street. I'm through talking!"

Matt would never get a better chance. "Why go out in the street, Beau?" With the words, he brought his right fist from down low into Beau's jaw with all the force he could drive upward from his sitting position.

The crack was louder than a gunshot, staggering Beau back into the black man, who winked at Matt as he took advantage of Beau's stunned condition to lift his pistol. "You asked for it, masta," he said. "Now go get it." With that he shoved Beau forward.

In seconds Matt learned that Southern gentlemen spent no more time learning how to brawl than how to use a shovel. Beau was, however, tough enough and stubborn enough to keep a man careful.

Soon the fight spilled into the street, dozens of men hitting, gouging and charging anyone who got close. Matt smashed Beau in the jaw again hard enough to feel the jolt all the way to the shoulder. Beau went down, and Matt didn't wait for him to get up, but left him, letting himself be drawn into the general mêlée.

He caught a glimpse of Roddy going down in the street after a blow in the back from a dirty-looking bear of a man and laughed out loud. Jaime Francisco Rodriguez y Candelaria would be the first to tell you he was a gunman, he did not brawl. This time, however, he had walked into the saloon with the man who started the fight, and he sure enough was in a brawl. The sight of Roddy reduced to rolling around in the dirt and manure in the street like some common gringo dissolved the last of Matt's black mood.

A shotgun boomed, and the sheriff and two deputies threatened, hollered and got everybody stopped. Confessing to his role in the whole free-for-all, Matt felt close to cheerful. His ability to pay for the damage instead of spending time in the city jail lifted his mood further. After settling things with the saloon keeper under the sheriff's eye, Matt retrieved Beau's gun.

"Guess you're out of a job now," the ex-Union soldier observed.

"I am."

"I heard of a man looking for help. Needs a strong back is all."

Matt felt more kinship with this man of a different race who had fought in his war on the other side than he did with the many who had fled West to avoid the draft. "A strong back and a hard head are all I got," he said. "I'll buy you a drink and you can tell me about it after I take this back to its owner."

"If you give him that back loaded, you're crazy."

Looking at the gun that was a twin of his own, Matt felt a spasm of unexpected regret. One more loss, and when exactly had he come to care enough about those hard, arrogant men it mattered?

"Did you hear me? Better empty that gun before you give it back."

Matt just shook his head and turned away.

RODDY WATCHED THE end of the fight on his back, pinned beneath two unconscious gringo pigs, cursing Matt Slade alternately in two languages. By the time he got free, Beau had pulled himself to a sitting position on the sidewalk, elbows on knees, head hanging between them.

Roddy would never be foolish enough to describe Beau's method of getting to that walk as crawling, and no one who wanted to grow older would describe Roddy's way of getting there that way either.

The two of them sat in unmoving silence for some time when footsteps approached in the street. Roddy didn't look up until something thudded into the dirt near his feet. Beau's pistol. Slade.

Beau looked up then too, still furious. "You know damn well when I said out in the street, I meant with guns."

"Aw, sure I did, Beau. But, you know, if I shot you, I think I'd feel real bad, and if you shot me, I know I'd feel real bad. So this way we got it over with and nobody got killed."

That damn grin. Roddy wanted to remove it with a knife.

After a moment's pause, Slade continued. "Of course, I didn't know you fancy fellows were so downright unhandy with your fists." He squatted down on his haunches and looked right at Roddy, then Beau.

"You know, right at the start of the war I envied the officers up there on those fine horses while the rest of us slogged away in the mud. Then at Gaines Mill we lost every officer, and I got real content in the mud, and I stopped envying them."

He took his hat off then, ran his fingers through his hair, and replaced the hat, no longer smiling. "And I reckon I envied you two for a while, coming from those high-class families and knowing all sorts of things I'll never know. Fact is, though, when I get mad, I'd rather sock a man in the jaw than shoot him dead, and when I ride with a man I can trust to keep my back safe in a tight spot, I'd like to call him my friend. But you two—those fancy granddaddies of yours not only made you too good for the likes of me, they made you too good for each other. It seems I surely do not envy you at all."

He left then, and Roddy felt quite content to sit quietly on the walk while the pain in his back subsided from a raging fire to a quiet throb. Of course, as that pain faded, other body parts began serving notice of damage done to them.

The world went on by, as if people in this town were used to bruised and bloody men in torn clothes sitting around. Footsteps echoed behind them on the wooden sidewalk. Horses, wagons and buggies passed in the street.

Finally, Beau spoke, "I'm going to kill him, you know."

"Only if you beat me to it."

"Not today, though.

Roddy didn't even reply. They continued to sit there as the hot summer afternoon faded, shadows lengthened and the air cooled.

The job scheduled after Denver had been the most lucrative kind of work, cleaning up a town overrun with riffraff bleeding ordinary citizens of all they could. Not only did towns like that pay well, Beau always negotiated a bonus for fast performance. They all looked on it as double money.

Three weeks after the fight, that job no longer waited. Beau had another lined up guarding mine payrolls in Southern Colorado, but the doctor's predictions of what riding a horse with broken ribs could do to his insides gave even Beau pause. Roddy expected to hear more furious threats to kill Slade, but the man's name never crossed Beau's lips, which worried Roddy more than he'd ever admit.

Sometime in the last year, Roddy had realized that his original premonition about Slade had come true. Except that the man hadn't brought trouble; he'd brought change. Because of Slade they lost the poison of Ward Carson. Carson's replacement, a blue-eyed, blond young giant who only gave the name Swede, spoke seldom and in heavily accented English, but Swede was a better man than Ward Carson in every way. Luke Goss also put the man he replaced to shame. As dark as Swede was blond, Luke's blunt, square features were indicative of his nature, solid as an oak.

Ignoring Slade had proved impossible. He got to them all. Broke got fixed, ripped got sewn up, worn got replaced. Everything Slade owned was ordinary, but he treasured each item.

Beau reacted first. With some justification, Beau saw himself as a gentleman of exceptional taste and a God-given gift for wearing clothes well. Overnight his shabby clothing disappeared, and he took care of the replacements, albeit by paying someone else to do it in one town or another. Then one day almost furtively Roddy polished the silver on his hatband and belt. Of course silver shining on a shabby outfit....

Beau threw in his cards for the third time in a row. Roddy didn't like the way Beau had been acting the last couple of days. Sick of Denver and inaction, Beau was all too capable of ignoring what anyone said about ribs splintering.

"I've been thinking," Beau said. "What if I had a single-footing horse? We had walkers back home that could glide across any ground."

Eager for a solution that would get them out of Denver without more trouble, Roddy agreed to a horse-buying excursion. Ready for anything different than the last weeks, Swede, Luke and Whitey joined him.

After inspecting and riding at least a dozen horses whose owners lied about their gaits, they did find Beau a single-footing horse. Roddy also found a big black mare that looked especially fine•wearing a silver-trimmed saddle and bridle. He named her Aurora, perversely pleased to own a black horse named for the dawn. Then Luke saw a bay gelding he liked the look of, and before the day passed, they owned five horses they needed to transport to Southern Colorado by rail.

Back at the hotel, Beau listened to their report stretched out on the bed with his legs crossed and hands behind his head. Assured that everything was ready and they could leave first thing in the morning, he mentioned the unmentionable for the first time since the fight.

"What are we going to do about Slade?"

Roddy had an answer all ready. "I suggest we cut cards. High card will shoot him. Low card will mutilate the body."

Beau gave him an irritated look. "You're starting to sound just like him. This is no joking matter. I'm not apologizing."

Roddy kept all traces of relief from his face. "Of course not." Across the room he saw Whitey and Luke having less success at controlling smirks.

Swede took the problem seriously. "This is Matt you talk about, Beau. Just go to see him and say we leave in the morning. He will come with us. He feels the same as you."

Beau glared at Swede. "You mean you've seen him? Where is he?"

"Ya, I see him. He learns from the blacksmith here in town."

Beau sat up. "Maybe he's finally learning something useful. Where is this smithy?"

THE BLACKSMITH DID only want a man with a strong back, but he had no problem showing a man a thing or two. Concentrating on shaping a shoe, at first Matt thought he'd made a mistake when his teacher, facing the doorway, stiffened.

"Taney and four others coming this way. You handle this yourself. I need a drink."

Matt positioned himself so he could see the doorway, but kept working, fighting off a sudden urge to whistle. He waited until they were all inside, leaning against the wall near the door, then stopped hammering, looked up and grinned.

"You fellows look some better than last time I saw you."

Beau got right to the point as usual. "I've decided I can't shoot you when I've a mind to unless you're with the rest of us. We're leaving in the morning."

"I'll be there."

Matt went back to work, but Beau didn't follow the others out. He stayed there inside the doorway, and when Matt glanced up again, said, "Tell me something, Matt. How the hell did anybody do that to your face in a fight? Did you have one hand tied behind your back?"

A knot formed hard in Matt's belly. He thrust the hot shoe into a pail of water and waited until the steam stopped hissing. "It was something like that."

He threw the cooled shoe on the dirt floor and used the tongs to pull another glowing red-orange piece of iron from the fire. He didn't raise his head again until the doorway was empty.

31

October 1874, Tavaras, New Mexico

SARAH SLIPPED IN the back door of the Blackburn house and stopped in surprise. "Why, Minna, whatever are you doing in the kitchen so late?" Minerva Blackburn, called Minna by family and friends, didn't ordinarily leave supper dishes unwashed.

Minna waved a soapy hand in greeting. "Earl Sanquist stopped by to talk to Henry, and Cecily came with him. Fortunately for me the dishes were cleared from the table, and I told her I was done in the kitchen. There's no way I'm letting Cecily Sanquist in my kitchen."

Minna scowled fiercely at the mere thought of the town busybody accomplishing such an invasion, and Sarah laughed. Minna was only an inch taller than Sarah and at fifty-five had a maternal figure, pure white hair, and soft blue eyes. An ideal model for a grandmother doll, Minna Blackburn didn't scowl often or easily.

Sarah sympathized. "I wouldn't want Cecily helping in my life either. She means well, but my mother used to say the road to hell is paved with good intentions. Let me help with these chores. I won't rearrange a thing."

Minna chuckled at this. "No, dear, you've been working hard all day. You don't need to do kitchen chores for me. If you're not too tired, I'd love to have company while I do this, though. Fetch a chair from the dining room and keep me company?"

"Is Laurie already asleep?"

"I'm afraid she is. She wore herself out playing after she finished her school work, and she nodded over her supper."

This disappointment was all too familiar, but since she couldn't change it, Sarah brought a chair into the kitchen and placed it so she could see Minna's profile. One advantage to working for a living was that no one ever accepted help with anything.

Sarah watched Minna bustling around and thought how the disaster in Heber had in the end been a blessing. Soon it would be three years since she had gotten off the stage in Tavaras and asked the town's sheriff if he knew of any work available. Henry Blackburn escorted her to Adelaide Canaday's café. Mrs. Canaday happened to need a new waitress.

The sheriff took Sarah to the boarding house and helped make arrangements there. Finally he offered his wife's services to watch Laurie while Sarah worked—for free. Of course that was out of the question. Sarah paid.

Before long Sarah found out the Blackburns' extraordinary kindness came from more than a charitable attitude toward a young woman on her own with a small child. Henry and Minna had raised four sons, none of whom now lived in town, although all visited regularly. The great tragedy of the Blackburns' lives was the loss of their only daughter at an age close to Laurie's.

Sarah soon accepted the Blackburns' oft-repeated offer to move in with them. Although she paid board, the advantages of living here were beyond price. The two-story frame house provided plenty of room for four people. Laurie had a room of her own for the first time in her life and the sort of loving care she might have received from grandparents.

Minna looked sideways as she washed the last of her dishes. "You know, I enjoyed Brad and Kate's visit more than ever before."

"It was their fifth visit since Laurie and I came here. I suppose you're getting to know them better."

"They really do care for you, you know, and they worry about you. So do Henry and I, of course."

Ah ha! The reason you enjoyed their visit so much, my friend, is that you've found a common goal in trying to push me into marrying Thad Stewart. What Sarah said was, "There's no reason to worry about me. I suppose I wish I could work shorter hours or fewer days a week, but my life here is quite pleasant."

"Sarah...." Minna hesitated then went on. "Since I've known you, whenever someone tries to talk about your husband or your family, you very adroitly change the subject, or you even disappear. Please don't do that now. If you don't want to discuss it, just say so, and we'll talk about something else. I'm enjoying your company tonight very much."

"Now, Minna, you exaggerate. People know my background."

"Generally, perhaps, but you are considered a mystery woman here in town, dear. Half the people think you must have cared for your husband so much you can't get over it and that's why you won't entertain a courtship of any kind. The other half think he must have been so terrible you're afraid of men."

Sarah stared at Minna in astonishment. It had never occurred to her she could be the subject of such speculation. Brad and Kate were the only people she could talk freely to about the past. She undoubtedly bored them to death talking about nothing else when they visited but couldn't stop herself. The lie she lived kept her from speaking of the past to anyone else.

Because she had chosen to keep her own name and to give her father's name as her "husband's," she couldn't even talk about Matt and use his name. Sometimes she ached to talk about him.

"Kate said she met him once," Minna said almost shyly.

"Yes, she did." *Three years after the last time I saw him, damn her, and I will never forgive her for what she did that day. We continue to care for each other, but it will always be there between us, and she knows it as well as I do.*

"Both halves of the town are wrong, Minna. You can't say every time a widow remarries that she didn't love her first husband. Perhaps I believed myself once that I had to stop loving him before I could care for someone else. I know now that's impossible. You must come to love someone else in a different way, and hold them both in your heart."

"You did love him very much then?"

"I remember once thinking I loved him more than any woman ever loved any man, and then I realized how silly that was, how vain, really, to believe I was even capable of that. But I never got over the idea that perhaps other people love as much, but none more."

Sarah felt heat in her cheeks and looked away, slightly embarrassed to have confessed this.

"But that's not what stops you from considering another man? You've discouraged several right here in Tavaras."

"Mr. Garvey is older than my father."

"Yes, he is, but some women like older men. If you don't feel that way, what about Mr. Norstrom?"

Sarah considered how to explain her objection to Norstrom. "My family are a rather sober lot, you know. I mean when I was little my brothers teased me, but when we grew up that sort of thing stopped. We were all very serious. Laurie's father was a terrible tease. He could joke about anything, even terrible, frightening things, and I came to see that can be a good way to diminish fears and make life sunnier. But you see, he was never mean about it. It was a gentle teasing that invited you to laugh with him, and Mr. Norstrom is just the opposite. He has a very clever tongue, but he uses it to wound and hurt. I don't like him very much."

"I see," Minna said. "I never thought about it before, but I do see what you mean, and what about Thad then? Why is it you're keeping him at arm's length?"

Now they came to the heart of the matter. The Blackburns and Stewarts had been friends since the families met on their sojourn to these parts many years ago, when the land was still part of Mexico. When the Stewarts decided their oldest son should take a wife and start producing grandchildren, they accepted Henry's suggestion that Sarah Hammond met every requirement perfectly.

The Blackburns wanted Laurie to have a better life as the step-daughter of the wealthiest rancher in the area—and a better chance of marrying well. The Stewarts wanted Stewart heirs, and Sarah had proven child-bearing ability.

Finding herself once again judged like a prospective broodmare amused Sarah at first. So did Thad Stewart's half-hearted suit, which suggested he wanted to please his parents with a minimum of effort. Recently, however, he had shown signs of taking Sarah's indifference as a challenge, and the Blackburn-Stewart matchmaking no longer amused her.

Sarah didn't want to hurt Minna's feelings but did want to make her understand, and stop pushing her at Thad Stewart. She said, "I met Thad only a few weeks after I first came to Tavaras. He's a very nice man and a good friend, I think, but I don't love him, and he doesn't love me. Do you think it would be wise to marry him and spend every night for the rest of my life lying in his bed wishing I were somewhere else?"

Minna looked taken aback at such frankness, but she pressed on. "Do you think you'll find what you had before again? Don't you think that maybe that only comes once, when you're very young, and that even if your husband had lived it would have—mellowed?"

"Perhaps," Sarah admitted. "Did Kate really tell you about us? Did she tell you I came west in the first place to marry someone else?"

"No, dear, she was very discreet. You shouldn't think she talked out of turn."

"I know she would never do that." *She wouldn't even tell Matt about Laurie.* Sarah told Minna how she came west to marry one man and fell in love with another. She left out Comanches and Kate's real part in events. To people in Tavaras, Kate was Mrs. Bradford Denham.

"One of the greatest lessons I learned," Sarah concluded, "was that nothing could be worse than to marry the wrong man and then meet the right one. That almost happened, and it would have been my fault, you see, for settling for someone I never even pretended to myself I loved. Love would come later, I thought. Now I know better. There has to be something there to build on right from the beginning."

"You've let that experience influence you too much. I know of many marriages that started only with respect and affection. Love came later."

"Perhaps. When the people didn't really know each other and they came to know each other inside the marriage, but I already know Thad well enough to know that if I married him it would be just like his parents' marriage, not like what I had, and not like what you and Henry have either."

"And what's wrong with Thaddeus and Amanda's marriage, pray tell?"

"Nothing, if that's all she wants. Mr. Stewart treats her well, but it's quite evident that she's not that important in his life, except as the mother of his sons, son even. Mr. Stewart is the kind for whom only the oldest son matters. The heir."

"That's unkind, Sarah, and untrue. Thaddeus himself would tell you you're wrong."

"I'm sure he would. In words, but not by actions. For him, and for Thad, I think, a wife is necessary only for children. Now Jesse, Jesse will make a husband much more to my taste, I think."

"Jesse is frivolous." Minna echoed the feelings of the whole Stewart clan toward the younger son.

"Since he's too young for me and his heart's spoken for, even if Julia Farrell is being a fool at the moment, it's irrelevant, but if Jesse is frivolous, then what I need is someone frivolous."

Minna abandoned the subject of the younger Stewart son. "If," she paused and gave Sarah a stern look, "and I'm not saying you're right about the Stewart marriage, but if you are, then there's no reason why your own marriage to Thad would have to be the same. Your marriage would be what you made of it."

"Exactly. And I'm going to start making it what I want by marrying a man who suits me. Not Thad Stewart."

"And what sort of man is going to suit you?"

"I don't know. I haven't met him yet."

"What was your husband like, Sarah? Kate said he was a Texan."

Minna was not quite able to keep the disapproval out of her tone, and Sarah smiled knowingly at the older woman.

"Yes, he was Texan, and I suppose he was every bit as outrageous as what you think that means. He was the only man who ever looked right at me and said I was beautiful, and it wasn't just courting talk. He meant it."

Sarah told Minna about pulling rainbows out of the sky. "He made me feel so special. But it was more than that too. I was fresh from the East, the spoiled and pampered daughter of wealthy parents. I saw myself as physically small and frail and female, which is to say not very capable. He made me see my own strength and believe in myself. If I'd been left on my own before I knew him, Heaven only knows what would have become of me, but when it happened, I marched off and did what I had to do. He gave me that."

"But your parents disowned you because of him."

"No, they didn't. My ex-fiancé told them some very ugly, wicked lies. They never knew anything about Laurie's father. It was what they came to believe about me that made them disown me."

"Is there no way to remedy that?"

"Oh, perhaps if I could go back East and see them in person, I could make them listen, but Major Macauley is an influential man from an influential family. Undoing what he did is probably beyond me now."

Minna finished the last of her chores, and the conversation ended. Sarah said no more than good night to Henry in the parlor and went upstairs to bed.

DEEPLY DISTURBED, Minna reported what she had learned to her husband. Her conversation with Sarah had her half convinced Thad Stewart's suit was doomed. Henry, however, saw the information only as ammunition.

"If what she wants is flowery talk, we'll just have to prime the boy a little. He can shower her with compliments if that's what it takes."

Minna stared at her husband in dismay. She had been present at Thad Stewart's birth and knew first the boy and then the man almost as well as her own sons. Much as Minna hated to admit it, she agreed with Sarah. Like his father, Thad would always put the Bar S first. She didn't agree with her husband. No script could turn Thad into the sort of man Sarah wanted.

Yet that night Minna let Henry talk her out of her doubts about the wisdom of persisting in plotting marriage between Sarah and Thad.

32

October 1874, Santa Fe, New Mexico

BRAD DENHAM LOOKED up from reviewing a contract to see Kate staring blankly at the eastern newspaper they'd been so pleased to find.

Stopping in Tavaras to see Sarah on the way to Santa Fe had been a mistake. Sometimes he thought seeing Sarah at all was a mistake. The women hugged and chatted and enjoyed each other, and he enjoyed both of them. And they all pretended that the conflicting tangle of emotions between them didn't exist.

Santa Fe was one of Brad's favorite stopovers. They had two rooms in the hotel, a sitting room and bedroom. The open windows let in the warm fall air and lively sounds of a bustling populace. Brad toyed with the idea of forgetting about business and taking Kate's mind off the problems with Sarah by luring her into a walk through town.

No, he decided, pleasure would have to wait until tomorrow. Not only had he promised to decide on this contract by morning, Kate wasn't going to enjoy sightseeing until she talked through her concern.

Why, he wondered, had he and Kate adopted Sarah so thoroughly in so short a time? Why now when things were so difficult were they unable to let go? Perhaps because they each knew they would never have children of their own. Myra failed a little more with each passing year, but whatever the future might hold for them all, the time for children had passed.

Kate threw the paper down. "What are you thinking about?" she asked.

"You, me, Myra—fate and fortune. Basically, that perhaps we feel the way we do about Sarah because we have no children and never will. If I had a daughter I'd like to believe she would be like Sarah. I'd want her to have a little less of that rigid New England pride maybe."

"It's Sarah I'm thinking about too, but not quite so benevolently. If I were really her mother, I think I'd slap her silly and hope to knock some sense into her."

"Harsh words for someone who can't raise a smile for a day or two every time we visit and leave."

"Oh, I know. Every time we see her she says she's ready to put the past behind her and get on with her life, and all she talks about is the past. Right now is the best opportunity for a better life she's ever going to have—she's not getting any younger—and she won't even consider it. She's going to spend the rest of her life slaving away at menial jobs with the only hope of respite if Laurie marries well. And Laurie's chances aren't enhanced by having a mother who's a drab!

"You think young Stewart is just what the doctor ordered?"

"He's not perfect. She says she doesn't love him and never will, he doesn't love her and never will. But life isn't perfect. Look at us. Look at poor Myra, for God's sake. The kind of love Sarah knew never comes at all to most people. It won't happen twice for her. She's going to have to settle for something less, and Stewart is a damn fine compromise."

Kate glared at him as if daring him to disagree, and he took up the challenge. "She is settling for something less. The problem is what she's settling for isn't what you think she should."

Instead of arguing, Kate got up and whirled around the room. When she sat down again she no longer seemed sure of herself but tentative.

"When you were at your business luncheon, I visited with the Delgados. They introduced me to a rancher, a Lucius Farrell. It seems his ranch is one of two very large operations that occupy a valley between Rye Wells and Tavaras."

Brad gave a low whistle. "The enemy."

"Yes, but when we were in Tavaras and hearing the Stewarts go on and on about how Farrell has lost his mind and is starting a range war he can't win, I believed every word. Yet when I heard Farrell today, I wanted to believe him, and he says it's the Stewarts who are causing the trouble.

Kate still seemed unsure of herself as she continued. "Farrell seems decent, honest. His daughter has just broken it off with her childhood sweetheart, and he brought her here hoping to cheer her up, which isn't working, by the way. She looks like an unhappy ghost. Then again, it's hard to see how he could cheer anyone up. He's one of those widowers who's never going to remarry. He talks about his wife as if she's still alive."

Brad thought of all the town gossip and news they had heard in Tavaras during their visit with Sarah. "But isn't that exactly what the Stewarts say? He was so devoted to his wife it was an obsession, and now that she's gone he's lost his equilibrium, which is why he's starting a range war he can't win."

Kate nodded. "That's what they said, but according to him, Stewart Senior has always fancied an empire, and now that he's reached that certain age when men take notions...."

Kate paused for emphasis. She and Brad often argued the matter. He maintained all men did not get notional at a certain age. Kate swore they did. Once Brad acknowledged her point with a nod, she went on.

"He's sure it's a temporary emotional aberration on Stewart's part. They've never been friends, but they've always been good neighbors. He also says his ranch would have gone to Stewart grandchildren anyway, because his daughter's sweetheart was the younger Stewart boy, and what caused their quarrel is the trouble between their families."

"Are you saying that you believe Farrell, and you think the Stewarts are liars?"

"No. Somebody's lying, but I wouldn't hazard a guess as to which side, and my impression was that Stewart Senior is still very much in control of everything he owns. He could be causing the trouble, and his sons could genuinely believe it was Farrell."

Brad considered her words, then said, "So you're not disqualifying young Stewart for Sarah over this?"

"No, that's not my point. The thing is...." Kate looked unsure again, then plunged on. "Aside from bringing his daughter here for a change of scene, Farrell is thinking about hiring some gunmen.

He's heard that Stewart is doing that, you see, escalating everything, and he feels he should protect himself if that's the case."

Brad saw how all their conversation tied in. A remark overheard in Denver last year had told him what Matt Slade had become.

"Kate."

"I didn't say anything. Farrell wouldn't listen to a woman on the subject anyway. I wanted to talk it over with you first. What if—what if she saw him again? What if she finally realized that the young man she loved doesn't even exist any more? Maybe she'd finally realize how impossible it is. She'd stop holding on to memories and start to live again. Am I so wrong?"

Brad selected a cigar from his silver case and went through the elaborate ritual of lighting it, taking time to examine the idea with care. "How many times in the last years have you and I sworn we would never interfere in her life like that again? In anyone's life like that?"

Kate made a face. "Two hundred and fifty-nine."

"And you've changed your mind?"

"A little. This time we'll do it your way."

"And what does that mean?"

"It means we won't tell her."

Brad couldn't help but laugh at that. "You realize the chances of anything coming of it would be small." He ticked off the contingencies on his fingers. "First of all, even if I recommend Taney's bunch to Farrell, there's no guarantee he'll try to hire them."

Kate nodded. "And even if Farrell tries, there's no guarantee Taney will take the job."

"Right. And finally, of course, even if both those things happen, Rye Wells is Farrell's town, and Tavaras is Stewart's town. Taney's men could go to work for Farrell, and Slade and Sarah might never cross paths."

They looked at each other for a moment, then Kate smiled at him. "See? It's all a matter of Providence anyway, and I'm not being an interfering bitch again."

"We're both interfering again. We just don't know how much."

"You'll do it then?"

"You introduce me to Farrell, and I'll find some way to recommend Taney's gunmen. I suppose it's not too dishonest. They probably aren't any better or worse than any others of their ilk."

Kate thanked him by making sure he forgot all about business for the rest of the afternoon after all.

33

November 1874, Goldville, Colorado

MATT CAME BACK to consciousness as a diver gone too deep breaks the water's surface to air, heart pounding, lungs aching, aware the depths had almost kept him this time. He made no effort to move; breathing took all his strength. Pain, medicinal smells and a strange, hostile voice filled his senses.

"If he doesn't come around long enough to get some water down in the next day, it's all over, and there's no use blaming me. He should have died days ago."

"I should have died years ago, and squirming out from under blame won't save your ass. He dies, you die." Beau's voice sounded gritty, different.

Matt got his eye half open and saw Beau nose to nose with the stranger. He caught sight of Luke and Swede. No Roddy, no young Rio. Oh, God. His slight movement stopped the argument.

"Matt!" Beau looked as strange as he sounded. It had been days since a shave, and Beau had slept in his clothes for at least that long. Matt tried to smile and knew he failed.

The stranger said, "We'd better not waste time on talk," and pressed the rim of a cup against Matt's lips.

The cool feel of liquid triggered a terrible thirst. Matt gulped greedily, then dove back into pain-free darkness.

Waking again to silence, Matt lay still, moving only his eye to examine the parts of the room visible in the dim light. A hotel room.

The light grew stronger, dawn not dusk. Increasingly alert, he remembered several short instances of consciousness in the same hazy detail as the first. Heavy pain weighed on his chest, intensifying and ebbing with each breath, but he remembered the cause of that.

Slowly, carefully, Matt turned his head. A second bed took almost all the floor space in the room. The occupant regarded Matt solemnly, and the sight made Matt feel a whole lot better.

"Have you decided after all not to die?" Roddy asked.

The amused cynicism of his expression was familiar, as was the flash of white teeth in the dark face, but Roddy's mustache blended into weeks of beard growth, and the long narrow face was thinner than ever before.

"The others?" Matt whispered.

"Luke and Swede have only minor wounds. Rio and Beau have serious wounds, but unlike us, they never tried to die. We have caused Beau much aggravation."

At this Matt managed a weak smile. A few minutes later Swede showed up, then Luke. Delighted to find Matt awake, they almost spilled the broth they carried. Their talk helped Matt orient himself—and remember.

Coming to this mining town had been a disaster. Goldville's town council lured Beau to take the job with promises of support, huge bonuses and outright lies. In fact the gang terrorizing the town could count on over thirty men in a showdown.

The few independent citizens lost what courage they had when faced with the possible consequences of their own actions. Mitigating the vengeance they expected from the Allertons after the gang killed Beau Taney and company became the town folks' only concern.

As Luke and Swede, surprisingly gentle nurses, spooned broth, Rio squeezed into the room. Two years ago, Whitey Bascomb had taken the marshal's job and a young wife in one of the towns they worked.

Only seventeen when he joined them, Rio probably answered to an ordinary name like Richard until he decided to re-christen himself with something more to his liking. He could be as wild as the unruly light brown hair and dancing green eyes promised, but even before this trouble he had earned the right to any name he wanted.

Hunched with worse wounds than the other two, Rio dropped onto the foot of Matt's bed and without prompting began relating what had gone on while Matt was oblivious.

"Swede carried you to the doctor's—like somebody my size would carry a baby."

Above average height, Rio was a lot smaller than Swede. They were all a lot smaller than Swede.

"Luke and me brought Roddy along. He bled a river right up the street. Beau had a leg shot out from under him. The bullet went right through and left a nice clean break, so he used your Yellow Boy as a crutch. Guess once you dropped it in the dirt he figured it wasn't sacred after all."

Rio paused to assess the impact of this information on Matt, then grinned irreverently and went on. "Sowers took one look at you and said he wasn't wasting his time digging for that bullet." He pointed to make sure Matt understood which one. "Said it would just kill you faster than you were going anyway. Then he looked at Roddy and said he'd already lost so much of that blue blood he wasn't going to make it either, to throw him on the tailings heap too."

Now Rio's cat's eyes were hard. "If Beau hadn't done something about that, I guess one of the rest of us would, but honest to God, Matt, he was scarier than I've ever seen him. He stuck the muzzle of his pistol between old Sowers' eyes and told him as soon as one of you died, so did he. I guess even that son of a bitch doctor could see not only he meant it but none of the rest of us was going to even try to stop him."

As Rio continued with the story while rolling himself a cigarette, Matt pictured it, a sullen, uncooperative doctor, and Beau, determined not only to impose his will on the doctor, but on God himself if necessary. It must have been some scene all right.

Seeing Roddy had finished his liquid breakfast, Rio lit the cigarette, then leaned over and put it between Roddy's lips. Starting to build himself another smoke, he continued with the story.

"After everybody got all patched up, you'd think it would have got better, but it got worse. Roddy'd kind of come to and look pretty perky and then sink right back and try to die again, and you were laying there like a corpse already. Old Sowers kept saying it was a waste of time. Seemed like every day he and Beau were hating each other a little more. The day after you woke up the first time, the damn fool started complaining, and he said something about all the fuss over 'the greaser and the white trash.' Beau didn't even go for his gun, he tried to tear his throat out. Swede had to kind of keep hold of him."

As Rio imitated a bear hug, Swede nodded and said, "It is a different kind of crazy he gets for sure."

Rio went on, "Yeah, well, he had me half-scared, and I'm on his side. You should have heard him. 'You are talking about Jaime Francisco Rodriguez y Candelaria.' Hell, I can't even say it right. He said it like Roddy does, you know, all Spanish?"

Matt glanced at Roddy, who looked as tired as Matt felt, except for his eyes, which were glinting with suppressed laughter. Roddy had heard this before, of course.

Rio stopped to light the second cigarette and spoke around smoke. "And then he says, 'And you are talking about Matthew Slade, and either one of them was born more man than you'll ever be.'"

Rio shook his head, "I know it sounds funny, telling it, but we were all starting to worry Sowers was going to give the two of you poisoned medicine or something, just to get at Beau, and he's the only doctor for miles around. So we talked Beau into going back to Kansas City for a visit. That's why he's not here now."

Beau had an old friend in Kansas City who kept mail for him and even answered some of the more obvious inquiries. Beau hadn't gone anywhere without Roddy as keeper since the two of them first partnered together. Was Beau ready for a trip like that on his own? Matt decided he was.

After some clean-up chores, the nurses all left to get their own breakfasts, leaving Matt and Roddy alone again. Exhausted by even the slight effort of listening, Matt drifted toward sleep when he heard Roddy's low voice.

"He blames himself for taking this job and bringing this on us."

"They did a powerful good job of sugar coating everything. We're lucky to get out of this alive, and there's no way it's Beau's fault."

"Yes. Like you, we are all surprised to find ourselves still alive." After a pause, Roddy said tentatively, "It has been more than six months since a spell. That one was not so bad."

Calling on the last of his strength, Matt said, "He'll be all right, Roddy. You've both been all right for a long time. You just never noticed." With that Matt let himself sink into sleep.

After only a few days, Matt found that while his body needed the bed rest to heal, his mind was like a caged animal inside his skull. The nights tortured him with a mixture of dreams, nightmares and memories.

Artillery boomed. Men and horses screamed. The smells of battle smoke, of sick, starving and dying men filled his nostrils long after he came awake drenched with sweat.

Far worse, however, were the times his mind conjured up Comanches, a courtroom, a jail cell, and Sarah, Sarah, not just near death in his arms, but dead. Then not dead but running from him, always beyond his reach, never looking back.

In the grip of those horrors, Matt never woke by himself. Roddy's hand on his shoulder brought him back to the hotel room to lie awake as long as he could, fighting sleep and memories.

In a strange reversal, the days provided his only real rest. As they passed the time playing cards and talking, Matt learned more about the men he rode with in those few days than in the years before and gave away more about himself.

Playing poker with bedridden men presented no problems for young innovators like Luke, Swede and Rio. They made the head of Roddy's bed the foot so that Matt and Roddy faced each other, then requisitioned a table the right size to fit over the two beds and extra chairs from what Rio described with a sardonic grin as "grateful" town residents.

A week after Matt rejoined the living, cards littered the table when the tapping sound of a man coming down the hall on crutches stopped all five men in mid-play.

In spite of the broken leg, Beau appeared impossibly rested and healthy. He must have enjoyed his visit to civilization mightily, although it had taken many reassuring telegrams to keep him there even a few days.

"You two look as sorry as you did the day I left," he said by way of greeting. "How soon before we can get out of this damn place?"

"Dr. Sowers says another week for Roddy. He's been up and about a little. Two for Matt," Luke answered.

Beau replied to this with a more varied spate of profanity than Matt had ever heard, then went on. "On the train, I had an idea. How about if we had the mayor's nice new carriage? You think these two could ride in that to the railroad?"

"Sure they could," Rio said, "but nobody in this town is going to let us borrow a carriage."

"This town owes us a lot of money. We'll take it in part payment."

Luke and Swede looked at each other, then down at the cards. Rio got busy with a cigarette, but Matt wanted out of this town, and more particularly this bed, badly.

"These folks don't see it that way, Beau. They figure since they hung the wounded and the extras their posse ran down, we didn't get the job done."

Luke, Swede and Rio looked at Matt in dismay, but the sight of Beau back in one piece had Roddy ready for action too. "They not only do not want to pay, the doctor believes we owe him fees for such extraordinary service, and the hotel wants room and board money. We are very heavily in debt here."

"Then to hell with taking the carriage in payment. We'll just impress the damn thing."

Looking stunned, Rio said, "What about a team? That pair of his is too snorty to be using to take Matt and Roddy over mountain roads in this shape."

Beau wasn't worried. "We'll use Sam and Aurora. We can get them going as a team in a day or two, and it'll take that long to convince the town fathers of the wisdom of paying anyway."

"Aurora?" Roddy's weak whisper was full of horror.

"Now don't you two start in about those spoiled damn bangtails. It will be good for them to do some real work for a change."

Beau switched to a more important subject, glaring at Matt. "If you weren't such a lousy shot, they wouldn't be giving us any trouble about paying, you know. I've never seen so many men with broken legs. You didn't get a one dead center."

Feeling better by the second, Matt defended with an offense. "I hear you used my old Winchester as a crutch."

"You dropped it in the dirt. I carried the new one, didn't I? Would you rather I used it with its pretty walnut stock for a crutch?"

Like Beau, Matt executed a lightning change of subject. "So where are we going after you collect our money from the town heroes?"

To Matt's surprise, Beau didn't just announce the name of a town and details of a new job. He sat in one of the chairs and pulled some papers from his shirt pocket.

"I wired regrets to all the ones who wanted somebody yesterday, or tomorrow for that matter, and all the ones who sounded like what they really want is their grandmother assassinated. That leaves these three."

Beau hesitated a moment, looking strangely unsure of himself. "Two of them are the usual, mining towns with trouble. The third is a rancher who says a long-time neighbor has gotten greedy of a sudden and is starting a range war. He says all he wants is to try to hold him off till he comes to his senses."

Swede accepted the unspoken invitation to give an opinion. "No more towns like this. All those people hide in back of locked doors and Matt and Roddy get shot to pieces. After, there is nothing but meanness."

"There aren't many towns like this," Beau said, but he wasn't arguing.

"If we're voting, I vote with Swede," Luke said. "Maybe we could use something different. A ranch might be a good place to rest up after this business."

Rio nodded, and Beau looked at Roddy.

"I am agreeable to this, Beau, but only if I do not have to listen to you on the subject of Matt and postholes."

"The way I feel right now, I just might help him dig. It has a safe sound." Beau matched the flashing white grin this response evoked from Roddy, then turned to Matt. "What about you?"

"I wouldn't mind learning some more about the cattle business. Where is this place?"

Beau looked down at the letter again. "Near Santa Fe. This rancher, Lucius Farrell, does most of his business in a place called Rye Wells, but it's about the same distance from another town called Tavaras."

"Can't ride the rails to New Mexico."

"Not for a few more years, I guess. Farrell says he doesn't figure things will hot up till spring. If that's where we're going, I'll wire him we'll be there before then. We'll get to someplace that smells better than this, heal up proper, and then start out."

All their heads were bobbing now, and so they decided. They were going to see if they could help a man named Farrell save his ranch near Tavaras in New Mexico Territory.

Matt and Sarah

1875

34

LUCIUS FARRELL ATE breakfast with his daughter in the big ranch house at the L&L. So when the graying, barrel-chested rancher appeared in the bare room attached to the bunkhouse where the ranch hands ate, the men anticipated a break in routine.

"Everyone can relax except Jimmy," Farrell said.

"I hear your saddle horse tore up his foot real good losing a shoe on those rocks yesterday. I bet you want me to take him to town," Jimmy Childers said.

Pouring himself a last cup of coffee, Matt listened to Farrell give the sandy-haired, freckled young cowhand instructions about the horse. Farrell wanted the damaged hoof repaired by the Tavaras blacksmith and no one else. He referred to the smithy in Rye Wells as a butcher.

"I'll take the horse if you'd rather," Matt offered. "The shirt I've got on is the last one I own without more mended than not. I need new shirts."

"You need a whole new wardrobe," Beau said.

Beau never missed an opportunity to point this out. The new Levi Strauss trousers particularly offended his sensibilities. Matt, on the other hand, considered Levis a wonderful wardrobe improvement. The tough cloth, reinforced with rivets at the seams, took months to break in, but his trousers no longer needed mending all the time, and his shirts still did.

Farrell took his time considering Matt's offer, tugging on his short beard. Finally he said, "It's not that my men can't walk into Tavaras, or Stewart's into Rye Wells for that matter, but I think it would be better if you just went along with Jimmy. Sheriff Blackburn and Thaddeus Stewart are close friends. I don't want to give Blackburn any call to accuse me of trying to intimidate anybody in his town."

Farrell smiled apologetically. "He doesn't know you, just your reputation."

Matt shrugged. "Time will pass faster with company."

"Will it ruin your ratio if I go along?" Beau asked.

"No." Farrell laughed. "But if any more of you go, I'll end up sending a roundup crew. I didn't think Tavaras impressed you that much."

When no once else volunteered, Farrell left, and Matt said to Beau. "He's right. The two times we've been to Tavaras, you got cross-eyed looking down your nose."

"I'm tired of cows and men," Beau said. "Even if that town's only whore would crack a mirror, I can admire the women from afar."

"Mr. Farrell's surprised to have you speak up like that," Jimmy said. "We all thought you fellas would spend your time twirling pistols and cleaning your teeth with knives, kind of go your own way and all."

Matt caught Beau's expression and smiled into his coffee cup. Neither man told Jimmy that before Goldville that's about what Matt's five companions would have spent their time doing. That ruckus had changed things. With Jimmy's outspoken innocence on one side and Beau's cynicism on the other, Matt looked forward to an interesting day.

"I CAN CHOOSE for myself, can't I, Mama?"

For the third time since they started for the general store Laurie asked for reassurance on this point.

"Within reason, sweetheart," Sarah said once more. "You know you can't have your good dress for summer made out of black silk."

"But I get to choose, and there's going to be lots to choose from."

"If the freighters only brought new goods to Mr. Michel yesterday, there should still be a nice selection." Giving this answer Sarah felt a tug at her heartstrings, remembering that at Laurie's age she had thought nothing of choosing material for three or four dresses at a time from bolts of cloth that filled entire rooms in Boston shops. At best there would be half a dozen suitable materials for Laurie to choose from.

"And it will be done soon because of Aunt Minna's new sewing machine."

"Sooner than by hand anyway. You can't wear a summer dress for a while, you know."

Sarah watched Laurie skip ahead and, far from admonishing Laurie to be more ladylike, had to admonish herself not to skip also.

The mildness of the late March day heralded an early spring, and their heavy winter coats still hung on pegs at Blackburns'. She planned to purchase material for a new dress for Laurie and for herself.

As they approached the store, more and more people filled the sidewalk. Sarah called Laurie back and took her hand. The freighters had delivered more goods than just bolts of cloth, and the whole town seemed to be going to, coming from or already in Michel's store. A tall, lean man in Levis and a faded blue shirt walked out of the store. Something about the way he moved, the way he was built.... Matt.

She froze, jerking Laurie to a halt. Hundreds, no thousands of times Sarah had pictured what would happen if they met again. She would run into his arms, which would be open, welcoming. They would come together with a joyous crash, and everything would be as it had been, should be. Now she stood and stared. Unlike in dreams, her emotions and fears and the lie she had lived for so long anchored her in place.

Staring, taking in every detail, she wondered how she knew him so instantly. Could a heart see in its own way what eyes did not? No words in that deep grainy voice helped her. She knew every inch of his body intimately, had traced the contours of each bone and muscle with her fingers and her lips. The changes jarred her, the beloved sameness called to her. The hat brim shaded his face, a face changed terribly whether in profile or full view as he pivoted toward her.

Dear God, he'd been hurt, hurt terribly. What could cause scars like that on just one side of his face? And the eye patch—that injury must have come at the time of the others that were healed. He must be blind in that eye. A wave of sorrow washed over her, but none of it mattered. Nothing mattered. That was still Matt's face. He was still Matt.

Blood drained from her extremities, pooling into a dead weight low in her stomach. Sarah labored for breath against the tight band constricting her chest as her lips began to tremble and her eyes to burn.

SHE WAS ON HIS blind side. Matt would have walked by had another woman not gasped and started to gape, causing him to turn and look. He stared once again into night sky eyes, shock smashing through him.

Boston! No longer the girl whose image floated agonizingly beyond reach in countless sleepless nights, but still Sarah, Sarah who had been his and still held all the parts of him that mattered, whether she wanted them or not.

The memory of Sarah was Matt's standard of beauty. He compared all things to that memory, and all fell short in some way. Until now. She was more beautiful than the memories, slimmer than when he'd first seen her so long ago but not the wraith of the courtroom. All the sweetness that first drew him to her still reflected from her eyes.

After the shock came the first swift surge of wild joy as he drank in the sight of her. At this distance Matt could see the brightness of her eyes well into tears, watch them brim and spill down her cheeks. One hand cupped as she raised it in a familiar gesture, and metal glinted in the spring sunshine.

Married! He'd expected that, hadn't he? More than married, there would be children.

Aware at last of the small figure holding Sarah's other hand, Matt glanced down into a smaller, younger version of Sarah's face, and into sapphire eyes identical to those that had looked back at him from every mirror until that night in the Charon jail. He saw something else, a difference in the tapering of the child's jaw line that gave her face a kittenish look. An aching, half-forgotten memory of his sister Betsy flashed through his mind.

Recognition almost took him off his feet, his knees started to buckle, and he swayed slightly where he stood. Jimmy Childers' hand on his arm steadied him, but Matt resisted Jimmy's efforts to pull him away.

"Come on, Matt, we should go. This isn't good."

Matt shrugged Jimmy off. He needed to see more of Sarah and of the little girl who leaned into Sarah's skirts and met his searching gaze, unafraid and curious. Gradually he became aware of the tenor of the scandalized, half-frightened conversations around him, and then Beau seized him by the shoulders.

"What the hell's gotten into you? I've never seen you act like such a damn fool. Move!"

Matt fought Beau's determined shove long enough to send one last incredulous look at Sarah, then let Beau push him toward the horses. Once he was moving, he lengthened his stride and pulled away from Beau, but on reaching Sam, he stood there, leaning against the saddle, staring at his package of paper-wrapped shirts. Beau came up behind him, took the package and shoved it in the saddlebags, then untied Matt's overcoat from behind the saddle and threw it over his shoulders.

"You all right?"

Soaked with sweat and trembling, Matt came out of his trance and realized the sight he must present and what conclusions Beau had drawn.

"If I start back now, will you wait for Farrell's horse with Jimmy?"

"You're not going anywhere by yourself like this."

"Yes, I am. I need to be alone. This isn't something to talk about. Understand me? Leave it alone."

"Put the damn coat on right then. If you can climb on the horse in one try, I guess you can sit him."

Matt swung up on the gelding easily enough. "Thanks."

"Yeah, well, if I find you've fallen off in the road somewhere when we come along later, it's going to make me mad enough to finally shoot you."

Matt didn't even try to fake a smile, just reined Sam toward the L&L.

At the ranch, Matt managed to get the saddle and bridle off Sam and turn him out. He retreated to the empty bunkhouse and sat on his bed. Unable to come to terms with what he had seen in town, he went back to the past. Except for the dreams that haunted him, most of the time Matt kept the memories of the time with Sarah buried deep in his mind.

Two or three times a year, though, he lost his resolve, went off by himself and let every moment of their brief time together unfold in his mind—the first time he saw her in her neat traveling costume, the first real taste of love, Sarah all around him, flesh against flesh, smiling at him, his as he was hers. Matt savored all those long ago feelings of what it was like, to be young and in love and to be loved in return. The sensations came back full strength, the honeyed taste of her mouth, the salt of her tears and sweat, the cloud of her hair covering them both.

He avoided the good memories because the bad followed inevitably behind, Sarah near death in his arms, the humiliation of the courtroom, the nightmare in the jail.

The meeting with Kate Pell and Brad Denham had always seemed a small thing, part of the bad maybe, but too small a part to dwell on. Now that day loomed large. Why hadn't they told him he had a daughter? Was Sarah already married to a man who believed that little girl was his?

Could he believe anything Pell and Denham told him? What would a young woman like Sarah do, finding herself with no family to rely on, far from home, expecting a baby and frightened? Would she marry some unsuspecting man, let him believe a child born far too early was his? Never, not Sarah. The husband must know the girl was fathered by someone else. He would have married her anyway, glad to have her. To have Sarah....

Matt heard voices outside. Shadows told him the day had faded away while he sat remembering. Beau and Jimmy had returned and some of the other men too.

Jolted from his reverie, Matt realized he was sitting with his hat and coat still on. Anything that heightened Beau's concern would be too much to deal with.

He catfooted across the room and got his coat and hat on the pegs beside the door fast. He heard Beau and Roddy outside, discussing the trouble in town, and Jimmy, trying to talk them into his idea of "making Matt feel better."

"Just leave him the hell alone," Beau said.

"But if he knew...." Jimmy was almost pleading.

"He knows enough about that little bitch already, leave him alone."

Matt resisted the urge to tear the door off its hinges and go wipe up the yard with Beau's body. Like everyone else who had witnessed the scene in town, Beau knew only what he thought he saw.

Dropping into a chair at the battered table the men used for poker games, Matt picked up the deck of cards as the door opened and men filed into the bunkhouse.

Incredibly, Jimmy had won the argument with Beau, for the gangly youngster headed straight for the table. Damn it, Matt thought savagely, not even tasting soap at the thought.

Jimmy sat across from Matt, not really too sure of himself. "Matt, if you want me to go away and shut up, you just say, but I thought maybe if you knew something about that lady, you'd feel better. She's a real nice lady, and she wouldn't ever do anything like that on purpose. She works real hard, and maybe she was just tired or something, and she got surprised."

Jimmy's voice tapered off, realizing perhaps that he wasn't making much sense. Everyone who was there thought Sarah was surprised, surprised and scared out of her wits.

But Matt perceived that Jimmy could tell him at least some of the things he wanted so desperately to know. He also knew he'd better not appear too interested. Both Beau and Roddy were listening hard, and trying harder to look like they weren't.

"I know she was just surprised," Matt said carefully. "She doesn't look like a lady who'd hurt anybody's feelings on purpose. What's her name?"

Relief slid across Jimmy's open face. "That's Mrs. Hammond. She works at the café right there in town, Mrs. Canaday's place."

Jimmy looked expectant, waiting for further encouragement, but Matt almost got lost again. Hammond! How could she still be Hammond? He struggled to frame an appropriate question. "Why does she work? Can't her husband provide a living?"

"She's a widow. She came here a few years ago with her daughter. They live with Sheriff Blackburn and his wife, but everybody says it's not charity, she pays the same as at the boarding house. She is sort of stiff-necked, they say. She's a Yankee from back East." Jimmy offered this negative tidbit with a worried look.

From Boston, Jimmy. She's from Boston, where she lived in a big house three stories high and had servants and everything she ever wanted.

"What's wrong with the men in Tavaras that a lady like that is still a widow?" Matt said.

Jimmy launched into a description of the men in Tavaras who had shown interest in the pretty widow and been discouraged, and the speculation the townsfolk indulged in as to the reasons for Sarah's behavior.

"But I guess that's going to end real soon now," Jimmy concluded. "At least everybody says Thad Stewart's going to succeed where those others didn't. After all he's good friends with the Blackburns, and they're in favor. She'll listen to what they say, I guess."

"Stewart's old enough to be her father!" Matt said—too vehemently, for Roddy shot him an appraising look.

"No, no," Jimmy assured him. "The Stewart we pointed out to you that time, that's Thaddeus Stewart who owns the Bar S. He has two sons, Thaddeus, Jr., we all always called him Thad, everybody does. Then there's the three girls. They're all married. Then there's Jesse. He's about my age."

"So it's Thad, Jr., courting Bos-, Mrs. Hammond."

"Well, he's trying. So far he's not doing any better than those others, but everybody figures she'll come around pretty soon. I guess it's not real nice, but the way things are, the Bar S making all this trouble, well, you know, around here we sort of enjoy some funning about it."

Matt wanted to keep squeezing Jimmy for every morsel of information and to ask about the girl, but he'd already shown too much interest. Roddy could be a perceptive devil, and Beau had too much to chew on. Matt had a lot to think over himself.

35

AFTER LOCKING THE back door of the café behind her, Sarah stood on the step, staring into the dark. Even when the March days warmed with the promise of spring, as the sun set, the temperature fell and winter returned. Sarah breathed deep of the fresh, cold air, clearing away the day's smoke and food odors. Although she seldom finished work before dark except in the longest days of summer, Sarah considered her job in Adelaide Canaday's café the best she ever had.

Addie had another employee, Mabel Lanning, who came in early in the morning and left after the lunch rush. Sarah started later and had time with Laurie in the morning. The café closed on Sundays, and Sarah also had one half-day off every week.

She had seen Matt on her half day. After that encounter she had felt nervous and expectant, sure Matt would seek her out. But as the days passed with no sign, the expectancy faded and a deep weariness settled like lead across her shoulders and in her heart.

The unremitting hell of the last week added to her misery. As soon as Matt turned away after the awful scene in front of Michel's, indignant friends and acquaintances surrounded her, determined to offer comfort. Not one person gave an iota of credence to what Sarah, searching her mind frantically, seized upon to explain herself.

Then, of course, there was Laurie. With a seven-year-old's belief in the omniscience of her mother, she asked question after question Sarah could not answer.

"Now that he knows about me, he'll come to see me, won't he, Mama?"

For once Sarah regretted telling Laurie the truth. No answer satisfied the child. Nothing stopped the steady stream every time they were alone. And each question cut like a razor. Every night as Sarah left the café she prayed that Laurie would be asleep, and she had not been, not once.

The emotional assault had peaked on Sunday. Sarah engaged in an unacknowledged war of wills with the Blackburns every week. They did their best to maneuver her into the church pew next to Thad Stewart, and she did her best to use Laurie as a small duenna between her and Thad. After church the Stewarts joined the Blackburns for Sunday dinner.

Sarah often thought Henry Blackburn's steel gray hair and the heavy lines of his face and body fit his personality exactly. Kind and honorable, Henry also was iron willed and chock full of strong opinions. On Sunday he started detailing Sarah's "ordeal" the minute everyone sat down to dinner.

Laurie put down her fork and made no attempt to eat, her young face pale and grim. Sarah trusted the memory of Heber to ensure Laurie's silence about their secrets, but her heart ached watching her daughter's reaction to Henry's words.

"I'm debating going to see Farrell, telling him to keep his gunmen out of town. He should know better than to let men like that come to my town, scaring respectable folks half out of their wits. Decent women like Sarah shouldn't be subjected to that."

"That would be pretty partisan, Henry. After all we've hired a crew of men like that ourselves. You can't tell them not to buy what they need in the town's stores because you don't like what they do for a living."

Sarah shot Thad Stewart a grateful glance. Maybe she had no intention of marrying him, or ever letting this nonsense Henry and his father were concocting proceed to a courtship, but Thad really was a decent man and more fair minded than either Henry or his father.

"Well, I can give him reasons to keep at least that one out of my town. I saw him myself a month or so ago. Not only is he a Texas gunfighter, the look of him is enough to scare a woman with a lot less delicate sensibilities than Sarah. He probably asked for whatever it was scarred him up so bad, and he probably looked meaner than a nightmare even before anyway."

Laurie's throat rippled in a retching motion, and something tore inside Sarah. She had told everyone that her reaction to Matt was because of his resemblance to someone she'd once known. Of course no one believed her.

Sarah stood up and dropped her napkin on the table, close to tears and making no effort to conceal the fact. "I can't bear any more of this talk. I've told you over and over the reason for my sorry reaction to that man. If I considered him frightening or evil looking, I would have averted my eyes, not stared. You will have to excuse us. Laurie and I are going to Gilbrides' right now."

Sarah slipped from the Blackburn-Stewart trap most Sunday afternoons by visiting her best friend in Tavaras, Emily Gilbride. That Sunday she showed up hours early, apologizing for interrupting the Gilbrides' dinner and in genuine need of Emily's gentle company.

Shivering now with the cold, Sarah left the café's back step. Her emotion had stopped the Blackburns from saying more about Matt in her presence. The rest of the town lost interest as the days passed, but Laurie grew more and more difficult each night.

The shortest route home from the café ran through this alley and the next, bringing her to Blackburns' back door. In this quiet little town, Sarah felt no fear walking through the alleys at night.

As she neared the only street she crossed, his voice came out of the darkness, surrounding her, enclosing her as in a rough embrace.

"Why didn't those friends of yours tell me I have a daughter, Boston? Why didn't you?"

"Matt? Matt!" Deciding where the voice came from, Sarah ran straight for him. As she got close enough to throw herself at him, hard hands clamped around her upper arms, holding her in a bruising grip. She stood on her tiptoes to keep from swinging in the air.

"None of that now. The time for that's long past."

Having failed so many times to make herself stop loving him, Sarah had long ago given up trying. From the beginning she dammed every negative feeling of anger or betrayal deep inside. At this rough treatment and rougher words, those feelings burst forth in a raging flood.

"None of that? After eight years, in an empty, dark alley you can't even spare your whore a hug, your slut a kiss? Damn you! Damn you straight to hell!"

"Quit that! You should never even hear words like that. You quit talking like that."

"Hear words like that! I've had words like that thrown at me, along with the garbage. That's what I am, remember? I'm a whore, a slut, a harlot."

"Quit it!"

"Not even good enough for a hug in a dark alley with no respectable citizens around to see, that's me, your whore, the mother of your bastard. Do you know what it was like to explain to a four-year-old that yes, she is a bastard, but it's not her fault? It's my fault because I'm a whore. I'm a...."

"Quit it!"

This time Matt shook her so hard she did stop her furious rant. "You quit that talk. You know you're not any of those things, and I never thought it."

"The hell you didn't! All those letters to the prison coming back marked 'Refused.' Me like a fool trying to visit you there anyway, and that disgusting guard saying you wouldn't see me. 'Prisoners don't get many privileges, but they don't have to see nobody they don't want to, and he don't want to see you.'" Sarah imitated the guard's sneering tone.

"And like a bigger fool I even went back to hear it again, and it wasn't any better, even if that time Brad kept them from pushing me up against a wall and telling me how I could visit with *them* in some back room."

"What are you talking about? I was locked up in that prison, and there weren't any letters. There weren't any visits. You never wrote, Sarah. You never came!"

The agony in his voice sliced right through her fury. The truth hit them both at the same time. Sarah heard his sharply indrawn breath that matched her own. His grip on her arms loosened and her heels hit the ground.

They stood there like that, turned to statues by the enormity of it.

"Tell me he couldn't do that to us, Matt. Tell me we wouldn't have let him. Even Carter...."

"Most likely it didn't even cost him much. Prison guards don't get paid a lot."

With a small moan Sarah burrowed in against him between the open edges of his wool coat. She wept, soaking his shirt with her tears. After a few seconds his arms closed around her, his chin pressed on the top of her head.

When her sobs let up, Sarah mopped up with Matt's handkerchief without leaving the warmth of his chest.

"I thought you were a-a-ashamed of me."

"How could I be ashamed of the best thing that ever happened to me? I'm sure ashamed of what I cost you, but I never regretted a second of the glory of it."

"You thought I just stopped loving you and went away."

"I did. I figured you saw it was no good." After a second he asked, "What's her name?"

"Laura, but somehow everyone ended up calling her Laurie from the time she was born."

"Laurie." His voice was so soft she could barely hear the word, as if he were trying it out. "Why didn't they tell me?"

"Because Kate always thinks she knows best. They weren't even supposed to be there. I was going to bring Laurie and meet you and talk to you again even if you didn't want to talk to me. Then Laurie got sick, really sick with a high fever, and I couldn't get there. I sent Kate a wire and asked her to meet you and give you back your money and talk to you. She said you didn't want to see me, that you turned and walked away, and I always knew she lied about it."

"She didn't lie. I did walk away, but then I went back and talked to them."

"That's lying. You know that's lying. Were you hurt already when she saw you?"

"I was."

"What happened?"

"A bad fight in prison is all."

Sarah closed her eyes and burrowed deeper against him. "That would be part of it too then, part of her thinking you aren't perfect enough. She thinks I should set my cap for somebody like Brad, Brad Denham. He was the one with her when she met you. I was so angry I burned every letter she sent me for months, but then Brad talked me around. Damn her. She helped me so much in the beginning, but...."

"Don't be angry at her. She was right, and you know it."

"No, she wasn't. She wasn't right."

"Sure she was. That Denham fellow is too old for you, but you've finally got your eye on somebody that suits."

"What are you talking about?"

"Stewart."

Sarah raised her head and tried to make out his features in the dark. "Are you telling me you think I'm going to marry Thad Stewart, or that I should?"

"Sure. He sounds like exactly what you need."

"Well, you just think again. There was a time when you told me I should marry Carter. Remember? Your ideas of whom I should marry leave a lot to be desired."

"Aw, come on, Sarah. Stewart isn't like Macauley. Even out at the L&L they all admit he's a decent sort, a real nice man."

"Nice? The world is full of nice men. I suppose you think any one of them is fine for me, as long as it's not you."

"Even Jimmy Childers says you've got too much Yankee stiff neck. Stewart's exactly what you should have, and you know it. Farrell's going to be wiped out if this land war really gets going, but the Stewarts won't be set back too much. He can give you everything you should have."

"Oh, I see, he's nice, and he's rich, and that makes him perfectly suitable as a husband for me and a father for your daughter. When you meet Laurie, you explain all that to her and see how far you get."

Matt stiffened. "What do you mean when I meet her? There's no reason for me to be meeting her. I'd scare her out of her mind."

"She's your daughter, she doesn't scare easily, and meeting you is all she's talked about for days."

"Why would she want to meet me?"

"Why wouldn't a little girl want to meet the father she's been hearing stories about since she was old enough to understand?"

"She thinks her father was somebody named Hammond."

"No, she doesn't. She knows her father's name is Matthew Slade. She knows we didn't marry and why. She's always known."

"Well, she doesn't know I'm him."

"Of course she does. What do you think I told her after we saw you the other day?"

Matt pushed her away from him by the arms again. "You can't mean it. Why would you do that to a little girl? Why couldn't you let her believe her father was some decent man she could be proud of? What's the matter with you?"

"The matter with me? Why should I tell my daughter lies about some made up paper cutout of a man when she has a real father who's more than enough for anyone to be proud of? Payne talked to me after court that day, you know. He told me that judge said they should have been pinning a medal on you, not sending you to prison."

"So you told her all of it. She not only knows she's illegitimate, she knows her father's a convict and a scarred up gunfighter. How could you do that to a little girl, Sarah? How could you do that to her?"

"Bastard, Matt. Bastard! That's the word that sticking in your craw so."

"Look, you marry Stewart, and...."

"I'm not marrying anybody I don't want to, and as it happens what I do is none of your business any more. You don't want to meet your daughter. You don't want any part of me. Well, that's just fine. You go to hell and don't want us!"

Sarah pulled away and took off running across the street and into the alley at the other side. Before she reached Blackburns', her blood pounded in her ears even more loudly than her own sobbing breath and her wet cheeks felt icy. She collapsed on the back steps, trying to stop the tears and regain control of her breathing. She couldn't go inside like this.

As the sobs let up, leaden weariness assailed her again. All these years she believed she had escaped the worst of Carter's wrath and at least lessened the impact of his vengeance on Matt. Now she saw what he had actually done to them. And even faced with the truth, Matt still wanted to push her off on someone else, still didn't want her.

For the first twenty years of her life she had been blessed with every good fortune. When Matt told her some people never got anything they wanted, she thought he exaggerated. But over the last years she had accepted that she was now one of those very people.

At last she pushed to her feet, ready to go inside. She did have some things—responsibilities, obligations and terrible answers for Laurie's questions.

MATT LISTENED TO Sarah's running footsteps fade, then followed her slowly out of the alley. He turned in the street, then stopped, totally disoriented. He couldn't remember in which direction he'd left his horse, and the shadows closed in on him, causing a moment of panic as if he'd gone totally blind. He started down the street in the direction he'd turned, then stopped again as he stumbled against the edge of the wooden walk.

Weaving down the street like a drunk. He stepped up on the walk and leaned his aching head against the front of some shop. The cold bit more sharply on the right side of his face.

Matt laughed or thought he did. What would the people of Tavaras think if they could see him now? Right now the fearsome Texas gunman was leaning against a wall because he couldn't stay on his feet without support, just a pain-filled one-eyed man, crying pain-filled one-eyed tears.

36

TIME HAD IN NO way dimmed Matt's memory of how relentless Sarah could be in pursuit of something she wanted. He vowed to stay away from her and from Tavaras. Sarah might be stubborn, but when she was proven wrong, she would do the sensible thing and marry Stewart.

Years of riding with men like Beau and Roddy had smoothed away some of Matt's rough edges. He recognized things like silk, satin and velvet these days. He no longer felt awkward and ill at ease in the offices or homes of men like Farrell, and he had most of what he'd earned from Beau and some of his poker winnings from the last years stashed away in a couple of banks.

He knew none of that mattered. Any association with a gunman would ruin Sarah's reputation in Tavaras in short order. She deserved a good life, and that meant a husband like Stewart.

As the enemy, the Stewarts were a common topic of conversation at the ranch. The L&L and the Bar S shared a huge valley, with the Bar S, almost twice as big, spilling out and spreading to the north. A smaller holding buffered the two large outfits for about half their mutual boundary in a pie-shaped wedge, but the Circle K didn't factor in the coming range war. The owner had died some months ago, and his widow wanted to sell out.

Using the pretext of needing to understand the enemy better, Matt not only listened every time conversation turned to the Stewart family, he probed.

Otto Kirkendahl had taken up his land first, Matt learned, claiming the heart of the valley and the best grazing for the Circle K. Farrell bought his land second; Stewart last. All three ranches prospered on the rich grass and plentiful water here at the foot of the Sangre de Cristo Mountains. Farrell and Kirkendahl used their land to provide good lives for their families. Stewart expanded, investing ranch profits in other businesses.

Several weeks after meeting Sarah, Matt saw the whole Stewart family in Rye Wells. An average-looking man in his sixties, Thaddeus had the rigid carriage and strutting walk of many short men.

His wife accompanied him, and Matt observed the woman with interest. Cynics at the L&L claimed Stewart chose a wife inches taller than himself with an eye to producing taller sons. Knowing what he did about Carter Macauley, Matt didn't reject the idea out of hand.

Two younger men joined the couple, and after a short conversation, all four headed for the town's shops. Old man Stewart had sure succeeded in siring tall, uncommonly handsome sons. Both had their mother's regular features, fine dark eyes, and almost black hair.

A full, curving mustache and ten extra years distinguished Thad from his brother, as did the self-confident manner that almost but not quite crossed into arrogance.

Matt had ridden to town alone to have a drink or two. His curiosity satisfied, he continued toward the saloon. No wonder every woman for miles around twittered at the mere mention of Thad's name, Matt thought, feeling cranky. No one could say he wasn't pretty enough.

Matt paid a high price for keeping his vow to stay away from Sarah. He couldn't sleep, didn't want to eat and spent a lot of time staring off into space. Not only Beau and Roddy, but Luke, Swede and Rio treated him like walking wounded.

Unable to explain, Matt avoided them as much as possible. He worked alone or with Jimmy, who didn't know him well enough to see what old friends did.

On a bright Sunday morning in late May, the erratic workings of Beau's slowly healing mind changed everything. Matt sat outside in the sun, splicing a frayed rope, when Roddy came to him.

"It has been a long time since a spell, and I thought he would conquer it this time, but he is losing the battle, I think. He says he wants to go to town to play cards. Now."

Matt glanced over to where Beau paced in a circle and saw all the signs. Eyes too wide, movements jerky, tension in every line.

"How long's he been like that?" he asked.

"Two days."

He needed to start paying more attention to what was going on around him, Matt thought. Beau never stayed on the edge like this for even a whole day. He either gave in to the insanity or beat it down.

"There won't be any place to play poker in town on a Sunday morning. Maybe we can talk him into a game right here."

Roddy shook his head, expression worried. "He does not want to play cards. He wants to make trouble. Tavaras is where he wants to go. I wonder if it has been too long since a spell. Maybe it has built up too long. Maybe that means this will just be worse than anything he ever did before."

Matt's mouth went dry. "Can you distract him long enough for me to get behind him?"

Roddy shook his head. "That only was good once. I know you don't want to go to Tavaras again, but Rio is young. He is a little crazy himself sometimes. Luke and Swede do not understand how bad it can get. I am worried."

Worried! Roddy would never know the sick fear twisting in Matt's gut. Even crazy, Beau would never hurt women or children on purpose, but he thought nothing of spooking wagon or buggy teams, of wild shooting that had bullets ricocheting, glass shattering and flying.

In his mind Matt pictured Sarah walking along with Laurie's hand in hers and Beau's mindless frenzy exploding over them. He threw down the rope.

"Slow him down any way you can. Tell him I want to come along and I need to clean up. Stall him, and when that won't work any more, I'll come with you."

SITTING IN CHURCH feeling like this had to be a sin, Sarah decided, toying with the idea of feigning illness, getting up and leaving. How had she let herself get into this mess? She was too tired to fight any more, that's how. That's how she felt all the time now, tired and spiritless, hopeless and miserable.

Sarah shot a resentful glance to her left where Henry Blackburn sat with his arms folded across his chest and a smug look on his face. A religious man who read a chapter of the Good Book every night, Henry should be ashamed to sit in church and gloat.

She glanced to her right at Thad Stewart's clean cut profile and gave serious thought to making a fist and hitting him right on the point of that nice strong chin. Of course, he had every trace of smugness off his face, but it still emanated from him.

Past Thad, Sarah saw Laurie squirming between Minna and Amanda. The two women had taken Laurie by the hands and pulled her into the pew between them this morning while Henry and Thad trapped Sarah. She wondered if the two families had plotted the rest of the day as carefully as that maneuver.

Staring down at her hands folded in her lap, Sarah saw them against the background of crisp blue and white checked gingham and felt even angrier. Without so much as a by your leave, Minna had unpicked the seams on one of her own older dresses and re-worked it for Sarah.

The dress now had neat white cuffs and collar. The skirt fell fashionably smooth at the front and the fullness draped gracefully at the back. Minna also claimed she had "found" an adorable straw bonnet.

Rather than force the older woman to lie, Sarah didn't ask where at the milliner's Minna found the hat. As a result of all this scheming, Sarah wore the most charming picnic outfit on any woman in church today, and they were all dressed for the annual church picnic.

Charming! Picnic! When Henry's deputy came and got him right out of the church to attend to some problem at the jail, Sarah didn't hide her satisfaction. At least Henry had to do something besides sit and wallow in his victory.

By the time the service ended and most of the congregation gathered around the table set up in the churchyard, Sarah felt if she forced herself to smile her face would crack.

Lavinia Young helped her husband choose a picnic basket from those piled on the table. Sarah watched, still wondering what would happen if she claimed illness. Probably the whole lot of them would follow her back to Blackburns' and pester her there.

Reverend and Mrs. Young decided on a picnic basket. He held it up and began touting the contents like a drummer selling miracle cures. Cecily Sanquist, who had prepared the basket, blushed and giggled. Her husband endured teasing from the men who would bid against him to drive up the price he would have to pay for his own food.

Sarah understood the necessity of a church raising money, but these picnic lunch auctions offended her to the core, and she had refused to participate in previous years.

Earl Sanquist manfully offered a first bid of fifty cents, and one of his friends called out, "Seventy-five cents!"

Sarah knew Earl would be forced to pay about two dollars for the basket, but as he raised his head, preparing to call out again, another voice, hard and with a brittle edge, rang out. "Ten dollars."

Sarah swiveled her head toward the voice along with everyone else, to see what they all saw—Farrell's gunmen, six men on horseback near the edge of the crowd.

Cecily gasped and ran for the church. Her husband threw a murderous look at the mounted men and followed her.

Sarah stared at Matt in disbelief, aware of the half-angry, half-frightened buzzing of people around her and the calls for Henry. Surely Matt wouldn't enjoy making this kind of trouble. No man could change that much. The outrageous bid hadn't been in his voice, but why was he with the others? How could he be part of spoiling everyone's day, starting something that could turn ugly?

Searching the faces of the other men, trying to find answers to her questions, Sarah saw that while the blond man next to Matt and one of the younger men wore trouble-makers' grins, Matt and the others looked grim.

NOTHING IN HIS nightmares ever frightened Matt more. The spring green meadow sweeping toward the cottonwoods that bordered the Tavaras River created a perfect setting for the whitewashed adobe church. The ladies in their colorful summer dresses represented everything good in a life no longer open to men like them.

Matt couldn't imagine anything worse they might have ridden up on with Beau like this. It must be like salt searing all the old wounds, a vision of everything Beau had once had and lost.

Matt saw Sarah and Laurie in the crowd and wondered if he would have to shoot a man he loved like a brother before the day was over. Beau teetered between sanity and madness like a man who had lost his balance on the edge of a cliff.

Occasionally, focusing Beau's mind dissolved the insane anger. Not understanding the scene in front of them anyway, Matt tried that tack. "What is this, Beau? What's money got to do with folks having a picnic after church?"

Beau fastened wide, fixed eyes on Matt. "They raise money for the church by auctioning off those lunches. The highest bidder eats with the lady who fixed the lunch. Only ladies don't eat with our kind. Their Christian devotion to their church doesn't extend that far."

Rio spoke from the other side of Beau. "They're going to try another one. Let me do it this time."

"Go ahead."

The preacher held up another basket nervously and began extolling the virtues of its contents. Without looking toward Beau, Matt tried sidestepping Sam closer, hoping to get a chance at a single, stunning blow.

Beau spurred his horse away, grinning madly. "Oh, no, you don't, my friend. Once was enough."

Where was Blackburn? Amanda Stewart and an older woman held Laurie between them. As the Stewart men conferred among themselves, Matt watched Sarah slip away from them unnoticed and work her way through the crowd. Close now, she looked directly at him, pushed her chin out toward him, then tipped her head toward the table with the baskets.

Behind him, Rio yelled, "Twenty dollars!"

Another woman ran for the church, and Rio's whooping laughter rang out, distracting Matt. Sarah repeated the same little motions then started back toward the table, where half a dozen angry men argued with each other. Aware finally that Sarah had left them, the Stewarts hurried to catch her.

Understanding came to Matt in a rush. Sarah's solution might work if he could bring Beau around a little. Matt glanced at Beau, assessing. "You said you wanted to play cards."

"I like what I'm doing here just fine."

"How about taking a gamble right here then? I'll make you a bet."

Beau fastened his wild gaze on Matt. "Like what?"

"I'll bid on the next one, serious. If the lady eats lunch with me, you and the others go find your card game or go back to the ranch. You leave these folks alone."

Beau looked toward the table and saw what Matt saw, Sarah talking to the heavy man in the clerical collar. Something flickered in Beau's staring eyes for a second. "That's the little bitch put a stick in your eye once before. You only got one eye left."

"That's my lookout. Is that your excuse? Maybe you're afraid of losing."

Beau twitched slightly. "And if I win, what do I win?"

"If I buy that lady's lunch and she won't eat it with me, I'll help you tree this town, Texas style."

Rio gave another whoop. "Do it, Beau," he urged. "Hell, I'd pay a hundred dollars just to see Matt get excited. This damn town deserves it anyway."

"I don't want to see more of what happened to you here last time," Beau said.

Beau was starting to steady, but Matt didn't let up. Suddenly he wanted this, desperately wanted a day with Sarah and his daughter and without a smattering of guilt for it.

"You only take easy bets?"

Beau leaned toward him, reacting to the challenge. "Damn you. Go ahead and get your face shoved in some more. And when it's done, you better pay off!"

A big man with a badge pinned to his vest joined the conference at the table, but as Matt fully expected, Sarah got her way, and the preacher held up another basket and started telling the crowd about the delicacies within.

A new worry occurred to Matt. "Most likely I haven't got enough money. It will be Stewart bidding."

Matt had succeeded in focusing Beau's mind all right. Furious with Matt, he snarled, "This is a damn church picnic! You think Stewart brought a big cash bankroll to a church picnic?"

"He won't need cash. He's the big bug in this town."

Beau's gray eyes narrowed, all signs of madness gone. "You bid," he said. "We'll count how much we've got among us. Believe me, there won't be that much cash anywhere else in town this morning. What's going to humiliate you won't be lack of cash."

The preacher stopped his nervous spiel and called for bids. Thad Stewart's voice overlaid the preacher's last words.

"Twenty dollars."

"Thirty."

All Matt could see was Sarah, Sarah looking like every good thing the world had to offer all bundled up in one delightful female package.

"Forty."

"Fifty."

Matt couldn't take his eyes off Sarah, and the bidding went along in ten dollar increments as if no one were talking about real money until Matt said, "One ninety."

Beau broke in then. "Excuse me for my suspicion, Reverend, but has Mr. Stewart got that much cash on him?"

"Stewart credit's good in this town!" Thaddeus Stewart shouted.

"Well, Matt's credit's good any place we've ever been, but I never heard of credit at a church picnic. You ever take credit, Reverend?"

The preacher's heavy cheeks turned dull red, but he admitted, "No. Our picnics are cash fund raisers."

Roddy pushed a wad of bills into Matt's hand. Matt grinned his thanks, but Roddy said bitterly, "Go pay the man and get your stick in the eye. You have made things much worse unless you have a plan too subtle for me."

Matt swung down off Sam and gave Roddy the reins. "You worry too much."

The crowd stayed silent as Matt approached the table. Careful not to look at Sarah, he observed the Stewarts closely, wondering if trouble might still come from that quarter.

Thad stood stiffly beside his father and brother, his color high, his face without expression. Jesse's face showed only suppressed amusement. Thaddeus Stewart's overt fury might lead to trouble if he were armed, but Matt saw no guns on any of the Stewart men.

Reaching the table, Matt counted out ten twenty dollar bills. "Keep the extra for the church, Reverend."

The man's mouth worked, his gray goatee bobbing, but he was speechless. At Matt's side, Sarah was not.

"That is a perfectly sinful amount to pay for a few pieces of fried chicken, Mr. Slade."

Matt dared to look at her then and saw in her face a perfect reflection of what he felt. "My friends told me it's not the food I'm paying for, but the privilege of looking at you when I eat it. I reckon that makes this a rare bargain."

Blackburn moved in then, pulling Sarah away from Matt by the arm. "You can reckon it was just a donation to our church," he growled, "because you're not eating anything in my town. You and your friends are getting out of here, or you'll see the inside of my jail."

Sick disappointment swept through Matt. Not only was he going to be robbed of a day with Sarah, but Beau's temper could be as destructive as his craziness.

The sound of horses moving told him that Beau and the others were pushing closer, but before he decided how to calm things down, Sarah shook her arm free and took flight.

"Henry Blackburn, if you think having badgered me into taking part in this ridiculous spectacle you are now going to cancel the whole thing because it didn't turn out the way you planned, you are wrong. You said I should be willing to give a few hours of my time to help the church, and here I am."

Sarah pointed dramatically to the small pile of bills still on the table. "Tell me that's not more money than the church usually raises with this whole immoral charade most years. Just tell me that."

Blackburn's jaw dropped. As Matt wondered why, the sheriff recovered and reasserted himself. "Now, Sarah, you stay out of this. You are not spending so much as a minute in this man's company."

Incredible. To hold a sheriff's job, Blackburn had to be smarter than that. Talking to Sarah like that pretty much guaranteed she'd dig in and find a way to get what she wanted. She had one hand on a hip now, and the forefinger of the other wagging at Blackburn's nose.

"I told you I didn't want to be sold at public auction like some poor slave girl through an obvious subterfuge like a picnic basket, but oh, no, you wouldn't listen. You pestered, and you bullied, and you harassed, and finally you caught me one night when I was too tired to argue any more. So here I am! And this man just bought me through the proxy of that basket, and I am going to eat lunch with him!"

"Not in my town you're not!"

Blackburn's roar would intimidate most women and a lot of men, but Matt knew which Yankee would win this battle.

"Fine!" Sarah shouted back. "We'll just eat outside of your town!" She turned to Matt and switched effortlessly to honeyed tones. "Will that horse of yours carry the two of us outside of the town limits?"

Matt knew he was grinning from ear to ear like an idiot, but he couldn't stop. "Oh, yes, ma'am. I reckon he'd be pleased to carry you anywhere. I know I would."

Sarah picked up the wicker basket and held it out, and when Matt took it from her, she took his arm.

"Wait a minute."

By now most of the onlookers, including the preacher, were trying to hide smiles. Everyone watching knew Sarah had won long before Blackburn's capitulation.

"You'll stay right here, right where I can see you're safe."

"Well, of course, Henry," Sarah said demurely. "I certainly wouldn't want to worry you."

Matt had to work at not laughing out loud. They moved far enough away to be out of anyone's hearing then stopped and stared at each other. Matt almost got lost in her eyes right there in front of the whole town.

"Doesn't Blackburn know why you Yankees won the war?"

"Henry thinks I'm a rather sweet little thing who could probably be faulted for a certain lack of spirit. The whole town thinks that."

"And who gave them such a wrong-headed notion?"

"I did, I'm afraid. Aren't you going to introduce me to your friends?"

Matt escorted her to where Beau, Roddy and the others sat on their horses.

Beau was polite to Sarah and unforgiving to Matt. "I may not know how you did it, but I know when I've been suckered, and you just suckered me. When I figure it out, all bets are off."

Matt grinned happily and asked Roddy to tie Sam in the shade. As they rode off, Sarah asked, "What did he mean about bets?"

Matt explained and said, "You tell people you did this to save the town a rough time, and they won't hold it against you."

"They won't hold it against me anyway. Now that they're over being frightened, they're enjoying the whole thing."

Right then Matt stopped caring about Beau's problems, Henry Blackburn's fury or the town's attitude. This time was his, a few grand, glorious hours to spend with Sarah.

"I thought all these years I'd never see anything so fine as you in Texas, but I was wrong. You are even more beautiful as a woman than you were as a girl."

I FORGOT, SARAH THOUGHT, looking up at him. I forgot that happiness isn't just a quiet, passive thing. It isn't just the lack of unhappiness. This is happiness, this wild, delicious feeling fizzing inside me.

If she said a word, tears would start, so she took his arm and pointed toward her favorite picnic spot.

Matt looked over to where Laurie stood with Minna and Amanda. "Can't she come with us?"

"Yes, of course, but I told her to wait until I signaled. I wanted her clear of any trouble."

Sarah waved her arm, and Laurie bolted, giving no one a chance to stop her. She ran all the way and stopped breathless in front of Matt. "You're my papa."

For a moment Sarah thought Matt might not be able to answer, but then he said, "I am."

Her face alight with excitement, Laurie's words tumbled out. "You didn't know about me, or you would have come to see us. You think it would be bad to come see us now, and that's why you didn't. I know I can't call you Papa, but I don't have to call you Mr. Slade, do I?"

Sarah wondered if Matt had been around enough children to handle this barrage, but he managed all right, ignoring everything but the last.

"I wouldn't like Mr. Slade either. How about Matt?"

Laurie subjected Matt to a non-stop unholy inquisition all the way to the best picnic area near the Tavaras River. Privately Sarah thought the narrow waterway would be better called a stream or creek, but Westerners had strange ideas about water.

She spread the cloth packed in the top of the basket over the soft spring grass and listened to Matt and Laurie with growing contentment.

Matt didn't make the mistake of talking down to his daughter, which was a surefire way any adult could earn Laurie's undying contempt.

Sarah made only an occasional comment as she set out the feast Minna Blackburn had prepared and packed as one part of the failed conspiracy.

Sarah's appetite had been poor these last weeks, and Matt looked drawn to her. The three of them demolished a vast amount of food in record time, even as Laurie continued her questioning, extracting answers that Sarah wanted to hear.

Of course, Matt painted a rosy picture of five years fighting other men's wars. He made it sound like a grand adventure, as if he'd never drawn a gun and no one would ever be rude enough to shoot back anyway. Still, Sarah saw the outline of the sort of life he led.

According to Matt prison life wasn't so bad either—three decent meals every day for the first time since he was a boy, a bath every week, clothes and shoes without holes, a warm bed in winter, and enough work to keep a man's mind off his troubles.

Only when Laurie asked about the injuries to his face did Sarah hear a hesitation that made her wonder how much of the truth he told. Sarah had no problem with him sugar coating that story for Laurie, and after all, he couldn't like talking about it, or even remembering.

He had been dragged into a bad fight in prison, he said. The prison doctor gave him drugs that stopped the pain. No, his eye wasn't just injured, the doctor took it out. The patch was so people didn't have to see the place where it had been.

Soon Matt turned the tables, and Laurie told him about the visits from Aunt Kate and Uncle Brad, about her room at the Blackburns' house, about how there was no real school in Tavaras and so Reverend Young and his wife took turns giving lessons.

Sarah leaned back against a tree and watched them and listened. The last time she felt this happy had been in Texas, and the meal was probably snake or crawdad, but she had been happy like this.

Sarah saw Mary Gilbride approaching, hesitant as always, and beckoned. "Come sit with us. I'll introduce you to Mr. Slade."

Mary's toe scuffed the grass. "Mama says I have to wait till every-one's done eating. I mustn't beg with words or with my eyes."

Like her mother, Emily, Mary had huge brown eyes that dominated the thin oval of her face. Those eyes could put a puppy to shame.

"I cannot imagine what your mother was thinking of, Mary. We know you'd never do anything like that. We're all done eating except for a bit of cake Minna put in here, and we'll just have to explain to your mother that you had to eat a small piece so that the rest of us wouldn't feel awkward eating in front of you."

In no time Sarah introduced Mary to Matt and served everyone pieces of cake. When they finished eating, she said, "Suppose you girls go and play with the others for a while. It's my turn to talk to Matt now."

Laurie started to protest, looked at her mother and got slowly to her feet. "You won't go without seeing me again, will you?" she said to Matt. "You'll say goodbye to me."

Laurie finally left with Mary, dragging her feet with reluctance as she walked toward the open part of the field where the children gathered.

Matt watched them go, looking almost puzzled. "I know she's mine, but a part of me can't believe I had anything to do with making something that fine. Was it hard, Sarah?"

Sarah told him about it then, about Flowers and her Sunday visits to the brothel and her friendships there. A long time ago she had told Matt things she never told another soul, and now she did it again.

"You must be one of the few ladies in the world who knows more about soiled doves than most men. I guess it goes with your talent for cussing like an artillery sergeant."

His tone wasn't particularly disapproving, but even so Sarah felt defensive. "I haven't fit anybody's definition of a lady for a long time."

"If that's so, they ought to change the definition."

Sarah's heart contracted sharply. "I thought I remembered everything, but I forgot how you make me feel. Oh, Matt, you make me feel so...."

As she paused, unable to find words to complete the thought, Matt eyed her suspiciously. "You're not going to start puddling up all over the place, are you?"

"Oh, heavens, no," Sarah said. "I learned a long time ago I'd better not cry around you unless there's a Comanche in sight."

They drifted into easy conversation then, about Texas and the years since. Matt told her about Beau, Roddy and the others. Sarah told him about the Blackburns and the Gilbrides. Their talk was casual, mostly a way of enjoying being together, until the subject of the trouble brewing between the L&L and Bar S came up.

"I understand how you can hire out to help people in trouble, but how can you take a job making trouble? How do you justify that?"

"We're not making the trouble. Stewart is."

"Maybe I don't want to marry Thad, but I know he's a more honorable person than that. The Stewarts don't want to expand their cattle operation anyway. They're the ones having stock rustled and water holes poisoned."

Matt bent toward her, intent. "Do you think I'm stealing cows and poisoning water?"

"No, of course not, but those other men...."

"Boston, believe me, Beau doesn't hire out to make trouble, only to handle it. We're not making this trouble, and Farrell's already stood for more than any man I've ever seen. He keeps saying Stewart will come to his senses, but Farrell's losing more cows than he can afford. I've seen the dead cows around his water—tracks of dozens more being run off. I've seen the cut fences, burned outbuildings, grass black from the fires last fall. Are you sure old man Stewart couldn't do this without anyone knowing?"

"He wouldn't. I've seen those people at least once a week for over three years. They just aren't like that. None of them would steal a penny, and they expected the L&L to belong to Stewart grandchildren anyway."

Seeing his look of outright disbelief, Sarah hesitated, then went on. "I shouldn't tell you, but Jesse Stewart would be marrying Julia Farrell this summer if things were different. They've been in love since they were children, but on her deathbed Lily Farrell made Julia promise to wait to marry until she was twenty. Hardly anyone knows, but that's one reason everyone's pushing Thad to marry. He thought he could continue to be fancy free and Jesse would produce all the heirs the family needed. Amanda Stewart thinks all the trouble has something to do with Mr. Farrell not wanting his daughter to marry a Stewart after all."

Matt relaxed back against the tree. "I know it's not Farrell, and if I believe you, and it's not Stewart, then who is it? Beau doesn't like to work this sort of job because he says usually a ranch goes under after they've borrowed and beggared themselves to fight a war. He says it's depressing even when you win. Who would want one of those ranches? Probably the L&L, since Farrell's smaller."

"No one. I mean, if someone wants a ranch that much, they can go buy one. There aren't any tales of buried treasure around here. There aren't any precious metals mined, and people have searched."

Matt still looked thoughtful. "What about a grudge?"

"I wouldn't know about that."

"Well, if Stewart's such an honorable sort, there's no reason why you can't marry him."

Determined not to quarrel with him again, Sarah said, "I'll tell you what. I'll marry Thad if I can choose a wife for you. I warn you I will choose a woman who looks like she spends all her time sucking persimmons, who is slovenly about her person and everything else, and who hates everybody, especially men. She'll believe all men are evil creatures, filled with ugly lust and base desire."

"We are all filled with lust and base desire. She sounds like a clever sort, just what I need. What's her name?"

Sarah threw a chicken bone at him. He caught it easily then paused with his arm still raised. "What's going on over there?"

Sarah followed his gaze and hissed. "I can't believe it! Those tasteless people and that wretched pony!"

"So what's going on?"

"The Hinshaws are Tavaras's wealthiest family. Their daughter Emeline—and don't make the mistake of calling her Emma or Emmy—is Laurie's age, and they've not only bought her a pony, a pony mind you, not a small horse, but every time there's some event in town like this picnic, they haul that fat pony around with Emeline sitting on it. She's terrified of the poor thing. She can't really ride it. What she does is she favors the other little girls who act as her handmaidens by letting them sit on the creature. I told Laurie if I ever see her on that pony, I'll know she did something I wouldn't approve of to get herself there, and she'll be in a peck of trouble."

"Are you telling me you're a mean mother, Boston?"

"Mean? You, you...! Sarah couldn't even think of an insult vile enough, and then saw the teasing glint. "You devil." Her tone made the words a caress.

The rest of the afternoon passed too quickly. Sarah didn't argue when Matt said he had to go. She wanted to throw herself at him, but she obediently packed the basket. As soon as they got to their feet, Laurie and Mary ran back across the field.

"You don't have to go yet, Matt. It's too early. Nobody's leaving yet."

"Now, some people are leaving, and I've got a long ride back to the ranch. I'll walk you and your mother home, how's that?"

"Yes." Laurie took a tight hold of Matt's free hand. His other held the picnic basket.

Sarah winked at Mary Gilbride and took her hand, and they all walked to where Roddy had tied Matt's horse. Their envy over Emeline Hinshaw's pony had only exacerbated both girls' fascination with horses, although they hardly ever got close to one. Henry claimed his saddle horse was too mean for children to even pet, probably to disguise his belief that girls and women should never touch anything so large and dirty.

Now Sarah watched while Laurie and Mary met Sam, who, it seemed, had a secret yen to be fussed over by young girls. Before Sarah realized what was happening, Matt lifted first Laurie, then Mary into the saddle. Sarah listened in awe as Matt explained that since this was a man's horse, ladies might find the gait a little rough, and if either of them did, they should just sing out.

His words gave them a face-saving way to admit fear, but Sarah was the one worried. She fussed around, making sure their skirts covered enough leg, then took a firm hold of each child's ankle. The horse hadn't moved a step.

Laurie looked down from her lofty seat with a queenly air. "Mama, you're going to scare Sam. I'm sure he's not used to someone fluttering around like that in petticoats."

Sarah stared up in astonishment, and Matt cleared his throat.

"She most likely has a point," he said. "You wouldn't want to strain the horse's tolerance."

Sarah looked at the horse, yawning as it waited patiently, and at her daughter, waiting anything but patiently, said, "Heaven forbid," and released her hold on the girls.

She picked up the basket from where Matt had left it and took his arm. As they moved off down the street, Sarah glanced back, saw both children looking disgracefully gleeful and stopped worrying. Pressing her whole side against Matt's arm, she gave herself over to enjoying every step of the walk to Blackburns'.

A short while later, Sarah raced out of Blackburns' back door, aware she was but seconds ahead of the return of angry, thwarted conspirators. Saying goodbye to Matt without begging for promises had been hard. The sight of the Blackburns and Stewarts hurrying up the street after them and Sarah's conviction that Matt wouldn't be able to stay away from her or from Laurie any more gave her the strength to behave properly. Watching Laurie's face scrunch up with unhappiness didn't make it easier.

Safely out of sight, Sarah slowed, catching her breath. Surely the Gilbrides wouldn't be upset about what had happened today, but Sarah wanted to be the one to tell them about it.

In ten years of marriage, the Gilbrides had been blessed with only two children, Mary, and a son who died the summer before Sarah came to Tavaras. Unable to handle his grief, Charlie Gilbride drank himself insensate.

When Sarah first knew Emily, her husband was the town drunk. Charlie lost his business and almost everything else, and Emily needed a friend as much as Sarah.

As their daughters became close, so did the mothers. In the last year Charlie had pulled himself together and started working again. Sarah enjoyed her peaceful visits in the little house the Gilbrides still owned, or at least co-owned with the bank. However, family finances made the picnic auction out of the question for the Gilbride family.

Charlie answered the door when Sarah knocked. A tall man, slightly stooped and with an unhealthy pallor, Charlie smiled as he invited her in. Sarah noticed the smile reached his eyes today and his thinning blond hair and short beard were neatly trimmed.

"We didn't expect to see you today, Sarah." Charlie held the door for her. "Not that it isn't a pleasant surprise, but we thought once they got you to that picnic, they wouldn't let you get away."

Sarah wondered if Charlie could see she stood not on his front step but on the air several inches above it. "The picnic didn't quite turn out the way everyone planned, and that's why I'm here, to tell you about it before anyone else does."

Sarah followed Charlie to the kitchen and turned down all Emily's offers of refreshment.

"Laurie and Mary are going to play in Blackburns' yard a while, and I better confess right away that I embarrassed poor Mary into eating a piece of cake, and you mustn't be upset with her. I really all but tricked her."

"Oh, Sarah, you'd say that anyway. She had a good lunch here, and she didn't need another bite." Emily scolded Sarah in the same gentle tone she used with Mary over minor transgressions.

"Minna packed enough goodies to feed an army. It would be a shame to waste that cake when there was a little girl around with room for it."

"Oh, all right. Enough about that. How was the picnic? You look so happy. Is Thad officially courting yet?"

Sarah laughed out loud at this, the absolute joy of her day too much to contain. She told Charlie and Emily about what had happened, and their astonishment only made everything better.

"How could you do such a thing? Weren't you afraid?" Emily was, like Mary, a rather timid soul.

"Oh, no, Em, if you met him, you'd like him. He is the most wonderful man, and I had the best time. I've been dreading this day so much, and then it was like the answer to a prayer. It wasn't just that I got out of being branded as Thad Stewart's private property in front of the whole town. I had a glorious, beautiful, superb day, but I haven't told you the part that concerns you yet."

Sarah told them about Hinshaws' pony, and heard Charlie make a disgusted sound. Charlie could say some very nasty things about young Miss Hinshaw and her pony. Then she told about Laurie and Mary, riding Matt's horse down the street.

"That's what I wanted to tell you, you see. Please don't be angry with me. You know I'd never introduce Mary to him except I like him so much. They were perfectly safe on that horse. It's very gentle and very well broke. I know half the town's going to be here telling you terrible things, and I wanted to tell you first. Please say you aren't angry with me."

Sarah looked back and forth between her two friends. Emily's face stayed blank with surprise, but Charlie smiled at her.

"Sarah, when we first knew you, there were people in this town we'd known all our lives who not only would cross the street to avoid me, they'd go out of their way to hurt Emily and Mary both, as if my weakness were their fault. If I started a list of good people I know, you'd be right at the top. If you like this Slade, that's good enough for me, and if anybody comes here trying to start a fuss, they'll get told so."

Such an outspoken endorsement embarrassed Sarah, but she smiled back at Charlie and said, "Em?"

"You really like this—gunslinger that much?" Emily asked.

"I really do."

"Then I agree with Charlie. He must be a very nice man." Emily's voice only quavered a little.

The three were silent for a moment, and then Charlie slapped his leg and started to laugh, really laugh. "I'd have given anything to see it! Little Miss Rich Britches sitting on that pony pasty-faced with fright, and our two riding the gunman's horse down Main Street!"

Charlie laughed out loud. Emily met Sarah's eyes and giggled. Sarah snickered. Soon all three of them were laughing so hard they had to hold their ribs and wipe their eyes.

Sarah wished she could tie ribbons around the day and keep it forever.

37

ON MONDAY AFTERNOON Henry Blackburn spurred his horse up the Bar S ranch road still filled with the same helpless anger that had started the day before at the picnic.

All right, pushing Sarah into taking part in something she found offensive had been a bad mistake on his part. Sarah had compared the church picnic to a slave sale before, for pity's sake. After all she came from an abolitionist family, and abolitionists all had more passion than sense.

After the years she had lived in his house, Henry would have sworn Sarah was incapable of that passionate scene. Henry did remember Lavinia Young's claim that Sarah had frightened her that time right after Lavinia washed some boy's mouth out with soap for cussing. Well, Lavinia could get rigid in her ways when she helped her husband with the schooling. Claiming Sarah threatened her with physical harm if she ever touched Laurie had to be female theatrics.

Until yesterday Henry had considered the stubborn streak that surfaced now and then Sarah's only flaw. Even when she stood on principle, she did it with quiet dignity.

In general, Sarah slipped through life quite agreeably. Maybe he himself felt a woman should have a mite more spunk, but Sarah would make Thad a perfect wife.

Thad. The boy needed a hard kick in the hind parts! Just thinking about it had Henry jerking on his horse. When the poor beast threw its head and stumbled, Henry soothed it with an apologetic pat.

Thad expected every woman he met to fawn all over him because they all did. Sarah wanted courting, and Thad acted as if being available should be enough. His reaction to yesterday's events had only been amusement.

"You can't blame her for getting even with us all, Henry. Not only that, but you know she's had a rough time the last years. If she enjoys being the center of attention for a little while, let her have her fun."

Fun! Thad was old enough and experienced enough to know how many women, faced with a choice between a decent man and a renegade, went for the renegade every time. Sunday's events had showed Henry his own mistake in thinking that Slade's scarred visage put women off.

The expression Lavinia Young and several other women got on their faces when Slade smiled hadn't escaped him. The damn man had that hungry wolf look that was the ruin of too many women, and when he smiled he looked just safe enough to tempt the especially foolish to try to tame him.

Thad didn't share this concern either. "A man like Slade isn't going to take Sarah seriously. They were probably both bored to death, but they enjoyed making us all look silly."

Henry had refrained from pointing out that Slade didn't have to get serious to ruin Sarah, or that his kind ruined things for the pleasure of it.

Sarah had already shown a weakness for the wrong kind of man. No matter what she said, it was too far fetched for belief that her husband wasn't the cause of the estrangement from her family, although in truth, to have fathered a little girl like Laurie, the man couldn't have been all bad.

As the ranch buildings came into sight, Henry took time to admire the sprawling adobe house set majestically on a slight rise, giving it command over low lying outbuildings. Thaddeus had done well for himself and his family. Growing up here Laurie Hammond would have luxuries so far unknown to her and a secure future.

The Stewarts considered Henry's worry unjustified, but they expected his visit. Jesse met Henry at the door and led the way to the office, where his father and brother waited.

"So what did that jackass Farrell have to say for himself?" Thaddeus asked.

"You were right. I wasted my time riding out there," Henry admitted. "The way he sees it, whatever Taney's intentions were, there wasn't any real trouble, and of course, he could hardly wait to tell me Sarah was right. He'd rather see his own daughter with Slade than with a Stewart. All the usual—you're making the trouble. He can't afford to keep his patience much longer, that sort of horse shit."

"That goddamn liar! I'm the one who's about out of patience. Well, come on in. I still think you're worried over nothing, but Rastus knows that whole bunch. He says he first met Taney right after the war. A cigar, a brandy or two, and he'll tell us anything he can easy enough. I sent for him as soon as you rode up."

Harlan Rastus was the Stewarts' answer to Beau Taney. Unlike Taney, he didn't ride with the same men from year to year, but took on a job and then hired others as needed. Here at the Bar S there were eleven men with him.

A big, likable fellow, with a ready smile, and a bushy red beard that failed to steal attention from the freckled bald spot up top, Rastus looked like the Illinois farmer he had been until four years of war weaned him from that life.

The big redhead settled into a deep chair in the book-lined room, sniffed a cigar, and accepted the brandy with undisguised pleasure. He got to the point before anyone else had a chance. "If all this fine treatment is in hopes of me giving the sheriff here a reason to jail Beau and his boys, you're out of luck. Not one of them is wanted anywheres for anything at all."

"That was too much to hope for, I guess," Henry said. "You heard what happened in town yesterday?"

"Sure. I saw Luke and Rio along the south fence this morning myself. Of course, they couldn't hardly tell it for laughing. They're getting some real miles out of it, but you're lucky Beau didn't smash that picnic and half your town to bits. When he goes crazy you don't want nothing to do with it. You could maybe just shoot him and get it over with, but then you'd have Roddy and the rest right down your throat."

"Crazy? It looked like pure meanness to me."

"Nah. Beau don't act like that sane." Rastus explained about Beau's problems. "He's been getting a little better every year since the war. Luke says after the Goldville ruckus he even made it to Kansas City and back in one piece without Roddy nurse-maiding him. Back in '66, '67, I'd have said Beau was hurt as permanent as them that lost legs and arms in the war, but maybe he's going to make it after all."

"You seem to be pretty cozy with men you're supposed to be primed to fight," Thaddeus said.

Rastus studied his cigar for a moment before looking at his employer. "The biggest surprise I had when I come here was finding Beau on the other side of this fracas. He admits he made a mistake taking the Goldville job. Maybe he's lost his instinct for what to stay away from, but I'll tell you right now, Farrell's paying somebody else to do his dirty work. Beau Taney's not sneaking around stealing cows and cutting fences."

"And you're so sure of it, you're fraternizing across fence lines you're supposed to be guarding!"

Henry wanted to signal his friend to back off a little, but couldn't catch his eye.

The gunman's face tightened into hard lines. "Mr. Stewart, I'll tell you honest, I'd rather fight with Beau than against him, and I'm hoping this won't come to fighting him. If it does, I'll earn my pay, but when it's over, if we're both still alive, I expect I'll feel the same about Beau as I do right now. I've known him nigh on ten years, and I ain't known you six months."

Henry searched in vain for some way to cool tempers when Thad intervened. "Dad only needed to hear what you just said. I suppose none of us realized there was such a—community feeling in your business."

"There's those I respect, and those I don't have nothing to do with. When Beau's got ahold of himself, he's a good man."

"So tell us about him," Thad urged. "Tell us about all of them. What about the Mexican. Rodriguez, isn't it? Would he be doing Farrell's dirty work?"

"Roddy?" Rastus made a sound close to a snort. "That fancy Spanish neck of his won't hardly bend far enough for him to look at a cow, much less steal one."

"You're saying he's nothing but a dandy, all he does is pander to Taney's problems?"

"Pander? Roddy?" Rastus roared with laughter.

When he finally caught his breath, all traces of anger had disappeared. "Beau used to fool himself he ran that outfit, but fact is Roddy never did a damn thing he didn't want to in his life. I guess you could say they're partners. Beau takes care of those things a white man can deal with easier is all. Not one of those six is your average gentle citizen, but if there's one you sure as hell don't want to go up against, Roddy's the one."

"He's more dangerous than Taney?"

"Well, let's put it this way. Beau'd come straight at you, and you'd know he was coming. Roddy now, if you got him riled, he wouldn't figure a gringo deserved any notice. I never cottoned to that Mex much, but I will say the less crazy Beau gets, the more human Roddy gets."

"So what about the others?" Thad asked.

"I'd ride with any of them. The young ones been with Beau a while. Nobody let him down in Goldville. They're good men."

It seemed Rastus was never going to mention Slade without a direct question, so Henry asked it. "What about Slade?"

Big white teeth flashed in the red beard then, and Henry knew the man had been playing cat and mouse, waiting for the question. Rastus drew out the pause, puffing on the cigar and blowing smoke out slowly.

"Well, as near as I could make out from Luke and Rio, Matt did enjoy that two hundred dollar chicken, but they were laughing so hard, I had some trouble catching all the words. I hope I'm not stepping on any sore toes here."

Grinning from ear to ear, Rastus looked less than concerned about anyone's toes, or feelings.

"Mrs. Hammond and her daughter live with my wife and me and are under my protection," Henry growled. "It didn't tickle me one damn bit to see her spending time with that scum over some silly female notion of fair mindedness."

"So you're saying a lady who lives at your house is too good to so much as eat with a man like Matt—or me? Is that what you're saying, Sheriff?"

Henry could have bitten his tongue. Once again Thad smoothed things over.

"You have to make allowances for Henry the same as you would for a father whose daughter was involved," he said. "You've told us you like and respect Taney and the younger men and you have reservations about Rodriguez. You don't count Slade as one of the young ones, do you? He must be my age."

The hard expression didn't leave the man's face, but he answered civilly enough. "Near as makes no difference. Matt's been with Beau maybe four, five years. We all worked the Colorado mining country about the same time, and so I got to know them pretty good. I like Matt. Everybody likes Matt. He's the best hope I've got of not having to go head to head with Beau here."

"How's that?"

Rastus swirled the last bit of brandy around in his glass as if deciding whether to answer, then shrugged. "Fill this up, and I'll tell you. No harm, I guess."

Jesse replenished the glasses, and they settled back again, Henry listening intently to the part of Rastus's information that seemed the crux of things to him.

"It's sort of hard to explain," Rastus said. "Beau and Roddy, either one would back the other all the way, no matter what. Right or wrong don't matter. But Matt, if he thought they were in the wrong, he'd take a bullet for them, but it wouldn't be backing them, it'd be trying to drag them out of it, you see?"

Rastus looked at the Stewarts and then at Henry and apparently saw no one took his point.

"It's like this," he said. "When Beau has one of his crazy spells, Roddy does anything he can to get Beau out of it in one piece, but he don't try to stop it. Now, Matt, he snuck up behind Beau once and gave him a smart tap behind the ear with his pistol and just put him to sleep. I saw him pitch Beau in a water trough once and dunk him under till he was so cold, wet and mad he pulled out of it. Yesterday, it cost him two hundred dollars, but he got Beau stopped, you see?"

Henry already knew about the bet from Sarah. "I understand what you're saying, but I don't see how it could take Taney's men out of this land war."

"The thing is, when Matt decides they're on the wrong side in this business, he'll walk away, and when he does, Beau and the rest will too."

"You make it sound like it's Slade runs the outfit, not Taney," Thad said.

"Nah, Matt don't run nothing but himself, but you might say he's their conscience, and they all think the world of him. If he walks, they all will. Beau told me on one of those jobs up in mining country they hired on to guard ore and payroll shipments. One day the mine owner invites them into his office. Kind of like you're doing with me here. He sets them up with some of his good whiskey, gets all friendly and then tells them the miners are giving him some trouble. They're wanting shoring timbers closer together in the mine and better food and more money, and he wants the ringleaders taught a lesson."

Rastus took a sip of his brandy and looked at his audience one by one as if to weigh their reactions. Henry knew the Stewart sympathies would all be with the mine owner. His own sympathies ran in the other direction, but so far as Henry could see, no one showed any reaction to the story.

Shrugging, the gunman went on. "Beau says he was sitting there, trying to decide what to say, and Matt just got up, slammed that glass full of good whiskey down on the fellow's desk and walked out. Not a word. Just walked out."

"Then what happened?" Thad asked.

"The rest of them followed him." Rastus grinned. "Except I expect a couple of them maybe gulped that whiskey down before walking out."

"So they refused to do the head busting." Henry said.

"You could say so. They packed up, saddled up, rode off and left that fellow to find himself some new guards and head busters. So I'm hoping that's how it will happen here. If Matt decides they're on the wrong side of something, he'll walk away and so will the rest of them like at that mine. Like they fought it his way at Goldville."

"That must be the third time you've mentioned Goldville," Henry said. "I never heard of it. What happened there?"

Rastus told them then about the Colorado mining town of Goldville. "Beau says as soon as they got there he saw they had more cougar by the tail than they could hold, much less hunt. He

SING MY NAME 273

told the town fathers what they could do with their town and got ready to hightail it out of there. And then they found themselves in what Matt calls an Alamo situation."

"It can't have been—they're all still alive," Henry pointed out drily.

"Maybe so, but they were surrounded by thirty, thirty-five of these Allens, no Allertons it was. Good citizens of the town all shut their doors and hid behind them. So Beau and Roddy and the others are having a war council, trying to decide what to do, and Beau looks around, and there's Matt, not paying any attention to the talk, and starting to look like a porcupine. Spare pistol in his belt, old Winchester he treats like a baby on a sling on his back, new rifle to hand. Matt says the others can do what they want, he's not getting hunted down through the streets like a rat. He's going straight at them, standing up.

"That was the end of the talk. They all just got up and followed him out into the street. You understand they didn't figure on getting through it alive anyway. It was just a matter of deciding how to go out. So they walked right down the middle of the street toward the livery. That's where most of these Allertons were waiting, expecting a try for the horses, you see."

Rastus paused for a swallow of brandy. "I heard rumors and all sorts of stories about it for months before I got here and heard the straight of it from Beau. I even heard they were all dead. You really never heard any of this, Sheriff?"

Henry shook his head. "It's hard to believe, but I take it no lawmen were involved."

"No law up there. That's the problem. Well, the truth is strange enough nobody needs to fancy it up. Beau ain't got over it yet. They're walking down the street, and these Allertons are pouring out of the stable and buildings all around. Beau never got a good count. He was up to eighteen when the shooting started, and that's part of what saved them, you see. Some damn idjit opened up with a pistol when they were still more than a hundred feet away."

Rastus paused again. More, Henry suspected, for dramatic effect than for the swallow of brandy he took. After a puff on the cigar, he continued.

"Beau starts warning his men to hold off till they're in decent range—just to steady the young ones, you know—when Matt opens up with the rifle, just levering the thing as fast as he can. He empties one rifle, throws it down, and in the quiet somebody yells out, 'He ain't going to die! I kilt him three times, and he ain't going to die!'"

Rastus grinned, enjoying his own tale. "And you might say that yellow stripe down that somebody's back got contagious, because right then a couple of them broke for the stables and got their horses and started whipping them out of town, and of course, Beau and his men are still closing the distance, and Matt opens up with the second rifle, and they get to pistol range, and all hell breaks loose, but more and more of those Allertons are just plain running. Beau says he never saw the like. They had odds of three, even four to one, but they just broke and ran."

Jesse was fascinated. "So Taney and his men came through it without a scratch?"

"Aw, hell, no. Not one of them took less than three bullets. Beau ended up sitting in the street firing away, with a leg broke. Roddy was on his belly, propped up on his elbows and still shooting. When things calmed down, Beau crawled over to Roddy and says he got sick just looking at it. Bullet went right in the groin and nicked an artery. So Beau and Luke are digging around in there next to Roddy's cojones, Beau trying to remember what he learned in the war about how to slow down the blood, and behind him he hears Rio and Swede, saying Matt's name over and over, so he turns around and Matt's down, just curled up in the street. When the shooting stopped Matt was standing there, kind of watching those Allertons running. Now Beau gets real tight lipped about the rest of it. This last part I heard from Luke Goss."

Rastus recounted then, the rest of what had happened in Goldville.

"Do you believe it?" Thad asked.

"Well, I might have got a detail or two wrong, but I heard stories all over about how Matt had a dozen bullets in him, and like that, and I'd say what I'm telling you is the truth of it. Luke says he was hit six times. Four bullets still in him, three in his chest. That would be killing him three times, all right."

"He couldn't have stayed on his feet."

"Oh, that he could do. With no big bones busted, a man can keep going when he's hurt pretty bad if he wants to enough, and Matt is one determined human being."

"What else do you know about him?" Henry asked.

"He's Texan, lost his family young. Joined the Rebs the day Texas started taking volunteers."

"Cavalry like Taney?" Henry asked.

"Infantry. Hood's Brigade. Matt fought a hard war, and it shows. He's a hell of a soldier. He's only passable with a pistol with the one eye, but he's as good with a rifle as any I've seen. Look, maybe you don't like what happened yesterday, but Matt's as decent as they come. He wouldn't be in this business, but he's got it in his head he looks too mean to do anything else, and he figures he owes Beau and Roddy for taking him on when he got out of prison."

"Prison?" Henry couldn't keep the triumph out of his voice.

"The carpetbaggers had him in prison in Texas for a couple of years over something," Rastus admitted reluctantly. "You know how it was."

"Texas juries don't even hang Texans for murder. He must have done something."

"I'm telling you it wasn't a Texas jury, it was Reconstruction carpetbaggers. As I remember the way Matt tells it, the charge was stealing, and I'll tell you right now, Matt never stole nothing. I'd trust him with my last dollar, and you can trust him around that little lady who lives with you too."

Rastus ground out the cigar violently and stood up, obviously angry he'd let slip what he had. He stomped out then without another word, banging the door behind him.

"I hope he's right about Taney quitting," Thad said ruefully. "Otherwise I suspect our army may not be passionately devoted to our cause."

"They're all like that," Henry said. "They've got more in common with each other than with us. They fight for money, and they'll earn it when the time comes. But I sure would like to know more about that prison sentence. An old friend of mine's in Austin these days. When I get home, I'm going to write to him and see what I can find out."

"You're reading too much into a simple thing, Henry. Sarah probably won't ever cross the man's path again, and he sounds decent enough anyway."

Henry thought grimly that if Harlan Rastus could be accused of lacking desired passion, so could Thaddeus Stewart, Jr.

38

"BOSTON."

Matt's voice came out of the darkness of the alley, and this time the arms Sarah ran to welcomed her better than in any dream. He lifted her off her feet for a hard, hungry kiss. She met his passion, matched it, ran her hands along the familiar, yet changed jaw line, then twisted her fingers in the thick hair at the back of his neck. Needs Sarah had long used grief and fatigue to suppress sang to life and chorused wildly.

When Matt stopped pulling her harder against him and started pushing her away, Sarah voiced her feelings with a wail, "Matt!"

"Ah, I'm sorry, Sarah. I never should have started it. The last thing you need is another fatherless child. I only came by to give you this."

Money. Cold rain on the back of her neck could not have stopped the thick heat of desire more effectively.

"Laurie is not fatherless. You are her father."

"That's a physical fact, for all the good it ever did either one of you. In all these years, it's one thing I never thought of. People don't start babies when they're dying. Leaning on me when I'm like this, with both of us fat and sassy might start twins this time."

His hands hard on her, holding her away, put Sarah in no mood for teasing, especially when he was half serious. "It's not quite that easy to start babies, and you know it. I suppose if it did happen you'd be telling me to get busy and marry somebody else and let him raise both your children."

"It isn't going to happen, because we're not going to get that—close. You know it's no good. It never was any good, and there's more against it now than there was then, too many years, too much changed. Maybe we never even knew each other so well back then, alone like that. All we've got between us are the same memories of a little time long ago...."

"And a daughter."

"And a daughter."

"You don't believe that any more than I do. If that's the way it is, then why is it in your arms I feel like I've come home for the first time since then?"

He stopped holding her away from him, and Sarah pushed in against him. Kissing his throat above the scarf around his neck, she felt the heat radiating from him, contrasting with the cool of the summer evening. His thorough arousal pressed hard against her belly through all the layers of clothing, and slight quivers spasmed his muscles erratically.

Sarah knew how easily she could break his control, have him in all the ways she so desperately wanted tonight. And giving the lie to his claim that they were strangers, she also knew the cost. If she seduced him when he was so sure it was wrong, he would leave this time and keep going, go as far as he thought necessary to protect her.

Almost sobbing with frustration, Sarah controlled the desire to let her weak knees give way and slide right down the front of him. "All right, I'll be good, but if you're not giving me anything else, you're not giving me money either. I've managed without help for a long time, and I'll manage for a lot longer."

"Just till you marry Stewart. I know you won't need it then. Let me make it easier for just that little while."

How could you love someone so much and all but itch to hit him? "You know, I think you're telling me how to discourage Thad. I'll just let him get—close, is it—and then he'll claim we're strangers and not want any more of me. Maybe the easiest way to cure a man of any desire for marriage really is to satisfy his carnal desire a few times. My mother always said so."

"Now you quit that talk. How exactly do you think we could be married? Do you see yourself living with a brood of young ones in a wagon, following me from gun job to gun job like a gypsy? Or are you thinking of cheap hotels in one town after another, with maybe a bunkhouse like where I'm living now in between for a change of scene?"

"Since you mention it, I see you doing something else for a living, but I will follow you like that if you don't want to change."

"Want to change? I never made a living doing anything else, and you know it."

"I do not. Before Webbs dragged you off, you had a good job. You told me so yourself."

"It was good enough for me then. I had decent clothes and a fancy horse and enough money to waste some in saloons, but it wasn't enough for a family."

"That's because you've got it in your head you'd have to be able to support me the way my father did. Maybe people can't be happy when they're hungry and cold and can't count on a roof over their heads, but having a big house and servants doesn't make anyone happy either. If I had servants to do everything, I'd just get fat again."

"You were never fat."

"Don't change the subject. You said that man you rode with got married. Whitey."

"He took a town marshal's job. You've had a good look at me in full light. Do you see me doing that? People don't like their lawmen looking so mean it scares them. Anyway, half her family still isn't talking to her over it."

"You look like a charming pirate, and we don't have to worry about my family not speaking to me, do we?"

"Maybe you need spectacles, and it's the whole town that would turn against you. I'm not ever sitting by and listening to people treat you like they did in that courtroom because of me again. They'd make your life not worth living and the same for Laurie."

"I don't believe that, and if you're right, there are other towns."

"Other, not different. If you'd never seen me again, you'd have married Stewart and...."

"I would not! I had no intention of marrying him, and I was fighting tooth and nail to keep it from ever getting to where people linked us together in any way before I saw you again."

Tears burned behind Sarah's eyelids. She didn't want to argue with him. To change his mind she would have to prove him wrong, and how could she do that?

"Please, please, Matt. I can't bear to quarrel again. If I promise not to tell you what you should do, what I wish you would do, will you not start on Thad again? Please, if you won't love me again, can we at least be friends?"

Still in the circle of his arms, Sarah felt him relax slightly.

"Take the money, and you can have this battle, Yank."

Sarah pushed the bills into her skirt pocket. It wasn't this battle, but the war she had to find a way to win, and the first step was to keep him from disappearing from her life again. "Can we walk a while? Just down the river path and back?"

The small sound he made might have been mirth or sorrow. "Why not? What difference can it make in this world if you and I walk another ways in the dark?"

A week later he waited for her in the shadows of the alley once more, and Sarah shamelessly used all her ammunition. She left him and got Laurie from Blackburns'. Other summers when she made it home from work early, she and Laurie sat on the back step in the summer nights. Blackburns would have no suspicion about this.

Laurie held Matt and Sarah each by a hand, swinging between them, chattering and happy, and unknowingly eased the tension. Sarah even got a good night kiss, a kiss every bit as paternal as the one Laurie got, but a kiss.

So they began what Sarah thought of as the summer of deceit. Two or three times a week, Matt waited for her in the alley. If the last customers dawdled and Sarah didn't finish her cleanup chores in the café until late, she and Matt walked down the river path and back. Sometimes they hardly talked at all. Sometimes they talked of the past, the goings on in town or at the ranch, but never of the future.

If the café had no late customers and Sarah and Addy said good night early, Matt waited while Sarah fetched Laurie.

The nights with Laurie were easier, for when Matt and Sarah were alone they walked apart, careful not to so much as brush against one another. Sarah thought sometimes she could hear the tension. It blocked out the sounds of the river and the summer night and grated over her skin.

Those nights when she slid into her bed alone, Sarah lay awake for hours, tortured by an ache so terrible she thought it should just kill her and be done.

In spite of so many nights without much sleep, Sarah's steps had a bounce in them. The fatigue that had weighed on her shoulders for years vanished. With Matt Slade back in her life, Sarah dreamed of the future not the past.

39

MATT NEVER PASSED up anything that let him take his mind off Sarah and his own inability to stay away from her. A cattle rustling puzzle served as a better diversion than most.

"Is it always like this?" Disbelief tinged Matt's voice as he stared at the repaired section of barbed wire fence.

"Yeah, it seems kind of strange, rustling cows and fixing the fence, but that's how it always is. Maybe they're hoping we won't notice," Jimmy said.

"Nobody could miss sign of two dozen cows bunched like that." Matt dismounted, led Sam up to the fence and began taking the twisted splice apart.

"What are you doing? You know we got orders not to cross onto the Bar S. We got to get back to the ranch and tell Mr. Farrell about this."

Busy with the fence, Matt didn't even look up. "You go back. A cow thief who fixes fences behind him is a fellow I want to meet."

"You go over there and you'll get yourself shot! You'll get yourself dead, and you'll start the real shooting war!"

"Nobody's going to shoot me when they can see I'm just tracking L&L stock. You go on back. I'll be along once I find out where those cows went."

Swinging back into the saddle, Matt rode through the gap he had reopened, intent on the trail. In seconds Jimmy was beside him, tight-faced and angry.

The tracks on Farrell's side of the fence had been as clear as could be on summer dry ground, but on the Stewart side the trail almost disappeared. The thieves had dispersed the tightly bunched cattle as soon as they crossed the fence line.

Jimmy's anger faded as the mystery intrigued him too. "They can't have just scattered them through the gap. The grass is good here. A few head would still be in sight."

Matt did not consider himself more than a competent tracker. Studying the ground, he said slowly, "I think they're still driving them, but they've got them spread way out. We're going to have to track one cow."

Hours later, with the sun almost straight overhead in a cloudless sky, they had deciphered the trail for only a few miles, and the faint sign disappeared completely on rocky ground.

Frustrated, Matt reined up, ready to admit defeat, when a rifle cracked. The warning shot furrowed into the ground a good twenty feet ahead of them. Horses closing in at a run sounded more ominous.

Matt raised both hands and watched Jimmy follow suit, the freckles standing out in the white of his young face. The first Bar S riders to reach them said nothing, just fired another shot in the air and waited. In minutes a dozen men surrounded Matt and Jimmy, including both Thad and Jesse Stewart.

Why, Matt wondered, were so many men in one place at one time on a working ranch? He waited to find out, already regretting giving way to his curiosity.

"Hard to believe we finally caught ourselves some cow thieves, bold as brass, right in broad daylight," said one of the men, looking to Thad Stewart. "Lucky they picked a spot where there's enough trees to choose a good one for a hanging, huh, boss?"

"You know I'm no thief, Pete! You got gall even saying it! Fear tinged Jimmy's anger.

Matt met Stewart's eyes, aware his life and Jimmy's depended on this one man Sarah described as honorable. He chose his words carefully. "Before you get around to any hanging, you mind telling me how you're calling us the thieves when we're sitting right on top of the trail of L&L cows pushed through the fence last night?"

"I've got to give you full credit for nerve, Slade." Stewart spoke without emotion. "You have to know we've been following that herd all morning. You've not only given us our best proof of Farrell's rustling, you've shown us where you started them into the rocks. What I can't see is why you're back here in the middle of the day. Were you afraid you left some sign you needed to slip back and cover? You didn't, you know. We traced all fifty back from where you pushed them through the fence, but lost the trail in the rocks and couldn't pick it up again."

Fifty! Maybe things weren't so bleak after all. "We're only following twenty-five," Matt said. "They were run through the fence sometime last night, and I'm the one ignored Farrell's orders and crossed the line. Maybe you won't listen to me, but you've known Jimmy long enough to know he's not a thief."

"I've known Jimmy long enough to know if Lucius Farrell asked him to hold his breath till he fell over dead, he'd do it, and I know you spent some time in prison for stealing. Cattle that time too, was it?"

"Why you son of a...." Jimmy tried to spur forward, but one of the surrounding men rode into his horse, the impact stopping Jimmy's horse and his words abruptly.

All the Bar S men looked to Thad, even Jesse. Matt forced a grin he didn't feel and shrugged. "You don't get three years for rustling in Texas any more than here. Of course, in Texas, if a man refused to 'fess up and told a story like I'm telling, we'd probably check it out, just to make sure he died embarrassed."

Thad considered, then looked around. "Rafe, take a look where we haven't cut up the ground and tell me what you see."

Hoping to Heaven Rafe was a better tracker than either he or Jimmy, Matt watched the man ride off a short distance and begin scanning the ground. The wizened little man rode back in what seemed far too short a time.

"It looks more like twenty-five than fifty," Rafe reported.

"They just got another couple dozen from somewheres else is all." Pete wasn't giving up.

"You willing to check back a ways?" Matt asked softly. "They strung them out as they brought them through the fence about two miles from here, but even a poor tracker like me can see it. Your man can probably follow it back right quick."

"He figures he gets close to the line, he can make a break for it is all. I say we hang them both." Pete looked like a regular cowhand, not one of Harlan's men, but he sure was a bloodthirsty sort.

Stewart ignored his man. "I understand you carry two handguns as well as two rifles, Slade. Suppose we just hold all of them for you for a while, and your reins, I think. You too, Jimmy."

"You're not leading me around on a horse like some little kid!"

Jimmy was angrier than Matt would have thought possible. He leaned over and touched the younger man's arm. "Better to get led around like a kid than hung like a fool. Let's let the man see the straight of things."

After handing over his gun and reins, Jimmy subsided into sullen silence. Rafe really was a first-class sign man, and soon they were back at the hole in the fence.

"It was the fact that fence was up and spliced got my curiosity bump itching so bad," Matt said. "Is it like that when you lose stock?"

"You know damn well what it's like. You're the one who...."

"Shut up, Pete." Thad's voice held no particular emphasis, but the man didn't say another word. "Yes," he continued, "that's what it's always like, and we've wondered about it ourselves."

"I think I might have an idea why now," Matt said. "You willing to take a look back a ways on our side?"

"No!" Jesse said vehemently. "If he's carrying another gun, over there he shoots you and claims he had a perfect right."

"I'll sit right here under guns if you want," Matt offered. "You'd better take Jimmy for a safe pass, though."

Jimmy shot Matt a furious glare. Thad, however, had already made up his mind. His men gave Matt and Jimmy back their reins, if not their guns. Thad and Rafe followed Matt and Jimmy a couple hundred feet back on to the L&L, every one of them studying the ground as they went. Once he was sure they realized how differently the rustlers had behaved on each side of the fence, Matt asked, "Are the tracks like that when you lose stock—clear on your side, next to nothing on ours?"

Thad pulled a cigar out of a shirt pocket, bit off the end and lit it. "I don't know. Dad and I decided we'd hold off with any retaliation as long as we could, see if Lucius came into his right mind again. We've given orders not to cross the line."

"That's exactly what Mr. Farrell says about you, or about your father anyway, and we've got the same orders. I just forgot them for a while this morning."

"How'd you make it through the war without a court martial?"

"Too many like me in the Fourth Texas to court martial us all."

"Well, we know where our fifty head went on to L&L range. Since we weren't going through the fence ourselves, we were backtracking to see where they were gathered."

Thad started giving orders long before the cigar was finished. He sent Rafe to see if he could figure out what had happened in the rocks. The rest of them rode the boundary fence to the place the rustlers had taken the fifty head through.

All the details that had confounded Matt to the point of ignoring orders were exactly the same. "I figure they want us to know what we lost, and they want you to know what you lost, but not what you gained, so to speak," Matt said. "Have you ever considered an outsider making this trouble?"

"No," Thad said flatly, "and I'm not convinced that's what it is now. You could have rigged this whole thing. It would buy Lucius more time before we get fed up and go after him."

"I suppose so. I suppose you could have done the rigging. That's an awful lot of trouble to go to, though," Matt pointed out.

"So much trouble you and Jimmy were caught flatfooted on our range this morning. Couldn't get it all done and get home in time."

"If you believe that, why aren't we wearing hemp neckties?"

"I don't believe it. I haven't made up my mind what I believe yet."

"Well now, that's a real comfort." Finally, Matt gave Thad a grin he really felt, and this time he got a smile back.

"I must say you didn't look particularly upset by it all. Do you have men clamoring to hang you often enough it no longer bothers you?"

At that Matt just broadened his grin, then looked down at the trampled ground leading up to the fence they had now opened up. "I sure haven't got over the notion I'd like to meet this neat thief. If Rafe did the tracking, we just might catch up in time to find out what's happening to those cows."

When they went back to get Rafe, however, he had gleaned some interesting information from the rocky ground. "There never was fifty of ours. That's why I couldn't find them. What they did was took twenty-five of ours and those twenty-five L&L, and then they joined 'em up on hard ground and drove them straight for the fence."

"Son of a gun!" Jesse exclaimed. "That explains the tally difference."

"Geeze, you're right," Jimmy said. "At least if they're doing it both ways it does. We can't match the count either."

Matt didn't understand until Jimmy explained. "We tally what we know we lost and subtract from what we know we had and we get a different number than if we do a rough count of what's on the range. Not the kind of difference you'd expect. A big difference."

The men formed a hunting party. Thad ordered one Bar S man back to ranch headquarters to report to his father and sent most of the other men back to their regular duties. Rafe, Thad, and Jesse joined Matt and Jimmy following the stolen herd across Farrell's range.

By late afternoon they started into the hills west of the L&L— government land, not Farrell's. To the west none of the new barbed wire was up. Although each year a few small bunches of cattle had to be rooted out of the hill meadows, most of the cattle stayed on the rich grass of the valley floor. The push for fences had come with the trouble between the ranches, except for Kirkendahl, of course.

Before his death Kirkendahl had fenced every acre of his land with barbed wire. Sitting on the best grass in the valley, and convinced his larger neighbors were overgrazing, he'd been delighted to finally find a way to keep their stock off his range.

As if by consensus, the five men halted as the shadows lengthened. Fifty bunched cows traveling across land never used for grazing could be followed at a run except for the broken, rocky terrain. Even so, the pursuers had been gaining on the herd with every mile.

"Where do you figure they're heading?" Matt asked, mostly to see if the others had reached the conclusion he had.

"It's rough country to push cows through, but I'd say over the ridge, then north. They'll drive them over Raton Pass and sell them in Colorado. Those mining camps won't even question brands, and they'll get more for them than we get legitimately." Thad set out Matt's analysis exactly.

"There's not much doubt we'll catch them," Matt pointed out, "but not before night. Jimmy, how about you go back to the ranch, tell Mr. Farrell and Beau what's going on. Tell them I'll be along in a day or two."

"The hell I will!" Jimmy burst out. "I'm not leaving you alone with a lynch mob!"

"Ah, now, nobody even got a rope burn out of all that talk, and you know nobody's going to shoot me. Just go on back and tell Mr. Farrell the whole story. With Beau and Roddy you maybe better leave out the hanging talk. Tell it gentle. Beau gets riled up easy, you know. It's bad for his nerves."

Jimmy leaned in his saddle toward Matt, for better emphasis. "You're bad for his nerves. He says you've been visited on him for his sins, and I thought it was just talk. From now on he gets all my sympathy." For emphasis Jimmy whirled his horse and spurred away, not looking back.

Thad gave a low chuckle. "He must think a lot of you. I can't believe he ignored orders and followed you this morning. It's not like him."

"He thinks I need a guardian, and he was right this time."

Thad sent Rafe back too. He left in a hurry, needing to catch Jimmy for safe passage over L&L land.

Matt and the two Stewarts pressed on until darkness made the going dangerous. Matt carried a small amount of coffee, some biscuits and jerky. Evidently the Stewarts made it to a main camp for lunch, or someone else worried about their meals.

The three men sat around a small fire, eating the few mouthfuls of food in silence. Passing the coffee cup to Thad, Matt noticed the male strength of the hand that closed around the tin handle.

When he urged Sarah to marry Thad, Matt saw her exquisitely dressed in impractical clothes. He saw her in huge, high-ceilinged rooms in a mansion-like house with maids hovering around. He saw her in shops ordering anything that took her fancy and people treating her not just with respect, but with deference.

When Stewart was in the picture at all, Matt saw Sarah standing beside him with a gloved hand resting demurely on his well-clothed arm.

Now Matt watched Thad drink, his throat undulating as he swallowed. For an instant coffee glistened on the man's lips, then his tongue slid across his mouth, neatening things the way tongues do. Matt shifted his gaze again to Thad's hand, curled carelessly around the cup. For the first time it hit home that Thad Stewart was a flesh and blood man, with the same needs and desires as all men.

The hand holding the tin cup would hold Sarah, run over her flesh and learn in the most intimate of ways all about the curves and hollows that made the irresistible whole. The fingers thrust casually through the cup handle would probe anything but casually into Sarah's most secret places, finding all the magical things Matt had found so long ago.

Matt's attention shifted back to the other man's face. The mouth outlined so neatly by the mustache would close over Sarah's. The tongue so efficient at wiping away traces of coffee would slip between Sarah's lips, plunge into the deepest sweet recesses.

Matt no longer saw a man sitting close to a small fire sharing a few swallows of coffee. Thad was in firelight all right, but naked, kneeling over Sarah. Sweat shone as he poised himself, ready to....

"Maybe Jimmy had it backwards. Maybe I'm the one who should be nervous if you plan to get even for that hanging talk here and now. Somehow, though, I'd expect a man in your business to be a lot faster and more decisive. Even if you're better than Rastus says, Jesse's going to kill you before you pull that gun."

Thad's words broke through Matt's self-induced reverie, but it took long seconds for him to replace the images in his mind with reality. Once he got that far, he took in the rest of the situation in an instant.

He had slipped the rawhide thong that kept his pistol in the holster without being aware of it. His hand held the grip, forefinger through the trigger guard. Thad still held the coffee cup, but across the fire, Jesse had his pistol out, pointing not at Matt's chest but his head.

"I'd say Jess figures if six slugs in the body won't kill you, he'd best just blow your brains all over these hills. Messy, but effective."

Matt let go of the Smith & Wesson, refastened the thong. Never in his life had he lost sight of where he was or what he was doing, except when it came to Sarah. If he kept this up he was going to end up chained to a wall in one of those asylum places. Had Beau ever found acting like a raving lunatic this embarrassing? And how did a man smooth something like this over when he still felt like shooting somebody?

Matt began carefully. "I can't blame you for getting a little edgy there, and I am sorry for it, but I was just woolgathering, nothing to do with this morning or today. If Harlan's been telling you so much about me, he must have told you I'm not good enough at this gun business to worry about. Beau keeps me around because I look mean enough to scare the opposition off without a fight."

"You're not selling that bill of goods at this fire." Thad's expression was as cynical as his words. "Harlan says you'll do to ride with. I'll give Taney credit for a good idea, though. The way you looked at me just now was enough to make a man start evaluating his life. Daydreaming could be a dangerous habit for a man like you, I'd think."

Matt managed a smile. "Any habit's dangerous, but that's not a habit, and it's not going to get to be one."

Jesse holstered his weapon and leaned forward. "Did you really stay on your feet after six bullets up in Colorado? Rastus says so, but I can hardly believe it. Did you?"

Grateful for the shift in subject, Matt said, "I'm not so sure about those six shots myself. Beau was sort of het up that day—he probably counted a couple places I nicked myself shaving. Anyway, it's your mind that's got to tell you to quit, and you've already seen mine tends to travel along a little slower than the rest of me."

So they got past the sticky situation, but after Matt rolled himself in his blanket, he waited sleepless for the dawn. The feelings coursing hot through him might all be new, but he recognized them easily enough—jealousy, possessiveness. And he had no right to be feeling those things. Already he liked both these Stewarts, and what he should be feeling was guilty, guilty for cheating Thad Stewart by continuing to see Sarah.

Because he could not summon the strength of will to stay away from her, Sarah clung to impossible dreams instead of facing the reality of a future that could be better than the past only as Stewart's wife. Somehow, some way, he had to find the strength to do what had to be done, and to live with the consequences.

Matt saddled up in the morning eager to catch rustlers, but the cow thieves had fled, leaving the stolen herd behind. In fact Matt and the Stewarts found a bonanza of more than three hundred head of cattle hidden in a meadow among the pines, all bearing either the Bar S or L&L brand.

"I will be damned!" Thad said. "From the looks of things some of these cows have been here quite a while. The grass is down to the roots in places."

"It makes sense, I suppose," Matt agreed. "It's a long ways north, so they're taking a small trail herd each time. They'll change their ways now. Are you willing to look for outsiders yet?"

"No, I'm not. For one thing, rustling's not all that's going on. What can an outsider stand to gain?"

Matt considered. "Land. One of these ranches, the L&L probably, and without the blame for beggaring Mr. Farrell."

"There's too much good land available in easier ways. That makes no sense." Then Thad added, "I'll tell you what. I'll keep an open mind about what I see if you'll do the same. Lucius may not have the resources to fight a range war in the regular way, but this operation would not only pay for itself, it would improve his cash situation considerably. If you see evidence he's paying someone else to do the dirty work, you don't look the other way. What do you say?"

Matt thought of Lucius Farrell's increasingly worried look lately and was still a hundred percent sure the man was not the world's best actor, but if this was all the Stewarts would give, he'd take it. "It's a deal."

The two men shook hands, then started pushing the herd home. A few hours later they drove right into a mixed search party of men from both ranches riding together in hostile silence, except for Beau and Harlan, who rode side by side, smoking cigars and discussing the news of the world quite amiably.

Recovery of an unexpected bonus in stolen cattle did nothing to soften anyone's attitude, but the extra hands allowed Matt to ride back to the ranch alone ahead of the rest to work on sorting out his troubled thoughts.

40

Sarah said good night to Adelaide Canaday and watched her leave the café through the front door before stepping out the back. Locking the door behind her, Sarah hoped for the first time that Matt would not be waiting. The night air was fresh and sweet with summer, but Sarah took her customary deep breaths with no pleasure, not even making the effort to raise her head or square her shoulders.

He was waiting for her in the alley, and Sarah forgot she didn't want to see him. She broke all the careful rules and threw herself in his arms. "Oh, Matt, I'm so sorry. It's such a long ride, and I wished you wouldn't be here, but you are, and I'm no good at all."

Sarah buried her face against his shirt and clung with all her strength, half expecting him to start peeling her away, but instead he bent, hooked an arm behind her knees and lifted her. She burrowed against his shoulder, willing to have him do with her what he would.

Too soon Matt lowered himself onto the big rock at the beginning of the river path. They had used this rock before, sitting silent in the nights, or finishing conversations before starting the last part of their walk to Blackburns'.

Quiet in his arms, Sarah wished she could stay like this forever, content and untroubled. With her face against his shoulder, she caught the slight scents of horse and leather, and the more basic male essence that was Matt himself. The strength of him cradled her, and Sarah wondered if she could soak up some of his strength for herself, suck it from him without diminishing him, as a child sucks life from its mother.

She voiced her thought without meaning to. "I'm stealing strength from you, strength and warmth, but I don't want to leave you without any."

"You can't steal from me. What I have is yours." He kissed her then, gently, across the forehead, on each eyelid, down the bridge of her nose and on the lips. How did he always know when she was just feeling sorry for herself and when she really needed comfort? For that matter how could so rowdy and rough a man manage a kiss so tender she felt wrapped in his love, cushioned and protected by it?

"Are you about ready to tell me what's wrong?"

Matt's breath blew softly across her lips, and Sarah reached for another kiss, but he raised his head.

"Start talking, Boston."

She wanted to tell him, but her thoughts chased each other into a hopeless tangle in her head. "You'll be angry with me, acting like the spoiled rich girl again. It's not me, not just me, it's the whole town, and the rest of them don't have you to make them feel better."

"The rest of them have better sense." Matt moved his shoulder slightly, a little series of shrugs prodding her into starting her story better than words.

Organizing her story enough to tell about it seemed like an impossible task, but she made a start. "We have a bank here in town, you know. Mr. Arnold Thompson came here several years before I did and set it up. At first no one would trust him with deposits; they only applied for loans. But he really did have a lot of capital behind him, and it has become a real bank. He owns it and manages it, and everyone in town calls him Banker Thompson, as if it's a title, like doctor or in the military."

"So you put your money in the bank and it's gone broke."

The very thought made Sarah smile against his shirt. "No, I never had enough money for banks, and I can't put all you've given me there. How would I explain it?"

"Tell them your family has come to its senses."

"Tavaras is too small a town for that. Everyone knows what does and doesn't come in the mail or by wire for that matter. You can't make me wealthy without making people think nasty things."

"Every penny I ever had wouldn't make you rich. So if the bank's not busted, what's Banker Thompson up to that's got you acting like a rag doll—he want to marry you too?"

Sarah almost giggled. "No, as a matter of fact you aren't the only man in the world who doesn't want to marry me. Even if Banker Thompson didn't have a wife, I'm sure I wouldn't be a candidate. No, you see, he has guests. His brother and two of his brother's friends. People here in town keep calling them Easterners, but they're not. I'm an Easterner. They're from St. Louis and Chicago, and that's only east of here, not the East. It's like the way they call a creek a river."

"Crick." Matt's shoulder moved again. "Now stop talking around it and tell me what Thompson and the fake Easterners are up to."

Sarah sighed, but with some more prodding and some questions, she finally got it all out so that Matt understood.

An arrogant man, Arnold Thompson repaid personal slights through his business dealings. Insulting him or even disagreeing with him could mean paying a higher interest rate for a loan or being refused. Everyone in Tavaras knew this, which was probably why, Sarah reflected, they curried favor with the title "Banker" Thompson. So when the brother and friends showed up, all Tavaras knew to be very careful around the visitors.

"And the thing is, they're terrible people. Banker Thompson is opinionated and rather boorish, but these others—they're ugly, cruel people. The brother is staying with the Thompsons, but the other two are in the hotel, and they're behaving terribly. They find fault, and they criticize, and they've even *accidentally* broken wash pitchers and things. They complained about all Mr. Michel's wares, said there wasn't enough of a selection and things were inferior, and they didn't buy anything, but they broke things."

Matt held her quietly as if he knew there was more, and after a moment Sarah told him more.

"They visited Mr. Hurtado, the barber, too. He's such a dear man, and they refused to pay for haircuts and shaves. At the livery they rented a buggy and said the horse was a nag and the buggy wasn't fit to drive and they brought the horse back in a lather with whip cuts and the upholstery was ripped. They're cruel. People here make a living for themselves, but losses like that make a real difference. No one's wealthy."

"So why isn't Blackburn doing something?"

"Well, I don't think they've done anything illegal, and of course no one's complaining to Henry."

"They're afraid of making this banker mad?"

"Yes, they are. Not everyone has a loan with the bank, but they all know they might need one sometime, and they won't get it if he decides they've insulted his brother or friends, and if they do have a loan, he's capable of calling it in on a whim. He's done that to people."

"Nice man."

"No, he's not, but he's not like his friends. They go on and on about the fortunes they've made from the railroads and stock and bonds. It should sound like some of the business talk I heard from my father and brothers at home, but it doesn't. My father would be mortified if anyone he associated with ever boasted like that. They're even worse with the Mexican shopkeepers. I heard they were down to the cantina at the other end of town. There's a woman there. You know, an, um...."

"You're sure getting delicate of a sudden. Sure, I know about her. She's in your friend Kate's business."

"Kate doesn't do that any more, and how is it you know that woman, pray tell?"

"I don't know her, not the way you're meaning. The first time we came to town we checked out both the saloon and the cantina is all."

Sarah could feel a huge aching lump forming at the back of her throat. "Matt, I don't think I could bear it if you're being so noble on me and then using that woman to...."

"The only thing I'm using is the crick," he put a slight extra emphasis on his proper pronunciation of the word, "that runs through the ranch. About the time my teeth are chattering and everything is shriveled up like prunes, I get myself all convinced I could of been a priest."

This tidbit fascinated her. "Does it work?"

"Sure, all the way till I get warmed up again. Of course if you don't start getting sensible before cold weather, I'll either die of pneumonia or they'll find me still there some morning, stuck in the ice. That would fix things permanent."

Knowing that the rigid self-control he had imposed on them both extracted a toll from him too pleased Sarah. She cuddled against him again. Still tired—weary—she no longer felt so cold and hollow. That made it easier to tell him.

"They hurt her. On purpose. For fun. After they accused Mr. Garcia of watering his liquor and having marked decks of cards and smashed half his place to pieces."

"How do you know that? Did Garcia talk to Blackburn?"

"No. The Mexican people try to handle their own troubles. They're afraid of American law, I think. But sometimes people act as if a waitress isn't really there. They keep on with their conversations. No one was very specific, but I heard enough. Kate says there are men like that. They...."

"I know."

He kissed her again, and Sarah almost started to cry at the sweetness of it. Being independent and responsible and—brave— had lost its attraction a long time ago. Perhaps sharing trouble didn't halve it, but having Matt there, holding her, caring, did make the problem seem smaller.

"So what are they doing to you?"

It tumbled out in an disorganized jumble, but in the end Sarah told him everything, almost everything, all but one little thing, and that was a mistake, or an accident. It had to be.

"Nobody can blame you if you tell Blackburn. You live there. Pass it on as just telling about your day. Does he owe the bank?"

"I don't imagine Henry ever owed anyone a penny for anything in his life, but I can't tell him. Don't you see? Addie has a little income from what her husband left her, and she can make payments on what she borrowed when she decided to open the café, but she borrowed against her house, and the café only barely pays for itself. It's something for her to do, and it really is sociable there. She enjoys it. So do I. We all do. If I complain, Addie's the one Thompson will take it out on, and what they're doing isn't illegal."

"In a town like this, the sheriff makes the law. If he wants to run them out, he will."

"I can't be the one to make trouble over such a small thing. It really is the whole town suffering, not just me, and probably no one else is acting so childish over it."

"How much longer are they supposed to be here?"

"Another week." Sarah's voice caught as she admitted this devastating fact she had only learned herself that day. "Matt?"

"Hmm."

"Could I have another kiss please?"

Her request resulted in her warm seat across hard muscled thighs disappearing as he stood up. "If you're feeling perky enough to ask, you're feeling perky enough to be dangerous. Let's get you home."

Sarah didn't argue with him but walked along docilely in the curve of his arm to the start of the path across the Blackburn backyard. There she did get another kiss, and a bouncing pat on the bottom that sent her up the path smiling. She was still smiling as she fell asleep, thinking about Matt taking a late night bath in the "crick" at the L&L.

41

THE NEXT DAY Matt stood in the space between two buildings across from Adelaide Canaday's café, observing customers as they entered and left. What Sarah had told him last night justified the state she was in, but it didn't account for the undercurrent of real fear. Maybe knowing what the men had done to some poor sad whore eking out a living in the cantina frightened Sarah, but he sensed something more.

Only days ago he had resolved to find a way to say goodbye to Sarah and Laurie. Today Matt intended to fix Sarah's problem. Knowing about all the years she dealt with much worse than this on her own made no difference; neither did the fact that a few words to Blackburn, and the sheriff would do the fixing.

The minute hand on Beau's gold pocket watch showed half past eleven. Matt put the watch away, lifted the barbaric Spanish spurs in his hands and admired the way they gleamed in the sunlight. Roddy called these his "walking spurs" but never explained. Beau, Luke, and Rio thought Roddy called them that because touching spurs like these to Aurora would have a man walking in an instant.

Matt, however, agreed with Swede, who maintained the name came from the unique sound the spurs made when fastened to a boot just right. Roddy had worn the spurs in Goldville, and Matt remembered the sound as downright inspiring.

Matt crouched to put the spurs on. Sam wouldn't take to the use of them any more kindly than Aurora. The spurs had come to town in his saddle bags, and right now small slivers of wood jammed the rowels in place on the shanks. He didn't want the spurs speaking their piece too soon.

SARAH'S GOOD MOOD from her time with Matt lasted until she got to work in the morning and faded as the minutes ticked away. When Addie went to deal with a deliveryman, leaving Sarah working alone with Mabel Lanning, Mabel twisted Sarah's nerves into a tighter knot.

"I saw what happened yesterday, you know. I figured it was your business to take care of, but you ought to tell Addie. If nothing else, you could do the cooking, and her and me could wait tables."

Tall, thin and graying, Mabel usually looked down her nose at Sarah. Now concern softened her features. Sarah wanted to hug her and didn't dare. "It was an accident, Mabel. I'm sure it was. He just reached for something as I leaned over, and...."

"Hah." Mabel made a sound of disbelief. "You know better than that. He didn't apologize, and he looked at you the way a fox looks at a chicken just before it bites the thing's head off."

"I'm sure you're wrong. No one would do that right here with people all around, and I'm going to be extra careful today. I'll stand back and be careful. I may be a fairly decent cook these days, but I'm not as good as Addie. I can't keep my eye on all those things for the lunch rush, and she can't hustle around well enough to keep those men happy and do other tables too."

Mabel gave another snort. "That's a fairy tale and you know it. Nothing's going to keep them happy. They don't want to be happy, and they want to make the rest of us miserable. If that's what you want, I'll keep my mouth shut, but if it happens again, I'm getting Addie right out of the kitchen, and after that it's up to her."

"All right," Sarah agreed meekly, her heart thumping. She really was going to have to be very careful, for Addie's sake as well as her own.

Sarah loved the café. Cozy and warm in the winter, in the summer the thick adobe walls kept most of the building pleasantly cool. The kitchen did get warm. A rosy flush always colored Addie's round face, but the heat never reached unbearable temperatures.

The wall between the kitchen and the café proper featured an open doorway and a pass-through where Addie set out prepared orders. By reaching into the pass-through, Sarah could pull one of the big coffee pots right off the stove.

Small tables lined the two walls at right angles to the kitchen wall, and two larger tables occupied the center of the small restaurant.

As she expected and dreaded, Banker Thompson, his brother and their two friends entered the café right at 11:30, early enough to appropriate one of the center tables. After the past three days of dealing with them, Sarah also knew the men would stay there as if rooted for hours. She braced herself as the ordeal she had described to Matt began.

A short while later, Sarah returned a plate full of food to the pass-through counter. The single bite Banker Thompson's brother had eaten made the entire plate fit only for the slop pail.

The waste filled her with rage, but that's what they did, what they had been doing for three days. They ordered, reordered, claimed she brought the wrong thing and sent food back for every flimsy excuse imaginable.

Making twenty trips to their table for every one trip most customers required exhausted her. Being unable to reply when they carped and criticized infuriated her.

Behind her Sarah heard the room ringing again with the calls of "Miss, Miss, Miss." In addition to sending each portion of each meal back to the kitchen one after another, bouncing her back and forth like a yo-yo, the four men demanded refills of their coffee cups constantly. When she was at the table with the coffee pot, only one would ever concede his cup could be topped up, but as soon as she put the pot down, the cries came again. "Miss, Miss, Miss." Often a cup had no more than a swallow gone from it.

Sarah reached for the coffee pot, her arm aching from the weight of it on so many trips. Beside her, Mabel whispered, "I couldn't understand why you weren't afraid of that man, you know, at the picnic, but he really is awful nice, so polite. And that smile could melt ice in January."

Sarah almost dropped the heavy pot as she whirled around. Matt. At one of the small side tables, totally absorbed in a newspaper. How could she have been too distracted to see him come in? And what in Heaven's name was he up to?

Panic flashed through her. If he made trouble, he would be the one Henry would jump all over. Even now, with the picnic past history, Henry still raged at the mere mention of Matt's name. When Thad and Jesse related their chase after the rustlers with Matt, Henry expressed genuine sorrow there had been no hanging.

"Miss, Miss, Miss!"

Flying by the center table, Sarah poured a dollop of coffee in the indicated cup then hurried over to Matt.

"What are you doing here?" she whispered. "If you make trouble, Henry will blame you, no matter what. You know that. Please, Matt...."

He cut her off without even looking up from the paper. "What I'm doing here is having something besides beef or beans for lunch. The question is what are you doing here. That other lady's taking care of me just fine, and those fellows are hollering for you again."

Close to despair, Sarah left it as hopeless. She couldn't win an argument with him here and now, and it was all her fault for not making it clear to him exactly how strongly Henry felt. If Henry had his way, Matt would be in jail on her account again in a minute. Soon Sarah had to push her fears to the back of her mind and concentrate on hurrying back and forth, trying to do her regular work and keep Thompson and his friends halfway satisfied.

The banker and his friends exhausted the subject of the poor food and service and moved on to bragging about their business deals. Yesterday, as they discussed railroads, stocks and bonds, Thompson's brother had reached out and touched Sarah, his hand running over her breast as she refilled his coffee cup.

Last night Sarah had convinced herself the touch was accidental. The man had raised his hand for some other reason. Now, faced with the rudeness, insults and sly looks, Sarah accepted that the humiliating touch had been deliberate.

Even so, this wasn't Charon—or Heber. Here in Tavaras people respected her. The café overflowed with friends and acquaintances. She would be careful, and it wouldn't happen again. In fact, with Matt sitting right there, she would be doubly careful and stand back from the table. If she extended her arms instead of leaning over, it would eliminate any chance for a repeat of yesterday's experience.

Thompson's brother didn't repeat yesterday's insult. As she picked up an empty plate from her careful distance, he closed his hand over one cheek of her bottom and pushed her forward so hard she had to throw her arms out and spread both hands on the table to keep from falling among clattering dishes. She hung there for long seconds, unable to gather herself to get away.

The man on her other side reached over and closed his hand around her breast, squeezing hard. "Well, now, that's better, honey. Standing back like that, why you almost made me think you didn't like us."

Sarah twisted away and bolted across the room toward the kitchen door, followed by perverse laughter. A hush fell over the café. Not one customer had missed what happened, except....

Sarah threw a frantic glance toward Matt and saw him still serenely reading the paper. How could he? She didn't want the café filled with gunfire, and she didn't want him in trouble, but her throat tightened and tears slipped down her cheeks.

Sarah had not seen Mabel go into the kitchen, but the older woman came out with Addie, even as the men started in again.

"Miss, Miss, Miss." The brother rapped a fork on a glass.

Addie paused there by the door, furious, but before she acted, Matt got up. He moved not toward the center table, but to the counter, reached around and picked up the coffee pot as if he'd been doing it every day for years. The sound of his walk sent a shiver all the way down Sarah's spine. His spurs hissed with each step.

Rooted to the floor of the doorway, Sarah watched as silently as everyone else. Matt walked up to the table, shoved the toe of one boot onto the seat of a chair, and rested the forearm holding the coffee pot on his thigh.

The brother Thompson sat in the chair Matt chose, and when Matt's boot toe prodded into the brother's leg, he squirmed angrily half off the chair.

"You know, I've been sittin' over there, listenin' to you folks," Matt said, his drawl so thick he sounded like a stranger. "It must be a fine thing to be used to all those fancy places way back East, but you fellows are overlookin' some of the advantages of a friendly little town. Say a nice lady like Mrs. Hammond gets some behind in her work? Well, somebody ups and volunteers to help her out. Like now. You fellows need some more coffee, and Mrs. Hammond's got other things to do, and so here I am volunteerin' to get your coffee. Of course, I'm not so pretty as her—and not so graceful either."

With his last words, Matt poured coffee into the brother's cup from a height of at least three feet above the table. The hot liquid splashed everywhere, fat drops burning the man's face, and staining his snowy white shirt and dove gray suit.

"Why you son of a...!"

"Well, that sure was clumsy of me. I'll get the hang of it in a minute here." Matt turned then toward the other man who had touched Sarah, but the pot sailed right over the man's coffee cup even as Matt tipped it to pour, and kept tipping. The pot turned upside down, the lid fell off, and the contents spilled right into the man's lap.

He shrieked, falling backwards screaming, pulling vainly at his trousers, trying to get cloth soaked with almost scalding liquid off his skin. Finally, one of the others threw first one and then a second glass of water at the man's groin, and the sound faded to a whimper.

"I'm going to kill that...."

Banker Thompson grabbed his brother by the arm and whispered furiously in his ear.

The two men helped the one on the floor stand and all four hurried toward the door. "All right, let's just get out of here."

Mesmerized by the scene, Sarah had lost track of Matt. She was as surprised as anyone to see him leaning casually against the frame of the door to the street. The further surprise was that for just a moment she saw him not as Matt, the man she knew and loved, the father of her child, but as others saw him.

A white shirt emphasized his deep tan, as the fitted cowhide vest and Levis emphasized the trimness of his waist and hips. Lean and leggy, every inch of him looked as tough as rawhide. The black patch and absence of his left eye made the stare from his right icier. The scars accentuated the harsh lines of his face and tight line of his mouth. Braver men than these bullies would pause at the sight. Sarah swallowed hard.

Matt's tone, however, was not particularly threatening, unless of course, you hadn't long ago come to love the deep, gravelly sound. "I guess I'm not much of a waitress, am I? I suppose this means I'm not going to get a pat on the ass, or my chest rubbed either. But you know, I would have figured gents like you, used to those fancy places back East, never would leave a restaurant without paying. Make a habit of that, do you?"

Their backs were toward her, and Sarah could only imagine their expressions. Banker Thompson returned to the table and threw down a few bills, then started for the door again. Matt didn't move.

"And I suppose in those fancy places fellows like you never walk out without leaving a smart sum extra on the table for the waitress," Matt said. "I figure no matter what happens, you want to make sure everybody knows how generous you are. Am I wrong about that?"

Thompson went back again and threw two more bills down, then looked toward Matt, who nodded and moved from the doorway. The footsteps of the four men echoed in the silence as they rushed out into the street. The spurs hissed as Matt returned to his table and sat down.

Before Sarah could move, Adelaide Canaday brought Matt to his feet again. Only a little taller than Sarah, but about four times as big around, Addie had a voice as deep for a woman as Matt's for a man, and she knew how to use it to be heard when she wanted. Now her voice boomed into every corner of the room as Addie held out her hand and introduced herself to Matt.

"I hope you know if I had any idea what was going on out here, I'd have run those no goods out days ago, banker or no banker."

Matt gave Addie his best smile, and Sarah heard Mabel make a funny little sound.

"I never doubted that for a moment, Mrs. Canaday," he said, "but maybe it's better like this. After all, nobody can blame you if there just happened to be a mean-minded Texan who likes pushing folks around eating here today."

Addie cocked her head to one side and regarded Matt for what seemed to Sarah like a very long time, then said more quietly. "Mr. Slade, if you try to pay for that meal, I'm going to be insulted, and you make sure you save room for a piece of apple pie, unless you'd rather have something else. It's yours for the asking."

By the time Addie disappeared back into the kitchen, low conversation started around the room again, but Sarah forgot about the customers as she went to Matt's table.

"You, Mr. Slade, might get yourself hugged and kissed in public with a performance like that."

Matt glared at her. "Well, you just slow yourself right down, Mrs. Hammond. They touched you before, didn't they? And you didn't bother telling me about that, did you? I've never been so close to emptying a gun in a man for the pleasure of it. I ought to erase the feel of his hand with a paddling."

She did feel guilty, just not enough to dim the joy of it. "I'm sorry. I really am. It was only once, yesterday, and I told myself it was an accident, that it had to be. He probably wishes you did shoot him, though. He's probably going to wish that for quite a while."

"He will, but you expected shooting, didn't you? You were worried I'd open up with a gun right here in a room full of people minding their own business. If that's what you think, what do you think the rest of these folks expected? You better get back to work before they start getting notions."

"They'd expect me to thank you."

"You thanked me. Now get."

If he hadn't destroyed her happiness, he surely had put a dent in it.

42

IN THE DAYS following the scene at the café, Sarah's mixed feelings resolved themselves into a determination to use this to prove to Matt he was wrong about the future.

After all hadn't half a dozen people gone up to him before he left the café that day, introduced themselves and thanked him? Didn't Addie say loudly she never expected to feel anything but contempt for a gunman, but this one she considered on the side of the angels? And Mabel, Mabel got a positively foolish look on her face every time anyone mentioned Matt.

At home, Laurie wanted to hear the story over and over, and of course, unlike the stories of long ago in Texas, Sarah could tell this one in front of others. While Minna admitted to Sarah privately that Matt's intervention had been a blessing, at the sound of Matt's name Henry's face flushed with anger.

The fact that people who had been afraid to come to their own sheriff for help now stopped him in the street to tell him how Matt had "run those gents out with a coffee pot" only enraged Henry further. Aware finally of the grief the bullies had caused in his town, Henry gave Banker Thompson an ultimatum, and the day after that his brother and two friends removed themselves to Rye Wells.

That did not mollify Henry, however. He continued to curse every time anyone mentioned the incident or Matt. When the next Sunday Thad not only refused to share Henry's outrage, but expressed gratitude, Sarah thought for a moment Henry's anger might spill over onto the Stewarts. A partisan man of passion himself, Henry Blackburn did not appreciate an open mind in others.

Not until Sarah pointed out that Henry's rants left her feeling he wished she had been kidnapped, ravaged and left to rot in the wilderness rather than helped by someone he didn't approve of did Henry slow down. In her presence only, she suspected.

Then there was what Sarah thought of as the visitation. When she looked up from a stack of dirty dishes one night to see Beauregard Emmett Taney and Jaime Francisco Rodriguez y Candelaria seating themselves at one of the café's center tables, Sarah's pulse quickened.

"Oh, bother," Addie said without looking up from her chores. "It's too late for customers. We should have locked the door. I'll tell whoever that is we're closed."

"No, please don't."

Addie looked up then and gasped. "You run out the back and get Henry. I'll deal with them until he gets here."

"No, please. They've come to see me. I'll finish my work later if you'll let me talk with them now."

Addie met Sarah's eyes, her surprise changing slowly to something else. She nodded and said nothing further.

Sarah picked up the coffee pot and three cups and walked slowly to the table. For the first time, she accepted that in one way Matt was right. These men differed from the shopkeepers, craftsmen, laborers and cowhands who frequented Tavaras. The difference showed in their eyes and faces, in the way they walked and carried themselves. The people who claimed dramatically that they smelled of death were wrong, but there was a difference.

At the table, Sarah smiled nervously as she put the cups down and filled two. "We don't have much left over tonight, but I'm sure I could find two pieces of pie."

"We didn't come to eat."

Sarah filled the third cup and sat down herself. The coffee had simmered on the stove too long, but she sipped the thick, bitter liquid, deciding how best to handle this.

Beau Taney examined her with cold gray eyes, making no effort to put her at ease. If Matt had not told her so much about these men, she would be terrified, but he had told her story after story.

She liked them, felt she knew them without ever having been closer than an introduction at the picnic.

Unlike Beau, Roddy hid his feelings, his face a neutral mask. Sarah knew Matt never told anyone what he had been up to this summer. He slipped away from the ranch at night without a word, and his friends minded their own business. Matt had borrowed those wicked spurs from Roddy, however, and everyone in the county had heard about the scene in the café by now.

"I suppose you've come to ask me if my intentions toward Matt are honorable," Sarah said. "They are, I assure you." She smiled, but got no smiles in return.

"Matt may suffer from a regrettable innocence where women are concerned, Mrs. Hammond, but believe me none of the rest of us has that problem. A woman who won't walk down the street with a man in daylight is sure as hell not serious. The people in this town think you're a sweet little lady who'd faint from a hard kiss, and you're sneaking around in the dark, having a lot of fun and laughing behind their backs. Your morals are your business, but it's Matt that you're using, and he can't handle someone like you. He'll never believe you're just playing games with him to inspire Stewart into proposing a little sooner."

The unfairness of that accusation washed Sarah's nervousness away in a wave of indignation. "Why you self-righteous ignoramus, who do you think you're preaching to?"

"Shut up!" Beau's voice was deep enough and loud enough to drown her out. "I'm telling you, you find a way to end it right now without hurting him any more than necessary, or your respectability is going to be an old memory. Do you hear me?"

What was only a memory right then was Sarah's self-control. Her temper took over, and she stood up, one fist on the table, and the other shaking in Beau's face. "Who the hell do you think you're talking to, Mister? If I had to listen to that, you can just listen to me! When you leave New Mexico, Matt will be staying with me, or I'll be coming with you, and if you don't like it, too bad! For your information, I'd be happy to sashay right down Main Street at high noon on his arm. Matt's the one so determined no one should know about us because of my damn reputation, and so far as I can see, that reputation is absolutely useless. So you just go right ahead and destroy it, and I might be so grateful I'd stop thinking how good you'd look all laid out in a black suit at the funeral parlor."

Temporarily out of breath, Sarah sat back down and glared first at Beau and then at Roddy. To her considerable satisfaction, Beau looked taken aback.

"This sneaking and hiding is Matt's idea?"

"Of course it is, and you know he's as stubborn as a stone. He says if people knew they would be cruel to both me and my daughter. He says I only imagine I could bear up to it for any length of time."

"So what's he planning on coming out of this?"

"Nothing, of course. I've been hoping what happened here the other day would help me convince him he's wrong, but it won't if most people are as open minded as you. You are a damn disappointment, Mr. Taney."

Beau regarded her thoughtfully. "Well, you are a damn surprise, Mrs. Hammond. How is it everyone around here thinks you're a gentle little thing, and both times I've seen you I'd want you on my side in a fight to the death?"

"I am gentle," Sarah said, and then realized how ridiculous that was under the circumstances and started to laugh. "Except when I lose my temper, and I seem to have done that the two times you've met me."

The cold hardness left Beau's face, and Sarah saw how a man like this could break a heart or two without even trying. "So why does everyone think you're going to marry Stewart?" he asked.

Sarah only just managed not to get angry all over again at the very sound of the name. "Because they think I should. I have never encouraged that man. I have gone so far as to state my lack of interest to Thad personally and to everyone else, but no one listens, and I am quite frankly tired of hearing about it. Matt's as bad as all the rest. He has some insane idea that how many cows the Stewarts own is more important than how we feel about each other. 'Marry Stewart, Boston. He can give you everything you should have.' I'm about ready to borrow his own gun to shoot him over it."

"Boston?" Roddy spoke for the first time.

Sarah turned to him. "He's calls me that sometimes. I grew up in Boston, you know."

Roddy got to his feet, giving her a trace of a courtly bow. "We are making you late in finishing your work, and it seems the misunderstanding is over now. Good luck to you, I think."

He gripped Beau's shoulder, strong brown fingers digging in hard. After exchanging a single glance with Roddy, Beau got up and followed him out. Sarah sat for a moment, puzzled by their abrupt departure, then collected the cups and coffee pot and returned to the kitchen.

Almost finished with the cleanup, Addie said nothing until Sarah washed the three cups and coffee pot and everything sat ready for morning.

When Addie finally spoke, her voice gave no hint of her attitude. "So it wasn't a coincidence that Mr. Slade was here just when you needed him."

"No, it wasn't," Sarah admitted. "I told him about those men the night before."

"And do you suppose you could bring yourself to tell me about this? A woman could die of fright with those two paying late night visits."

Sarah told her employer then about everything that had happened since the picnic, about Beau and Roddy's misconceptions, and about Matt's attitude. When she finished, she asked, "So is he right, Addie? Do you feel exactly the way Matt says you will? Shall I stay home tomorrow and from then on?"

"If you mean am I dismissing you because of your choice of men friends, no, Sarah, I'm not. But I think meeting him in the dark like that is extremely foolish. If you were seen, depending on who saw what, I might not have a choice. If he worries about you so, why hasn't he thought of that?"

"I think because he's sure we won't be seen, or recognized anyway, and also because he keeps thinking we won't go on."

"Maybe." Addie sighed. "To be honest, if I hadn't met him, I'd be appalled. But I did meet him, didn't I, and I liked him. Mabel is so taken with him, she's acting like a silly girl. The fact remains, he's more than a little right. There are people in this town who will judge harshly and never relent. Can you accept that?"

"If we can have a life together, I can accept anything. I'm afraid Henry may be one of the ones who won't relent, though. It will be a sorrow, but I've lived through enough of that."

Addie gave Sarah a hug. "If that's the way you feel, then you do what you must. Nothing anyone says is going to stop you anyway."

BEAU HAD COME CLOSE to balking when Roddy signaled he wanted to leave the café immediately. Roddy had been a half-hearted companion from the start.

"Matt is a grown man. This is his business, not ours."

Beau, however, thought Matt needed a little help in this department. Matt was just plain naive where women were concerned. He treated whores like ladies, and ladies like angels. In the end Beau talked Roddy into helping with the effort to convince little Mrs. Hammond she was playing with fire and going to get royally burned if she kept it up.

Since Roddy had been so reluctant to interfere, he should have been pleased at the unexpected way things turned out. Instead he had given a clear signal: I know something about this you don't. Do this my way.

Although impatient, Beau let it hang between them. Halfway back to the ranch, Roddy pulled up, ready to talk. "I got us out of there because of the name. Boston."

"So she's a Yankee. What of it?"

"It's more than that. You were not in a bed next to Matt in Colorado for days and nights."

"He told you something?"

"No. It was what he would not tell. You see, his sleep was not easy. The stronger he got, the more dreams troubled him. As I got better, I would hear him and wake him. There was never any sense to his words, but sometimes he would cry out, and then one word was clear. Boston. I too thought of the city. I asked him if he had been there. He said no, and he was upset. He would not talk about it."

Beau pulled a cigar from his pocket and prepared to light it, thinking hard. "That would explain the picnic. He knew what would happen that day. Knew it."

"Yes, and it also explains the way they acted when they met in town that first time. You have to look at it in a different way."

Beau shook out his match and dropped it, watching where it fell near his horse's front hoof to be sure no spark flared. "It had to be before he went to prison, and I don't see Matt involved with a married woman."

"Maybe the husband was already dead. Maybe she married another after he went to prison."

"Maybe." Beau took a puff on the cigar, then said. "I'll tell you one thing that isn't maybe any longer. You were right that this is Matt's business. I guess we just sit tight and hope it works out."

"Sometimes, for an intemperate man, you can be almost reasonable."

Beau laughed out loud and started his horse moving again.

TO SARAH'S RELIEF, she did not have to decide whether or not to tell Matt about the visitation. Beau and Roddy mentioned seeing her themselves. What stunned her was Matt's attitude.

"I suppose now Mrs. Canaday knows what she shouldn't."

"She knows I've been seeing you. She's not ready to throw stones. She liked you."

"Easy enough to like somebody that helps you out of a fix—for a while."

"And Mabel thinks you're the most charming human being she's run across in years. She giggles."

"That poor old lady most likely has so many problems she doesn't see the straight of anything."

"As a matter of fact her no good husband ran out on her years ago, leaving her to raise two children by herself and without even the option of remarrying if she wanted to. Generally, she hasn't a kind word for any man."

"Look, Sarah, this whole business makes it clear where we're heading. A few people know today. The whole town will know tomorrow. Maybe I can't talk you into marrying Stewart, but I can sure stop you from getting hurt over me. It's not fair, but you're going to have to figure out what to tell Laurie. Make her understand somehow without telling her if we go on people will be calling you names in the street."

Sarah, who had been looking at everything from exactly the opposite point of view, could hardly believe her ears. Nor could she force herself to once again give him assurances of renewed secrecy. Angry frustration made her do the one thing she had vowed at the beginning of the summer never to do. She pushed him. More than that, she clawed.

"What names would they be calling me in the street, Matt? Terrible dirty names that imply I'm the kind of woman who would have a child out of wedlock? My goodness, a delicate little thing like me probably would just die of shame over such slurs."

Matt grabbed her by the shoulders. There would be bruises from his hold. "I told you before I don't want to hear that kind of talk. You just quit it."

"You're walking out of my life. I'll talk any way I want to, and I think maybe I'll start by telling everybody the truth about Texas over Sunday dinner this week. I'm tired of living in a prison myself, a prison with walls of lies."

"If you think you're threatening me with that, forget it. We both know you won't do that to Laurie, so there's no use even pretending. You listen to me now. Enough poison can kill anything, even love. If we end it now, what's between us is still more good than bad and so are the memories. If we keep on, what will happen will poison it all, and we won't even be able to look back without having to see it through ugliness. It just wasn't ever meant to be. Fate played an ugly trick on us, but we came out of it with more good than was meant anyway."

His hands had stopped digging into her shoulders long before he finished, and now he cupped her face.

"Marry him, Boston. Let yourself have something good. If you're trying to pay for some sin, it was mine, not yours, right from the start."

Desperation assailed Sarah, along with terrible grief. What did you do with a man who loved you too much to love you? How could she make him understand? Now Sarah's fingers dug into his flesh.

"If I can't make you see that for me something good can only be with you, I can't. But for your own sake you ought to ask yourself if perhaps you really just don't think that what we might make together is worth any effort. Would any circumstances ever have been ideal enough? What if things were backwards, Matt? What if when you got out of prison instead of Beau and Roddy you fell in with some businessmen and now you were wearing an expensive suit and people tipped their hats to you on the street and called you sir, and you visited some little town like this and there I was with paint on my face, wearing a red dress that didn't cover everything it should? What if Carter succeeded with me beyond his wildest dreams, and you escaped unscathed? Would you see me on the street and pretend you didn't know me? Would you come around in the night and give me money and tell me all the reasons it was still no good, not even worth enduring some ugly words or nasty looks?"

He moved under her hands and started to speak, but Sarah reached up and put her fingers across his lips. "Oh, no. I don't want an easy answer right now. You wait until you're alone with those cows out at the ranch someday when you have time to look deep into all the corners of your heart. Perhaps I don't even want to know what you find."

She pulled away from him then and walked unsteadily home alone. Not a single tear fell until she was in bed, and then Sarah cried until she was sure she would break into pieces.

43

THE NEXT WEEK passed slowly, one day drifting by after another as Sarah watched from somewhere outside herself, going through ordinary day to day motions and feeling nothing. For once she took the easy way out with Laurie.

She told the child Matt would be too busy at the ranch to come to town for a while. Perhaps that only postponed the reckoning, but dealing with Laurie's questions heightened Sarah's pain to an unbearable level, and she took the coward's way out.

Everyone else believed Sarah was coming down with something and plied her with endless tonics and advice. Adelaide Canaday's sympathetic behavior hinted she knew the truth, but mercifully, Addie only gave Sarah an occasional pat on the arm as they worked and offered neither advice nor tonic.

After a Sunday dinner at which Sarah ate little and tasted less, she wanted to crawl upstairs and hide in her bed, but for Laurie's sake and to escape any well-intentioned ministrations, she made the walk to Gilbrides'. Emily showed an unwanted insight.

"I can't imagine what you two could have quarreled about that has you dragging around like this, Sarah, but it will pass. Learning to get past difficulties is part of learning to live together."

Sarah jerked her drooping head up. "What! What are you talking about, Em?"

"I'm saying that the first lovers' spat always seems like the end of the world, and it never is. If you and Thad have had a difference of opinion...."

"Thad!" Sarah spit the name as a curse and didn't care. "Thad! How could we have a difference of opinion? I don't know what any of his opinions are. I don't care what any of his opinions are. I wouldn't care if the whole family was overcome with a sudden urge to move to China and acted on it. What's gotten into you, Em? How could you think such a totally insane thing?"

Charlie appeared in the kitchen doorway, probably wondering what all the racket was about. Sarah included him in her outraged glare.

"Well, if you're not ready to admit your feelings toward him have changed, I'll hush up," Emily faltered, "but really, you aren't keeping a secret. Everyone in town sees it, and we're all very happy for you. You're a pretty woman, Sarah, but this summer you've caught fire. You look positively beautiful, more beautiful with each passing week. Only love does that, and there isn't any reason to be shy about it. Thad is a wonderful man. The only surprise is that it took you so long to see it."

Sarah stared at Emily's sweet face, mouth curved in a smile, dark eyes showing real concern, and almost groaned. Life this summer had come to revolve around Matt's voice reaching out for her from the shadows of the alley behind the café, late night walks on the river path, and an occasional kiss that left her aching for more.

Through her genuine astonishment, Sarah saw the people who had been in the background of her days all summer. While she focused on Henry's anger at Matt, most of the time he acted gruffly hearty, pleased with her. And Minna, hadn't Minna recently made some silly remark about being glad that Sarah had finally realized all good men weren't teasing Texans?

Today, she remembered vaguely, Thad had taken her arm and walked her to church. Did he do that often? He'd been solicitous about her health and—possessive! What had been going on around her these months while her mind and heart were elsewhere?

Sarah examined her friends again. Emily still looked tentatively pleased. Charlie's expression was unreadable.

"I assure you," Sarah said in a low voice, "that you are absolutely and totally wrong. I apologize for imposing myself on you today when I'm in such a miserable state, and I think I had better take my leave."

"Oh, no, don't do that. Please, Sarah, I won't say another word on the subject if it upsets you so, although I do admit I can't see why you feel admitting you've fallen in love with Thad at last is so terrible."

"Em, I swear if you say that man's name one more time, I'm going to do violence," Sarah said through her teeth. "Hard as it may be for you to believe, I cannot conceive of any intelligent woman looking at that man twice so long as Matt Slade walks the same earth!"

Defiantly Sarah watched Emily's face register shock. There! It was out, and even if she hadn't meant to talk about it, what did it matter any more?

"Oh, ho," said Charlie, walking into the room and sitting down at the table too. "I'm not an expert on romance like the women in this town, but I've been having some trouble believing Mr. Don't Say His Name Again started striking sparks of a sudden after all these years. No wonder you're in such a misery. You must know taming a man like Slade is an unlikely proposition."

"And you can't be in love with him," Emily added. "Why you only met him at the picnic. You didn't hardly talk to him that day in the café. Cecily said...."

Emily's voice tapered off in embarrassment over admitting she had listened to the town gossip.

"Cecily wasn't there," Sarah said, then sighed, "but as it happens she's right. The thing is...."

Charlie listened in attentive silence, and Emily made only tiny sounds of distress as Sarah told them the story, all that she had told Addie and everything since.

"So you see," she said, "it's all my fault. I knew better than to push him but that's just what I did, and he's gone, and maybe I'm not going to die, but I wish I would, and there's no use thinking about going out to that ranch and telling him I'll follow him around for the rest of his life. There's Laurie."

Emily was horrified. "Oh, Sarah, meeting that man alone at night! You're not, not...."

Only the fact that Emily couldn't even say it made Sarah aware of what she hinted at, and the thought didn't even embarrass her. It was a sore point and just made her cranky. "No, of course, I'm not. I barely got a few kisses out of him all summer. He says the last thing I need is another fatherless child, and let me tell you there is nothing in the world more irritating than a virtuous man."

Charlie chuckled, caught Sarah's look, choked it off and left the kitchen. In a few seconds he was back, patting at his mouth with a large handkerchief. "Sorry. Caught something in my throat."

"Oh, you don't have to pretend. You're probably appalled at how utterly wicked I am, and you should be. I'll go."

"No, you don't." Charlie stopped hiding the smile. "We've had a good close look at human failings in this house, and nobody's going to get lofty over your problems. But I'll tell you one thing, if what you say is true, you can stop moping around, because he'll be back. It may take him another week or two, or a month or two, but he'll be back."

"Don't try to make me feel better, Charlie."

"I'm not trying to make you feel better. I'm telling you something I know because I was born male. Not one man in a thousand worries more about a lady's well being than what he wants for himself. If Slade's that one, he'll be back, not because he wants to, not because he thinks it's right, but because he won't be able to stay away. And the fact is he's right about the way some people in this town will feel, although they won't speak out the way he thinks. It will be talk behind your back and snubs, but you bring him over here, and we'll show him there are folks and there are folks."

With Charlie beaming at her and Emily worrying over her, Sarah made herself smile at them. They cared about her, and convincing them of the truth wouldn't make this heartache go away. Neither one of these gentle people would ever understand.

The only way to make anyone understand Matt's peculiar strength would be to describe the young man who had loved her so passionately in Texas, who drove her outside of self and beyond awareness of anything but the two of them, and who never lost sight of the pistol for so much as a second.

Most men were flesh and blood and bone. In Matt each bone had a core of iron.

USUALLY SARAH ENJOYED the expectant hush in the church just before Reverend Young began the service, but today a growing sense that she was sitting there in a totally unsuitable dress distracted her. She realized that her conservative New England background made her see the deep rose dress as unsuitable and that women in this part of the country didn't share the conviction that only solemn colors should be worn for worship.

A made-to-order gift from Kate, the dress had appealed to Minna from the day she first saw it, but Sarah never went any place she would wear something this gay. Today the dress doubly offended her as both unsuitable and a travesty of contrast with her funereal mood.

The terrible headache that followed another sleepless night had left Sarah putty in Minna's hands this morning as they prepared for church, and Sarah stared at the result in dismay.

She thought of Thad's pompous, possessive compliment on the way to church and fought a wave of nausea. The contest of wills over who would sit where in the pew had lost its importance to Sarah, but not to Laurie. She inserted herself between her mother and Thad with a fierce scowl, earning a look from Thad that a grown man should never be caught giving a seven-year-old.

I'm going to have to do something about it soon, Sarah thought. *Maybe we'll just move on. That would be easiest, just leave the whole mess behind.*

A stir rippled through the small church, a combination of murmurs and cloth rustling as people moved around. Too young to pretend not to notice, Laurie twisted in the pew, then to Sarah's horror, climbed to her knees, one arm waving frantically. "Matt! Mama, Mama, it's Matt!"

Instinctively, Sarah reached for her daughter, took hold and pulled her back to a sitting position with a thump. "But Mama, Matt's here!"

"Well, he'll be leaving at a dead run rather than have anything to do with a little girl with manners like that," Sarah whispered furiously. "And what will he think of the mother of such a hoyden? You behave yourself until the service is over, do you hear me, young lady?"

"Yes, Mama." Laurie smiled back unabashed.

Blood pounded at the back of Sarah's ears, which must be as red as her cheeks. Embarrassment barely entered into it. She closed her eyes for a brief second, restraining herself not just from looking to the back of the church but from getting up and running. Relief rushed through her in a cleansing flood, and deep inside some part of her took wing and began to soar.

"Mm, hmpf!" Reverend Young stared straight at her. "If we are all ready."

Sarah gave the preacher a smile so brilliant he blinked.

The last amen still echoed when Laurie launched out of the pew in an undignified run. Sarah shook off Henry's attempt to restrain her with a glare that would have put a lesser man on his knees. Bobbing and weaving through the people in the aisle, Sarah didn't quite run, but she didn't politely wait her turn either.

She paused only to exchange a look with Charlie Gilbride who smiled and gave her shoulder an encouraging pat. "Go get 'im, Mrs. Hammond."

In the churchyard, the only thing that marked the tall figure in the well cut dark gray suit as Matt was Laurie, wrapped around his neck and clinging hard. As Sarah approached, Matt gave Laurie a last hug and put her down. She clutched one of his hands with both of hers, content.

Through the whole service, Sarah had pictured Matt sitting in the last pew dressed about the way he had been in the café. The suit made him a stranger, a terribly attractive and slightly nervous stranger. The tanned column of his throat above the snowy shirt started her fingers twitching. She wanted to smooth the collar, touch him.

Instead she stopped at a very proper distance. "I am absolutely certain, Mr. Slade, that neither my father nor my brothers ever attended church looking half so fine as you do this morning. That is a most elegant suit."

The nervous look waned a little as he smiled back at her. "Do you really think so? I never even owned a suit before, and when I asked Beau for help, he started talking about shirts with ruffles and pointing to some suit stuff the color of a Yankee uniform. We almost got to blows before he said this was good enough."

"Well, if this is the end result, I'd say once Mr. Taney settles down his taste is impeccable." Sarah said clearly, then lowered her voice. "You'd be a sight for sore eyes in rags, Matt."

Reassured about the suit, Matt grinned at her full strength, himself again. "A fellow would have to look awful good to even be allowed in the same town as you. You make that dress look like a wildflower used to wrap up an angel that fell from the sky and landed right in this church."

It was outrageous; it was ridiculous; it was Matt. Sarah heard a small gasp behind her and didn't even turn to look. She smoothed her skirt and murmured, "Do you really like this dress? It's one of my favorites." As she said it, it became true.

In moments they were through with how glad they were to see each other and grew serious.

"I don't want to make you late for Sunday dinner, Boston. Blackburn's already trying to think of something to hang me for, but I need to talk to you for a minute."

"Dinner is never ready until at least an hour after church, and I'm not allowed to help, you know. They say I labor over enough food during the week." Sarah took his free arm. "We have time for a walk."

They strolled silently, surrounded by Laurie's bubbling conversation, but at the end of the path where brush and cottonwoods screened them from the world, Matt ensured their privacy.

"I need to talk to your mother alone, Laurie. Do you think you could scoot back up the path a ways and keep watch?"

Happy to be of service, their small sentry skipped off, and Matt turned to Sarah. "It didn't take me this long to answer your question, you know. I knew the answer before you stopped talking that night. What took me so long was deciding what to do about it."

"And the fact that you're here says what you decided, doesn't it?"

"Maybe not the way you think. There's no joy in fighting the whole world, and maybe I'm the one who can't stand it. I know I can't ever sit by again and watch people treat you like they did in Charon."

"It won't be like that. The worst that will happen here is that some people will avoid us. It won't be the same. We're not the same. You'll see."

"I see that whatever's between us is too strong to leave us be. We're going to have to take this all the way to the end, no matter what that is."

Sarah tipped her head up. "If you have at least come that far, there is something I have to tell you."

"Like what?"

"I really need a kiss."

He shook his head at her as if disagreeing, but his arms slipped around her. "Maybe I could use some of that myself. After all there's a crick right handy."

His lips touched hers, warm and firm, and then the taste of him filled her senses. Sarah began to lose herself totally in the deepening kiss, when Laurie's high shrill voice cut through.

"Matt! Mama! Somebody's coming. Somebody's coming."

Matt ended the kiss, in no particular hurry. "I think I have to teach her some of the finer points of picket duty."

As Laurie came running to them, Sarah took his arm in proper fashion, and the three of them started demurely back up the path to the church.

SARAH KNEW SHE was the cause of the terse conversation around the Blackburns' Sunday dinner table, but she had too much else on her mind to worry about it.

When she and Matt returned to the churchyard, she had introduced him to some of the people still lingering in sociable groups. Avoiding those who looked askance at them, Sarah chose the curious, and then wished she hadn't.

Every single one of the women reacted to Matt exactly the same way Mabel did, gaping at him with the expression of a silly sheep. Of course Matt was charming, and of course he was handsome. The eye patch and scars only emphasized the roguish look that had always been there, didn't they? Did that mean she had to stand by and watch every woman he met turn to a giggling jelly?

When she said something to Matt, what he said only made it worse. Snubs she could bear, but this had to stop. All he had to do was stop smiling at them. His smile tied knots in her own stomach, but those other women needed to let their own men take care of their stomachs.

Sarah still had half a jealous mind on the new problem, the other half listening to Laurie's happy review of the day's events, as she walked to Gilbrides', when Thad Stewart's voice intruded.

"Sarah." Striding faster with longer legs, he was right behind her. "Wait a moment, would you. I'd like to talk to you."

Sarah turned, almost sighing out loud. Much as she'd rather put it off, she needed to deal with this problem. Laurie pressed against the front of Sarah's skirt, facing Thad.

"Could this be a private talk?" Thad asked.

"Run on along, sweetheart," Sarah said. "I'll be right behind you."

"No," Laurie said defiantly. "He's going to try to kiss you."

Thad directed the same glare toward the young chaperone he had used that morning in church. Sarah almost laughed out loud. For strength of will, she would bet on Matt's daughter every time, but this was no place for a contest.

"He's not going to do anything of the kind. Now you go along. I do need to talk to Mr. Stewart, and I do not need your help. Go."

It took a few more stern words, but finally Laurie went.

"I should have given her a ride on my horse long ago, I suppose," Thad said.

Sarah saw no need to reply. Awkward around children, Thad had never had any chance of buying Laurie's approval, much less affection. Sarah got right to the point.

"I'm sorry for any embarrassment you suffered this morning, but I was honest with you from the start. Perhaps the fault was that I like you too much to be as outspoken as necessary, but I have been honest."

"No one could accuse you of leading me on, Sarah. You've always been so quiet, so ladylike. I guess we all just expected you to go right along with our plans."

"If my unnatural lack of temperament deceived you, I'm sorry. Since I've been on my own, I suppose I store my energy to fuss only over the truly important things."

"And in the years you've been in Tavaras the only truly important things have been making sure that Mrs. Young knew better than to try any form of corporal punishment on your daughter—and Slade. Is that it?"

"Yes, I suppose that's an accurate assessment. Be honest, Thad, your pride may be hurt a little, but that's all. You're not in love with me and never have been. It even occurred to me that a half-hearted pursuit of a woman who isn't interested is one way you've satisfied your father's sudden desire that you marry without actually getting near the altar."

At this Thad threw back his head and laughed out loud. "You are too perceptive by half, you know." Still smiling, he went on. "The problem is that the quiet little lady who was the subject of the half-hearted pursuit turned into a vibrant beauty this summer. That dash of spice in with all the sweetness makes for a far more desirable package, you know."

"My mirror says I look the way I've always looked, but you are not the first to tell me otherwise. Emily says it's the look of a woman in love, and if that's true, don't you think you'd better find a woman of your own to add spice to?"

"No." Thad was serious now. "I think Slade's going to rip you to pieces. I like him myself, you know, but he can't help what he is any more than the rest of us can help what we are. Even if his intentions are honorable, what can he give you? Do you really think he'll marry you, and if he does what kind of life would it be, drifting around from one troubled place to another?"

"Yes, he will marry me, and as for the rest—it's not as if he likes what he does. He is close to the men he rides with, but he doesn't like fighting other men's wars for a living. That decision is his. I've made mine. Whatever he does and wherever he goes, I'm going with him."

"You're going to get yourself hurt, and when it's over, you're going to need a friend to help you put yourself back together, and when that time comes, I'll be there."

"And if you're wrong and I'm right? Will you still be a friend then?"

"If you are right, I'll dance at your wedding, but I don't expect to ever have to subject myself to that."

"Fair enough," Sarah said. "Now if you'll forgive me, if I don't get along to Gilbrides', Laurie's going to have Charlie down here to save me."

Sarah continued her journey to Gilbrides' with at least something to think about other than female reactions to Matt's smile.

44

ONLY TWO DAYS after his call to religion, Matt rode into Tavaras in the early afternoon. Maybe it had taken several weeks of agonizing for him to decide what to do, but now that his mind was made up, he saw no reason to pussyfoot around.

"Matt, Matt! What are you doing here? Are you going to see Mama?" Before he had Sam tied in front of Michel's, Laurie leapt for his arms, sure of her reception. Not hugging her was impossible. Mary Gilbride peered up at him shyly, much less sure of herself.

"I thought I'd have dinner at Mrs. Canaday's and walk your mother home, but first I've got errands to run, starting with some things to buy here." Matt nodded toward the store.

"Can we help? We know where things are in Mr. Michel's, really we do."

"Sure. I'll most likely need help."

Michel seemed friendly enough, but after all, Matt was spending money there, wasn't he? The men at the ranch had given him a list of items to bring back for them.

A short while later Matt and his small escorts left the store, all three of them working on peppermint sticks. With the girls in the saddle, Matt led Sam to the Tavaras blacksmith. Peter Alford and the men lounging around his shop were downright sociable, and careful of their language with two little girls listening round-eyed to every word.

By late afternoon, Sam had new shoes, and Laurie and Mary reluctantly admitted they needed to get home for supper. Matt led his small procession to Gilbrides', where Emily ran halfway down the front walk to meet them before Matt finished lifting Mary to the ground. The little girl introduced Matt to her mother with perfect manners, staring at the ground the whole time.

"It certainly is good to meet you at last, Mr. Slade. I don't believe anything that ever happened to Mary thrilled her so much as riding your horse the last time. Can you stay for a while? My husband will be home any minute."

Matt tried a tentative smile at the pretty dark-haired lady and watched her nervous look change to something else. Women really were soft-hearted creatures.

"No, ma'am, thank you. If I don't get Laurie home, the sheriff will be after me for kidnapping for sure. Another time maybe."

"Soon, I hope. My husband really would like to meet you. We told Sarah to bring you by for coffee some evening."

Matt took his leave and started toward Blackburns', but he had not gone far before Sam's passenger had a suggestion. "I'm sure I could ride faster. Can't we go faster?"

"For you to try anything faster we need a saddle that fits you better. The stirrups have to be short enough for you to use them."

The young face so like Sarah's fell, and Matt couldn't stand it. "I guess I could give you a little taste of going faster now. How's that?"

"Yes. Oh, yes, please."

So he swung up behind her, holding her with his free arm. The miracle of finding he had anything to do with creating this wondrous separate person still rocked Matt back on his heels every time he saw her.

Loose strands of pale blonde hair blew back across his shirt, silky, and finer than anything he could think to compare it to, and in the bright sun her skin appeared translucent. Her weight didn't seem enough for her size. Her bones felt fragile. How did a man protect something this precious, this vulnerable? The tidal wave of feelings slamming through Matt told him there was no effort he would not make.

He pushed the gelding gradually into a slow jog. They covered almost a block at the bouncing gait before Laurie confessed her disappointment. "I d-don't like this. It's t-too r-rough."

"That's why you need stirrups. You have to learn how to take the bounce. Let's try this."

The rhythmic rock of Sam's canter was more to Laurie's liking. They went all the way to the church, around the church meadow, and then back to Blackburns', walking only the last few steps. Minna Blackburn peered out the front window, unhappiness all over her face. He lifted Laurie off Sam, holding her for several hugs before putting her down.

"Thank you, Papa. I had a wonderful time."

"Laurie...."

"I know, but I only say it when no one else can hear."

"Your mother's right about this, you know. Someday you'll forget, or you won't see somebody who can hear you, and it will cause us all a lot of grief." Talking sternly to a seven-year-old was one more thing he had no idea how to do. He must be the world's most downright useless father. How could he stay stern when she looked at him like that? Matt winked at her, provoking another hug and an unrepentant grin before Laurie ran toward the house.

NOT ONLY DID MATT eat dinner at the café, he stayed after the last customer left and helped with cleanup chores. It would be hard to decide which was funnier, Sarah thought, the sight of Matt stacking chairs on the tables and sweeping the café floor with a gun tied low on his thigh, or Addie's reaction. Nothing had ever flustered the older woman so.

When Matt started wiping dishes, Addie threw up her hands and stopped fussing, and then they all had a grand time. Addie told stories of her trip west as a young bride; Matt told war stories; Sarah told some of the ways Aunt Lucy scandalized her whole family. It felt so good, so right, to have him there like that.

After saying good night to Addie, they walked the river path hand in hand. How many miles had they walked like that in the dark? Tonight Sarah felt more than the warmth of his hand. Electricity ran between them. The night air felt soft on her skin. The little river sang a special song, and each rustle of a leaf added to the magic.

Through the summer the wanting had tortured her. Now slow, deep anticipation took hold. Waiting would not be easy, but Sarah knew she would wait, perhaps even with a modicum of patience.

Entering Blackburns' darkened kitchen, Sarah passed through the dining room toward the light in the parlor, smiling to herself, still tasting the last kiss. The tableau that greeted her in the parlor banished all her good feelings. Hard years had taught Sarah nothing if not how to recognize trouble at a glance.

Laurie huddled in an upholstered side chair in her night dress with her knees drawn up to her chest, red-eyed from weeping. Her face was set in hard lines that showed every bit of the stubbornness she had inherited from two strong-minded parents.

Standing in front of the bookcase with his arms folded over his chest, Henry had fury in every line of his massive body. The whiskey bottle on a nearby table and glass with traces of liquid still in it told their own story. Henry only drank when he was beside himself.

Slumping in a chair that matched Laurie's, Minna looked as miserable as only a person caught between a rock and hard place can look.

Sarah took all this in at a glance, and even as she emotionally girded herself for war, Laurie jumped up and ran to her.

"He says I have to stay away from Matt!" she wailed. "He says I can't even talk to him. I told him no. I told him I won't. You tell him. Tell him I won't. Tell him he can't make me!"

Sarah took Laurie firmly by the shoulders and pushed her far enough away to look her in the eye. "I think, young lady, you knew perfectly well I would straighten this out as soon as I got home. There was no need for a scene like this, and you knew that too. You not only want me to countermand Henry, you want to make sure I rub his nose in it, and I am afraid, my darling daughter, you are about to find out that getting what you want can sometimes be quite devastating. Now you go upstairs, and I want to hear the bedroom door shut."

"But, Mama...."

"Don't but, Mama, me. Get upstairs! And shut the door!"

Laurie didn't eavesdrop any more than most children, which was to say she would listen if a chance presented itself. Her running footsteps echoed on the stairs and the bedroom door slammed shut before Sarah turned to Henry.

"I'm sorry you've been subjected to this, Henry," she said, "but as it happens, no matter how dreadfully she's behaved tonight, Laurie is right. She can see Matt any time she wants to, she can talk with him any time she wants to, and she can go anywhere he's willing to take her. It is a sorrow to me that you have taken such a dislike to Matt without even getting to know him, but even so I think this situation is in great part my fault. I've abdicated too much of the responsibility for my own daughter to you and Minna these past years."

Sarah realized Henry was too angry to respond when Minna answered. "That's not true. Caring for her has never been anything but a pleasure, and the fact is in raising young ones there are always difficult times like this."

"Perhaps so, but the difficulties should be mine, not yours."

Henry finally spoke, the tendons in his neck straining with the effort at control. "Do you have any idea what we're talking about here? I was out at the edge of town all afternoon or I'd have stopped it. He had those little girls all over town with him. He had them down at Alford's listening to the devil knows what out of the trash that hangs around down there."

"Matt told me what they did this afternoon. If it will make you feel better, he said the men at Alford's were all very careful with little girls around. He didn't know that the unemployed and unemployable of the town spend their time there, and the fact is that none of those men is going to offend someone like Matt. They watched their tongues."

"I think, Sarah, it's time for some unpleasant frankness between us. I'm old enough to have seen a good number of women ruin themselves over men like Slade, and I don't want to see it happen to you. There's only one thing a man like that wants from a woman."

"I can manage unpleasant frankness quite well, Henry, so I'll tell you if all Matt wanted was carnal, he would have had it months ago. The only virtue between us is his, not mine. What he wants, however, is a lifetime, and we're going to have it, with or without the blessing of people like you. You are not my father, and you are not Laurie's grandfather, and even if you were, I am a grown woman, and your approval or disapproval of what I do or do not do is neither necessary nor relevant."

Sarah's bluntness brought a sound from Minna that was more a moan than a gasp, but Henry was far from through.

"What you're calling virtue isn't natural in a grown man, Sarah. He had Laurie all over town today, alone with him on that horse.

Maybe we all protect you women too much, and maybe we keep you from protecting yourselves from what you don't understand. The fact is there are men with unnatural appetites. There are men...."

But Sarah, who knew more about the perversions of the human condition than she cared to, understood immediately. Henry's slander on Matt left her shaking with outrage. It also sent fear shivering through her. She had no doubt how Matt would react if he heard anything like this. Sarah didn't wait for Henry to finish searching for a way to speak the unspeakable.

"I'm afraid I do understand what you're talking about. More than that I understand that you are so determined to get your own way, you're going to throw enough filth around that some will stick where you want it to. I'm not even discussing this with you. I am telling you. I am telling you that I'm going upstairs, packing a bag, and Laurie and I are leaving here tonight. I shall tell Laurie nothing except that our disagreement is so deep, it's better that we don't live here any more. She will still regard you with affection and respect and still call you Uncle Henry and Aunt Minna."

"Sarah, please!"

Sarah ignored Minna's appeal and continued. "If, however, there is ever so much as a whisper that you have repeated that calumny against Matt to anyone, under any circumstances, I will see that my daughter regards you with contempt, with fear and with hatred. I will assure that she crosses the street to avoid you. I will see that she never speaks your name except as a curse. I hope I am making myself very, very clear, Henry. You can cost yourself my daughter's respect and affection, but you will not cost me my hope for the future."

Whirling for the stairs, Sarah didn't wait for a reply. In her bedroom she pulled out the old carpetbag and began throwing things into it without thought or care and then went to Laurie's room.

"What are you doing, Mama?" Laurie no longer looked like a furious avenger but like a sorry and frightened little girl.

"I'm packing. We're going to Gilbrides' tonight and moving to the boarding house tomorrow. I told you that you might not like this devil once you let him out of his bottle."

"But, Mama, I just wanted you to tell Uncle Henry...."

Laurie started to cry again, and Sarah relented and hugged her. "Some lessons come hard, don't they, sweetheart? I did tell him, but

I can't make him change his mind about what he believes. If we kept it from ever coming to a confrontation, perhaps we could have lived with our differences, but you pushed everyone too far, and now we can't pretend any more. We said things that were better left unsaid."

Sarah kissed the woeful face. "Now you get dressed. We have to go."

"But he's wrong about Papa."

"He's wrong about *Matt.* Do you want a spanking added to your troubles tonight?"

A soft knock sounded on the door, and Sarah threw the dress she was folding into the bag in a wad. She was through with this business tonight and had nothing else to say. The tap came again.

"Come in. It's your house."

Minna came in and sat on the edge of the bed, looking very old. Sarah stayed steely. Her decision was made, but still she felt sorry for Minna, caught in the middle. Laurie crawled across the bed and put her face against the older woman's shoulder, making Sarah wonder if there were any other knives that could be twisted in her heart tonight.

"Sarah." Minna's voice was quiet and controlled, but the blue-veined hands patting Laurie's back trembled. "I suppose you know I've come to ask you to reconsider. In all the years of our marriage, Henry has only cried once, the night our own daughter died, but you have him very close again now. When you apologize for giving over too much responsibility that is yours, you apologize for the wrong thing. The disservice you did us was in giving the impression you were a passive woman who needed guidance in her life."

"You mean a weak woman who would let someone else run her life."

"No, I don't, but I won't bandy words. There's no intention of insult, you know. Most people admire an agreeable woman very much."

"Hogwash," Sarah said flatly. "Most people enjoy taking advantage of women like that, but I will agree I have misled you, and evidently a lot of others. I work hard, I'm too tired to fuss over trifling matters, and life is easier when one floats with the tide, so to speak. But this isn't trifling. This is my whole life, and I'm going to have it."

"I think I feel great sympathy for your parents, Sarah. You're right, of course, Henry and I are no substitute, but it must have been like this for them, I suppose, over Mr. Hammond."

"No, it wasn't," Sarah said sharply. "I told you the truth about my parents once. If you choose not to believe me, I'm not debating it now."

"No." Minna hugged Laurie, her white hair mixing with the pale blonde. "Will you stay the night, at least, and reconsider? I confess there is no possibility Henry is going to apologize. He's too proud, too stubborn and he believes he's right. I am sure, though, that he could bring himself to promise you not to interfere again. Couldn't that be enough, Sarah? Please?"

Sarah stopped pretending to pack. She was too upset to think and making a mess. Sitting on the bed, she buried her face in her hands. "All right, Minna. We'll wait and see in the morning, but Henry will have to back down. I will not."

Sarah didn't raise her head until after Laurie's arms wrapped around her neck and the door shut softly behind Minna.

45

PERHAPS AT BLACKBURNS' only an uneasy truce endured, but the attitude of the rest of the town encouraged Sarah no end. Oh, a few of the good citizens of the town avoided her on the street, but whatever objections they had to her behavior, they whispered among themselves.

Matt as a suitor caused their disapproval; Matt as a suitor provided a shield against outward displays of disapproval. And most of the town considered Matt and Sarah's courtship grand entertainment. They called Matt "Mrs. Hammond's gunslinger."

As the days shortened with the approach of fall, Matt continued to attend church. Sitting in the same pew as the Gilbrides, Laurie inserted herself between Sarah and Matt just as she had between Sarah and Thad. Instead of glaring at her, Matt winked, and a contentment spread through Sarah that made church seem holier.

Sarah and Laurie no longer ate Sunday dinners with the Blackburns and Stewarts. According to Matt, a tasty cow always fell over dead at the L&L on Saturday evenings, and Matt brought enough beef to feed a hungry dozen with him every Sunday morning. Emily Gilbride popped the roast in her oven, and they all shared the feast after church.

The trouble between the ranches had stopped with the recovery of the stolen cows. Tension eased slowly as each side started to hope the other had called off the war. Sarah tried not to worry about what would happen when Farrell decided he no longer needed a private army. Matt would stay—or she would go.

Matt still came into town two or three times a week, in the afternoon now, and no longer alone. Luke, Swede, Rio, and Jimmy Childers each accompanied him once or twice, courtesy visits. Sarah liked the young men, but the café with no liquor, no cards and only respectable women bored them. In fact, Tavaras itself was too sleepy for them. They preferred Rye Wells.

Beau and Roddy often kept Matt company. They rode in before dinner time, visited the barber or a shop or two, ate at the café and stayed with Matt till closing time. While Matt helped Sarah and Addie close up, Beau and Roddy visited the saloon or cantina, then rode back to the ranch with him.

Hard men with an edge Sarah could not see in Matt, Beau and Roddy showed, by the hours they spent in a quiet family restaurant, an affection for Matt that gratified Sarah. Matt looked at it another way.

"They came from good families, and even if they'd die before saying so, they're liking a little taste of that again just fine. Don't worry about them. If they get bored, they'll disappear."

But they didn't disappear. When Matt came to town, Laurie and Mary tracked him down in minutes. Her sense of fairness overcame Mary's shyness, and she took it upon herself to compensate for Laurie's favoritism, adopting Beau and Roddy. Before long the residents of Tavaras grew used to watching Laurie on Sam and Mary on Aurora, following the three men around town.

In the café, Laurie glued herself to Matt until she had to leave for supper at Blackburns'. Mary divided her time equally between the others. The first time Sarah saw Mary on Roddy's lap, she almost dropped the coffee pot. Mary had the look of an experienced adventuress. Roddy looked bemused.

"It's good for him," Matt said. "I bet Roddy hasn't been near a child since he was one. They both need a good dose of regular folks."

Regular folks—Matt's description of everyone in the world except men like him and criminals, and as the weeks passed he gave no sign of admitting the majority of those regular folks would accept him. The end of the job with Farrell would force him to take the next step, Sarah supposed, but that didn't stop her from luring him further down the path herself.

"Will you take me to the harvest fiesta, Matt? It's the one time every year the whole town drops everything else and concentrates on having a good time. People come from miles around." Saying this, Sarah thought of her mother, who would die of shame over a daughter issuing a man such an invitation.

"What's a harvest fiesta?" Matt asked cautiously.

"It's as if there's a huge party through the whole town. Addie locks up right after lunch. The streets are hung with lanterns, the women bring wonderful food, and whole steers and hogs are roasted. Everyone dances and enjoys it all until dawn. Laurie and I always have a good time, but we could have a better time if you were there."

"If everybody comes from miles around, it would be a good time to make trouble. Most likely I need to be out at the ranch with a rifle."

"Oh, I see." She felt her mouth forming a pout and couldn't stop it. Sure she could get him to say yes, she had done foolish things in anticipation.

"Now, don't give me that pitiful look. I'll talk to Beau and be here if I can."

"I thought they'd all like to come. I thought...."

"It would be a good time to make trouble, you know, and this is still Stewart's town. Some of his men are sure to be here, and after they've had a few drinks, you don't want hotheads like Beau and Rio around."

"Perhaps not. You'll try to be there, Matt? Really try?"

"I'll really try."

After that Sarah returned to fantasizing about what would happen at the fiesta. After all a promise to try from Matt was the same as a blood oath from any other man.

PERHAPS, SARAH THOUGHT, somewhere in the world there was a woman so talented she could keep a bland smile pasted on her face and follow Peter Alford's ponderous and unique ideas of dance steps. Not here in Tavaras at the harvest fiesta, of course. Perhaps in Brazil.

Sarah sincerely wished Mr. Alford would go seek that woman out. The soft leather of the new shoes that had so delighted her mere hours ago provided no protection from Alford's thick-soled boots. Her feet, at least, were beginning to feel numb. *I should be thankful for small favors*, Sarah thought bitterly.

When the music ended, Alford escorted Sarah toward their starting place. Emily and Charlie waited there, sitting companionably on one of the many makeshift benches scattered along the streets. Aware that Matt was returning a giggling Mrs. Alford to her husband's keeping, Sarah refused to look at him. The sympathy in Charlie's face didn't help. Emily came to the rescue.

"I'm starting to feel very thirsty, and I haven't danced half so much as Sarah. Would you and Matt get us something to drink?"

With these words to her husband, Emily Gilbride proved acts of mercy can be performed in the most ordinary ways. Glancing toward the punch bowl on a board and barrel table mere feet away, Emily shot her husband a meaningful look. "I especially like that lemonade of Mrs. Hooper's. Do you suppose you could find us some of that, please?"

Married long enough recognize much less broad a hint, Charlie agreed instantly. "We'll find Mrs. Hooper's best. You and Sarah wait right here now."

Sarah sank gratefully to the bench beside Emily, not even watching Matt make excuses to the waiting Michels, and not sparing a thought for what the rough wood seat might do to clothing she had dreamed and schemed over.

It seemed a lifetime ago, not merely hours, that she had made a ceremony of putting on everything new from the skin out, delighting in delicate undergarments, slipping the new peach faille dress over her petticoats with something approaching reverence. The stylish princess bodice and delicate ruching at her wrists and neck lent a subtle elegance.

Tonight the mirror had finally shown Sarah what Emily meant by "you caught fire." She piled her hair high with no thought for hat or bonnet, and her neck became a slim white column. Short tendrils of hair she could not catch up made a soft frame for her face, a stranger's face.

Delicate pink, more artful than any rouge, spread across her cheekbones, emphasizing the slight hollowing below. The woman who as a girl despaired of every padded curve turned her head this way and that, watching her reflection as shadows played across those hollows.

Now Sarah slumped on the bench, feeling as lumpy as burned porridge. Pulling the hem of her dress up slightly, she stared glumly at the scuff marks left on her shoes by Peter Alford and half a dozen like him.

Emily took Sarah's hand. "Your evening isn't going quite as planned, is it?"

"Oh, Em, I want people to like him, but it would be just fine if they liked him a little less. I've only had one dance with him, and Mrs. Alford has managed two, and there's Mrs. Michel, just waiting to pounce again, and Lavinia Young is right behind her. Isn't Reverend Young supposed to believe dancing is sinful?"

"You are getting desperate. You know perfectly well that's not our belief here. And you can't really blame us. I looked forward to my turn myself. If you want a monopoly, perhaps you should think about someone less charming, say Thad?"

Starting to snap an angry reply, Sarah recognized Emily's look of exaggerated innocence and caught herself. "It wouldn't be so terrible if Matt realized what's going on. He thinks all those men want to dance with me."

"They do. Every person here has commented on how lovely you look tonight."

"Ha," Sarah said with disgust. "Mabel dragged her poor son here tonight just to make him ask me so she could dance with Matt. Addie browbeat her friend to make him cooperate. He told me so himself. And I wager Mr. Alford never even attempted dancing with anyone at all before tonight. Why he's worse than...."

Sarah broke off, unwilling to admit that the disaster of her one dance with Matt compounded her misery.

"Perhaps it will help Matt's attitude to find himself so popular."

"It will not. He thinks they're being nice to him because they feel sorry for him."

"What!"

"You don't have to tell me how silly it is. I was ready to quarrel with him over it, but Beau and Roddy both swear he really believes it. They told me any time they want a lesson in, in—fisticuffs—they can get one by teasing him about it. You know how stubborn he is, and he's decided women are all kind souls, and when they get close and see how badly he was hurt, they feel sorry for him, and so they're nice to him."

"Oh, my. Oh, dear." Emily couldn't go on for a moment for her laughter. "If you have any sense at all, you'll let him cherish that belief for the rest of his life."

"If he doesn't see the truth tonight, he never will."

Sarah and Emily were still talking quietly, when a large figure loomed over them. As Sarah looked up in surprise, her wrist disappeared in a huge hand, and the hand's heavyset owner jerked her to her feet.

"So you're the lady that likes fighting men. If Slade's fool enough to leave you, you can dance with me."

Already in a miserable mood before this stranger grabbed her and assaulted her with his aggressive, too loud voice, Sarah pulled back and tried to twist her arm free.

Even as she recognized one of Harlan Rastus's men, strong whiskey fumes explained his behavior. He was not, however, too drunk to easily capture her other wrist and pull her into disgustingly intimate contact. With time to think Sarah might have danced with him rather than fuss, but he gave her no time.

She kicked the elegantly pointed toe of one scuffed shoe into his shin with all her strength, then brought the graceful little heel down as sharply as her weight would allow on the arch of his boot.

"Ow! Damn it!"

She managed to jerk one arm free, but he used the other to yank her toward him. A sharp crack knifed through Sarah's confused, spinning senses. For a second she thought her neck had snapped and her head was floating away. Then she felt Matt's arms around her and saw the drunk at their feet, shaking his head and feeling one side of his jaw. The sound had not been her head coming off, but his.

"Are you hurt?"

The concern in Matt's voice put the world back together right side up. "No, just a little dizzy," Sarah assured him.

Matt pushed her toward Emily and stared at the man on the ground. "Is Harlan hiring idiots these days?" he asked without any particular emphasis.

"Aw, hell, you weren't around, and she likes our kind. I just wanted to dance with her."

"Maybe you should have asked proper when you were still sober enough to find your feet."

"The only thing wrong with my feet is that little bitch just kicked and stomped me. She...."

"You use that word again, and Harlan won't find enough of you to carry off in his saddlebags," Matt said, anger starting to show, "and you can forget any apology, just pick yourself up and make yourself scarce."

"Speaking of idjits, that's big talk for a man all dressed up with no gun on him. You notice I'm not naked."

The words had no visible effect on Matt, who stood glaring down at the gunman, but Sarah panicked.

Breaking away from Emily, she lunged for the nearby table and seized one of the heavy metal trays there. Crumbs showered over the last cookies that fell as she swung the heavy weapon with all her strength at the head of the rising gunman. He crumpled back to the ground, any sound he made covered by the solid thunk of the tray on his skull.

Sarah looked from the still form to Matt, as astonished by what she had done as he was. Without a word, he crouched down, feeling for a pulse, then gingerly probed the part of the skull that had taken the blow. Finally he looked up at her. "Well, you didn't kill him anyway."

"He was going to s-shoot you."

"He isn't drunk enough to shoot an unarmed man in front of a hundred witnesses. They hang you for that. They might even hang a woman for attacking a man from behind and knocking his head clean off."

"He said he was going to shoot you!" Hysteria crept around the edge of Sarah's voice.

Henry shouldered through the crowd ringing the scene, followed by Thaddeus and Thad Stewart.

"I should have known there'd be trouble wherever you were, Slade. What the devil's going on here?"

Sarah was incapable of explaining, none of the witnesses offered a word, and Matt didn't appear inclined to help. He got to his feet and replaced the tray on the table with exaggerated care, then half sat there himself, arms crossed.

The very look of him was almost more than Sarah could bear. He had presented himself at Blackburns' tonight not in the familiar gray suit he wore to church, but in black broadcloth, cut in the same impeccable way. His shirt had no ruffles, but a pleated front showed above the matching vest.

She didn't want to explain anything to anyone. She didn't want to dance any more with heavy-footed clods. She wanted to throw herself into Matt's arms and have him carry her off away from everyone and into the night.

"Well, what the hell happened?" Henry barked.

Sarah looked at Matt, at Henry, then back at Matt, her mouth moving but not forming words, her eyes begging for the help she couldn't believe he wasn't giving.

Finally, Matt cleared his throat and gave Henry a partial answer in a curiously flat voice. "That man said something."

Matt didn't seem inclined to say more anyway, but right then Harlan Rastus pushed through the crowd and walked over to the fallen man, prodding the limp form with the toe of a boot with obvious disgust.

"Hell, Matt, I'm sorry. I heard Joe was making trouble over here. I should of talked harder at the whole bunch before we started for town. I hope you knocked some sense into him."

"If he wakes up any smarter you have Mrs. Hammond to thank."

Every eye turned to her, and Sarah shrank toward Emily.

Harlan examined her as if measuring every one of her few inches, and winked. "Well, now, I'd say the lady is a real good reason for putting Joe here down, but...."

"Harlan, I am not funning with you." Matt's voice was no longer dead but half-choked with suppressed laughter. "Mrs. Hammond took something your friend there said as being a threat to me, and in mortal fear for my life, she leapt to the rescue and about killed the poor man."

Matt's last words were almost lost in laughter, and he gave up the struggle and started to roar.

Harlan gave Sarah one brief, incredulous glance, threw back his head and joined Matt.

As smiles and laughter broke out through the whole crowd, a disconcerted Henry turned to the nearest bystander. "Are you telling me Slade didn't do that?"

"Oh, he knocked the fellow down for getting rough with Mrs. Hammond, but it was the lady laid him out for sure, Sheriff."

Matt was still laughing hard, and the laughter spread like contagion through the crowd. Sarah couldn't believe it, and she couldn't bear it.

"Matt Slade, if you don't stop laughing at me, you'll be sorry! That tray didn't break over his head the way it would on yours!"

Matt looked right at her, getting control of himself for a split second with obvious effort, then broke out laughing harder than ever.

Emily poked Charlie so hard in the ribs, he almost stopped laughing himself. "Let's let the ladies compose themselves, Matt. We need to replace that spilled lemonade anyway. Come on now."

Charlie all but hauled Matt off by the arm. Henry and a still chuckling Harlan pulled the drunk to his feet, and the crowd slowly dispersed. A night in jail was the least Harlan's man needed and deserved, Henry declared, and left with him.

Sitting on the bench next to Emily, Sarah decided that things simply could not get worse.

"Will you honor me with one dance while Slade's exercising the better part of valor, Sarah?"

Looking up at Thad, Sarah almost lost control. Tears brimmed.

"Oh, come on now. It's not that bad. I think what I have to say might cheer you up."

He took her hand, bringing her to her feet and guiding her toward the dance area with no more consideration of her desires than his drunken hireling had shown, but with considerably more finesse.

The Stewart men were among the few Sarah had met in the West who danced the way she had been taught. Smooth and practiced, Thad led her now with an infuriating ease. Blast him.

Head bowed, Sarah stared at a button on his suit.

Ignoring her attitude, Thad addressed himself to the top of her head. "You know, I hoped Slade would be here tonight. I expected with liquor flowing freely there would be a scene like that one, and I thought it would show you how impossible your hopes are. It never occurred to me, I would be the one proven wrong."

Surprised out of her passive resentment, Sarah raised her head to see a rueful expression on his face.

"I couldn't see how a wolf like that would ever fit in with the rest of us civilized citizens, but he will, won't he? In fact he makes some of our ordinary citizens look hot tempered."

When Sarah still said nothing, Thad went on. "Not only would I have expected a brawl from one end of town to the other, or even a shooting, but nine men out of ten, including me, would have lost their tempers and given you a thorough tongue lashing then and there for usurping male prerogatives like that. I suppose all you'll get is a quiet scolding when he gets you alone. I'll keep my promise. I'll dance at your wedding and behave impeccably, and I'll let Dad and Henry think you've given me reason to believe you might change your mind to keep some of the pressure off you for a while."

The music stopped, and Sarah found her voice and a tiny smile. "Thank you. You are making me feel better." She even let him talk her into a second dance.

Matt didn't looked particularly concerned when Thad returned her to him with a few polite words, but Sarah only got two swallows of lemonade before he had her upper arm in a firm grip. "I need to talk to you someplace private. Let's go."

Marching down the street toward blackness and quiet like a child on the way to the woodshed, Sarah thought about Thad's prediction of a tongue lashing with first disbelief, then anger. By the time Matt pushed her into the shelter of a darkened doorway, she was more than ready to lash right back.

Matt cupped her chin in his hand. "I'm sorry I laughed at you, Boston. The sound that thing made hitting his head, I was sure you killed him and I was going to have to watch you in a courtroom again. When his heart was still thumping away, the relief of it made me shaky, and I just got foolish. But nobody likes to be laughed at. I shouldn't have done it, and I'm sorry. Are you still mad?"

Sarah's indignation collapsed in a teary heap. "I'm not angry. I was s-scared. He did have a gun, and you don't, and I didn't think I could hurt him. I only meant to stun him so you could d-do something. I didn't think I was strong enough to h-hurt him."

His fingers smoothed across her eyebrows then brushed away the tears. "You were always stronger than you thought, weren't you? And I'm not exactly defenseless."

Pulling her close, Matt slipped her arms around his back and guided her hand down to his waist. Sarah felt straps and then the holster and gun.

"Roddy would skin me if I ever went anywheres without some kind of weapon."

"Is that a d-derringer?"

"Beau would skin me if I ever put much faith in a lady's gun. That's a full-sized man-stopper."

Sarah hugged him with all her strength. "Thad said you'd be angry with me for usurping male prerogatives."

"Did you tell him I'm just a dumb Texan. I don't even know what those fancy words mean?"

"You know every one of those ten dollar words. Is that what I did?"

"I'd rather have a woman who likes me in one piece enough to do something more than stand around making squealy noises or fall down in a faint like a dog-run sheep. Promise me you won't ever get in the middle of things to where I can't think for worrying about you is all."

"I promise," Sarah said, meaning it. "Would you like to know what else he said?"

"I don't know. Would I?"

Sarah told him then the gist of what Thad had said.

"That poor man has his smarts in all the wrong places." His voice fell to the deep rumble she loved so well just before his mouth closed over hers. This kiss was hard and possessive, his tongue invading, branding.

From the street came footsteps, the rustle of a skirt, a female giggle, then a lower male voice. "Mrs. Hammond's gunslinger" were the only words Sarah heard clearly as the couple moved on by.

"Do you mind being called that?" Sarah whispered against his lips.

"At first I liked it, but lately it's come to me I'd rather be Mrs. Slade's than Mrs. Hammond's."

As his meaning hit her, Sarah jerked her head back. "Matt?"

"It's a good thing all Stewart wants is a parlor ornament. He needs to find himself another woman anyway. If you're still willing, we'll work it out, but I need to tell you. All the years. I can't say I never...."

"I don't want to know," she whispered. "Don't tell me what I don't want to know."

"You need to know. I've been with other women, and you need to know, but I've never done what could make a baby with any woman but you."

Sarah reared back, trying to see him in the dark, feeling suddenly lighthearted. "And that's as much because you don't want that part of you we're both so fond of turning black and rotting off as because of me, isn't it?"

"A little of each maybe."

She couldn't keep the laughter out of her voice. "Well, I'm holier than you are, although if I didn't have Laurie it might have been different. I did get kissed a few times."

"Did you now."

"Yes, and not one of them tasted right."

"How did Mr. Stewart taste?"

"Bland." Sarah stood on her tiptoes and pulled herself up to his mouth. All that stopped this kiss with them both standing was the sound of more footsteps in the street.

"This isn't a good place for misbehaving, is it? We'd best get back before the sheriff comes hunting anyway. Maybe by the time we get back there my trousers will be fitting again."

Catching her breath after the kiss, Sarah teased, "Why, Mr. Slade, here I thought you had another hideout gun on your person."

"You better not go on to say anything more about derringers, or I'll hand you back to Stewart personal."

"Kate told me you have nothing to worry about there."

"Didn't you keep any secrets from that woman?"

"A few, but she was the first woman I ever met I could talk to about those kinds of things. I suppose she still is. And I didn't think I'd ever see you again. Do you mind terribly?"

"I don't. But when she comes to visit, I think I'll hide in the hills."

"Then I'll tell her she can't visit. I'm not sure I ever want to see her again anyway."

"Boston."

"If she'd told you about Laurie all those years ago, you'd have come for us in San Antonio, wouldn't you?"

"I would, and maybe it wouldn't have been any good. Maybe we'd all have starved to death by now or we'd be starving with a passel more kids and hating each other over it."

Sarah wanted to argue, wanted him to be as angry over the lost years as she was, and yet she didn't want him different. "I haven't told her about us, you know. You'd be proud of how, how forgiving I've been because I have written to her, but I haven't told her about us. We can surprise her and Brad when they visit again."

"You surprise them with me, and they'll end up buried with 'died of surprise' on their tombstones."

"It would serve them right," Sarah said, unable to keep a trace of bitterness out of her voice.

Matt let that pass, and they strolled back toward the festivities, teasing each other as they went. Laurie ran up to them as they arrived back at the center of town.

"Where have you *been*? Everybody's talking about you." Laurie's unhappy gaze fastened on Matt. "Mrs. Sanquist says you took Mama somewhere dark to kiss her."

Searching the crowd, Sarah spotted Cecily Sanquist and glared at her. Matt leaned over with his hands on his knees. His deep voice reached not just his daughter, but everyone in the block.

"Well, if you see that Mrs. Sanquist again, you tell her she is *exactly* right. I did kiss her. I kissed her thoroughly, and I liked it so much I'm going to do it again first chance I get."

Matt paused, winking reassuringly at the worried young face, and Sarah shot another glance toward Cecily, watching with satisfaction as the other woman paled.

Matt went on, lowering his voice for effect, in tone only; it was not one whit less forceful. "And the best part about it was," he paused for effect, "your mama never hollered whoa."

He straightened then, taking Sarah by the hand. "Now, you'd best go back with your own friends, because I came here to dance with your mother, and I am going to dance with your mother. Anyone who gets too close might just get knocked down and danced on."

Happy again, Laurie ran back to where the children congregated, but Matt didn't take Sarah among the dancers. "She's worried I'll embarrass her, isn't she? And I guess I did."

"No," Sarah answered. "She's worried something will happen that will take you out of our lives again. She couldn't bear it, and neither could I."

"We'd better set her down and tell her then."

"Can we leave it just a while? As soon as she finds out, she's going to post notices all over town explaining her right to call you Papa to all and sundry."

"All right, we'll wait a while. Now suppose you tell me how come when you dance with that Stewart fellow it looks so easy, and you and I are like two left wheelers hitched together by mistake."

Sarah would never have broached the subject so directly. "I don't know. Where did you learn to dance?"

He shrugged. "It's not something you have to learn, is it? During the war the ladies from some of the towns used to take pity on us and invite us to socials. Nobody said anything about learning. We just hopped around and had fun."

"Hopped around?" Sarah echoed faintly.

"Sure." He eyed her warily now. "You're not going to tell me I have to have lessons to dance with you, are you?"

"No," Sarah said, grabbing him. "I'll hop."

It took a circuit and a half of the dance area, before Sarah managed to throw away every admonition of every dancing master she'd ever known. She hopped, she bounced, and as it all came together, Matt used a hand on her waist to add impetus, and she flew.

"We never did get anything right the first time, did we, Boston?"

"No, but we work things out superbly."

Wild and boisterous, this was not what she had dreamed of when anticipating the evening, and she didn't care. Sarah laughed until her ribs ached and her throat hurt. When they stopped for a few swallows of punch, Matt kept one hand possessively at her waist or her back, and that, coupled with his words to Laurie, kept the rest of the town at bay.

A line of gray light along the eastern sky heralded the coming dawn when the music stopped and everyone began drifting homewards.

Laurie had long since joined most of the youngsters, asleep in a quiet corner on straw covered with quilts put there for the purpose. Sarah's shawl was her pillow, Matt's coat her blanket. He scooped her up so gently she never waked and carried her to Blackburns' dark and quiet house.

Sarah showed the way upstairs holding a lamp high. Silently, as if he had done it many times before, Matt lifted and turned as Sarah removed everything but the chemise that could serve as night dress tonight.

Laurie roused only once, just enough to murmur a sleepy, contented, "Good night, Mama. Good night, Papa."

Sarah only shook her head, kissed her and tucked her in, then watched Matt do the same.

Full of people now, the house reverberated with hushed conversation. Matt's polite words garnered only scowls in return from all except the amused younger Stewarts.

"If Laurie doesn't wake in the morning, maybe you'd better let her sleep in," Matt said in parting, "but I'll see you for breakfast, Mrs.

Hammond." He kissed her then, quickly and on the cheek, but easily enough to let everyone know how things were.

Sarah stood at the front door after he was gone, staring at the place where he had disappeared into the dark.

"What did he mean about breakfast?"

Reluctantly, Sarah turned to Minna. "Matt's staying with the Gilbrides, and we're all going to have breakfast there and then go on to church. Don't look like that, Minna. You have enough extra guests you won't miss me, or Laurie either since I suspect she will sleep till afternoon."

Sarah refused to be troubled by Minna's look. She said good night sweetly and floated upstairs. In the few hours before breakfast and church, she intended to relive and savor every moment of the night.

CONFOUNDING ALL LOGIC, after the night's revelry and no sleep at all, Sarah felt no fatigue, just a profound inner joy. Walking to church on Matt's arm with the Gilbrides right beside, they saw more smiles and nods of greeting than not. Work it out. They were going to work it out.

In the churchyard after the service, people stood in small groups visiting, and Matt and Sarah spoke to several others before Reverend and Mrs. Young approached. After greetings, the preacher launched onto one of his favorite topics.

"You know, Mr. Slade, you have a good carrying bass voice in song. I do believe rejoicing voices are one of the finest ways to honor the Lord. Mrs. Hammond's voice is pleasant, of course, but I fear it too timid to carry far toward the Heavens."

As Young droned on at length on the subject of hymns and song, Sarah glanced at Matt, intending to share the memory the words evoked with a look, but the memory was already there on his face and in the intensity of his gaze.

The churchyard sounds faded away. Sarah no longer stood in her Sunday dress amidst a sociable group of people. She lay naked on blankets in a hollow in a hill, screened from the world by a row of stunted, thirsty bushes. She no longer breathed the fresh fall air of Tavaras, but the thick summer heat of Texas.

Matt's forehead touched hers, their lips brushed. She saw not one sapphire eye but two, his face young and unscarred. He kissed the corners of her mouth, the bow, then along her jaw line, down her neck. He touched his tongue in the hollow above her breastbone, moved down to her breasts and gently pulled a nipple between his teeth.

As he kissed his way down her belly, Sarah cupped her hand around the back of his neck, felt the knobs of his spine with her fingers as she caressed each one, tapping between them as if playing a piano. The pleasure reached a crescendo that brought a low moan from her.

Sing, Sarah. Sing my name.

A hand grasped Sarah hard by the elbow and shook, pulling her around in a quarter turn.

"I need to talk to you, Sarah. Now."

With her lock on Matt broken, Sarah returned through time and space to the churchyard, but the transition bewildered her. She stared uncomprehending at Adelaide Canady's stern countenance.

"I also need to talk to Matt," Addie said in the same tone, and jerked Sarah along, taking Matt by the arm in the same manner and pulling them toward the edge of the crowd.

The sight of Matt, struggling back to New Mexico himself now that the spell was broken, cleared away Sarah's fog, and what they had done hit her. A ruddy flush spread under Matt's deep tan, and he stared at the ground intently.

The silence of those in the churchyard dinned in her ears. One glance at all the staring faces had Sarah staring at the ground too. She tried to swallow but her mouth was too dry. A dizzy rush swept over her, and she thought she might faint.

"Do you two have any idea what you were doing?" Addie scolded, not quietly. "I thought that silly goatee of the Reverend's was going to start smoking any second, just because it was in your line of vision."

Bless her. She was trying to help, but surely they were beyond help. Dear God, let her have stopped us before we got too far, Sarah prayed.

Matt didn't scuff his toe in the dirt, but he gave that impression as he looked at Addie with his head lowered.

"I reckon I never worried about something so small as a beard. I get nightmares the whole town will go up in flames, and the bucket brigades will empty the wells, then dry up the river. The town will be burning away, and folks will pray for rain and never guess the only hope is to throw Sarah and me under water and hold us there till we turn blue."

At this Addie stopped even trying to keep her face stern. "Matt Slade, you are absolutely the most endearing rascal who has ever crossed my path. But I warn you, if you don't let Sarah get you roped and tied soon, I'm going to stop eating so much of my own cooking and start chasing you myself."

Matt gave Addie a smile still tinged with embarrassment. "No Texan would be dumb enough to run from a lady like you, Mrs. Canaday. We'd all find something to stumble over, fall down and get ourself caught."

"Get on with you." Addie wagged a finger at him, then included Sarah. "You two better go for your walk, and I suggest you walk briskly. Don't stroll."

Incredibly, Sarah could see people shaking their heads now, beginning to resume their conversations. She hugged Addie hard. "Thank you," she whispered.

Matt and Sarah walked the river path but she did not take his arm. He kept his hands in his pockets. She crossed her arms over her ribs. Neither of them spoke. They had said everything that needed saying already this morning without words—in Texas.

46

MATT REINED BACK and spoke a few reassuring words automatically without really paying much mind to the nervous antics of his horse. He was only halfway to Tavaras, and Sam had jigged most of the way, refusing to settle into a flat-footed walk, even shying slightly when a puff of breeze or rabbit disturbed the weeds near the road. The totally atypical behavior from a rock-steady animal reflected Matt's mental state.

What the devil had gotten into him yesterday? Beau claimed it was natural for a man to have second thoughts after making such a commitment. Matt had a hundred second thoughts.

In his whole life he'd never bought anything bigger than a horse, and only two of those, for that matter. So he'd gone off and shaken hands with that old lady like some rich fellow or something. And back at the L&L everyone slapped him on the back and told him what a fine deal it was and all.

Easy for them, they hadn't agreed to a mortgage, had they? Close to ecstatic, Jimmy Childers went on and on about the rich grass and good water. Of course that's how Jimmy got the whole thing started, talking about how Kirkendahls raised a big family on that place and never wanted for anything, sent two of their boys to school back East even.

So Matt rode to the Circle K yesterday to talk to Mrs. Kirkendahl. Just to see. And the way things started out, it was a miracle how it finished. For it started with Matt looking down the muzzle of a gun again, a situation that made him feel downright cranky.

"Do you point a gun at every visitor you get before you even say howdy or ask his business?" he asked, staring in disbelief at the tiny gray-haired woman pointing a shotgun at him.

Velma Kirkendahl might be small, but the shotgun never wavered as she held it on him with one hand and drew a pistol and fired three signal shots with the other.

"I don't have to ask your business. Either Stewart or Farrell is tired of asking nice and sent you to try to scare me into selling. When my boys get here, they'll be reading a little Gospel to you, and then you're going back where you came from and telling whichever of those greedy buzzards you work for I won't sell this place for a fraction of what it's worth. I'll sit here till I die, doing nothing but keeping the fences in good shape so their cows can't get in. And when I'm gone, I hope one of my own will honor my memory by doing more of the same!"

Knowing he was wasting his breath arguing with such hostility, still Matt tried. "Ma'am, I work for Mr. Farrell, but I'm here on my own. Folks say this place is for sale. If that's not so, you don't need to be shooting me over it. I'll just turn around and go. No hard feelings."

"You move, and I'll blast the chest out of that horse. You'll still be here to talk to my boys."

Matt gave up trying to reason with her then. A hard knot of anger formed in his stomach. Did he want to live someplace where every time you set foot on a neighbor's property you took your life in your hands? Did he want Sarah and Laurie in such a place?

Matt and Velma Kirkendahl kept their places like statues for some time until two sturdily built blond men about Matt's age rode up on blown and lathered horses.

"Lord, Ma, we heard those shots and figured you were in trouble. You run the others off?"

Matt listened to Mrs. Kirkendahl explain her version of events to her sons. There seemed to be no doubt in her mind that Farrell had sent a gunman to intimidate her into selling for pennies on the dollar.

Matt waited until the family was through conferring, angrier by the minute. "If you've got some notion Farrell's paying me to scare folks off their land—or could—you're crazy. I came here on my own because Jimmy Childers made this place sound real fine, and so far as I can see he's as crazy as you. Even the grass around here looks sour to me. So you'd better make up your mind whether you're crazy enough to backshoot me, because I'm leaving."

Having already decided who was giving the orders, Matt gave the old woman a hard look, ready to wheel his horse, when one of the Kirkendahl sons spoke up. "Well, I'll be.... Ma, that's Mrs. Hammond's gunslinger."

"You can't know that, Willie," said the other.

"Well, I've heard the talk. One-eyed, scarred up, deep voice, rides a plain horse and don't even blink looking down a gun. How many like that you think Farrell's got?"

Matt relaxed slightly. Better to ride out of here without the gun at his back if possible.

"Maybe he's telling the truth, Ma. Maybe he's proposed to Mrs. Hammond."

The little woman looked up at him like an inquisitive magpie. "So is that the way of it? Has Mrs. Hammond accepted a marriage proposal?"

His personal life was no business of these insulting people. Matt stared back at them with his mouth set in a hard line.

"Cat's got your tongue, does it? Maybe you think you need to own a ranch before Mrs. Hammond would have you?" She paused, considering. "Of course, that didn't help young Stewart, did it? Maybe you're just so vain you think she'll jump at the chance when you get around to asking?"

"I don't figure on asking," Matt said through his teeth. "I'm going to say yes next time *she* asks *me*."

For the first time the woman's eyes lost the beady look as they flew wide open. She stopped pointing the shotgun at Matt and let it droop toward the ground as she started to laugh, and in seconds both her sons were laughing with her. Matt only held out another few seconds before he grudgingly let go of his anger and started to smile.

And that, he thought now, soothing his fretting horse once again, was how he'd gotten himself into trouble. After letting his anger dissolve he ended up with a tour of the ranch, and then in the house talking to the Kirkendahls over coffee. The sons, Willie and Tom, had businesses in Rye Wells and were set on town life. Two other Kirkendahl sons would have followed in their father's footsteps, but one had lost an arm in the war, the other his life.

"I don't hold it against the boys," their mother told Matt philosophically. "Otto never could accept it, but the fact is we left what our folks had back East and came out here, made new lives for ourselves. Young folks do that, need to, but their Pa and me, we put our lives into this place, and I'm not letting it go for nothing, and I can't stand to think of the buildings deserted, cows getting out of the sun in my house. Willie and Tom here are tired traveling back and forth, helping me keep things together, and their wives are tired of making do without them more often than not, but I'll stay here till I drop rather than give this place away."

Matt explained how sure he was that Farrell was not sending agents to try to buy the place, and that most likely Stewart wasn't either. Yet he didn't doubt the Kirkendahls. Men had been pestering them, becoming increasingly aggressive, and claiming to represent Farrell or Stewart.

In the end, convinced that a family would really occupy the home she loved, Velma Kirkendahl offered Matt what he recognized as a bargain, and offered to carry a mortgage to boot.

"I'm going to be living in town with Willie and his wife. It would be good for us all to know I have an income of my own. Maybe I'll even travel, see a bit of the world." She gave Matt a knowing eye. "And I don't suppose Banker Thompson would be giving you a loan."

So they ended up shaking on it, and now he faced his own doubts—and had to keep a secret from Sarah. As he'd told the Kirkendahls, "If Sarah finds out, if I won't bring her out here, she'll walk. Until the trouble is over for sure, I'd as soon no one knew."

The Kirkendahls agreed in the end, but like everyone else, they believed the big ranches had settled down and the range war was over without really ever getting going. Beau expected to get notice any day now, but Matt didn't share the sanguine view. He had a feeling those clever trouble makers had only backed off to reconsider and he had just bought himself into the middle of the trouble.

Tavaras came into sight, and Matt forced himself to stop going over it in his mind. It was done. From here on out he would hold tight to the belief that Sarah meant it when she swore she would be happy in city, town or the middle of nowhere so long as they were together. Right now he'd better concentrate on getting Sam settled down to where little girls could ride him.

Henry Blackburn stood waiting at his front gate when Matt brought Laurie home that afternoon. Blackburn didn't fake any friendly feelings.

"I need to talk to you, Slade. Come in a minute."

Quite aware Blackburn considered him an interloper, usurper and worse, Matt started to say a polite no and go on when Laurie stepped protectively in front of him. He hated the conflicting loyalties tearing at Laurie. Thinking he might find some way to work out a truce with Blackburn, Matt reconsidered and accepted the invitation.

In the house, Mrs. Blackburn tried unsuccessfully to send Laurie upstairs to do school work. The fact that a few words from Matt had her skipping off didn't ease the situation, but what else could he do?

Blackburn didn't offer a chair in the parlor but led the way to the dining room. Evidently a table between them was more to his liking. As soon as they were seated, Blackburn pulled an envelope from his shirt pocket, took out the enclosed letter and pushed it across the table.

"I got this yesterday. It's from an old friend in Austin. I think you should read it."

Matt looked at the couple across the table in surprise before picking up the letter. He read newspapers when he could get them and the Bible he kept in his saddlebags daily. Unused to script, he worked through the letter slowly.

The letter spoke for itself. Blackburn had asked his friend to find out about one Matthew Slade who had been sentenced to the Texas penitentiary sometime between '66 and '70 for crime or crimes unknown. The friend had taken his task to heart, corresponded with the prison warden and the judge, who had long ago returned to Illinois. He even visited Charon and talked to Curtis Payne. Reading it in the words of a stranger was an odd experience, like looking at his own life through the wrong end of a telescope. Parts of the letter Matt read two or three times, including the last paragraphs before the writer changed to other subjects.

I fear my investigation has been more lengthy than what you contemplated, Henry, but once I started, the story fascinated me. The judge and the lawyers, indeed everyone involved, admit Slade did not commit any crime, and I believe all concerned struggle with their consciences for their part in extracting a terrible and unjust vengeance.

It is, however, the thought of the girl that haunts me. As ever in our society, she too was judged, and one could even say executed, for she lost her life, did she not? Her only friends in Charon were the riffraff of the town, and none of them would talk to me. Most of the townspeople believe she turned to prostitution, although she disappeared from Charon shortly after the sentencing.

The men involved deserve their nightmares, I think, the coward's thousand deaths.

As he read, a hardness came over Matt. Two months ago, even one, that letter would have given the sheriff the weapon he wanted. No longer. Now Matt would fight for Sarah, for Laurie and for a future. Through with it at last, Matt dropped the letter on the table and pushed it back toward Blackburn.

"I suppose you think you can use that to make me get up and walk out of here, ride out of town and out of the territory without even saying goodbye."

Before Blackburn could answer, a small, choked voice said, "No, Papa, no."

Matt whirled to see Laurie in the doorway, both hands pressed to her mouth, as if she could take back the word. She threw herself into his arms, weeping.

"It's my fault! It's my fault! I said it, and now you'll go away, and it's my fault, and Mama will hate me!"

Some instinct always told Matt how to deal with Sarah's emotional ups and downs, but the agony tearing through the small body heaving in his arms panicked him. His attempts to soothe her only provoked further howls of fear and grief. When Mrs. Blackburn came around the table and tried to help, things got worse. "Don't touch me! I hate you! I hate you both!"

That outburst broke Matt's paralysis. He took a firm grip on the small chin and forced her to look at him. "Now you quit that. You don't hate anybody, and we all know it."

"You're going away! You're going away because he's making you, and because I said, I said...." Upset she might be, but she wasn't going to utter the forbidden word again right then.

"I'm not going anywhere, at least not without you and your mother," Matt said firmly. "Your Uncle Henry and I were just starting to talk things over and state our positions, so to speak, and if you didn't eavesdrop, you wouldn't have heard something that scared you."

"But I said...."

"You sure did, and if you hadn't been disobeying your mother for weeks, toying at it, it wouldn't have slipped out so easy, would it? But as it happens the Blackburns have a letter right there that tells them all about Texas anyway, so it's not so bad. Maybe we don't even need to mention this to your mother."

The teary eyes seemed to take up about half of her face, and then she pressed against his shirt and sopped up quite a few more tears. When the sobs faded to hiccups, Matt gently detached her. "How about you go back upstairs and wash your face and blow your nose and give us a chance to finish up our talk? I'll let you know when we're through."

"You'll go away."

"Laurie, do you think I'm a liar? I'm telling you I won't walk out of this house without seeing you again, and if I'm leaving this town for good, you're coming with me."

She didn't argue any further then, just slid from his lap and disappeared through the doorway. She was seven years old. Matt took no further chances. He got up and closed the door.

"I guess that says about all there is to say, Sheriff. I can't believe you plan to use that letter to make trouble for Sarah, but if you have any notion of letting her read it, I'll have both of them gone from here before you can talk to her. I'll take your word on it, but you'll have to make your decision before I leave."

His face no longer set in angry lines, Blackburn looked out and out confused. "Trouble?" he repeated. "Trouble for Sarah?"

"You're Laurie's father," Mrs. Blackburn whispered.

Now Matt felt as confused as Blackburn looked. He sank back down at the table. "What did you think that letter said?"

Mrs. Blackburn's troubled expression cleared rapidly. "We thought it told how you had ruined another young woman in Texas. The letter doesn't use names except yours, almost as if there's still reason to fear that Army officer. All we saw was what happened to the girl in the letter. You didn't go after her when you got out of prison and marry her then."

Blackburn had finally caught up. He got to his feet, cursing, and pulled a whiskey bottle and one glass from the sideboard.

"Feel like sharing?" Matt asked mildly.

The sheriff didn't respond but splashed liquid in a second glass and thumped it down on the table. "You didn't look for her when you got out, because three years is a long time, and you couldn't be bothered. Why saddle yourself with a wife and a child when you could fiddlefoot around the country with a gun strapped on too low?"

"Henry, that's unfair. He probably couldn't find them."

"I'm afraid I could have, Mrs. Blackburn," Matt said softly. "When I got out, Kate P... Mr. and Mrs. Denham met me and gave me money. They asked me if I wanted to see Sarah, but they didn't tell me about Laurie."

At this Blackburn warmed the air with a spate of oaths that would have given Beau's best serious competition. Matt wondered if the man would snatch the glass back rather than have a person of such deplorable ancestry and character drink from it.

Mrs. Blackburn, however, was through making prejudgments. "Henry, hush up, sit down and let him explain. If Laurie overhears any of that and repeats it, I don't want to have to explain to Sarah."

Women were a never-ending source of amazement to Matt. In this mood, Blackburn might give a Comanche pause, but after his wife's sharp words, he tossed down the contents of his glass in a swallow, poured more and sat down.

Grateful to Blackburn's friend in Austin who had told the worst parts of the story for him, Matt tried to make sense of the rest.

"My goodness," Mrs. Blackburn said when Matt stopped talking. "All those years. I should have seen it quicker. She described her 'husband' to me once. Doesn't anyone know except Denhams?"

"I have a notion Mrs. Canaday knows. I've caught her looking at me kind of knowing when Laurie's right there, and maybe Gilbrides too, but no one's said anything. Once we're married, I'd as soon friends like that know. It's not fair to ask Laurie to keep pretending about something so important to her."

Blackburn had calmed down, his glass stayed half full, and the belligerence disappeared from his attitude. "Even if they didn't tell you about Laurie, why the hell didn't you go after her when you got out of prison?"

"Because I knew what kind of life I was facing, and I thought she should have better."

"And what about when you saw her here? If she held off every man who looked at her for eight years, why the devil didn't you just carry her off and marry her the minute you saw her here?"

The total turnabout was so sudden, Matt had to smile at the other man. "I guess I never thought about it quite like that. There was Stewart and everybody saying he'd win her over. Seemed like he'd be better for both of them—a fine house, servants, all the things she grew up with."

"And how has that changed? What kind of future do you think you're going to make for them?"

Now Blackburn sounded like a father checking a suitor's prospects, but Matt saw no reason to trust him with any extra secrets. "I'm not sure yet. We only just decided the other night we'd find a way."

"You mean you only just decided," Mrs. Blackburn said. "There's never been any doubt in Sarah's mind."

At this Matt smiled at the older woman. He was going to end up liking one of these people for sure. He watched her face soften. Women.

"You must know we would never use anything in that letter to hurt Sarah. She should know that herself," Mrs. Blackburn said.

"Oh, I didn't figure you'd be judging too harsh, but Sarah's had a bad time over it, and she's skittish. In fact there's a few things I caught from Laurie a while ago that sound worse than Sarah let on. I'm going to have to coax it out of one of them."

Henry picked up the letter. "So if Sarah lived through this, what can be in here that you won't let her see?"

Matt didn't answer. "If you didn't know the girl in the letter was Sarah, what did you think you could use to drive me off?"

Matt returned Blackburn's wary regard in kind until Mrs. Blackburn broke the stalemate. "Actually, we knew that if we showed Sarah the letter, she would be so angry that we investigated you, she'd pack her bags and leave, so Henry thought showing it to you we might—you might get the impression...."

"I might not know how dead set Sarah is and be tricked into disappearing."

"Yes. I'm sorry."

"I still need your promise she won't see that letter."

Blackburn tapped the edge of the pages against the table. "Maybe you'll get it, but you'll have to tell me why."

Fair enough. Maybe. "What that letter will tell Sarah that she doesn't know is that Macauley did this." Matt touched the eye patch then the scars. "That was—is—his name. Major Carter Macauley. I told Sarah it happened in prison by accident, a brawl. From the beginning she blamed herself for everything. I never got her over saying if she hadn't been with me I'd have gotten out of Comanche country by myself in no time, no trouble. That's not the truth of it, but I never convinced her. She says I went to prison for the crime of saving her, and I never got her to see the truth of that either."

Matt took a sip of whiskey, trying to decide how to put it in words. "It wasn't what happened between us. If she got out with that lieutenant in command of the escort, Broderick his name was, and if everything else was just the same, Macauley would have shaken his hand and acted like a gentleman. It was me, what I was, what I am. A no-count Rebel drifter, Secesh trash. And he was right, you know. Even if her folks found out they were wrong today, they wouldn't want me walking through their front door."

"It seems to me Sarah had a better perception of who was the trash and who was the gentleman," Mrs. Blackburn said.

Pushing back his chair, Blackburn disappeared into the kitchen for a moment, came back with an ashtray, placed the letter in the middle, and held a match to a corner of it. The three of them were watching the paper curling into ash when a hesitant tap sounded on the door to the parlor.

"It's all right, Laurie, come on in," Matt said.

Laurie climbed back on his lap. "Why are you burning the letter?"

"That's sort of like the way Indians smoke a pipe. A peace symbol you might say."

"Are you going to tell Mama what I said?"

"I'm deciding. Now suppose you tell me what some of that other stuff you were spouting was all about. Your mother never shot anybody."

Laurie gave a one hundred percent female look. "I'm not supposed to tell about that," she said primly.

"You've been spilling secrets all over like a leaky canteen this afternoon. If I have to find out what you were talking about from your mother, I'm going to have to tell her what made me want to know."

Matt gazed steadily into the blue eyes so like his own and felt their relationship shift as Laurie realized her usually indulgent father was tough enough to win out in this matter.

"Mama says I don't really remember. I was too little, and I've just told myself the story over and over. She says you don't need to know. It would upset you and you can't change it."

Matt said nothing and waited until she gave in and started the story, but the real test was keeping control of his face as he heard about Heber. Sarah had told him after people in that town found out about her, they were so cold and unfriendly she decided to leave. To Matt's amazement, Laurie glossed right over the shooting of the ticket agent.

"Mama says she didn't mean to hit him. She meant to shoot near his head, and he moved."

Laurie described vividly the other men bumping into each other, pushing to get out of the station as the shot echoed, but she didn't show much emotion over that part of the story either. Out of everything that had happened that day, only the fact that her mother took the stage tickets without paying worried Laurie.

"Mama says it wasn't stealing. She says the stage company would make Mr. Holthoff pay for the tickets and it would serve him right."

Her voice went up at the end of this as in a question. Finally sharing the experience, Laurie wanted reassurance. Matt looked to Blackburn, who was equally dumbfounded. "There couldn't be a want out on her, could there?"

Blackburn shook his head. "No, she'd be too easy to find. How many men would go into a court and admit they were doing that to a woman with a small child and had an ear shot off for their trouble?"

The sheriff's face lit up with a grin. "I can't believe she's fooled us that much all these years, slugging some woman in the jaw, shooting ticket agents, steal... I mean, running off with compensatory tickets. Three years in my house, and I feel liked I've never met her."

Matt tried to tell Blackburn what he had seen so long ago watching the determined young woman march over to take on the Webbs when Broderick's courage failed. "The woman you know is real enough. Sarah will always be like that—as soft as she can be, and as strong as she has to be. You Yankees sure raise up some fine women."

Blackburn glanced at his wife and nodded. "I'd agree with that. Maybe you and I do have some common ground."

47

AT THE SOUND OF horses, Matt grabbed his rifle from beside the front door and moved out onto the porch. One week tomorrow since he'd moved here, and already he'd had his first lesson as to why folks in these parts threw down on visitors before asking their business.

Beau and Roddy. They waved a greeting and headed their horses straight for the corral by the barn. Matt took the opportunity to duck back into the house, finish running a comb through his wet hair. This visit was unexpected, and he was doubly glad he'd had time to bathe, scrub off the blood and gore, get into clean clothes and almost forget the stink.

Footsteps echoed across the porch as Matt set the coffee pot on the stove. Beau and Roddy walked in without knocking and settled comfortably around the scarred table in the homey big kitchen. Matt avoided the shining furniture in the rest of the house.

"It's still hard to take in," Beau said. "You and Jimmy each rattling around in a house all your own. You're like kings without subjects."

"Jimmy's been staying here. Two of us rattle the same here."

Matt sure enough considered this house a palace. A wide porch ran the whole length of the first floor, painted the same dove gray as the traditional wood siding. The house had so many rooms if Velma Kirkendahl hadn't left most of her furniture, Matt never would have figured out what they were all for.

"I'd rather you have it than sell it piece by piece," she said. "If Mrs. Hammond—Mrs. Slade—would like it and keep it, we'll come to terms."

The second, smaller house on the property had been built during the war for a Kirkendahl son and his family, but that son's home had long been a grave at Vicksburg.

Jimmy Childers jumped at the chance to work for Matt. Maybe the pay was the same, but a house instead of a bunk meant a chance for a family of his own, and if he was the entire ranch crew, well, as Jimmy said, that made him the foreman.

Roddy pulled out papers and a tobacco pouch and started building a cigarette. Beau already had a cigar angling from the corner of his mouth. Matt dropped into a chair himself, not trying to hide the bone weariness or the discouragement. And yet he knew the attack could have been much, much worse.

Restless in the night, up and roving around after returning from a visit with Sarah, he'd heard the faint sound of gunshots, roused Jimmy, and they'd gotten there in time to stop the worst of it. There were only nine dead cows, three more wounded so badly Matt finished them himself, and another dozen that would probably make it with nursing.

The threat to his future and Sarah's started a deep fury, but the waste appalled him. He didn't merely cut out the best meat and make one huge pyre of the carcasses, as he knew they did on the L&L. He and Jimmy did rough butchering from the middle of the night on, removing entrails mostly so the meat wouldn't be ruined.

Come daylight Jimmy borrowed Farrell's heaviest wagon, and by late morning he had started for Rye Wells. The priest and the preacher in the town would know how to distribute the meat. Any wounded stock that didn't make it could go to Tavaras over the next days.

"Jimmy says Farrell lost fifty."

Beau shifted the cigar, the better to answer. "Closer to sixty all said and done. Another twenty or so in bad shape. Whole place smells like burning meat. You were right all along. It's not over."

"I'm surprised to see you," Matt said. "I figured you'd be swarming all over the L&L hunting the killers."

"The cattle churned the ground up so bad trying to get away, there's no sign worth following," Beau said. "And we're not looking for more trouble till dark. For that matter, I bet tonight's going to be peaceful, except for one of the ranch hands getting nervous and shooting one of us, but we'll be out there, just in case. We decided to come commiserate, and make sure you know your south fence is as safe as we can make it. How do you figure this? They've never touched this place before. They left a widow lady alone, but you're fair game?"

Velma Kirkendahl had not left her good china, but what she did leave intimidated Matt. He pulled three tin cups from his own stash and set them on the table, pouring coffee with considerably more grace than he'd shown in the café months ago.

"I figure men who round up cows in the dark and start shooting when they can't even see well enough to make clean kills don't care much who or what they're hurting. They thought they could buy this place for nothing is all. Those agents visiting Mrs. K and supposed to be from Farrell and Stewart are the ones we're looking for—or their friends."

They chewed it over a while, then Beau said, "I told Farrell if they come after you hard, he's going to need new men. We'll move over here. Six of us—seven with Jimmy—could cover this place pretty well, and when it gets that personal, to hell with defense. It's time to start fighting back. I think Harlan and a couple of his men might feel the same."

Matt was more moved by the casual offer than he wanted to let on. "I can't afford you."

"You've got credit." Beau rocked back in his chair then, hands folded behind his head. "Ah, hell, Matt, you must know how much we're going to miss you, you and your irritating ways and that rigid moral compass of yours."

Surprised, Matt looked from one to the other. "You're not supposed to miss me. Sarah knows she'll be running a rest home for between times mercenaries."

"You cannot become respectable with us in and out of your house," Roddy pointed out.

"Then we'll pass on respectable. Sarah says you're the only family I've got. If you disappear for good, she'll take it like she married into a family that doesn't like her."

Roddy looked around the cheerful cream-colored room now as if he hadn't looked closely enough before. "It would be good to feel someplace is home again, I think," he murmured. Then in a more normal voice, "You will of course be forthright when our welcome wears thin."

"Sarah will."

They laughed at that and started discussing the travel difficulties, speculating when the railroad would come to Santa Fe, but Beau was uncharacteristically quiet, and soon he changed the subject.

"If we're family, isn't it time to level, Matt? What's between you and Sarah? Laurie's yours, isn't she?"

It shouldn't have come as a surprise, but it did. Matt got up and refilled the coffee cups, trying to decide what to say.

"You can tell me to mind my own business short of a fist in the jaw."

At that, Matt smiled. He dropped back in his chair and said, "I don't feel that way about it, and I couldn't deny Laurie if I tried, but Sarah's had some bad times, and it scares her." He paused, fiddled with his cup, then looked right at Beau. "You can pass some awful hard judgments on women, you know."

Beau pretended the cigar needed tending, rolled the end in the ashtray. "You taught me better ways to judge men, you and Roddy. Educate me some more."

Matt nodded and looked back over the years. Such a long story, and where did it begin really? For him it began with the first sight of her, so fine, and belonging to a Yankee like every good thing seemed to. But to tell it.

He started with waking up from Webbs' kick, hung over, but not enough so he couldn't recognize that his small beginning on a decent life had disappeared. He told it all, even the night in the Charon jail, and what Sarah had told him of her part, even though he now knew she had prettied that up some.

When he finished there was silence around the table. Roddy's face was inscrutable behind a haze of smoke. Beau was, as always, easy to read, sympathy, anger.

Matt tried to make light of it. "So you see, you're all the family I've got, and you're more respectable than all Sarah's got, a retired whore and her lover who's married to somebody else."

Beau sat up straight, eyes cold. "Didn't you ever think about going after Macauley?"

"I thought about it a whole lot for three years, but when I got out.... Between us we changed her life a whole lot for the worse, but her friends told me she was all right. I figured she'd marry somebody like Stewart. So long as she got away from Macauley, he didn't matter much. And I guess I never got over feeling sorry for him anyways."

"Sorry for him!"

"He never even knew what he had—and lost. He's a fool."

"Maybe he's a fool, but you defy description."

Matt shrugged, ready to leave a difficult subject alone now. "Either of you hungry? I've sure got a lot of beef needs eating around here."

"I can't believe you saved any," Beau said, still outraged.

"Food sounds good to me," Roddy said. "Listening to such a tale is very hard work, you know. Beau is ready to break a sweat."

Matt grinned at them both and got busy. The meat was only half cooked when Jimmy got back, dirty, tired and disgusted. But he carried reciprocal gifts of fresh bread, butter and even a pie. Their simple meal turned into a feast.

Halfway through the meal, Jimmy gave a start. "Uh oh, I almost forgot, and I think she'd skin me. Here, Matt." He pulled an envelope from his shirt pocket. "Mrs. Kirkendahl tracked me down in town special to give me this for you."

Matt turned the sealed envelope over and over in his hands. Sure enough his name was on it. No one had ever sent him a letter before.

"What do you suppose it could be? I'm not supposed to pay her any more money until the first of the month. I'm sure. I asked that lawyer fellow twice."

"Why don't you open it and find out?" Beau suggested.

Leery of something so strange, Matt did so slowly, ignoring the others' impatience. He read it through and then sat staring into space, thinking about the spidery words covering the pages.

Finally he looked at his friends, curious and waiting. "What do you all know about mortgages?"

Jimmy shrugged, Roddy looked blank, but Beau said, "More than I'd like to, I guess, but that old lady's half in love with you. You can't tell me she's making trouble over the loan."

"No, not her. Listen to this." Leaving out the sociable bits at the beginning and end, Matt read them the heart of the letter.

Something that seems very strange to me has happened in the few days since I moved in here. It involves you, so you should know, although I cannot see what you might do. I only just got settled when a man came to see me.

He was friendly in a smooth way, and said he represented the United Territorial Mortgage Company of New Mexico and that company was buying mortgages in these parts. He wanted to buy your mortgage from me and he offered the principal amount less what he called a discount. He said then I could have all my money now instead of in small payments over many years, and for his company it was an investment.

I told him no. I told him I like having an income. He stayed friendly, but I could see he was angry when he left. I never heard of such a thing, but my boys told me it is done all the time, this buying and selling of loans.

The next day, he came back again, and he came when I was alone. This time he offered to pay the full amount of your note without the discount. He was no longer so friendly, and I believe he thought I might sign his paper because it would be easier than saying no. He was mistaken of course. When I told my boys about this, they did not like it at all. They said this offer was not good business. There was no sense to it.

The fact is that man came back a third time yesterday. I was alone in the house again. This time there were two of them, and one did not look comfortable in his suit. The fancy talker this time offered to pay what he called a premium, and he did not intend on taking no for an answer.

As you know, I may be an old lady, but I am not an old fool. After his second visit I took to keeping a pistol near to hand, and I ran the both of them off. Willie and Tom are very upset. They tried to find those men to read them some Gospel but could not. They are keeping watch over me like a child. Can you make sense of any of this? If you know those men and could help Willie and Tom find them, I would be grateful. I do not like being watched over this way.

Finished with the pertinent part, Matt looked to Beau. "If somebody buys my mortgage at a discount, they pay Mrs. K less than what I owe her, but they get the full amount from me and all the interest?"

"Right. She gets less, but she gets it now, and it ends her risk that you might not pay. But your loan is pretty small for any company to want to bother over, and you aren't what most experts would consider a good risk. Even at a considerable discount, it's surprising any mortgage company would be interested."

"So her sons are right. These offers are bad business."

"They're worse than bad business. They make no sense. Somebody wants you owing them instead of her pretty bad."

"But what good does that do them?" Matt asked.

"None, unless you don't pay. Then they foreclose."

"But this place is worth more than I owe. I paid her more than half already. Maybe I should have paid her the whole price. I could have."

"No." Beau was adamant. "You need operating capital. You keep the cash you've got set aside and pay the damn mortgage. Nobody can foreclose unless you don't pay."

"But I can pay so why...." Matt stopped talking, thinking about what he could pay and what would change things so he couldn't. Pieces of the puzzle fell into place with almost audible clicks in his mind.

He said to Jimmy, "Mr. Farrell has a mortgage, doesn't he?"

"That's none of my business, Matt," Jimmy said, embarrassed. "All right, yes, he does. I think maybe he borrowed more these last months, but he deals with the bank in Rye Wells. They wouldn't sell him out."

Matt looked at Beau again. "What about Stewart? Do you think he's got loans? Would he borrow against the ranch?"

"Sure," Beau answered. "It would be the easiest way, borrow against a going concern to get investment funds for...."

Matt watched first Beau, then Roddy and Jimmy catch up with his own thoughts.

"Buy the loans, start a range war so no one can pay, foreclose and own the valley," Roddy said. "But why?"

They could come up with no answers to that basic question, but they did sketch out a plan of action. Leaving Jimmy to keep lonely guard, Matt saddled up and rode back to the L&L with Beau and Roddy.

Farrell didn't want to believe it and had a hundred reasons why Matt had to be wrong, but in the end he agreed to talk to the Rye Wells banker if only to disprove the idea. Matt rode home, feeling impatient, but at least staying awake all night presented no problem. His mind churned the whole thing over and over, and long before dawn he had fastened on a further idea.

Beau, Roddy and Farrell stomped into Matt's kitchen in mid-morning, continuing an argument that had undoubtedly been going on since yesterday afternoon when Farrell's banker admitted selling the L&L loans to the United Territorial Mortgage Company of New Mexico. Farrell wanted to talk to Thaddeus Stewart—forthwith.

Matt agreed. "We'll just ride over and talk to him."

With Farrell, Beau argued politely. With Matt, he laid down the law. "Like hell you will. You can wait till Sunday and see them in Tavaras without any risk. They'll shoot you on sight if you ride over there."

"There could be a whole lot more trouble before Sunday," Matt pointed out reasonably, "Enough maybe to have twenty men charging onto the L&L like an army. We know as much as we're going to know without Stewart talking to Banker Thompson. If just two of us ride over there, we'll be all right."

"You are not going over there without me," Beau said flatly.

"And how's it going to be better if you get shot too?" Matt asked.

"Harlan won't shoot me," Beau said.

"He won't shoot me either. Harlan isn't the problem."

"No, *you're* the problem. As usual. I'll shoot you myself before I'll let you go over there without me."

Unable to refute such impeccable logic, Matt gave in.

48

AFTER CONSIDERABLY MORE acrimonious debate, Roddy agreed to start on to Tavaras alone and wait for the others there. If the Stewarts were about to be visited by their enemy, the fewer of his gunmen accompanying him, the better the chance of getting to talk.

None of the men remarked on the sprawling majesty of the Stewart home. Drawing close, they paid far more attention to the number of men in the yard, all straightening now from attitudes of bored waiting to at the ready. Harlan Rastus lounged near the ornate double doors to the house. Recognizing him, Matt relaxed slightly. Too soon. Thaddeus Stewart burst from the house.

"Murdering son of a bitch!"

Matt rode on the far right as always, his blind side to his companions. Now he jumped Sam into Farrell's horse so hard it careened into Beau's mount, even as Stewart snapped off a shot that whined over their heads only for lack of care in the aiming.

Off balance on his staggering horse, Beau still managed three retaliatory and much better aimed shots before Matt could stop him. Splinters from the front door sprayed around Stewart's head.

Harlan's roar kept it from turning into a short, one-sided war. "Nobody shoots, damn it!" The big redhead yanked Stewart's gun from his hand.

"You traitorous bastard, get off my land and take the rest of that useless bunch with you!" Stewart shouted at Harlan.

Quite beyond any concern for his own safety, Stewart charged to Farrell, trying to pull him his off horse, still shouting accusations.

Dismounting, Matt caught Stewart from behind and trapped his arms, surprised at the strength rage gave the smaller, older man. Physically restrained, Thaddeus attacked Matt with words, spraying spit with his fury.

"You skulking, backshooting bastard. A bullet would be too quick. I'll see you back in a cage where you belong. I'll see him there for paying you and you for taking his money! You missed your shot! You missed your chance! Did you think if you killed my boy Sarah would have you? She was playing with you, playing! Even killing my son wouldn't get you that woman, and you didn't kill him!"

Matt had been two ugly days without sleep, and at the mention of Sarah, he lost his temper. "You old fool, Sarah Hammond was mine before you ever set eyes on her. She's been mine every day of all the years since, and I don't have to kill anybody to prove it!"

Thad, speaking calmly from the doorway, defused the situation. "I think I'd like to know what you mean by that, Slade, but that's not why you're here, is it? Let Dad go."

Matt saw Thad leaning against the splintered door, his left arm bandaged and useless in a sling, and understood the fear driving his father to such crazed behavior.

"Get inside!" Thaddeus shouted at his son. "I'll handle this. You shouldn't be up."

Realizing his son's presence made restraining Thaddeus unnecessary, Matt did let go.

As his father ran to him, Thad said, "Now, Dad, the doctor admitted that getting pitched off the horse did more damage than the bullet." Thad looked back to the visitors. "Even Jess agrees the time for patience is past, Lucius. Did you plan on breaking in on my funeral? Slade's not quite as good with a rifle as they say, although I'll admit it was a tricky shot."

"Too tricky for the shooter, I guess," Matt pointed out. "If it was me, you'd be dead."

"Well, now I should be. I was riding a horse with more looks than sense. He spooked at a shadow and got me a hole in the arm instead of the heart. Then he took to pitching so hard the next shots were clean misses. Bad luck for the assassin, good for me."

"I do believe I could hit a target the size of a man from a considerable distance—even on a spooky horse," Matt said evenly.

Thad smiled slightly at this but didn't answer. "So why are you here?" he asked Farrell.

"To tell you who shot you, if you'll listen," Farrell said. "It's Matt's idea, and I thought it was crazy, but damned if I don't believe it myself now."

Jesse Stewart had moved into the doorway behind his brother, and Matt could see him speak, couldn't catch the words, but Thad nodded slowly. "All right," he said, "we'll listen. That's all. Listen."

Beau gathered the reins of all three horses. "I'll stay here. I like the company better."

A man would need a map for a week or two until he could memorize the layout of the house, Matt decided, following his reluctant hosts into the depths. Settling into a deep chair in what they were calling an "office," Matt ran his eye over the bookshelves. Did anyone read those fat volumes, or were they there for show?

Farrell deferred to Matt. The idea was his so he could explain it. Angry interruptions from Thaddeus changed to incredulous silence when it finally hit him that Matt was not speaking as an employee of Lucius Farrell.

"So Rye Wells admitted selling your notes to this company?" Thad asked Farrell.

"Sure enough. They see it as only good business. The request to keep taking my payments and front for the buyer struck them as a little strange, but they get a fee for it, so why not?"

With his emotions under control again, Thaddeus showed signs of the man who was building a multi-faceted empire. "That still leaves why. It's easy to say they want the land, but why this particular land?"

"I had an idea about that too," Matt said. "But maybe this notion is—personal."

"When you own them, dead cows are personal as hell," Thaddeus said. "If you're lucky, you'll never find out how personal a shot son can get."

Matt nodded. "The day I was in Mrs. Canaday's place, waiting for Thompson and his friends to start harassing Mrs. Hammond, I wasn't really listening to what they had to say. It just sounded like braggarts' talk. But last night some of it kept coming back to me. They were boasting about how smart they were, rich and going to get richer. They talked about friends in high places, speculating in bonds and land—and railroads. If smart men knew where a railroad was going to go, and they could get hold of the land it was going to go over cheap, would it be worth their while?"

No one answered him for a minute, and Matt waited for a rebuttal of his unsophisticated reasoning. It didn't come.

"This valley is only one of the ways they could lay track to Santa Fe," Thad said finally. "And it's not the best way. They'd have to be able to manipulate the choice of route. They'd have to own more than our land, say a big chunk of the company building the road. It would be worth their while, all right. Getting title to as much land along the route as cheaply as possible would be only part of it. So they saw your name on the land transfer from Mrs. Kirkendahl and couldn't resist going after you. That's personal all right, and it was their first mistake."

Matt didn't quite agree with that. "I think the first mistake was they didn't know any of you better. They didn't know about you and Miss Farrell, for one thing." Matt nodded toward Jesse, then looked at the senior Stewart. "You hired gunmen because they started a rumor Mr. Farrell was hiring gunmen. He did the same, same reason, but it happened you got men who know each other, and we aren't in any froth to go at it. They thought it would be easy to start a war, but it never happened."

They talked it over a while longer. Then the Stewarts argued over whether or not Thad would ride to Tavaras with his father and brother. Matt felt no surprise when Thad got his way.

What did surprise him was how harshly they all brushed off Mrs. Stewart's worried inquiries. This was business, none of her concern. No son of his would ever speak to Sarah like that, Matt vowed to himself, at thirty or at three.

When Matt walked outside and saw Roddy in the yard with Beau, he didn't even remark on it, knowing that Roddy had also most likely not come straight in but worked his way around from the other direction. With Harlan, eight grim men rode to Tavaras. As they entered the town, people on the walks stopped and stared, recognizing enemies riding together, recognizing trouble.

Not old enough to recognize trouble, Laurie and Mary came flying down the walk as the men approached the bank, Laurie into Matt's arms, Mary managing to get a hold on both Beau and Roddy at the same time.

"Why are you here with them? Are you going to see Mama?"

Matt gave his daughter a single hard hug then set her down. "We think that Banker Thompson might be able to help us get the trouble around here stopped, and we're going to talk to him. You and Mary need to stay here out of the way so you don't hear any words your mamas wouldn't approve of." Matt winked at her. "Beau and Roddy are going to wait here too. How about you keep them company?"

Laurie and Mary agreed readily, and Matt was relieved to see Beau's small shrug. He hadn't expected to win the point that easily.

Thaddeus made no suggestions. He gave orders. "You stay here too, Jesse. And you."

He thrust his chin at Harlan, who had been wearing a hard look ever since the scene in the ranch yard. If the old man had the smarts Matt suspected, he'd be taking time to give Harlan an apology when this was over.

The teller gaped as they walked in, the Stewarts leading the way straight to Thompson's office.

"No, you can't—I mean, you shouldn't...." No one even looked at him, and the ineffective words drifted off behind them.

The last one through the office doorway, Matt took in the unexpected in an instant, his hand snaking for his gun at a speed Beau would have applauded. And he knew it was no good. Three men in the room, not just Thompson, one with a pistol already in his hand, the barrel centered on Matt's chest. Too late, too slow.

Three shots rolled together as one, an assault on the ears, and Matt watched red flowers burst on the man's chest, the back of his head explode and spatter on the wall. An artist's hand, only slightly darker than his own deeply tanned skin, holstered the Colt Beau maligned, and Matt met Roddy's dark, cynical eyes.

"It is good you are retiring from this business, my friend. You will never have the right attitude. I will go reassure the girls—and Beau."

Roddy disappeared back through the doorway, leaving Matt and the others with an unpleasant scene. Thompson fell to his knees, vomiting up a fat man's lunch. His brother alternately made excuses and confessed in a non-stop shrill stream. The dead man was the Eastern friend who had assaulted Sarah, and Matt thought Mrs. Kirkendahl would say he looked uncomfortable in a suit.

As Farrell and Stewart Senior broke into the confession with question after question, Thad slumped against a wall, gray-faced and giving every sign of joining Thompson on the floor any second. Matt decided the older men could take care of the mess. He could use some fresh air himself.

"How about some help out of here?" he asked Thad.

"Neither one of you turned a hair. What's the right attitude, a killer's?"

Matt felt something harden in his belly. Someday he might call this man friend, but Sarah spoke the truth when she said what was between him and Roddy and Beau dwarfed ordinary friendship and made them family.

"I've seen too many good men die to mourn one like that," he said. "Would you like it better if my blood were soaking that fancy rug right now?" He put an arm around the other man and helped him to stand straight.

At the door to the street, Thad stopped him. "But that's what he meant isn't it? You don't have a killer's instincts."

Matt hesitated, deciding whether explain at all, and then how. "I've done my share of killing. He meant I don't always expect the worst like he does. Roddy doesn't think much of most folks, and today he was right. I'm going to get your brother and Harlan to deliver you to Mrs. Blackburn for some fussing over, and then I'm going to embarrass Roddy for a while before I go tell Sarah it's over."

"Will you explain what you said to Dad this morning about Sarah always being yours?"

"No," Matt said bluntly. "When you're feeling better, you tell the Blackburns I said they could tell it. I'm not doing it again."

SARAH HESITATED IN the dark outside Blackburns' house, aware she would never come "home" this way again. The house blazed with light, making her even more chary of entering, of seeing knowledge in all the eyes. So many people knew now. Today Beau and Roddy and the Stewarts, and Addie, who finally asked as they discussed the future. Last Sunday, when Matt left town early, Sarah told Charlie and Emily Gilbride about Laurie, about Texas and the past.

All these friends reacted with sympathy, hugs and wishes for a better future. They were better people, better friends than those who had caused her so much pain over the years, but Sarah also suspected they accepted the past because of Matt. They assumed he planned to marry her and make the future right.

Busy with her work, Sarah had not known about the ranchers' visit to the bank until it was all over. Henry had jailed both of the Thompsons, and the town mortician had the dead man's body by the time the café filled up with relieved, celebrating men. Laurie and Mary were right in the middle, soaking it all in.

No one explained clearly. Understanding dawned in bits and pieces. Sarah had grasped the basics when a careless remark let her know how close it had been. A gun centered on Matt's chest, a finger tightening on the trigger. She hugged Roddy until he protested.

"You will break ribs, and admitting such a small person did that to me will be my ruin."

She let go then, but later came up behind him as he sat at a table, hugged him around the neck and kissed the lean cheek.

Thank you, Roddy, thank you, for keeping Matt safe.

Matt, acting so unlike himself, telling her about the ranch, but so quiet, not meeting her eyes. Sarah tore herself from unsettling thoughts and entered the house.

"No, no, don't get up." Her words had no effect on the men, and Sarah dropped into a chair quickly. She had expected Thad to be here with Henry and Minna, staying overnight rather than further aggravating his wound with the trip home, but his father's presence surprised her.

"Matt said you'll have to stay alert for trouble a while longer— until they all realize they've been found out."

"Yep." Thaddeus had never looked so mellow in Sarah's experience. "But Harlan rode back, and he can take care of it. Jesse can help. Lucius probably ran him off his place before dark."

Jesse had stayed in the café with Lucius Farrell for a very short time, nervous with an eager excitement Sarah understood so well. Lucky Julia.

"Will they catch the others? Is it really over?"

"It's over, sure enough," Henry said. "Exposing their scheme will stop it, but it wouldn't surprise me if none of the others are ever caught. They'll be running and hunting holes to hide in already. Thompsons won't serve much time, you know. The only one who paid full price was the one Rodriguez executed today."

Sarah nodded, agreeing with the satisfaction in Henry's tone more than his words. "The dead man was the one who shot you, wasn't he?" she said to Thad. "I'm so glad it wasn't worse. Matt said you shouldn't have come to town; you got gray. Are you feeling better now?"

"You're embarrassing me, Sarah. I have a feeling men like Matt and Rodriguez don't think a wound like this deserves a bandage. I almost lost my stomach over the demonstration of why Dad hired men like that to handle our trouble." Thad gave her a sheepish smile. "So are you looking forward to being a rancher's wife after all?"

Sarah looked down at her hands in her lap, afraid her feelings showed on her face. "There was so much going on. Matt didn't get to describe it very well. You must know all about it. What's it like?"

Sarah regained her composure as Thaddeus gave her a good description of the Circle K, complete with his opinion. "With the benefit of Childers' experience, he'll make a good living, no doubt about that. But there's no room to expand."

Expansion might be the Stewart creed, but a good living would suit Sarah fine. She wanted a home, a home filled with love and laughter and Matt.

"Surely Matt is going to take you to see the house soon, isn't he?" Minna asked. "I've never been there, but I hear it's very nice."

"Tomorrow," Sarah said. "Addie has already all but given my job to Juanita Sandoval, and she's going to start work tomorrow. Matt said he'd call for me with a buggy right after lunch."

"Laurie will enjoy that."

"Just me tomorrow. He said Laurie could have a private viewing the day after and that made her happy."

Henry made a disapproving sound. "So when exactly are we going to get this marrying done? Sunday?"

"W-we haven't decided yet." Sarah stared at her lap again, unable to deal with more people assuming something she was no longer brave enough to assume herself. Matt had acted so strange, so withdrawn.

In the few minutes they'd spent alone in the alley before he left with the others, he had never once spoken such words as marry, marriage or wife.

No obstacles stood in their way any more. Perhaps he had realized he didn't want to marry a woman who had borne him a bastard child, a woman who imposed no restrictions on their relationship and fought his, a woman he knew so well in every way. The biblical way— Bible.

Sarah needed an excuse to escape the awkward silence that had fallen over the room anyway.

"It's been such a full day, I'd better check on Laurie and retire myself. Henry, may I look at your Bible? I won't keep it. Matt said the strangest thing today. He said he wants to discuss two verses with me tomorrow, and I need to read them."

"And when did your gunslinger get that familiar with the Good Book?" Henry asked with amazement.

"He said church people visited the prison and gave Bibles to anyone who would take one. He doesn't know chapter and verse like you, but he knows it better than I do."

"So what are you going to look up?"

"First Corinthians, Chapter 7, verses 1 and 9."

A strange look flashed across Henry's face. "Bible's on the table by the bed. You'd best get up there and read them," he said without expression.

"But you know it! I can see you know those verses. Just tell me. Please?"

Henry shook his head, then said, "I suppose there's nothing in that book that can't be read out loud around women folk, but those verses.... You go upstairs and read them. Get now."

Sarah's stomach curled into a knot, but Henry's expression told her pleading would be a waste of time. She took the stairs slowly, unable to imagine what biblical verses Henry would refuse to quote for her.

Lighting the bedside lamp in Blackburns' bedroom, Sarah paged through the Bible and found the verses.

> *7:1 Now concerning the things whereof*
> *ye wrote unto me: It is good for a man*
> *not to touch a woman.*
> *7:9 But if they cannot contain, let them*
> *marry; for it is better to marry than to*
> *burn.*

Tears blurred her vision as Sarah closed the Bible and replaced it on the table, blew out the lamp and floated to her own bedroom on a wave of friendly laughter coming from downstairs.

49

MATT AND SARAH spoke only a few meaningless words on the trip to the Circle K. Everything that mattered passed between them when their eyes met.

Sarah sat still on the buggy seat, and inside her feelings jostled each other, shouted, and tumbled till she thought she would explode with the joy of being alive. Sensation after sensation assaulted her and then settled deep inside to compound with the others. There was heat and strength where Matt's arm pressed against her. Crisp and fresh, the fall wind tugged at her bonnet and kissed her cheeks, leaving her snug in the plum-colored wool dress and gray shawl that almost matched Matt's suit.

In years past the fall wind carried traces of regret for Sarah when she remembered autumn in New England. Never again, she thought. The drabness of the grasslands made the pines in the distance greener, the sky bluer, and she was home.

Sam trotted along at a good clip, the sound of his hooves and the buggy wheels blending into merry background music. When they turned onto the ranch road between high gateposts, Sarah knew without Matt saying anything. She examined the land on each side of the road as she had never before studied mere ground, and when the buildings appeared, stared even harder. Matt stopped in front of the house.

"You go look around inside, and I'll put the horse up."

Behind her, Sarah heard the buggy leaving, but she stood spellbound looking only at the house, their house. Thaddeus hadn't mentioned the porch or the porch swing creaking slightly now as it moved in the breeze.

She pictured her family sitting there on warm summer nights, Matt's arm around her and her arm around Laurie. In her mind she saw other figures, small figures in Matt's lap and hers.

Sarah walked up the steps, crossed the porch and went inside. By the time she heard the door open and close as Matt came in, Sarah had been in every room except one. She had run her fingers over each piece of furniture except the ones she now studied from the doorway.

Matt moved behind her as she stood there, holding onto the doorframe of the cream and blue room, almost hypnotized by the big four poster bed covered with a colorful quilt.

"I can't believe she left such beautiful things."

"She took all the furniture from one of the upstairs bedrooms—it fits where she is now she says—and some other things the sons' wives wanted."

He kissed the back of her neck then, nibbled at the edge of her collar. All the emotion that had been building through the long months of summer surged in a hot tide. Sarah whirled in his arms, ready to accuse him of torture, but saw the truth in the pale blue gaze in the split second before his mouth closed over hers. She clung to his neck. He carried her to the bed without stopping the kiss.

In a frenzy, Sarah tugged at clothing, Matt's and her own. Unbuttoning her dress only exposed her shoulders and the tops of her breasts. The shell of her corset guarded her upper body, but Matt's fingers slid under, reached a nipple, and Sarah made a soft sound deep in her throat, half pleasure, half frustration.

Her own effort to touch, to feel him without any barrier of cloth was more successful. After yanking his shirt and under vest out of his trousers, she slid her hands over his back, her hands alive to the feel of smooth skin and firm muscle.

They both abandoned the fight with the clothing on their upper bodies at the same time. Sarah tugged at the buttons of his trousers. Matt pulled skirts and petticoats up and aside, drawers down. Sarah reached him first, curled her hand around the hard length of him and started to stroke.

"Ah, Sarah, no, don't...." He pulled her hand away, trapped both wrists together in one hand and held her as his other hand explored her own swollen heat.

"That's not fair," she moaned. "Matt...."

He cut her off with a kiss and rolled onto her. She felt the hard heat of him probing where she wanted him, needed him. Matt thrust down and entered her; Sarah thrust up and enveloped him. Their double effort brought them together in a coupling as violent as their first so long ago, but this was passion met and matched, so very different.

The joy of him slid and slipped through Sarah, rippled across her, at first a quicksilver thing she could not grasp and hold on to, but then came the power of it, snaking through her, coiling deep and low, then lifting, taking her to a place once familiar, now so strange as to be new. She cried out with pleasure again and again. The final peak came with his as if triggered by it.

Even after Matt shifted most of his weight from her, Sarah lay quiet with her eyes shut, sure she could hear peace and contentment in this room.

"Some things never change, do they, Boston?"

She opened her eyes just enough to look at him. "Such as?"

"I'm still too fast and too rough for you."

Wiggling to her side to face him, Sarah said, "Did you hear anyone hollering whoa?"

A lazy grin replete with exactly what she felt was her only answer. Matt reached behind him then and his hand reappeared with his hat, which he threw toward one corner of the room. Then he tugged at the ribbons still holding her bonnet on.

"Maybe the world's full of folks who got eager enough to do this with their clothes on, but we may be the only ones tried it with hats."

The perky little bonnet so carefully chosen to match her dress sailed after his hat.

A worrisome thought occurred to Sarah. "Jimmy...?"

"I told him if he showed his face around here before full dark, he'd lose more than a job." Matt ran his fingers through her hair, searching out hairpins and loosing the thick blonde cloud.

"There," he said. Then he unfastened the rest of the buttons down the front of her dress, in a slow ceremony.

"Let's have a look at you, lady."

An unexpected wave of shyness washed over Sarah as she waited for him to remove the clothing they had pushed and pulled aside. The feeling melted and she laughed as Matt teased his way through her wardrobe.

"This is like peeling an onion," he complained, working on her corset. "A man who had to do this often wouldn't have strength for more. This thing's like the shell on a turtle." He tapped a nail on a stay, and indeed it sounded like a shell.

"Everyone in town watched us leave thinking we'd be up to exactly what we're up to out here. I was the only one in the world convinced you were going to stay noble until I died of it, and so I wanted to look respectable."

"If they all know anyway, you could have worn a sack with nothing under. You're not going to wear yourself out putting all this on every day are you?"

"Of course not. This will be for town. Here I'll dress the way I always have for work."

His fingers stopped on the hooks of her corset. "It isn't what you should have. It isn't going to be any easier, harder maybe."

Sarah cupped her hands along his jaw. "I don't want easy, Matt. I want you, or maybe just having you makes hard things seem easy. I don't know. I know I'm happy."

He let her fingers smooth the frown from his face. "Do you suppose the preacher can be talked into marrying us Sunday? Beau and the others want to be there. They'll be moving on soon."

"I think Reverend Young has come to equate getting us safely married not only with our salvation but with his own. It's a major goal in his life."

"Well, he's right isn't he? And I have a confession to make." The teasing glint danced in his eye now. "After Beau told me how a man is supposed to get down on his knees and make a fool out of himself proposing and all, I decided to just bring you out here and do this. I figure now that you're in the family way again, you have to marry me."

Sarah gasped with laughter. "Why you arrogant male, you, first of all you can't know we've started another child, and second, I managed to have a baby once without a husband. I could manage again."

"But you won't," Matt said with a confidence that did in fact border on arrogance. "We both know you aren't going to walk around with a bustle on your belly and no husband, embarrassing yourself and Laurie and me."

The word picture he painted had her laughing again, but still, her own fears compelled her to say, "Matt, sometimes it just doesn't happen, like Charlie and Emily. I'm not past the age, but we lost the best years for children. Will you be terribly disappointed if there are no more? No son?"

Surprise flashed across his face. "To have you and Laurie makes me twice blessed. I didn't mean to sound greedy. If there's no more, I'll never be anything but content." He kissed her then, a surpassingly tender kiss.

"But I'll be almighty surprised. I'm expecting such a passel I wonder if your friend Kate could maybe tell you how we space them out some. I don't want you to be like those women I see with one for every year, looking just plain worn out by it. If I'm right and there's another along so quick people wonder, will you ask her?"

"She'd probably be happy not only to tell us, but to give us personal, private lessons."

"Telling will do fine. After all we've got till the first one comes to practice and work it out, and talking about practice...."

Matt finished with the corset in short order, and the rest of her clothing followed. Sarah held her breath as he examined her inch by inch, her fears returning.

"What's this?" His fingers brushed the marks he questioned.

"The skin stretches from a baby, and...." Sarah couldn't finish, afraid of what he would think of a body that was no longer a girl's but a woman's.

He kissed the marks, dispelling more of the satisfied aftermath of their coupling, beginning to heat her blood again.

"I think I like that, like knowing I marked you by loving you," he said.

Ah, little did he know. It was her heart and her soul that he had seared with a brand she had never been able to cover over, cut out, or ignore, even when she tried, and she had tried.

Sarah tugged his tie off and started on his collar. "You have a lot more on than you did in Texas yourself, you know."

"As I recall, fig leaves would be more."

His suit and shirt joined her dress, folded on a chair. Petticoats, stockings, and drawers mingled in a careless heap on the floor. Delighted with the subtle differences between the body of the boy-man she had first known and the muscled contours she now traced,

Sarah examined him as minutely as he had her. She was far less happy with the ugly, puckered scars on his chest where bullets had torn into him.

Then she found the ruler-straight line of the scalpel cut on his throat, always hidden by neckerchief or collar and tie before. He tried to distract her, bent his head and kissed the crest of first one breast and then the other to no avail. Sarah slid her fingers through his hair, pushed the strap that held the eye patch in place over the top of his head and removed the whole thing.

"Don't! Sarah, don't! You can't be looking at that."

Pulling away from her, Matt sat up, leaving her nothing to look at but his back. Sarah stared at him in astonishment. He had never seemed self-consciousness about his face.

"You can't tell me you're supposed to leave that on twenty-four hours a day. It can't be good for you."

No answer.

Sarah sat up, wrapped herself around his back, cheek on his shoulder. "Matt, I can't lie to you. I loved your face. When you were asleep and I was the one watching, I'd examine every line and angle, wonder what the magic was in the way you're made that drew me to you even when I believed you were a murderer. And it hurts to think no one else will ever see you the way I did then—Laurie, our friends— but I already love this face too, because it's you. We're not going to look the same forever anyway, you know. The years bring changes."

"I know that. Sometimes when I see Mrs. Kirkendahl I think of you at that age, and I hope you're like that a little. Only I want to still be there."

"You're going to be. We're going to take very good care of each other and live to see great-grandchildren." Sarah kissed his shoulder.

He turned around then, giving her a good look at the scarred hollow that should have been a sapphire eye as intent as the one regarding her now. "Can you live with that?"

She touched his chin, traced his mouth, smoothed his eyebrows with her fingers and ever so lightly brushed across the eyelid on one side, the absence on the other. "The problem is I can't seem to live, really live, without you."

Against her will her voice changed then from soft with love to harsh with pent up anger. "But I want to meet him one more time, just one more time to point a gun straight between his eyes and send him to hell where he belongs. I know it was Carter. I knew it from the first time I saw you again, but I didn't want to face it."

He tried to interrupt but she wouldn't let him. "You knew about my family from him, and there was only one time you could have seen him, in jail, and the morning after we were in court I went there, and they said you were gone, and for the first time they let me inside. There was a man scrubbing up a bloodstain, so much blood, and the sheriff said it was a drunk with a bloody nose, but it wasn't. It was your blood. That was your blood. You were locked in a cell, and they let him do that to you because of me. I want to kill him. I want to see him again just long enough for him to see the hate, and then I want to kill him."

Matt took her into his arms, holding tight. "No, Sarah, I want you to promise me right now, you'll let go of the hate and the anger."

"How can you say that! He...."

"No. You listen to me now. He stole enough from us. We're not giving him anything more, and hating is giving him feelings we've got better ways to use. Whatever he's getting out of life, he's getting less than us. Promise me now you're going to use everything inside you loving me, Laurie and any others we get for the trying."

With the last words, he loosened his hold, tipped her chin up and tried a small smile. In spite of herself Sarah reacted to it, the corners of her mouth pulling up.

"I can soak up all the loving you can manage all by myself, like the desert does the rain, so swear it now, Sarah. He gets nothing, and I get everything."

"I swear," Sarah said huskily. "You get everything."

Then Matt wrapped Sarah in rainbows and made all the colors shine.

Epilogue

Texas, June 1881

CAPTAIN J.T. EDLER SANK into the hotel room chair, leaned his head against the back and closed his eyes.

"Are you all right, Jim? Was it as dreadful as we feared?" Jenny asked.

He pried his eyes open and smiled at his wife. "For the most part, it was exactly what you'd expect. Senator Carter Macauley enjoyed rubbing my nose in the fact he has the power to have me assigned as a drudge to this commission, and I boiled with hate and resentment, but you can stop worrying. I'm not going to climb in a whiskey bottle and pull the cork tight behind me tonight."

"I know that, but if there's anything I can do to make you feel better...."

Edler closed his eyes again as her voice drifted off. Jenny knew nothing of the sort. She'd endured almost two years of his nightly drunkenness after what happened in Charon years ago. Fearing the effect taking orders from Carter Macauley again would have on her husband, Jenny had left the children with friends and accompanied him on this trip, and he was glad of it.

If Macauley had stayed at Fort Grissom.... Edler hated admitting to himself what he knew to be true. So long as Macauley's arrogant, bad tempered presence served as a constant reminder of his own guilt and cowardice, he'd never have crawled out of the bottle. His first sober day had been the one after Macauley followed his ambitions East.

Edler rolled his head towards his wife and watched her working on a piece of embroidery. How did she stay so serene?

"You must be having a harder time of it than I am," he said. "Keeping Mrs. Senator Macauley company is above and beyond the call of duty. Why don't you come down with something tomorrow. You can stay here in peace, and maybe I can convince the head big wig I need to stay with you."

A smile crossed Jenny's face although she kept her head bent to her needlework. "Let's save deceit and maneuver for the days ahead. You don't need to worry about me, although she may be his match for arrogance. She told me her family made him a senator, said it just like that."

"One of the commissioners hinted at the same thing. We know he would never have married someone from a family of modest means for love."

"No, and I suppose it's a good thing she's useful to him. There are no children, and I'd worry about her physical well being otherwise."

"There's a brother. Maybe there are nephews to continue the Macauley dynasty. After the way he used to go on and on about it, it's hard to believe he's abandoned the idea."

They sat in silence for a while. Edler finally roused himself to say, "I don't have to be back on duty until three. What do you say we ask downstairs and see if there's some quiet little restaurant we can walk to and get away from everybody."

"We may get away from the commissioners, but I understand the whole town is packed with Confederate veterans."

Edler laughed. "Yes, it is, and they're the bright spot in all this. The commissioners had no idea when they decided to meet here that the place would be overrun with a Rebel reunion, and by forcing me to attend resplendent in dress uniform, Macauley ensured that they recognized the whole group as a government commission. Even shut in that meeting room, we heard Dixie and Rebel yells right outside the door so regularly they must have set up a schedule. You should have seen Macauley's face. He was so red I kept hoping he'd fall over with apoplexy."

"Jim."

He grinned at her, unrepentant, then sobered. "You know it's Hood's Texas Brigade down there. Slade was one of Hood's men."

"I know," Jenny said quietly, concentrating on her needle placement.

"Did you ever wonder why it was always Sarah I thought I saw in my drunken wanderings, never Slade?"

"I know why."

Edler regarded his wife with astonishment. She had assured him a thousand times he bore no guilt for what happened to Sarah and Slade, and nothing she said ever made any difference. Being here, enduring Macauley again, fighting the old feelings—for the first time he wanted to talk about it. "Tell me then because I never figured it out myself."

Jenny's hands stopped, and she put the embroidery down. "You hope to see Sarah because you believe there's a chance she found someone, married and has a decent life. You dread seeing him because you believe he will be begging on a street corner or something equally degrading. You blame yourself, and you can't bear it."

Her words hit like a punch in the stomach. "I'm not sure I'm sober enough to hear that much truth."

"You must be. You haven't slammed out of the room."

"No, I haven't. And I'll even admit to you I saw another woman that brought it all back right here this morning. Her back was to me, but she was small and had that unusual shade of blonde hair. Instead of rushing over and sticking my face in hers and scaring her half to death, I walked away. You'd have been proud of me. Surprised, but proud."

"I am proud of you, and we're going to get through this. It's only a few weeks, and we'll be fine."

"It may not even be a few weeks. The head of the commission is already showing signs of realizing there's no reason on earth for my presence. Let's pray that he continues to see the light and sends us home early."

Edler got to his feet and stretched, feeling better than he had a short time ago. "Now what do you say we go see if we can find that Rebel-free lunch."

SARAH GLANCED AT THE grandfather clock on the wall of the hotel ballroom. Almost noon. Across the room Matt stood amidst a group of laughing, talking men. She considered excusing herself from the group of women chatting around her and going to get him. Laurie would be back with the boys all washed up and ready for lunch soon.

As Sarah watched, the man beside him slapped Matt on the shoulder, and Matt slapped right back. Better to let him enjoy himself for another few minutes, she decided.

One of the other women detailed the difficulties she and her husband had endured traveling from California to attend the reunion, and Sarah made sympathetic sounds. For her and for Matt, the trip had been the easy part. Deciding on a year to attend the annual reunion around pregnancies and babies had been the hard part.

In fact convincing Matt that this year was the best they would get for a long while had taken some doing. She definitely had a bustle on her belly again, and no matter that she sailed through every pregnancy and gave birth easily, Matt still treated her like a porcelain figurine that might shatter if he didn't fuss enough.

She had felt shy about taking part in the festivities more than six months along—until last night. Last night had been the reunion ball. Of necessity all her dresses were some version of loose-fitting wrappers. A blue silk trimmed with ivory lace and ribbons, her gown for the ball was pretty, but still—a wrapper. Matt banished her concern in nothing flat, of course.

"It has to be against nature for a woman to look more beautiful with every year that passes, Boston, but you do."

Smiling at the memory, Sarah watched Matt break away from the group of his friends and start toward her. He stopped at her side and slid an arm around her, his hand resting on the side of her swollen belly.

Not one of the women in the group, all of whom had met Matt earlier, got so much as a mildly disapproving look on her face. Instead the group broke out with various versions of the silly sheep look. Sarah heard a giggle and suppressed a sigh.

Matt said, "Ladies, I hope you'll forgive me if I steal my wife away. We promised our young uns lunch someplace quieter than this."

As if to emphasize his words, a group of men broke out with whoops and yells across the room.

Matt left his arm around her as they walked out into the hotel lobby. The sight of a man in a cavalry captain's uniform at the desk caught Sarah's eye.

"Matt, look! That's Jenny Edler and her husband." Sarah hurried forward, calling out as she went. She hugged Jenny hard.

"I can't believe it," Sarah said, finally letting go. "What are you two doing here? Does the government think it needs to keep a close eye on these old Rebels?"

Jenny laughed at that. "No, Jim has been dragooned into serving on a commission to deal with the Indians. They definitely had no idea they would be right in the middle of the reunion."

Looking past Sarah, Jenny's expression changed to one of wonder. "Is that who I think it is?"

Sarah beamed at her. "Yes, it is. Mrs. J.T. Edler, I'd like you to meet my husband, Matthew Slade."

Matt swept his hat across his middle and dipped his head in a way that came off as a courtly bow. "It's a pleasure to meet you, ma'am. I understand while your husband was saving me, you did the same for Sarah. We are in your debt."

Jenny's eyes went wide and her mouth fell half open. At least she didn't giggle.

J.T. Edler had stayed a step back. Now he moved beside his wife and spoke almost angrily. "Jenny had the courage to help Sarah, but you know damned well I walked away like a cowardly dog and let him tear you to pieces with his fist and that ring. He thought he killed you, and he almost did."

Matt answered softly. "The doctor told me the reason I lived was that you carried me there and helped him get me fixed up before the swelling stopped me breathing. He said another thirty minutes would have been too long."

Sarah shot Matt a narrow-eyed look. Until this minute he had steadfastly maintained he remembered nothing from the time he blacked out in the jail until he was in the infirmary at Hartsville. Then again, perhaps she hadn't been too forthcoming with him about Carter's visit to her in Edlers' bedroom.

Edler stuttered, "I can't b-believe.... How can you s-say grateful.... I s-should have stopped him. I should have...."

Matt shook his head. "If you stopped him that night, he'd have been back another time. Then who would have done what you did? I'm grateful, Captain."

Edler's eyes glistened, and Sarah thought she saw his lips tremble for a second before he squared his shoulders and drew himself to attention.

"You're too generous," he said, "but thank you. I am the one in your debt. You need to know, however. He's here. United States Senator Carter Macauley is here. He's on this commission."

Rage seared through Sarah. She grabbed for the gun Matt had holstered at his waist, hidden under his suit jacket. He knew her too well. His hand clamped over her wrist before she got near the gun, and he met her eyes steadily until she regained control and smoothed out her expression. Neither of them said a word—or needed to.

Matt turned back to Edler, his tone unconcerned. "So Macauley's on this government commission the boys have been serenading? What are they really up to? The last of the Comanches were rounded up and shipped off five, six years ago."

"It's genuine. The commissioners are meeting with men who took part in the last action against the Comanches. Then we're heading to Tucson, and using that information to formulate the best plan for dealing with the Apaches."

"God have mercy on the Apaches," Matt said sincerely.

Edler looked surprised at the sentiment, but before he replied, cries of "Mama, Papa," came from the stairs. Matthew and B.J. ran straight across the lobby. Laurie followed at a more lady-like pace.

Sarah watched the expressions on the Edlers' faces as they saw Laurie, then glanced back and forth from Laurie's face to hers, to Matt's.

Thirteen now, Laurie was developing the kind of beauty Sarah never saw in her own mirror. No stubborn chin for her, but Matt's tapered jaw line. The sapphire eyes lit her face, and her hair had taken on a golden cast these last years.

Like Laurie, five-year-old Matthew showed clear signs of his inheritance from both her and Matt, but two-year-old B.J.—Sarah was beginning to hope that someday B.J. would show the world the face she had first seen across a campfire so many years ago.

Sarah said to Jenny, "I wanted to write to you many times, but I was—leery about who might see a letter."

Jenny tore her gaze from Laurie. "You were right to be cautious. You must have quite a story to tell."

Matt said to Edler, "We're on our way to lunch, Captain. We'd be pleased if you and Mrs. Edler would join us, and the ladies can catch up with each other."

Edler nodded. "We were on our way to lunch ourselves. We'd like that."

Still alert to danger after the news that Macauley was in the same town, Sarah started at the sound of half a dozen men thumping down the stairs. As they appeared in the lobby, she saw him. Major, no Senator Carter Macauley.

The broad forehead reached back into his hairline now. He was heavier of body and ruddier of complexion, but her family would still describe him as a fine figure of a man.

Sarah's fury rose again at the thought that he had ever been that close to her children. They wouldn't be out of her sight again from now until they left town tomorrow. Matt had to be thinking the same thing. His face had gone hard and still.

The other men walked out into the street, but Macauley caught sight of their little group and strode toward them.

"Captain Edler, this afternoon, we're going to need...."

His words stopped as he took in Matt, Sarah and the children. He froze, nothing moving but his head as his eyes darted from Matt to Sarah, Sarah to Laurie and back, then to the boys.

"You should have died," he said, fastening at last on Matt.

"You did your best," Matt said, "but your best wasn't good enough."

The two men stared at each other, stiff and hard-eyed. Nausea rose in the back of Sarah's throat. Was Carter armed? If Matt shot him here and now, what would the law do to Matt?

A shrill, loud voice broke through the ugly silence. "Senator! I'm so glad I caught you. I've changed my mind. I will accompany you to luncheon."

The owner of the voice walked from the stairs to Macauley and grasped his arm firmly. She might have been pretty once, but now her corset made no indentation where a waist should be. The fashionable cuirasse-style dress looked like a cruel joke, and a sour expression spoiled her face almost as much as the doughy cheeks and several chins.

"Senator! Who are these people?"

Her voice didn't just hurt the ears. It grated right up the spine and back of the neck. The hard look disappeared from Matt's face, and something else Sarah recognized only too well began to dance in his eye.

Macauley showed no sign of acknowledging his wife's presence or answering her, and she responded by raising both her voice and the level of whining discontent in it.

"Senator, introduce me!"

B.J. made a sound of distress and held his arms up to Sarah. Even though Matt fussed every time she lifted the toddler in her present condition, Sarah picked him up and whispered soothing words, patting his back.

Matt once again swept his hat over his middle and inclined his head. He treated Mrs. Macauley to his very best smile and when he spoke his deep voice drawled like thick, warm honey.

"Now, ma'am, don't you be upset with your husband," he said. "We only crossed his path for a short time years ago. He most likely can't remember our names."

For a few fleeting seconds, Sarah saw Mrs. Macauley's heavy features relax into the look of a silly sheep, then the woman scowled, regarding them all with suspicion.

Matt put his hat on, signaling they were on their way out of the hotel. Now his voice was full of laughter. "I am Matt Slade, and this is my wife, Sarah Hammond Slade." He rested his hands on Laurie's shoulders for a moment. "This is our daughter, Laurie." He moved one hand to the top of Matthew's head. "This is our son, Matthew."

He took B.J. from Sarah's arms and positioned the boy on his left shoulder with his arm under the small bottom. B.J. wrapped his arms around Matt's neck and pressed his smooth cheek against Matt's scarred one.

"And this is our son, B.J. We seem to be a pro-lif-ic family. Now if you will excuse us, these young uns are hungry, and we need to get them fed."

Sarah put a hand very lightly on Matt's right arm, not wanting to impede his ability to use it. As they walked away, she heard the shrewish voice behind them.

"That's her isn't it? That's the woman you almost married, and she's still no better than she ought to be. Can you believe she's here in that condition?"

Laurie and Matthew led the way to the street. Matthew held the door and then skipped to catch up to his sister. Knowing that terrible voice wouldn't grate over her nerves again, Sarah dared to look at Matt and couldn't help starting to laugh herself.

"Pro-lif-ic people don't have an eight-year gap between their first and second child," she said.

"That woman won't give him time to do the arithmetic."

"You aren't calling her a lady?"

He shook his head. "Shrew."

"Harridan."

"Nag."

"Termagant."

"Scold."

When they ran out of words and laughter, Sarah turned serious. "Do we need to worry about him?"

"No. Cowards don't go after people who can fight back. I'm not chained up, and you're not sick in bed."

"Do you think I'd look like that if I'd married him?"

"You might. You'd have to do something to keep him away, and I bet that works fine. No man would want to try to make that woman sing."

He grinned at her, and Sarah grinned right back.

"Do you think Edlers will still join us for lunch?" she asked.

"I expect they'll be along. In their shoes I'd be running out of that hotel."

Matt reached his right arm around her and gave the side of her belly a possessive pat before pulling her close to his side. Sarah pressed against him.

She hoped he was right about the Edlers.

But she never looked back.

Author's Note

The bits of information about Hood's Texas Brigade in *Sing My Name* are historic fact. Along with General Thomas J. (Stonewall) Jackson's Stonewall Brigade, the Texas Brigade was one of the premier brigades of General Robert E. Lee's Army of Northern Virginia.

Annual reunions of the brigade were held right through the first third of the Twentieth Century. The idea that a federal government commission met at the same time as one of those reunions and in the same town is, of course, strictly mine and fiction.

For more information about the Texas Brigade, see:
www.hoodstexasbrigade.org.

Ellen O'Connell

Made in the USA
Middletown, DE
22 January 2020

83531651R00241